CORDUROY MANSIONS

Alexander McCall Smith

WINDSOR

PARAGON

First published 2009 by Polygon
This Large Print edition published 2010
by BBC Audiobooks Ltd by arrangement with
Birlinn Ltd

Hardcover   ISBN: 978 1 408 46130 3
Softcover   ISBN: 978 1 408 46131 0

British Library Cataloguing in Publication Data available

Printed and bound in Great Britain by
CPI Antony Rowe, Chippenham and Eastbourne

This book is for
Andrew Sachs

1. In the Bathroom

Passing off, thought William. Spanish sparkling wine—filthy stuff, he thought, filthy—passed itself off as champagne. Japanese whisky—Glen Yakomoto!—was served as Scotch. Inferior hard cheese—from Mafia-run factories in Catania—was sold to the unsuspecting as Parmesan.

Lots of things were passed off in one way or another, and now, as he stood before the bathroom mirror, he wondered if he could be passed off too. He looked at himself, or such part of himself as the small mirror encompassed—just his face, really, and a bit of neck. It was a fifty-one-year-old face chronologically, but would it pass, he wondered, for a forty-something-year-old face?

He looked more closely: there were lines around the eyes and at the edge of the mouth but the cheeks were smooth enough. He pulled at the skin around the eyes and the lines disappeared. There were doctors who could do that for you, of course:

tighten things up; nip and tuck. But the results, he thought, were usually risible. He had a customer who had gone off to some clinic and come back with a face like a Noh-play mask—all smoothed out and flat. It was sad, really. And as for male wigs, with their stark, obvious hairlines, all one wanted to do was to reach forward and give them a tug. It was quite hard to resist, actually, and once, as a student—and when drunk—he had done just that. He had tugged at the wig of a man in a bar and . . . the man had cried. He still felt ashamed of himself for that. Best not to think about it.

No, he was weathering well enough and it was far more dignified to let nature take its course, to weather in a National Trust sort of way. He looked again at his face. Not bad. The sort of face, he thought, that would be hard to describe on the Wanted poster, if he were ever to do anything to merit the attention of the police—which he had not, of course. Apart from the usual sort of thing that made a criminal of everybody: 'Wanted for illegal parking,' he muttered. 'William Edward French (51). Average height, very slightly overweight (if you don't mind our saying so), no distinguishing features. Not dangerous, but approach with caution.'

He smiled. And if I were to describe myself in one of those lonely hearts ads? *Wine dealer, widower, solvent late forties-ish, GSOH, reasonable shape, interested in music, dining out etc., etc., WLTM presentable, lively woman with view to LTR.*

That would be about it. Of course one had to be careful about the choice of words in these things; there were codes, and one might not be aware of them. Solvent was clear enough: it meant that one

2

had sufficient money to be comfortable, and that was true enough. He would not describe himself as well off, but he was certainly solvent. Well off, he had read somewhere, now meant disposable assets of over . . . how much? More than he had, he suspected.

And reasonable shape? Well, if that was not strictly speaking true at present, it would be shortly. William had joined a gym and been allocated a personal trainer. If his shape at present was not ideal, it soon would be, once the personal trainer had worked on him. It would take a month or two, he thought, not much more than that. So perhaps one might say, *shortly to be in reasonable shape*.

Now, what about: *would like to meet presentable, lively woman.* Well, presentable was a pretty low requirement. Virtually anybody could be presentable if they made at least some effort. Lively was another matter. One would have to be careful about lively because it could possibly be code for insatiable, and that would not do. Who would want to meet an insatiable woman? My son, thought William suddenly. That's exactly the sort of woman Eddie would want to meet. The thought depressed him.

William lived with his son. There had been several broad hints dropped that Eddie might care to move out and share with other twenty-somethings, and recently a friend of Eddie's had even asked him if he wanted to move into a shared flat, but these hints had apparently fallen on unreceptive ground. 'It's quite an adventure, Eddie,' William said. 'Everybody at your stage of life shares a flat. Like those girls downstairs. Look

3

at the fun they have. Most people do it.'

'You didn't.'

William sighed. 'My circumstances, Eddie, were a bit different.'

'You lived with Grandpa until he snuffed it.'

'Precisely. But I had to, don't you see? I couldn't leave him to look after himself.'

'But I could live with you until you snuff it.'

'That's very kind of you. But I'm not planning to snuff it just yet.'

Then there had been an offer to help with a mortgage—to pay the deposit on a flat in Kentish Town. William had even gone so far as to contact an agent and find a place that sounded suitable. He had looked at it without telling Eddie, meeting the agent one afternoon and being shown round while a litany of the flat's—and the area's—advantages was recited.

William had been puzzled. 'But it doesn't appear to have a kitchen,' he pointed out.

The agent was silent for a moment. 'Not as such,' he conceded. 'No. That's correct. But there's a place for a sink and you can see where the cooker used to be. So that's the kitchen space. Nowadays people think in terms of a *kitchen space*. The old concept of a separate kitchen is not so important. People see past a kitchen.'

In spite of the drawbacks, William had suggested that Eddie should look at the place and had then made his proposition. He would give him the deposit and guarantee the mortgage.

'Your own place,' he said. 'It's ideal.'

Eddie looked doubtful. 'But it hasn't got a kitchen, Dad. You said so. No kitchen.'

William took this in his stride. 'It has a *kitchen*

4

space, Eddie. People see past an actual kitchen these days. Didn't you know that?'

But Eddie was not to be moved. 'It's kind of you, Dad. I appreciate the offer, but I think it's premature. I'm actually quite comfortable living at home. And it's greener, isn't it? Sharing. It makes our carbon footprint much smaller.'

And so William found himself living with his twenty-four-year-old son. *Wine dealer*, he thought, *would like his son to meet a lively woman with view to his moving in with her. Permanently. Any area.*

He turned away from the bathroom mirror and stooped down to run his morning bath. It was a Friday, which meant that he would open the business half an hour late, at ten-thirty rather than ten. This meant that he could have his bath and then his breakfast in a more leisurely way, lingering over his boiled egg and newspaper before setting off; a small treat, but a valued one.

There was a knocking on the door, soft at first and then more insistent.

'You're taking ages, Dad. What are you doing in there?'

He did not reply.

'Dad? Would you mind hurrying up? Or do you want me to be late?'

William turned and faced the door. He stuck out his tongue.

'Don't be so childish,' came the voice from the other side of the door.

Childish? thought William. Well, you've got a little surprise coming your way, Eddie, my boy.

2. *Corduroy Matters*

The flat occupied by William and Eddie was on the top floor of the four-storey building in Pimlico known as Corduroy Mansions. It was not a typical London mansion block. The name had been coined—in jest, yet with a considerable measure of condescension—by a previous tenant, but Corduroy Mansions had stuck, and a disparaging nickname had become a fond one. There was something *safe* about corduroy, something reassuring, and while corduroy might be an ideological near neighbour of tweed, it was not quite as . . . well, tweedy. So while William would have been appalled to hear himself described as tweedy, he would not have resented being called corduroy. There was something slightly bohemian about corduroy; it was a sign, perhaps, of liberality of outlook, of openness to alternatives—of a slightly artistic temperament.

Corduroy Mansions had been built in the early twentieth century, in a fit of Arts and Crafts enthusiasm. It was an era when people still talked to one another, in sentences; that had since become unusual, but at least the occupants of all the Corduroy flats still conversed—at least sometimes—with their neighbours, and even appeared to enjoy doing so. 'It's got a lived-in feel,' one of the residents remarked, and that was certainly true. Whereas in more fashionable blocks down the road in Eaton Square, or the like, there would be flats that lay unoccupied for most of the year, or flats occupied by exotic, virtually invisible people, wealthy wraiths who slipped in and out of their front doors without a word to neighbours, everyone with a flat in Corduroy Mansions actually lived there. They had no other place. Corduroy Mansions was home.

The staircase was the setting for most of these personal encounters, although every so often there would be a meeting at which all the tenants got together to discuss matters of mutual interest. There were the meetings that took place in William's flat over the new carpet for the stairs— an issue that took six months of delicate negotiation to resolve—and there was also a meeting over what colour to paint the front door. On these occasions it was inevitably William who took the chair, being not only the oldest resident, but also the one most endowed with the *gravitas* necessary to deal with the landlord, a faceless company in Victoria that appeared to ignore any letters it received.

'They're in denial,' said William. 'We've got them for the next one hundred and twenty years and they're in denial.'

But the landlord eventually did what was required, and although Corduroy Mansions could not be described as being in good order, at least it did not appear to be falling down.

'This old place suits me,' remarked William to his friend Marcia. 'It's like an old glove, familiar and comfortable.'

'Or old sock, even,' said Marcia, sniffing the air. Marcia was always ready to detect a smell, and she had often remarked on a slight odour on the staircase.

Marcia was a caterer. Ten years previously she

7

had set up Marcia's Table, a firm that specialised in catering for small weddings, board lunches and the like. Actually, to call Marcia's Table a firm was to dignify it beyond what it deserved. Marcia's Table consisted of Marcia and nobody else, other than the helpers she engaged to serve and clear up: young Australians, Poles, Romanians, eager all of them—to a fault—and totally free of the casual surliness that plagued their British contemporaries. It was Marcia who planned the menus, bought the supplies and cooked. And it was Marcia who frequently brought leftovers to Corduroy Mansions and left them in William's flat. He had provided her with a key—in an impulsive gesture of friendship—and would sometimes come home to discover a pot of goulash sitting on the cooker, or half a plate of only-the-tiniest-bit-soggy chicken vol-au-vents, or cocktail sausages impaled on little sticks, like pupae in a butterfly collection.

It was thoughtfulness on her part, touched, perhaps, by the slightest hint of ambitious self-interest. Marcia *liked* William; she liked him a great deal. It was a tragedy, she thought, that he was on his own; what a waste of a perfectly good man! For his part, he had never shown any interest in her beyond that which one has in a comfortable friend—the sort of interest that stops well short of any gestures of physical affection. She understood: a woman can tell these things, especially one as sympathetic and emotionally sensitive as Marcia believed herself to be. No, William had shown no signs of wanting *closeness*, but that did not mean that he might not do so in the future. So she continued with her culinary overtures and he, replete on vol-au-vents, reflected on his good fortune to have such a friend as Marcia. But in his mind she was just a friend, firmly on that side of the line.

The stumbling block, Marcia thought, was Eddie. If William were truly on his own, and not sharing with his son, then she felt it likely that he would be more receptive to the idea of a relationship with a woman. Having his son there distracted him and took the edge off his loneliness. If only Eddie were to go—and it was surely time for him to fly the nest—then her own prospects would be better.

Unfortunately, Marcia had once let slip her low opinion of Eddie, incautiously describing him as a 'waste of space'. It had been unwise—she knew that—but it had been said, and it had been said when Marcia, who had been visiting William after catering for a rather trying reception, had had perhaps two glasses of wine too many. Eddie had been in the flat, listening to the conversation from the corridor. Nobody likes to be described in such terms, and he had pursed his lips in anger. He waited for his father to defend him, as any father must do when his own flesh and blood, his own DNA, is described as a waste of space. He waited.

'That's a bit hard on the boy,' his father said at last. 'Give him time. He's only twenty-four.'

Perhaps Marcia regretted her slip, since she said nothing more. But then Eddie heard William say: 'Of course, there's a theory in psychology that many men only mature at the age of twenty-eight. You've heard of that? Seems a bit late to me, but that's what they say.'

Eddie had turned round and slunk back into his room, a Polonius in retreat from behind the arras. That woman, he thought, that *blowsy* woman is

9

after my dad. And if she gets him, then she gets the lot when he snuffs it—the flat, the wine business, the old Jaguar. The lot. She has to be stopped.

Then he thought: twenty-eight? *Twenty*-eight?

3. Dee is Rude about Others

As William locked his front door behind him that morning, he heard the sound of somebody fiddling with keys on the landing downstairs. This was nothing unusual: the girls, as he called them, had a difficult lock, and unless one inserted the key at precisely the right angle and then exerted a gentle upward pressure, it would not work. It was not unusual, he had noted, for the locking-up process to take five or ten minutes; on one occasion he had gone out to buy a newspaper and returned to discover one of the young women still struggling with the recalcitrant lock.

As he made his way downstairs, he saw that it was Dee on the landing below.

10

'Having trouble with the key?' he asked jauntily.

She looked up. 'No more than usual. I thought I'd got the hang of it and then . . .'

'Keys are like that,' said William. 'They never fit exactly. I remember an aunt of mine who used the wrong key for years. She was determined that it would work and she managed to force the lock of her front door every time. But it took a lot of force. She had lost the right key and was in fact using the back door key. The triumph of determination over . . . well, locks, I suppose.'

Dee stood back and allowed William to fiddle with the key. After a few twists the lock moved and he was able to withdraw the key. 'There we are. Locked.'

They started downstairs together. There were four floors in Corduroy Mansions, if one included the basement. William owned the top flat, the girls were on the first floor, and in the ground-floor flat lived Mr Wickramsinghe, a mild, rather pre-occupied accountant whom nobody saw very much, but who kept fresh flowers in a vase in the common entrance hall.

'The others have all left for work?' asked William.

'Some of them. Jo's away for a couple of days. I've actually got the morning off, so I'm doing a bit of shopping before I go in at lunchtime. Caroline and Jenny are at work, if you can call it that.'

William raised an eyebrow. 'From that, I take it that you don't.'

Dee sniffed. 'Well, look at Caroline. She's doing that Master's course at Sotheby's. Fine Art. She goes to lectures and drifts around the salerooms. Very taxing.'

11

'Very pleasant,' said William. 'But she'll have essays to write, won't she? 'The Early Giotto' and that sort of thing. And articles to read? The *Burlington Magazine*, I suppose.'

Dee was not convinced. She worked in a health-food shop, the Pimlico Vitamin and Supplement Agency; she knew what hard work was.

'And Jenny?' William asked.

'Her job consists of going to lunch, as far as I can tell,' said Dee.

'There must be more to it than that,' said William. 'Being a PA to an MP must involve something. All those letters from constituents. All those complaints about drains and hospital wards. Surely those must take up a lot of time?'

'Oh yes, I suppose they do. But still she seems to have a lot of time for lunches.'

William smiled. 'Have you met her boss? The MP.'

'Oedipus Snark? Yes, I met him once. He came round to the flat to deliver some papers to Jenny.' She shuddered involuntarily.

'He didn't make a good impression?'

'Certainly not. A horrible man. Creepy.'

They had now come out of the front door and continued to walk together along the street. William walked to work; Dee was heading for the tube.

'His name hardly helps,' said William. 'Oedipus Snark. It's very unfortunate. Somewhat redolent of Trollope, I would have thought. What was the name of Trollope's villain? Slope, wasn't it? Snark and Slope are obviously birds of a feather.'

'Creep.'

'Yes,' said William. 'That would be another good

12

name for a villain. Creep. Of course that's a name with political associations already. You won't remember CREEP, but I do. Just. Watergate. Remember Watergate?' He realised that of course she would not. Just as she would know nothing about Winston Churchill or Mussolini; or Kenneth Williams or Liberace, for that matter. 'CREEP was the name of the committee that President Nixon—he was a president of the United States, you know—had working for his re-election. The Committee to Re-elect the President. CREEP was the acronym.' Dee seemed to be paying very little attention to him, but William was used to that. He was terribly old by her standards. She was twenty-eight and he was in his late forties (well, early fifties if one was going to be pedantic). He was old enough to be her father, a thought which depressed him. He did not want to be a father-figure to the young women who lived in the flat below. He wanted them to look upon him as a . . . friend. But it was too late for that. Being realistic, there were just not enough shared references in their respective worlds to allow for much of a friendship. The most he could hope for was a reasonably neighbourly relationship in which they did not condescend to him too much.

'How does Jenny get on with Snark?' asked William. 'Does she share your low opinion of him?'

Dee became animated. 'Yes. She really does. She hates him. She thinks he's gross.'

'I see.'

'But then everybody hates him,' Dee continued. 'Even his mother.'

William laughed. 'Surely not. Mothers rarely hate their sons. It's a very non-maternal thing to

13

do. Particularly if one's son is called Oedipus.'

He waited for her to react. But nothing came.

'Oedipus—' he began.

'But this one does,' interrupted Dee. 'Jenny told me all about it. She can't conceal it. She hates him intensely.'

'How does Jenny know all this?'

'His mother has spoken to her about it. She said, "I wish I didn't dislike my son so much, but I do. I can't help it." She paused. 'And she's plotting against him.'

William was silent. Mothers should not plot against their sons . . . and nor should fathers. And yet was that not exactly what he was doing? He was plotting against Eddie in that he was making plans for Eddie's exclusion from the flat. But that was different: he was not working for Eddie's downfall, merely for his moving out. It was a different sort of plot, but nevertheless he felt a degree of shame about it. And yet at the same time, he felt a certain satisfaction at the sheer cunning of his idea. Eddie could not abide dogs and was petrified of even the smallest and most unthreatening breeds. It would not be necessary, then, for William to buy himself an Alsatian or a Rottweiler; a mere terrier would do the trick. If a dog moved into the house, then Eddie would have to move out. It was a very simple and really rather clever plan.

William smiled.

'What's so funny?' asked Dee.

'Nothing much,' said William. 'Just an idea I've had.'

4. A Generous Offer

'Half the time,' said Dee, 'I can't follow what he's going on about. It was Watergate this morning. Watergate and some guy called Nixon.'

'Old people wander a bit,' said Martin, her colleague at the Pimlico Vitamin and Supplement Agency. 'I had an uncle—or something—who lost all his nouns. He had a stroke and all the nouns went. So he used the word 'concept' for any noun. He'd say things like 'Pass the concept' when he wanted you to pass the salt.'

Dee frowned. William was not *all* that old. But there was no need to correct Martin on that; the interesting thing was the salt issue. 'He ate a lot of salt?'

'I think so.'

'Well, there you are,' said Dee. 'Sodium blockages. You know I'll never forget when I went for iridology the first time and the iridologist looked into my eyes and said, 'You eat a lot of salt.' And it was true. I really freaked out.'

Martin looked concerned. 'How do they tell?'

'Sodium rings in the eyes,' said Dee. 'It's pretty obvious.'

Martin was silent. Then, after a few moments, 'Could you tell? Yourself, I mean. Would you be able to tell if you looked into my eyes?'

Dee smiled. 'Maybe. Do you want me to?'

It took Martin a minute or so to decide. Then he said, 'Yes. It's better to know, isn't it?'

'Of course you must know anyway,' said Dee. 'You must know whether you eat too much salt. Do

15

you?'

Martin looked away. 'Maybe sometimes.'

'All right.'

There were no customers in the Vitamin and Supplement Agency at the time and Dee pointed to a chair in front of the counter. 'Sit down, Martin. No, don't close your eyes. I'm going to have to shine a light into them. Just relax.'

There was a small torch beside the cash register. They used it from time to time to look into the mouths of customers who wanted something for mouth ulcers or gingivitis. Dee reached for this torch and crouched in front of Martin. She rested a hand on his shoulder to steady herself. His shoulder felt bony; Martin did not eat enough, she thought, but that was something they could deal with later. For now it was sodium rings.

The torch threw a small circle of weak light onto his cheek. She moved it up closely until it was shining directly into his right eye.

She felt Martin's breathing upon her hand, a warm, rather comforting feeling. Then it stopped; he was holding his breath.

'See anything?' he asked.

'Hold on. I'm just trying to see. Yes . . . Yes.'

'Yes what? Are there any sodium rings?'

'Yes. I think so. There are some white circles. I think those are sodium rings all right.'

She turned the torch off and stood back. Martin stared at her balefully.

'What can I do?'

'Eat less salt for starters.'

'And?'

'And the sodium rings should disappear.' She paused. 'But there were other things there.'

16

He looked at her in alarm. 'Such as?'

'Flecks. And quite a few yellow dots. I don't know what those mean. I suppose we could look them up.'

They were interrupted by the arrival of the first customer of the morning. He wanted St John's Wort and a bottle of Echinacea. Dee served him while Martin tidied the counter. Afterwards, when the customer had gone, Martin turned to her. His anxiety was evident.

'Should I cut out salt altogether?'

She shrugged. 'We need a certain amount of salt. If you cut out salt altogether you'd die. So maybe just a bit less.'

He nodded. There was a mirror in the washroom and he would have a quick look at his eyes in that. If he could see the sodium rings himself, then he could monitor his progress in getting rid of them.

'It's not the end of the world,' said Dee reassuringly. 'People live with sodium rings for a long time.'

'And then they die?'

'Maybe. But you're not going to die, Martin. Not just yet. As long as you take sensible precautions.'

Martin looked thoughtful. 'Supplements?'

Dee shook her head. She knew that Martin was already on a number of supplements—they all were—and probably needed nothing else. No, the yellow flecks she thought she had seen in his irises pointed to colon issues.

'I think that you need colonic irrigation,' she said. 'Those yellow flecks I saw are probably related to the colon.'

Martin said nothing.

'Colonic irrigation is the answer,' Dee

17

pronounced. 'We all need it, but very few people take it up.'

Martin swallowed. 'You have to . . .'

'Yes,' said Dee. 'It's not a very savoury subject, but it's no use running away from it. The transit time for food through the system should ideally be less than twenty-four hours. The average time for British men—of which you, Martin, are an example—is over sixty hours. Sixty hours!'

Martin swallowed again. 'And it involves . . .'

'Yes,' said Dee. 'It does. But we don't need to go into that. One doesn't have to look.'

She stared at Martin. She liked this young man. There was something innocent about him; something fresh. And yet when she had looked into his irises . . .

She smiled at him. 'Don't be too concerned. It's not as bad as you think it is. I've had colonic irrigation. I went to Thailand and had a special course of it on Ko Samui. But you don't have to go that far.'

'You don't?'

'No. Not at all.' She reached out and patted him on the shoulder. 'How old are you again, Martin?'

'Nineteen. Twenty next month.'

'Twenty years of impurity,' mused Dee. 'Look, why don't you let me do it for you? It's not difficult, you know.'

Martin looked down at the floor. He was not sure what to say. It was such a generous offer.

5. Unmarried Girls

Dee might have had a low opinion of her flatmate Caroline's work, but for all that it was about as removed as was at all possible from the factory floor—in so far as any factory floors remained— still it required a measure of talent, and considerable application. And that was not all: in addition, the annual fees for the course amounted to seventeen thousand pounds, and that was just for tuition. On top of that one had to live, and for most of the people on the course with Caroline— and for Caroline herself—the living was the expensive part. One could not do a Master's degree in Fine Art and just *exist*. There were certain standards to be kept up, and those were expensive.

Caroline had the distinction of having had her photograph featured in *Rural Living*, a fact she carefully concealed from her flatmates. Not that this was difficult: Dee's reading was more or less confined to the vegetarian and alternative therapies press—*Anti-oxidant News*, for example, or *The Healthy Table*; Jenny read political biographies, and little else; and Jo, as far as anybody could ascertain, read nothing at all. So there was little chance that any of them would have spotted her in the magazine, immediately after the property advertisements and just before the editorial on rural policy.

The publication of full-page photographs of attractive young women of a certain class was one of the great traditions of British journalism, better established than the rival—and vulgar—tradition of plastering naked women across page three of the *Sun*. The *Rural Living* girls could not have been more different from their less-clad counterparts in the *Sun*, separated by social and cultural chasms so wide as to suggest that each group belonged to a fundamentally different species.

Rural Living girls were photographed in a rural setting, although from time to time one might be featured in a cloister or some other suitable architectural spot. Generally they wore clothes that were not entirely dissimilar to their mothers'. Indeed, in the case of those girls of very ancient breeding, where long bloodlines had not been synonymous with commercial success and where genteel penury was the order of the day, the clothes they wore *were* in fact their mothers', having been passed on with relief when it was discovered that fashions had come full circle and the outfits were once again *à la mode*.

The girls were always unmarried, even if some of them were engaged. The engaged girls had their pictures in the magazine as an encouragement to others to make suitable marriages when the time came. None of the fiancés was unsuitable; quite the opposite, in fact. So this meant that unengaged girls should put behind them any temptation to marry unsuitable men—of whom there was always a more than adequate supply—and marry, instead, boys who would in the fullness of time be the fathers of girls who appeared in *Rural Living*. And if there was a degree of circularity in this, it was entirely intentional.

Of course, Caroline's parents would never have sought out the placing of their daughter's

20

photograph in *Rural Living*. It was well known that anybody who did so would be quietly and tactfully made aware that that was not the way it worked. The best route to inclusion was to come to editorial attention in a social context; another way was to know one of those photographers whose work was regularly published in the magazine. These photographers wielded considerable power—as photographers, and picture editors, often do. They could make or break political careers, for instance, simply by photographing their subject in a particular way. There was many a politician, or politician's wife, who had been photographed in such a manner as to make him or her an object of derision. A former prime minister, for instance, was regularly portrayed as having extraordinary eyes, rather like the eyes of one possessed, and his wife was portrayed as having a perpetually open mouth, the mouth of one who was rarely silent. Now neither of these portrayals was accurate or fair. The Prime Minister's eyes were not those of a maniac: photographers who did not approve of him simply achieved this effect by omitting to turn on the anti-red-eye device on their cameras. This created the impression that the Prime Minister was a messianic lunatic, which he was not. Similarly, when photographing his wife, these photographers simply waited until her mouth opened in order to breathe and then they snapped her. It was all extremely unkind.

Caroline had been spotted by a photographer called Tim Something. Something was a freelance photographer who specialised in covering events such as May Balls at provincial universities such as Oxford and Cambridge. He also covered picnics at

Glyndebourne, regattas at Henley, and the occasional charity cricket match. His photographs were competently executed rather than brilliant, but then none of his subjects was particularly brilliant, and so it was a good match.

Something had been in Oxford to cover the award of an honorary degree to an influential financier, having been commissioned to photograph the event for the financier's company. Afterwards, he was having a cup of coffee in a coffee bar when Caroline came in with two of her friends. He had been drawn to her looks, which were typical of a certain sort of English girl who, although not overly intellectual, nonetheless has intelligence sufficient to animate the face.

Something had watched her discreetly from his table. He noted the style of her clothes—there was no sign of the ubiquitous blue jeans that virtually everybody else in the coffee bar was sporting. He noticed the single strand of pearls that she was wearing; the subdued, pastel-shaded blouse; the shoes (everybody else was in trainers). And he said to himself: Oxford Brookes, the university where girls of a certain background can go and be well placed to meet boys at the 'real' Oxford University, in so far as any of these would be considered by such a girl to be worth meeting.

He watched her, and then acted. Crossing to her table, he cleared his throat and said, 'Look, I know you don't know me, but would you like to have your photograph in a magazine?'

Caroline looked up at Something. 'What magazine?'

'One that mostly features dogs and horses,' he replied.

6. Tim Something Takes a Photo

'Tim Something,' said Caroline. 'He's a photographer. I'm sure he's all right.'

'Not a name to inspire confidence,' said her father, Rufus Jarvis, a semi-retired partner in Jarvis and Co., a land agency in Cheltenham.

Caroline smiled. 'But you can't judge people by their names,' she said. 'It has nothing to do with them. You called me Caroline, for instance.'

There was a silence. They were sitting in the kitchen of the Jarvis house in Cheltenham, a rambling old rectory with a large Victorian conservatory and a monkey puzzle tree in the garden. Rufus Jarvis stared at his daughter. She had been a very easy teenager—no rebellions, as far as he could recall—but now that she was twenty-one, were resentments going to start to come out? Did she resent being called Caroline?

'Caroline is a perfectly good name,' he said. 'It's not as if we called you . . .' He thought for a moment. Bronwen was a problematic name, to say the least. Or Mavis. A girl called Mavis these days might have every reason to resent parental choice. But Caroline?

'Oh, there's nothing wrong with being called Caroline,' said Caroline. 'I was just making the point that you chose it, I didn't.'

'Well, you can hardly complain about that,' said Rufus. 'Parents can't very well say, 'I'm not going to call you anything until you're twelve, or sixteen, or whatever, and then you can choose for yourself.' For heaven's sake!'

Caroline sighed. 'No, listen, Daddy, you're not getting the point. What I'm saying is that parents choose names and children don't. So you can't judge anybody by their name. Because it has nothing to do with them.'

'All right. But you must admit that there are some names that just don't . . . don't inspire confidence. That's all. This chap, Something, how do you know . . . ?' He did not finish.

'He's perfectly respectable. And he wants to put my photograph in *Rural Living*.'

Rufus frowned. 'In the front? Where they have the photo of the girl?'

'Yes.'

'But are you looking for a husband?'

Caroline laughed. 'I don't see what that's got to do with it.'

'Come, come, my dear,' said Rufus. 'It has everything to do with it. Any chap—unmarried chap—reading *Rural Living* will see that you're not yet married. Hello, he'll say. Nice-looking girl, that. That's how it works, my dear. Half of Mummy's friends appeared in *Rural Living*. Mummy herself—'

Caroline gasped. 'Mummy? Her photograph was in?'

'Yes, it was. And she looked extremely attractive, if I may say so. I saw it and I said to myself, there's a looker! And the rest, as they say, was history.'

Caroline was silent. She was shocked, indeed she was appalled, to discover that her father had found her mother in a *magazine*. Like everybody, she did not like to think that she was the product of . . . well, all *that*. And between her parents too! She had fondly imagined that her parents had met

24

at . . . a dance, perhaps (and not too close a dance). They had had a formal and courteous relationship and then, after a decent interval, she had appeared on the scene. That was how she liked to imagine it. Anything else would have taken her into the Freudian territory of the 'primal scene', where the child, witnessing the closeness of parents, interprets the situation as one involving violence.

When she had recovered her composure, she glanced at her father and said, with a certain note of reproach in her voice, 'I didn't realise that you got Mummy from a *catalogue.*'

Rufus found this amusing. 'A catalogue? No, it was hardly like that. After I saw her picture in the magazine I got somebody who lived near her father to get me invited to a do they had. That's how I met her. Of course there were lots of other men all about her and I had to join the queue, so to speak.'

'Daddy!' This was unbearable. That her mother should have entertained advances from anybody but her father was inconceivable. How could she? It was almost as if she had discovered that her mother had a history as a courtesan: talked about by men; the subject of heaven knows what dark ambitions and fantasies.

That was where the discussion stopped. Caroline had discovered enough about the expectations that might be raised by the publication of her picture— which had already been taken—and she decided to contact Tim Something and get him to withdraw the photograph. She did not want a husband—at least not yet—and she certainly did not want people to think that she had agreed to have her photograph featured in this way purely for that

25

reason.

She telephoned Tim Something. 'That photograph,' she said. 'I don't want you to use it.'

'But it's great. They liked it a lot. That picture of you standing next to the monkey-puzzle tree in your old man's garden. Fantastic. Have you ever thought of modelling? I know a guy in London who's always on the look-out for likely vict— subjects. I could do a few portfolio shots. You know the sort of thing. You looking into the middle distance. You smiling. You've got a great smile, btw.'

She began to shout, but then calmed down and spoke more evenly. 'You're not listening to me,' she said, adding, 'btw. I said that I'm withdrawing my consent. You know what that means? No. *Nyet. Nein.*'

It was a moment or two before he replied. 'Too late,' he said. 'Sorry.'

'What do you mean too late?'

'I mean that they've made up the magazine. It'll be ready for printing.'

Caroline drew in her breath. 'Then they'll just have to stop,' she said. 'I'm withdrawing my consent.'

'Too late,' he said. 'Really. It's just too late.' He paused. 'Of course you could get them to over-print it with a sign saying Sold. That's what they do with houses that are off the market by the time the magazine goes to press.'

'Are you trying to be funny?' she hissed.

'No,' said Tim Something. 'Just helpful.'

7. Proustian-Jungian Soup

Caroline thought: It's odd, sitting here, letting one's mind wander, and who should come into it but Tim Something, of all people. Strange.

She had not seen him for two years; her photograph had appeared in *Rural Living* during her last year at Oxford Brookes and then there had been the gap year in New Zealand looking after the children of a family who lived in Auckland (whose fifteen-year-old son had made a pass at her; *fifteen!*). Now here she was doing her Master's in Fine Art, sitting in a lecture on seventeenth-century Dutch painting, and a photographer whom she barely knew—and rather disliked—suddenly came into her mind. It was odd, but that was how the human mind was: a Proustian-Jungian soup of random memories and associations.

Proustian-Jungian; she rather liked the term, and might use it in one of her essays. She was overdue with one of them—a discussion of influences in

27

Veneto-Cretan painting—and she was finding the going rather difficult. There was a literature on the subject but a lot of it was in German, and Caroline's German was almost non-existent. She could ask the way to the station, perhaps, in that language, and had indeed once done so in Frankfurt, only to be answered in perfect, almost non-accented English. But when it came to influences in Italian art, it was a different matter.

The Proustian-Jungian line would certainly help. She had been looking at a photograph of a small Veneto-Cretan treatment of the birth of the Virgin Mary, a popular theme in the art of the time. In this painting, the Virgin Mary's mother was lying in a large four-poster bed, across which a rich, brocaded green cover had been draped. The mother was composed, and was being served a tray by a serving girl, next to whom was standing a saint, his halo providing a measure of illumination for the eating of the meal on the tray. In the foreground a group of angels stood around the newborn babe, who was, curiously enough, already standing, at the tender age of a couple of hours, although admittedly lightly supported by another serving girl, or early au pair perhaps.

It was the *reading* of the painting that was all-important, and only the naïve would see this painting as being simply about the birth of the Virgin Mary. There was far, far more to be gained from looking at it closely, but . . . what exactly? That was the difficulty.

Her thoughts, however, were interrupted by the voice of their lecturer, who had pressed the button to bring a fresh slide to the screen. Thoughts of the Veneto-Cretan were replaced by thoughts of the

Dutch Golden Age and the significance of light.

'These paintings,' said the lecturer, a small man in a velvet jacket, 'are really about water, because whenever a Dutch artist paints land, he is really painting land as seen through the water that suffused the very air about him. It is this omnipresence of water that gives to the light of that period its particular quality. As we see here in this landscape by Pieter de Hooch. See. Here and here. And here.'

Caroline felt herself becoming drowsy. It was warm in the lecture theatre, and she had woken up rather early that morning. The Dutch light, she felt, was soporific; it had perhaps had that effect on de Hooch as he sat at his easel all those years ago.

She felt a gentle dig in her ribs. 'Don't go to sleep,' her neighbour whispered. 'Poor Dr Edwards will be very offended if he sees you. But he is boring, isn't he?'

She half turned to the young man sitting beside her. He had started taking notes at the beginning of the lecture but now appeared to have stopped. James was a special friend of hers; they often sat next to one another in lectures, lent each other notes, and went off for coffee together. He was easy company, amusing and undemanding and, most importantly, quite unthreatening to women.

'I can't help it,' she whispered back. 'His voice . . .'

James patted her forearm. 'Quite. But listen, I need to talk to you. Have you got a moment after this?'

'Of course.' She hesitated. 'A problem?'

He put a finger to his lips. Dr Edwards was looking in their direction. 'Wait,' he said.

29

'Afterwards.'

At the end of the lecture they left the lecture room together, abandoning a small knot of members of the course who wanted to take up with Dr Edwards some point about the Dutch Golden Age. Coming out of Bedford Square, they went into the coffee bar off Tottenham Court Road where, at any hour of the day, they knew they could always find a table.

'So,' said Caroline. 'What's up? Have you got an interview? Or even an offer?' James was applying for jobs at various galleries and had been passing on to her the woes of his fruitless quest.

He shook his head. 'Nothing like that. Actually, this is a personal issue. I don't want to burden you . . .'

'Listen,' she said. 'Who's your best friend on this course? Me. And what are best friends for? To be burdened. So . . .'

He looked at her gratefully. 'I couldn't talk to anybody else about this,' he said. 'It's not the sort of thing . . . well, it's not the sort of thing I've found very easy to talk about. Ever.'

She nodded. 'I can imagine . . . Not that I know what it is, of course, but if I did, then I'm sure I'd see what you mean.'

James toyed with the spoon that the barista had placed beside his café latte. 'It's not easy.'

'No.'

'Well, you see, it's about me. About who I am. About what I feel.'

Caroline looked at him encouragingly. 'For most of us, that's quite an important issue. Yes?'

He looked at her. 'Caroline, you do know that I'm . . . well, you know that I'm . . . you know . . .'

She laughed; this was hardly a disclosure. James, after all, had admired the paintings of Henry Scott Tuke—more than once. 'But of course. And so what? Surely that's not an issue.'

'No, it isn't. Except that . . . well, except that I think I'm not . . . you know.'

Caroline frowned. 'You've just discovered that you like . . . girls?'

James sighed. 'Yes. I think I may be straight. Here I am at twenty-two, committed to art history, and discovering that I may be straight. How bad is that?'

'Now, that is a problem,' agreed Caroline.

8. *The Merits of Italian Wine (or some of it)*

While Caroline sat in the coffee bar with James, listening to his unexpected and unsettling disclosure, William was busy taking delivery of a large consignment of Brunello di Montalcino, eighteen cases in all, of which seven were already promised to clients and three were semi-promised. A semi-promise was where the client said that he would take something and the merchant said that he would set it aside, both knowing that neither meant it. Failure to take up a semi-promise had no consequences for the client but he could nonetheless treat such a failure as cause for minor umbrage—mild disappointment, perhaps, that something he might have wanted had been sold. But there were limits to this umbrage and if the merchant thought these limits had been surpassed, he could come back with a remark about making

31

firm orders in future. Clients who traded in semi-promises did not like firm orders and would usually let the matter drop at that point.

William's assistant, Paul, a young man of nineteen, was late that morning and came in to find William stacking the last of the cases of Brunello. William looked pointedly at his watch and then at Paul, who was dressed in the outfit that he wore every day—denim jeans and a T-shirt of a colour somewhere between grey and white. He wondered whether it was always the same pair of jeans and the same T-shirt, but it was difficult to tell. Paul seemed clean enough to him and was never, as William put it when commenting on the unwashed who appeared to circulate in London, 'slightly off'. Indeed, Paul wore something, some cologne or aftershave, that had a pleasant, slightly sandalwood tang to it. William had once discovered a bottle of white wine from the Veneto which seemed to have exactly the same nose to it as Paul's cologne. He had called out to Paul, 'My goodness, Paul, this Italian white smells exactly like—' And had stopped himself before he said *you*. One man—even a *new man*, which William would claim to be—did not comment to another man on how he smelled; there were taboos about this, and the most that any man could do of another was to wrinkle his nose slightly, or perhaps waft the air in front of his nose with a hand—a gesture into which all sorts of alternative and innocent meanings could be read.

But now there was the issue of time-keeping, rather than smell, and William looked again at his watch and then glanced at Paul.

'Not my fault,' said Paul. 'Somebody on the

32

District Line. Everything stopped.'

William rolled his eyes. He suspected that Paul's excuses for being late were not always true; indeed he thought that Paul, for all his merits—and he was a willing worker—had little idea of the difference between lies and the truth. This suspicion had been aroused on a number of occasions, most recently when, in the course of a desultory conversation during a slack period in the wine shop, William had commented on a newspaper report about a government minister found to have been lying.

'Can't blame him,' said Paul. 'Poor geezer. All those journalists after him like that. Can't blame him.'

'I beg your pardon,' said William. 'He is a minister of the Government. He should not tell lies.'

'A few porkies,' said Paul. 'Everybody tells porkies now and then. Specially if somebody's trying to get you.'

William found himself almost speechless. 'Porkies!'

'Yeah, porkies. What difference does it make if he says that he didn't do it? Nobody's been hurt, have they?'

William was silent for a few moments. 'You don't mind being lied to? You don't mind? When you trusted somebody and then he goes and lies to you when you're paying him your taxes . . .'

'Don't pay all that much tax,' Paul had said, looking reproachfully at William. 'If I earned more, then I'd pay more tax and maybe I'd feel a bit different. But as it is . . .'

Now, glaring at his assistant, William resorted to

sarcasm. 'You seem to live in a highly suicide-prone area, Paul. How many this year? Four? Amazing. Other people don't seem to suffer from quite as many person-on-track delays as you do. Extraordinary.'

Paul shrugged. 'Awful, isn't it? You'd think that they might choose a time when people didn't need to get to work. Why jump in front of a train when people need to get to work?'

William found himself being drawn into the exchange. He had started off talking about punctuality, but the conversation was entering deeper waters. 'People don't think about these things,' he said. 'They're usually very upset. But let's not dwell on that. There but for the grace of God go I.'

Paul looked at him in astonishment. 'What?'

'Never mind. It's an expression that means, it could happen to anybody. They don't teach you people anything these days, do they?'

'I wouldn't choose the District Line,' said Paul.

William opened one of the cases of wine and held a bottle up to the light. 'Look at this lovely stuff. You do know that they gave this to the Queen when she visited Italy last, don't you? They had a state banquet and served Her Majesty Brunello di Montalcino.'

Paul stared at the bottle. 'They could hardly give her Lambrusco.'

'Ah, but that's where you're wrong, Paul,' said William. 'Lambrusco has its place. Not the sort of stuff that we get in this country, but the real thing. They make it around Reggio Emilia and Parma. And I've tasted some very fine examples of it in the past. Out there it's much drier.'

'It taste like sherbet here,' said Paul.

'Perhaps. But that's because it's the sweet version. The locals drink it dry, and eat some fresh Parmesan cheese with it. It's delicious.'

William replaced the bottle of Brunello in its case. At this point the telephone rang and Paul, being closer, answered. He smiled as he spoke, and William began to wonder whether it was to be one of those long personal calls that irritated him so much. But then Paul mumbled something and handed the receiver to his employer.

It was Marcia.

'I'm coming round at lunchtime,' she said, 'with some very interesting news.'

'What is it?'

'You just wait.'

9. Marcia's Idea

Although Marcia had a habit of parking her van half-way over the pavement, she had never been given a parking ticket.

'The wardens are sweeties,' she once said to William. 'Or at least the male wardens are—in my experience. If you talk to them reasonably, they understand that you don't mean any harm. It's the female ones who are the problem. They're ruthless. Fortunately, I've never had any dealings with them, but my goodness, they're a bunch of frumps. Amazons. And they take out all their sexual frustrations on drivers—all because they can't get a man. Not one of them, I believe, has a man. Can you credit it?'

William had smiled. He was used to Marcia sounding off about all sorts of matters, and used to discounting most of what she said. She was full of prejudices, but in spite of that he found her entertaining. Nothing she said was *really* nasty; untrue, perhaps, and extreme, but not downright nasty.

That afternoon, she parked her car immediately in front of the wine shop, in a spot where the council might once have considered establishing a paid parking place but in the end decided not to. It was just right, Marcia thought; it was a car-shaped space that *needed* a car, or, as in this case, a modest-sized van, and she was doing no harm in leaving the van protruding just slightly over the pavement.

'There you are,' she said, as she walked into William's office at the back of the shop. 'Was that the coffee you were putting on?'

'No, not exactly. But I can if you wish.'

She lowered herself into the chair on the other side of William's desk. 'There's a dear. Thank you. As I said on the phone—'

'You have some important news to impart to me.'

'Yes, I do.'

William busied himself with the coffee as Marcia began to talk. 'Eddie,' she said.

William stiffened slightly. 'Eddie?'

'Yes, Eddie.' She paused, and looked at him across the room. 'You were telling me that you were keen to get Eddie into his own place.'

William unscrewed the top of the coffee canister and sniffed at the contents. Smells. He was very sensitive to smell, and coffee grounds were one of his olfactory favourites.

'Yes,' he said. 'Eddie is twenty-four now and I have been thinking about helping him to move on. There was that place in Kentish Town . . .'

'You told me about that,' said Marcia. 'The one that had no kitchen and a front door at a forty-five-degree angle.'

'Yes. Not the best of places. But he could have made something of it.'

'But didn't.'

William sighed. 'No. He didn't.' He turned and met Marcia's stare. 'Look, Marcia, Eddie may have his little failings but he is my flesh and blood, you know . . .'

She held up a hand. 'Of course he is. Of course. And as his father you love him dearly. I know that.'

William turned back to the coffee. Did he love Eddie dearly? Would it be possible for *anybody* to love Eddie dearly? William's late wife had done so, but that was because she was his mother. Every mother loves her son dearly—or should. Even after the son has done something egregiously terrible—tried to shoot the Pope, or something equally awful—the mother would still love him. There had been that man, of course, who *had* shot the Pope; what must his mother have thought? Perhaps it would depend on whether the mother was Catholic or not, thought William. A Catholic mother might find her maternal affection *stretched* if her son did something like that. But then again, she would have remained his mother and might have argued, 'Well, dear, you must have had your reasons . . .'

The thought occurred to him that Marcia had found a flat for Eddie. That would be all very well, but the problem lay not so much in the finding of flats—there were plenty of those—but in getting

37

Eddie to move into one of them.

'You've found somewhere suitable for him?' he asked. 'He's difficult, you know. He's very fussy when it comes to flats. Corduroy Mansions seems to suit him rather too well.'

Marcia shook her head. 'No, I haven't found him a flat. But I've found a way of encouraging him to move out. It's something you and I have already discussed.'

William poured two shots of espresso into a cup and brought it over to Marcia.

'There,' he said. 'Strong.'

She looked at him appreciatively. 'Remember you said you'd had the idea of getting a dog. You said that Eddie can't stand dogs and that if you got one, then he would probably be inclined to move out. Remember?'

William laughed. 'Yes, I do. I had planned that but the problem, you see, is that I can't envisage keeping a dog for ever. What would happen once Eddie had taken the hint? You can't take dogs back to the . . .'—he waved a hand in the air—'to the dog place.'

'But—'

William was emphatic. 'No, you can't.'

'I know that,' said Marcia, rather crossly. 'But the point is that you could have a *temporary* dog.' She paused, taking a sip of her espresso. William made such delicious coffee, and yet there he was single; such a waste . . . 'Let me explain. I was catering for a dinner party in Highgate the other night. Quite a do, and some fairly well-known faces there. The host is a newspaper columnist. Not that I read him. But somebody must, I suppose. Always preaching to people, telling them what to do; holier than

38

thou. Anyway, when I took things round before the guests arrived I got talking to him. They have this dog, you see. Odd sort of creature. A mongrel, I'd say, but he said it was a Pimlico Terrier. Now there's a coincidence—you living in Pimlico. Have you ever heard of Pimlico Terriers? No? Neither have I.'

She took another sip of her coffee. 'Anyway, he said that they liked this dog but they wished they had some sort of dog-sharing arrangement. He said that they had friends who had a set-up like that—the dog was shared by two households. If one set of people had to go away, the dog went to the other. It divided its time.'

William nodded. 'A useful arrangement. People sometimes have that sort of thing for their elderly relatives.'

'Exactly. So it occurred to me: why don't you talk to them about sharing this Pimlico Terrier with them? You need a dog, but not a full-time dog. They have a full-time dog that they would like to convert into a part-time dog. If job-sharing is all the rage, then why not dog-sharing?'

10. Oedipus Snark MP

Jenny was on her way to Dolphin Square, where she was to meet Oedipus Snark for what he described as *dictée*. She had asked him why he called it that, and he had replied, 'Dictation, my dear Jennifer, is such an *authoritarian* word. If I were to give you dictation, I would feel so like a . . . like a *Conservative*. Dictators, no doubt, give

39

Oedipus
Snark MP

dictation. Whereas *dictée* is what we used to have at the Lycée in South Kensington. Our dear teacher, Madame Hilliard, would dictate a complicated passage to us—Proust perhaps, with its dreadfully long sentences—and we poor *élèves* would write it all down in our little *cahiers*. So sweet. That's why I call this taking of letters on your part *dictée* rather than dictation. See?'

Oedipus Snark had an annoying habit of adding *see?* to his observations. At first Jenny had been largely unaware of it, but then, after she had worked for him for a few weeks, she became acutely conscious of it and resented it greatly. She had even sent a letter about it to an agony aunt, in which she had written: 'I work for a man in public life. He has his good points, I am sure, but I am finding his turn of phrase more and more irritating. At the end of many of his sentences he adds the word 'see'. He is not Welsh; when Welsh people say that, or 'look you', it sounds rather nice, but he is not Welsh. Should I say something to him about this, or should I try to put it out of my mind?

The work is otherwise interesting and I do not want to lose my job.'

The agony aunt had published this letter, and her reply.

Dear Anxious,

There is often nothing worse than some little mannerism in others that we become aware of and then look out for. I have a teenage son who adds 'and stuff' to virtually everything he says. When I ask him what time it is, he says, 'It's eight, and stuff.' By comparison, what your boss says is mild, although I fully understand that my telling you that other people have worse verbal mannerisms must be scant consolation. I always remember the advice given by a rather wise psychiatrist, who said, 'the contemplation of the toothache of another in no way relieves one's own toothache'. That, I think, is broadly true.

What should you do? Well, the same doctor also said, 'verbalisation precedes resolution'. And that, I think, is also very true. So I suggest that you talk to your boss and say that there is a little matter that is worrying you. Stress that it's just you—that it's an odd sensitivity you have—and then tell him what it is. My bet is that if you are frank—and if you mention that you have many faults yourself— he will be accommodating and will try to stop. Alternatively, of course, he may sack you.

The final part of this advice had persuaded Jenny that perhaps it was best not to say anything, and so

41

she merely closed her ears to the 'see'. And there was so much else to take exception to in Oedipus Snark that linguistic mannerisms were soon overshadowed. Jenny became used to the false excuses that he gave—'diplomatic excuses', he called them—but still it made her uncomfortable to be party to them. Like all MPs, he received regular invitations to visit schools and libraries in his constituency, and he was in the habit of turning all of these down, without exception. 'I shall, alas, be tied up with parliamentary business on that day' was the standard excuse. It was then followed by fulsome praise of the school's efforts: 'May I take this opportunity to tell you how many people have expressed their admiration for the high standards that your school has achieved over the last year. I really must congratulate you: it is not easy to motivate students in these distracting days, and you seem to achieve this with conspicuous success.' This was said to every school, and had even once been inserted into a letter to a local baker, who had written about European regulations and their baneful effect on small bakers.

For invitations to functions that were several months away, more inventive excuses were necessary. It was difficult to turn down an invitation received in, say, March for an event that was to take place in October. But Oedipus Snark was not loth to do this, and he had even told a pensioners' action group that he could not attend a meeting planned for six months hence. 'I very much regret that I shall be unable to attend,' he dictated, 'on the grounds that . . .' He paused, and looked at Jenny as if for inspiration. 'On the grounds that I shall be attending a funeral on that

42

day. There!' he said. 'That settles that.'

Jenny looked up from her notebook. 'But . . .' she began. 'But, how could you know? Funerals are usually arranged only a few days beforehand. They'll know that you can't possibly be booked to go to a funeral six months ahead.'

Oedipus Snark glared at her. 'Oh yes?' he challenged. 'And what about cases where people are given six months to live? You have heard of those, I take it? Well, there you are. It's perfectly possible that if somebody has been given six months to live and has told his friends, they'll pencil his funeral in the diary. Perfectly possible.' And to underline his point, he added, 'See?'

Jenny had bitten her lip, both in reality and metaphorically. She told herself that she was not in a position to change him in any respect and that she should therefore simply accept him for what he was. After all, he was a democratically elected Member of Parliament, even if the turn-out in his constituency at the election had been only thirty-two per cent. He had been chosen, and it was not for her to dispute the choice of his electors. In those circumstances, her job was to help him to do the job that he had been elected to do; or to avoid doing it, as was the case with him. But she realised that she did not like him, and never could. And that, she later discovered, was exactly what Oedipus Snark's own mother thought about him too.

'Don't talk to me about my son,' Berthea Snark had said to Jenny when she first met her. 'Just don't talk to me about him.'

11. A Flexible Diary

Oedipus Snark's two-bedroom flat in Dolphin Square was on the third floor, affording him a wide view, just above the tops of the trees, of the unlikely Italianate gardens. It was a place much favoured by politicians. 'From my window,' he was fond of saying, 'I can see into the flats of twenty-two other members of the House of Commons. With binoculars, of course.'

He knew the locations of the many political landmarks: the house where de Gaulle had lived and from which he had run his campaign, the counterpoint to that infamous hotel in Vichy; the flat where Lord Haw-Haw had stayed; the one where Christine Keeler had entertained; and so on. 'Success in politics,' he had explained to Jenny when she first went to work for him, 'is purely about one's address book. There is only one person who can afford not to have an address book, Jenny. You know who that is?'

She did not. 'Who?'

'I'll tell you some other time,' he said.

It was typical of the evasive answers to which she would soon become accustomed. Even a simple question—such as an enquiry as to what time it was—could be evaded. 'It's rather late,' he said to her once when her watch had stopped and she had asked him the time.

'But what's the actual time?'

He looked at his wristwatch. 'After four,' he said, 'and I must get up to the House.'

That answer, she reflected, revealed two things

44

about his personality. The first was this tendency not to provide an answer to a question, however innocuous; the second was the extent to which the universe—even time—revolved around him. Four o'clock was four o'clock universally—at least for the sixty-odd million people living in the GMT zone—but for Oedipus Snark the significance of four o'clock was what it meant in *his* life, according to the exigencies of his diary for that day.

Jenny arrived shortly before ten that morning to find Oedipus Snark sitting in the converted bedroom that served as his office. It was not a large room, but it was big enough to hold two desks—a generously proportioned one for him and an extremely small one for Jenny. In fact, Jenny had earlier discovered that her desk came from a primary school that had closed down and sold off its furniture cheaply. The desk's provenance had been revealed by the initials carved by a child into the underside of the lid, and also by the small pieces of dried chewing gum parked underneath. When she had pointed these out to Oedipus Snark, he had laughed.

'I remember doing that as a boy,' he said. 'I used to stick chewing gum under the dining-room table and then take it out and revive it by dipping it in the sugar bowl.'

Jenny winced. Could germs survive in the medium of dried-up gum, or did they die a gummy death? She extracted her handkerchief from her bag and used it to prise the small nodules of gum off the wood. Oedipus Snark watched her, amused.

'You're not one of these people who're pathologically afraid of germs, are you?' he asked. 'Like the late Howard Hughes. The germs

45

eventually got him, of course.'

'No. It's just that I don't like the idea of little pieces of gum on my desk. It is a school desk, isn't it? For a very small child?'

Oedipus Snark frowned. 'Don't think so,' he said. 'Compact, I suppose. But that's an advantage these days.' He paused. 'Going back to germs, tell me what do you do with the handles of public loos? Do you touch them?'

Jenny looked away. She was not sure whether she wanted to talk about that. As it happened, she made sure that she never touched such handles with her hands, and would resort to gymnastics, pulling the chain with her foot if necessary, rather than risk the very obvious bacterial contamination that awaited those unwise enough to put their hands on such things. But she was not going to tell Oedipus Snark that.

'What do *you* do?' she asked.

He sniffed. 'I am not one of those obsessive-compulsive types,' he said. 'And we all know that a few germs are necessary for the immune system to keep itself in trim. That's why there's so much asthma these days—people are not exposed to enough germs.'

She realised that he had not answered her question. She persisted. 'So you don't touch the handle?'

Oedipus Snark nonchalantly picked up a piece of paper from his desk and began to read it. 'This is a letter from Lou Portington. Remember her? Rather large party. There's one loo I wouldn't touch, even with gloves on! Hah! See?'

Jenny settled herself at her minuscule desk and picked up her notebook.

46

Oedipus Snark continued: 'She wants me to go to a dinner she's holding for the French Ambassador. At her place. How kind of her.'

Jenny made a note in her notebook. 'And the date?'

Oedipus Snark put down the letter. *'Problema.* La Portington has alighted on the twenty-second, which no doubt suits His Excellency but which is the evening I've agreed to speak at that substance abuse conference. I was due to open it, wasn't I?'

Jenny consulted a diary. 'Yes. You agreed to that eight months ago. They wrote the other day with the programme. You're on at seven-thirty. The first plenary session.'

'Pity,' said Oedipus Snark.

'Yes.' Jenny made another note in her book. 'Shall I write and give your regrets?'

'Please do. Say that I'm terribly sorry, but I just can't manage it.'

Jenny nodded. 'I'm sure that she'll find plenty of people happy to have dinner with the French Ambassador.'

Oedipus Snark looked up sharply. 'I meant that you should give my regrets to the substance abuse people. Usual thing. Sorry to cancel etc., etc. Urgent Party business.'

She looked at him. Hateful, she thought. Hateful Snark. Dissembling, lying Oedipus.

12. Berthea Snark

Those were the very thoughts, as it happened, that Berthea Snark was entertaining about her son at

47

that precise moment—an example of what is known as Proustian synchronicity, where the stream of consciousness of one person matches another's and where, for a few moments, both flow in the same direction and at the same pace, like waters conjoined. This instance of synchronicity, though, was not all that surprising, for if Oedipus Snark crossed the mind of anybody at any particular time, there was a reasonable chance that his mother was also thinking of him at that same point, given that she thought about him thirty or forty times a day—possibly more. This was not just because she was his mother, but because for the past two years she had been writing her son's unauthorised biography—a task that required frequent contemplation of the subject. Such is the lot of the biographer: to live with the subject, to inhabit his skin, to enter his mental universe, to such an extent that biographer and subject become one.

Where a mother writes her son's biography, this notion of becoming one with the subject has, of course, an additional, striking resonance. She and Oedipus had indeed been one, when she had nurtured the Liberal Democrat politician *in utero*. Not that a pregnant woman thinks of the baby she is carrying as being political: a mother may *wish* for a Liberal Democrat baby, but may not think of the matter as determined. And there is always the possibility that the child will grow in a political direction not contemplated, or approved of, by the parent; how many parents have seen their children espouse views radically different from their own?

Berthea Snark did not disapprove of her son's political party, which struck her as being largely

48

benign, perhaps even a *touch* too well-meaning, but only a touch. Nor did she disapprove of the parties to which he was in opposition. She quite liked the Labour Party for some of its policies and the Conservatives for some of theirs. It all depends, she said. Why should everybody embrace the herd instinct which required one to regard one set of politicians as being always in the right while demonising another set? But what she did disapprove of was her son's hypocrisy. He might be a Liberal Democrat on the surface, but he was not, she believed, a liberal democrat inside. And that was a most serious matter. Authenticity, in Berthea's view, was all.

As Oedipus Snark discussed with his assistant, Jenny, the breaking of his undertaking of eight months' standing to open a conference, Berthea Snark was preparing herself a cup of coffee in her house in a small street not far from Corduroy Mansions. This street, a cobbled mews which meandered briefly before ending in a modest row of garages, had become fashionable only recently. Berthea and her husband, Hubert Snark, had not had to pay present-day inflated prices for their home; they had acquired it for a song thirty years ago, when Oedipus was six. The mews house had been his childhood home and the place in which he first dreamed of reaching that promised land only a short distance away—Westminster. For just as small American boys may, in their log cabins, dream of the White House, so may small British boys, in their mews houses, dream of the House of Commons.

Berthea's husband had been a largely absent father. When Oedipus was at primary school at the

French Lycée in Kensington, Hubert had begun an affair with Jane Sharplie, an Oxford philosophy don and a Fellow of Somerville College, and had drifted away from the marriage. Berthea had been aware of the affair from the beginning; she was, in fact, a colleague and friend of the other woman, and had reviewed one of her books—favourably— in *Mind*.

'I know what's going on,' she announced to Jane. They were sitting in the Friends' Room at the Royal Academy in Piccadilly, having met to view a well-received exhibition of French painting.

'Then you are fortunate,' said Jane, sipping at her coffee. 'There are few of my philosopher colleagues at Oxford who can say the same thing. I, for one, must admit quite frankly that I don't know what's going on. I am working on the question, but cannot truthfully say that I have yet found an answer.'

Berthea smiled. 'As a philosopher,' she said, 'it's your privilege to misinterpret what I say. But when I said I knew what was going on, I did not mean that I had achieved any insight into the meaning of things; I simply meant that I know what's going on between you and Hubert.'

Jane put down her coffee cup. 'Oh that,' she said nonchalantly. 'I thought that you meant . . .'

Berthea smiled again, more sweetly this time. 'No,' she said, 'I meant the other thing.'

There was a silence. A fussy-looking man seated at a neighbouring table glanced at the two women before returning to his copy of the *Burlington Magazine*.

'I don't want you to think that I'm angry,' said Berthea. 'Many women would be, but in my case . . .

50

Well, frankly, Jane, you're welcome to him.'

Jane looked at her friend. 'I didn't start it,' she said.

Berthea nodded. 'Of course not. I've never taken the view that the tango requires two. Such an old-fashioned attitude to dancing.'

There was a further silence as this comment was digested.

'So there we are,' said Jane. She added, 'Would you mind terribly if he moved to Oxford? He could always come back to Pimlico for . . . for the occasional weekend.'

'Not in the slightest,' replied Berthea. 'But I wouldn't want him to keep a room in town. We don't have all that much space and I would like to use his study as a waiting room for my patients. I consult in the house, you know.'

Jane was quick to agree. She looked at Berthea appreciatively. 'You're being very mature about this,' she said.

Berthea's coffee was getting cold. She lifted the cup to her lips and drained it. 'But that's why he's leaving me,' she said. 'Because I'm mature.'

They returned to the exhibition, still having a couple of rooms to visit. In the final gallery, where they found themselves faced with Vuillard and other post-Impressionists, Jane suddenly realised what Berthea's remark might mean. If Hubert was leaving Berthea because she was mature, did that mean that he was coming to her because she— Jane—was immature? Or that Hubert himself was not sufficiently mature for Berthea? Either way, she was not sure that she emerged with a great deal of credit—at least in Berthea's eyes.

They peered together at a Vuillard interior. For a

51

brief moment they turned and glanced at one another, and smiled. What was a man, a mere man, to come between two women friends who went back a long time? *Nothing*, thought Berthea.

They moved on. Another interior, a Montparnasse bedroom.

'I take it you've discovered that he snores,' Berthea remarked.

13. Stevie Phones Eddie

Marcia left William in a thoughtful state. Her visits usually gave him something to reflect upon—Marcia brimmed with ideas, not all of them useful—but on this occasion he felt that what she had said was well worth considering. He had prepared himself for a show-down with Eddie over moving out, and had decided that the best tactic to adopt was to insist—and he would have to insist—that Eddie pay rent out of the small fund his grandmother had left for his benefit, but which, crucially, was entirely controlled by William. This rent would be an economic one, thus forcing Eddie to choose between a cheap rent elsewhere or an expensive rent at home. Eddie did not like to spend money—if it was his own, the money of others being a different matter—and might just prefer the cheaper option. It was a long shot, perhaps, but worth trying.

The time was ripe. A few days earlier, William had overheard the alternative offer being made over the telephone when he had picked up the receiver in his bedroom at precisely the moment

Eddie had lifted it in the kitchen.

'That you, Ed?'

He recognised the voice of Eddie's friend, Stevie.

'Yup.'

And it's me too, thought William, *because I live here*. He was just about to put the receiver down and leave Eddie to get on with his telephone call when he heard himself mentioned. Nobody could resist that, especially when it was on his own phone in his own house.

Stevie's nasal voice continued. 'Your old man.'

'Yup. What about him?'

'Pretty fed up with him, aren't you?'

William held his breath. And what about me? he thought.

'Yup.'

William clenched his teeth.

'Mine gets on my nerves too. Blah, blah, blah. On and on about getting a job and a mortgage and so on. Blah, blah, blah.'

'Yup. Blah, blah, blah. Old-speak.'

William, on the point of interjecting 'blah', stopped himself in time. There was more to come.

'Got a place at last. Found it yesterday. Kennington. Not bad at all.'

'Oh yeah?'

'Yep. De Laune Street. Heard of it?'

Eddie had not. 'Sounds posh. Not?'

'No, not. But it's got three bedrooms. Five hundred and sixty quid a month each. I need one other person. Maggie says she'll take one of the rooms, but only three weeks after the lease starts. That's a bit awkward but I said OK, that's cool. So there's her and me. I thought you might like the other room. Get your old man out of your hair.'

53

William's eyes widened.

'Well . . .'

Take it, thought William. I'll pay.

'Nice place,' said Stevie. 'You know that pub we went to last month with Mike? Remember? It's round the corner.'

There was silence. William imagined Eddie doing the calculation. Currently he lived rent-free in a better area. He also received free food and heating, and paid no discernible taxes. If anything went wrong and a tradesman was required, then it was William who made the arrangements. And Eddie, as far as his father could remember, had never used the vacuum cleaner, nor washed up, nor even loaded the dishwasher, in spite of frequent hints and requests. Eventually William had tired of piles of unwashed crockery and accepted that he would have to do everything himself—in a tight-lipped way, of course, but keeping before him, like the prospect of release from servitude, that glorious moment when his son would announce that he had found a flat and was moving out. Durance vile, though, was proving to be drawn out.

Eddie spoke. 'Can you give me time to think? There's quite a lot going on round here that I have to sort out.'

'Next week, Ed,' said Stevie. 'Next week, max. I have to tell the guy next week or he gives to it to somebody else. Students, I think. He doesn't really want students, but he says they're offering to pay a bit more rent and he has to know.'

'Students are bad news,' said Eddie.

William slipped the handset back into its cradle. He had heard enough—too much, in fact. Eddie

54

had said that there was a lot going on—but what exactly did he mean by that? And as for the comment about students . . . One has to laugh, he thought, and he did then; looking up at the ceiling, he laughed at his son's sheer effrontery. One had to like the young man, one really did. Perhaps he should just let him stay, resign himself to the fact that some people were *meant* to stay at home, like those Victorian and Edwardian women who never married but lived at home to look after their parents. And then, when the parents were no more, they became companions to other women, richer ones, and lived in that beholden state for the rest of their days.

But there was a difference. Those daughters looked after their parents, whereas it was he who was looking after Eddie. That was a major difference. And then those women busied themselves with all sorts of activities—sewing, making things—whereas Eddie . . .

No, the decision was made. And now, sitting in his office, staring at the empty chair recently occupied by Marcia, he realised that the endless rehearsal of options could be just that—endless. Upon reflection, the rent scheme looked less and less likely to achieve its objective. Eddie would simply refuse to pay up, and even though William controlled the purse-strings of the grandmother fund, he doubted whether he would be able to stand up to a furious Eddie should he turn off the monetary tap. No, he would have to be more subtle, and Marcia's idea of obtaining a dog under a dog-share scheme seemed the perfect answer. Eddie hated dogs. He was scared of them in an utterly irrational way. And there was a physical reaction too: dogs made his eyes water—not uncontrollably, but at least to the point of irritation. And if a dog licked him, his skin itched.

He picked up the telephone and dialled the number Marcia had left. Would this dog be *licky*? he wondered. He hoped so.

A voice answered at the other end: a slightly impatient voice, the voice of one who rather resents being telephoned by a caller who will almost certainly be less *significant*.

'Look,' said William, 'I'm sorry to phone out of the blue, but I was given your number by Marcia. She did some catering for you recently and she said that—'

The voice cut him short. 'If you're wanting to sell me something, I'm afraid—'

'No, I'm not. Not at all. It's just about your dog.'

There was a surprised silence at the other end of the line. Then: 'My dog? Freddie de la Hay. Do you know him?'

14. The Names of Dogs

William had treated himself to a taxi—this was, after all, a special mission and he needed time to think. He would need to come back by taxi too, since he was unsure about taking a dog on the tube. William reflected on the fact that while dog-owners notice the dogs of others and what they are doing, non-dog-owners tend not to be aware of what dogs are up to and what rules, if any, they obey. Had he seen dogs on the tube? There was a guide dog who travelled regularly on the Victoria

56

ROVER PHOENIX

Line; William had once spoken to its owner, breaking the rule of silence that made strangers of multitudes, and had heard how this intelligent dog could distinguish the various lines by their smell. The Victoria Line, the owner claimed, smelled quite different from the Northern Line or the District and Circle Lines; but only a dog would know.

Guide dogs, of course, were different, and usually not subject to the same rules as lesser dogs, but when it came to recalling whether he had seen ordinary dogs travelling on the tube, he was not sure. But then he remembered: he had seen a dog on the Northern Line a while back, being carried by its owner, a middle-aged woman in a low-waisted green dress who had talked to the dog throughout the journey. William remembered this because he had been struck by the conversation between woman and canine. The woman had looked into the dog's eyes as she addressed it, and it had looked back at her with every indication of understanding and agreement. He had thought: she yearns for conversation, here in this great city,

57

and only the dog will oblige.

But even if the dog-sharing arrangement were agreed that day, he would not want to travel back on the tube with a dog who would still be a stranger. And what if one had to pick up one's dog to travel on an escalator? He was not sure he would be able to lift this Freddie de la Hay, who could for all he knew be a very large dog, the size of a Rottweiler perhaps and with a disposition to match, who would respond to William's attempts to pick him up by savaging him, right there in the tube station, at the foot of the escalator beside the admonitory notice, Dogs Must Be Carried. What a scene that would be, as the crowds, anxious not to be delayed, stepped around the scene of carnage, one or two muttering, 'Well, you shouldn't bring large dogs on the tube.'

The thought made William worry. In his eagerness to enter into this arrangement, he had forgotten to ask for any information about Freddie de la Hay. All he knew was that he was a Pimlico Terrier, a breed that he had never seen, nor indeed heard of before. And as for his name . . . He looked out of the taxi window as he mused on the subject of canine names. From one point of view, the name of a dog said nothing about the dog itself and everything about the owner. But then, *mutatis mutandis,* that was the case with human names too, except in those comparatively rare cases where people chose to call themselves something other than the name imposed on them by their parents. John Wayne was really Marion Morrison—not a name by which a macho film star might wish to be known. And Harry Webb, had he sung under that name, might never have been as successful as he was as Cliff Richard. Such changes were understandable and necessary, perhaps, if creativity were to flourish. Of course, the new names chosen were usually much more suitable than those given at birth. John Wayne was clearly a John Wayne rather than a Marion Morrison. And the same must be felt by those boys who were called Beverley but became something else, out of sheer self-defence.

William remembered one such from school, a small boy with an intensely freckled face whose second initial was B. When it was discovered that this was for Beverley, a name that is technically available for both boys and girls, his life had become a torment of derision. Such is the cruelty of children, and of boys in particular, displayed in full vigour when difference or weakness is discovered. William tried to dredge the full name out of his memory: George Beverley Jones. That was it. And this George Beverley Jones had suddenly disappeared one day, absent from school—driven out, no doubt, sent somewhere else where the name might not follow him. Even now, in his taxi to Highgate, William felt a flush of embarrassment and regret at the ancient childhood cruelty. He had been one of those who had called out *Beverley!* in the corridors; everybody had.

Of course it was easy for parents to make a mistake, even if they chose popular names. What is unexceptional at one time might at another be ludicrous, or simply unfashionable. Elderly ladies called Euphemia—and there must be very few left—had been nothing unusual as girls, and no doubt never dreamed that their name would later come to be regarded as quaint. In fifty years' time,

59

the same conceivably might be said of the legions of Kylies, who already might be feeling a certain suspicion that they were touched with the mark of a particular decade. While Euphemia could be shortened to Effie or even Ef, there was not much that one could drop from Kylie. One might become Ky, perhaps, he mused; there was a certain ring to that.

River Phoenix, thought William. Now there was a name! Rover Phoenix would be the canine version, and it was just as effective, just as redolent of whatever it was that made River Phoenix such a desirable name. Rover Phoenix would be a good-looking dog; compact, decisive, with a baritone bark and a light in his eye. An American dog, no doubt; certainly a dog who would go down well in California, in the back of an open-topped car, his ears catching the wind. Rover Phoenix.

Mind you, he reflected, there are traffic jams in California, and we should not imagine that open-topped cars there proceed with much greater dispatch than London taxis, caught, as William's taxi now was, in a slow-moving line of grumbling, irritable humanity. Even so, he was nearing his destination, and he felt a curious sense of anticipation, tinged with the realisation that what he was doing was somewhat absurd. Why should he be forced to get a dog in order to persuade his son to move out? It seemed quite ridiculous. It was Marcia, again. He always allowed himself to be persuaded by her to do things he really should not be doing.

He should stop the taxi; he should ask the driver to turn it round and go home. He could phone the dog's owner and explain that he had decided that

60

they should not go ahead with the whole ridiculous scheme. He could so easily do that.

But then the taxi driver half turned in his seat and said, 'Number eight, wasn't it?' And William said yes, it was.

As they stopped at the front gate, somewhere inside the house a dog barked.

15. *An Experiment*

'This way,' said Manfred James. 'We'll go into my study, I think.'

William looked at Manfred. The columnist was a tall man somewhere in his forties, wearing a small pair of unframed glasses and with a slightly distracted, scholarly air to him. The disdain that William had picked up on the telephone was present in the flesh, he thought; his host's aquiline nose was carried at such an angle as to look down on his guest, as if slightly displeased—if noses can express such things. He had welcomed William at the front door and led him into a book-lined room off the small entrance hall. As William stood there, glancing at the bookshelves, the barking that had greeted his arrival abated. That would be Freddie de la Hay, shut away in some room at the back. Dogs barked, of course; he had not thought of the implications of that for Corduroy Mansions. Would Freddie de la Hay's barking carry to the flat downstairs and disturb the girls? Eddie would not like it, but then that was the whole point of the exercise. The more Freddie de la Hay and Eddie got on each other's nerves, the better.

'Tea?' asked Manfred.

William accepted, and Manfred went out of the room, gesturing casually for his guest to sit on the small leather sofa backed up against a wall of shelves. As he sat down, William glanced at the books behind him. They seemed to be arranged in no particular order: *Poland's Past* rubbed shoulders on one side with *Schopenhauer Delineated* and on the other with a small book on the history of rope-making in Bridport. Then came *Garner's Modern American Usage* and a line of vintage Graham Greenes, as tatty and desolate as the territory they described.

A few minutes later Manfred came in with two mugs of tea. 'You may conclude only one thing from my shelves,' he said, noticing the direction of his guest's gaze, 'and that is that I have not bothered to organise the books according to any of the accepted patterns.'

William accepted the mug of tea offered him. 'It's difficult. I find that—'

Manfred, lowering himself into a chair opposite the sofa, cut him short. 'Alphabetical arrangement is not the only option,' he said. 'And I'm always slightly suspicious of people whose books are arranged alphabetically. OCD issues. One isn't a bookshop, you know. Nor a library.'

William shrugged. 'It must be helpful, though. I find that when—'

'The late Alistair Cooke had a wonderful scheme,' Manfred continued, 'whereby he placed books on the United States in such a position on his wall of shelves as to reflect their geographical situation. Books on Montana were at the top and those on Florida were down in the bottom right-hand corner.'

William smiled. 'I once read about how the Victorians—'

'Yes,' said Manfred, 'shelved books by male authors separately from those by female authors, out of a sense of propriety. Frightfully funny.' He took a sip of his tea, staring intently at William over the top of the mug. 'Now then, Freddie de la Hay. It's an extraordinary coincidence that Maria—'

'Marcia,' interrupted William.

Manfred looked slightly annoyed. 'Of course. Marcia. That Marcia should have discovered that we wanted to *share* our dog. And then discovered that you would be quite keen on an arrangement of that sort. Isn't London extraordinary? There will be a *consensus ad idem* somewhere for every matter under the sun. And this applies to selling things too. If there is one person wishing to sell a collection of the stamps of Fiji, there will be some other person anxious to buy just such a thing. London, I think, is the perfect market. Ideas. Things. People. Every vendor will find a purchaser.'

'I'm a wine merchant,' offered William. 'I sometimes go to the wine auctions and you find that even the most obscure—'

'Yes, of course,' interjected Manfred. 'Now, Freddie de la Hay. He's a remarkable dog, you know. We found him down in Kent, in a little place called Sutton Valence. Charming spot. A friend had put us in touch with a breeder down there and we chose him from a litter of four. He was by far the most intelligent-looking of the lot. I can't stand an unintelligent dog, can you?'

63

'It depends on the personality,' said William. 'You find that some dogs who are a bit dim are very affectionate, and then—'

'Of course,' interrupted Manfred. 'That's to be expected. But we wanted to carry out a little experiment with our dog and so we wanted one that was up to the challenge.'

William frowned. 'Experiment?' He decided that the best way to conduct a conversation with the columnist would be to use sentences of only one word. In this way, a contribution could be made before Manfred had time to interject.

'Yes. An experiment. We wanted to see whether one could raise a dog for the twenty-first century.'

William stared at him. 'Oh?'

The columnist adjusted his glasses; behind the lenses, the eyes were large. The aquiline nose tilted higher. 'Do you realise the damage that dogs cause to the environment?'

William thought for a moment. 'No,' he said.

'Well, I can give you the figures. Or rather, I could look them up, I have them somewhere. If you work out how many cattle dogs get through with that disgusting dog food of theirs, you can extrapolate how many acres of rain forest are felled for pasture to feed those cattle. *Quod erat—*'

'*Demonstrandum,*' supplied William.

The nose tilted again. 'Exactly. So we have tried to bring up Freddie de la Hay to be a responsible world citizen. This has two dimensions to it. One is behavioural, and the other is dietary.'

'Dietary,' muttered William.

'Yes. Freddie de la Hay, you see, is a vegetarian.' Then he added, 'For starters.'

16. *An Invitation to Bake is Misconstrued*

Caroline's tête-à-tête with her friend James in a coffee bar off Tottenham Court Road proved to take longer than she had anticipated. She had no further lectures to attend that day, but she had thought that she might spend the late morning and afternoon writing an essay that, even if it was not yet overdue, had about it an air of impending tardiness. For the most part, her course assignments went smoothly, but every so often she found herself working on something where her thoughts never seemed to rise above the banal. This essay was one such project.

James, however, wanted to talk, and the claims of friendship were stronger than the promptings of academic obligation. His problem, too, was not something that could be disposed of in a few minutes; it was a matter that could affect the entire direction of his life.

'Are you sure?' she said to him. 'Are you quite sure?'

He nodded. 'Yes. I really am.'

'You see,' she said, 'this is not something that one normally gets wrong, is it? One either feels a particular way, or one doesn't. Do you see what I mean?'

He frowned. 'But if it's a question of taste, can't one's tastes change as one goes through life?' He warmed to the theme. 'Think of music. I used to like the *Carmina Burana*—now I can't stand it. I can't take Orff. And Britten—I used to think he was tremendously boring, but now I actually enjoy his music. I saw *The Turn of the Screw* the other day at the ENO, by the way. I loved it.'

Caroline considered this. Had her own tastes changed? They had, she thought, but she was not sure the analogy was entirely appropriate. 'I don't know whether it's quite the same thing,' she ventured. 'It's not like a preference for red wine over white. I don't think it's that simple. It can't be.'

James looked at her searchingly. 'But if you read what the developmental psychologists have to say, isn't it true that people go through stages? I read that it's standard stuff for boys to be fond of other boys when they're growing up and then to start liking girls instead. Maybe that's what's happening to me. I'm going from one stage to another. Just a little bit later.'

Caroline stared into her cup of coffee. She was not sure whether she should be expressing an opinion on developmental theories. What did she know about all this? Nothing, really. All she knew was that there were people who liked one or the other, and some who liked both. Perhaps that was where James was. He was one who liked both. And if that was the case, then there was not very much that anybody else could do about it, even if they wanted to. James would have to decide what to do.

They rehearsed various possibilities, but forty minutes later they were no further on. 'Why don't you wait and see what happens?' she said eventually. 'Give it a year. Then if you really are going through some sort of change, you'll know about it. See how things turn out.'

James looked thoughtful. 'But if I'm to make a choice—and maybe you're right, maybe that's what

I should do—then surely I'll need to try being straight? Which means I'll need to find a girlfriend.'

Caroline agreed. 'Fine. No problem with that. Find one.'

'But that's hardly fair on the girl,' said James. 'Nobody wants to be an experiment.'

That, thought Caroline, is why I like you. You're so decent, so good. In general, men were only too willing to treat women as experiments.

'I think you should just tell her,' she said. 'You should explain the situation.'

James looked doubtful. 'But will anybody want me if I say that?'

Caroline knew the answer to this. 'Listen,' she said. 'There are hundreds of girls—thousands—who believe that they can win over a man who appears not to be interested. These girls think that they just need to show him what he's missing. They really do. Such men are seen as projects.'

James laughed. 'Then they're wrong.'

'Misadvised,' said Caroline.

'I don't want you to think that I believe there's anything wrong about it,' said James. 'I suspect I could be equally happy either way. It's just that I'm not sure which way I am.'

The conversation had come full circle, and Caroline now looked at her watch. 'I have to go to Blackwell's,' she said, 'and then I want to go back to my flat.' She hesitated. She did not want to leave him in the coffee bar, uncertain about who he was, but nor did she want to stay too long. She would ask him to accompany her. He was easy company and he would be no bother.

'Look, James,' she said. 'Would you like to come

back to Corduroy Mansions with me?'

He gave a start, and spilled a small amount of coffee on the sleeve of his shirt. 'You mean—?'

Caroline realised that he had misunderstood. 'Of course not,' she said quickly. 'I'm sorry, I didn't mean you to think that. Oh dear.'

For a moment he looked crestfallen. She swallowed hard. 'Listen, James,' she went on, 'I find you really attractive. And you are, you know. Anybody would find you attractive. But you and I are just friends, aren't we? There would be no point in changing the nature of our relationship.'

He nodded. 'I suppose you're right. But that's what everybody's going to think, aren't they? They will want me as a friend and that's all. How will I ever *know* what I want if all I'm going to get is friendship?'

'Oh come on, don't talk such rubbish. As I told you, there'll be plenty of girls wanting to . . . to get to know you better. Plenty.'

'I hope so.'

She rose to her feet. 'Come on, let's go to Blackwell's. Then, when we get back to Corduroy Mansions, we can bake something together. I want to make some biscuits.'

He looked at her mournfully. 'There you are,' he said. 'Would any woman ever invite a straight man to cook biscuits with her?'

Caroline was about to dismiss his objection out of hand, but then she thought, yes, he's right. No woman would ask a completely straight man to cook biscuits with her. It just wouldn't happen.

17. Brutalism in Architecture

'Arts and Crafts!' exclaimed James. 'Is this your place, Caroline? Corduroy Mansions.'

They had walked together up Ebury Street and turned into the side street on which, along with several other less distinguished blocks of flats, stood Corduroy Mansions. James, who had a strong interest in architecture, was ecstatic.

'Look at your chimney,' he exclaimed. 'Pure Domestic Revival! And the sharply sloping roof. And the dormers. Oh, Caroline!'

'Those dormer windows are fake,' Caroline said. 'William—he lives on the top floor—says that there's nothing in the roof, just empty space.'

James became even more enthusiastic. 'Fake windows! Even better. Can you think of one contemporary architect, just one, who would bother to put in fake windows?'

They were standing on the pavement outside Corduroy Mansions, both looking up at the building's cream-painted brick façade and at the fake windows jutting out of the roof. Caroline tried to think of a contemporary architect who would resort to such decoration, and could not. Her problem was more profound, though: she was having difficulty thinking of *any* contemporary architect, whether or not he would resort to fake windows. She was weak on architects but she knew that there was one, at least, who was iconic. What was the name of the man who designed Stansted airport? Norman Foster. That was it.

'Norman Foster?' she ventured. 'No, he wouldn't, would he?'

James laughed. 'Certainly not. Mind you, he's all right, compared with some of them.'

'Stansted airport,' suggested Caroline. 'I quite like it.'

'Lots of air,' said James, making an extravagant, airy gesture above his head. 'And lots of light. Unlike most of Heathrow, which is a glorified *souk* these days.' He gave a shudder. 'All those low ceilings and tatty carpets and flashy shops. When you go to an airport abroad now—virtually anywhere—you find clean floors—stone floors—and ceilings that allow you to breathe. Everything has become so mean in this country.

'Mind you,' he went on, 'one shouldn't just pick on Heathrow. There's the British Library, a lot of people still hate that. I think it's rather nice inside though. That poor architect. I don't think he deserved all that criticism.'

He turned away from his inspection of the building and looked at Caroline. 'Do you think that architecture and morality are linked, Caroline?'

Caroline had been thinking about biscuits, and wondering whether she still had any lemons in the fridge. It would be nice, she thought, to make lemon biscuits rather like the organic ones Prince Charles baked for his Duchy Originals. They were delicious, those biscuits, but a bit of a treat, not being all that cheap. She could afford them—her father gave her a generous allowance—but when one shared with others one should be careful about what sort of food was left lying around in the kitchen. Not that any of them would eat food that was not theirs (a nibble, perhaps, now and then); it was more a question of *tact*. Dee had no spare money for expensive food; she largely lived on food supplements and brown rice. And the others, though not as hard up as Dee, had to watch what they spent. Oedipus Snark paid Jenny a pittance, she said, and although Jo seemed to find sufficient funds to go on regular paintballing weekends in Essex—a bizarre activity even for a man, and doubly so, thought Caroline, for a woman—even so, she was always grumbling about the price of essentials such as milk and bread.

'They're not essential,' Dee had once snapped. 'You don't need cooked grains. And milk is bad for you, as everybody knows. It's full of chemicals that the cows pick up when they eat the chemical-covered grass. Chemicals, Jo, chemicals. There was an article about it in *Anti-oxidant News*.'

Jo had ignored this. 'Back home in Perth,' she said, 'you never thought twice about buying something like milk. You just bought it. Here—'

Caroline's train of thought was interrupted by James.

'When I was at Cambridge,' he went on, 'there

was a Fellow of Peterhouse called David Watkin. Heard of him? A very amusing, interesting man. He said that modernism in architecture involved a frightening, stern morality. Everything must be functional, stripped bare, stark. Brutal. Hence the South Bank Centre.' He paused. 'I think he's right about modernism.'

'Oh,' said Caroline. 'So . . .'

'Of course,' James continued, 'we all know that buildings express an attitude to the world. And that means we can judge them morally.'

'Stansted airport?' asked Caroline.

'Open. Reasonably friendly. Not scary. It's OK from the moral point of view.'

Caroline was intrigued. She enjoyed James and his conversation. What would it be like, she wondered, to be married to somebody like him— somebody who would keep one entertained all the time? The world would be always be interesting with James by one's side. She looked at him again. He was very good-looking; there was little doubt about that. And yet, and yet . . .

'Give me an example of an evil building,' she asked. 'Can you?'

James did not take long to come up with an answer. 'Anything commissioned by Mussolini,' he said. 'Or designed by Speer. Fascist buildings. Soviet architecture—you know, those great horrid blocks of flats that showed such contempt for the people who lived in them. Treated them like ants. Las Vegas—virtually everything there.' He thought for a moment longer. 'Or that Romanian dictator's palace. You know, the one who was shot in his long winter coat when people rose up against him.'

'What about prisons? Don't they express . . . well,

72

cruelty?'

'I'm trying to think of famous prisons,' said James. 'I suppose, by their very nature, prisons will look unfriendly and hard. They have very small windows, you see, and that makes a building look threatening. The Bastille? San Quentin?'

'Yes. Those are certainly cruel buildings.'

James sighed. 'But look at modern fortress architecture. Schools with tiny windows and large swathes of concrete. Look at the Hayward Gallery, in all its brutality. How could they do it, Caroline? How could anybody *make* a thing like that?' He sighed again. 'And here's this lovely building, your Corduroy Mansions. Crumpled—if a building can be crumpled. Utterly friendly and human. A building that says, 'Come in, love.' That's what it says: it calls us 'love', like a tea lady. A building that one would like to sit down and have tea with. That sort of building.'

They both looked up at the comfortable brickwork.

'Those are our windows up there,' said Caroline.

James smiled. 'Lovely. Lovely windows.'

Caroline looked at him appreciatively. What other man would compliment one's *windows*? As her younger sister would say—with the elongated teenage vowel that signified utter approbation—he's sooooo sympathetic.

Was there a possibility? That business about stages—was there any truth in it? she wondered.

No, she must put all of that out of her mind. James was here to bake biscuits. Nothing more.

18. On the Sofa

James enthused further about the building, on the staircase and on the landing. 'Original doors,' he said. 'Worth their weight in . . . well, not quite gold, but very nice anyway. And look, your fittings, Caroline. The handle. To die for!'

Caroline thought this a little exaggerated, but said nothing. She had never inspected their door handle, and now, viewing it through James's aesthetically keener eyes, she realised that it was rather attractive. Vaguely Art Nouveau, she thought.

They went inside. 'Not much to get excited about in here,' she said. 'Our furniture is pretty ordinary. A bit run-down, in fact.'

James looked about him. 'I see what you mean. It could certainly do with a makeover. However, that sofa looks tempting.' He lowered himself onto the sofa, stretching his legs out in front of him. 'I could be very comfortable living here.'

Caroline raised an eyebrow. 'Well, there's no room, I'm afraid. Four people is about as many as this flat can hold.'

'Four girls,' mused James. 'Four girls living together in Corduroy Mansions. Tell me about them. I know all about you, of course, so you can skip that bit, but what about the others?'

'We all get on well enough,' said Caroline. 'I'm the most recent arrival. I've been here for six months—the others have all been here for a couple of years. Jenny found the flat. She knows the person who owns it. In fact, the owner is some sort of distant cousin of Jenny's father. She's a woman who lives down in Dorset. She's let this place ever since she inherited it from a friend. Wouldn't you like a friend to leave you a flat? Wouldn't that be a nice surprise?'

'Very,' agreed James. 'And also very unlikely. But who's this Jenny person? Tell me about her.'

Caroline slipped off her shoes and settled herself on the threadbare chintz sofa beside James. 'She's a few years older than me. Twenty-seven, I think. Everybody's older than me in this flat. I'm the baby.'

James laughed. 'You're twenty-three, aren't you? Same as me.'

Caroline did not think of James as being twenty-three. He looked young enough, of course—he was often asked for ID in the off-licence—but he talked as if he were much older. He knew so much, that was why. He was one of those people, she thought, who just seemed to know a great deal. And he spoke so *wisely*, as if he had thought for hours about everything he said.

'Jenny works as a PA,' she went on, 'for an MP. A man called Snark. Oedipus Snark.'

James frowned. 'I think I've read about him,' he said. 'Something in the *Evening Standard*. There was a picture of him and they said something like, 'If you think Liberal Democrat MPs are nice, meet Oedipus Snark.' Something like that. I had to laugh. Poor Lib Dems—they really are nice. As are the others, come to think of it. I've got nothing against the Tories or Labour. They're all rather sweet, don't you think?'

'Jenny hates him,' Caroline said. 'She'd agree with the *Standard*.'

'Then why does she work for him?'

Caroline had discussed the issue with Jenny and had received a curious answer. 'Because he fascinates me,' Jenny had said. 'Like a snake. You know how you go to a zoo and you see these deadly snakes in their glass enclosures and the snake looks at you with his little eyes. And you think: I'm only that far away from a painful death, only that far. If it weren't for the glass . . .'

She told James this. He shrugged. 'Forgive my saying this, Caroline, but isn't that the sort of thing that some women—I'm not saying all women, but some women—do? They find themselves fascinated by dreadful men and they stay with them—as employees or wives or girlfriends or whatever. And the horrible men know that this is how they feel and so they just carry on being ghastly because they're certain the women won't leave them. And they don't.'

'Maybe.' And then she added, 'Sometimes.' She was thinking of a girl she had known at university who had taken up with a boyfriend who talked about soccer all the time, got drunk regularly at weekends and was ill on the stairs. They had all said that she should leave him, but she had said that he was getting better and that underneath it all he was really very gentle. She had remained with him and they had eventually married; he had been drunk at his own wedding and had threatened the vicar. She shuddered at the memory.

'It's interesting that it should be like that,' James said. 'Men who find themselves with difficult women are far more likely just to leave, aren't they? They put up with so much less than women do. You people are heroines, you know. Heroines.'

76

'It's kind of you to say that, James.'

'Well, I do mean it. The more I think about women, the more I like them. Isn't that interesting? I used to be wary of girls, you know.' He paused. 'You don't mind my saying that, do you, Caroline? Present company excepted, of course.'

'Of course.'

He leaned back in the chair. 'I used to think that women were . . . well, rather bossy. That's why I preferred playing with other boys rather than with girls. I didn't like being bossed about.'

'Understandable.'

'Yes. But now I find that women don't really want to push me around. I suppose I've got more confidence. I know what I want.'

Caroline thought, but you don't, do you? That's the whole point: you don't know what you want. 'Did your mother push you around?' she asked. For a moment she entertained an absurd mental image of the infant James in a pushchair, being propelled around a park by his mother and, even then, gazing at the architecture of the park buildings and commenting on the fine ironwork.

For a few moments James was silent. 'My mother?' he asked.

'Yes. Your mother. Was she . . . dominating?'

There was something odd in James's eyes as he looked at Caroline. 'My mother,' he said quietly, 'was completely absent from my childhood. I never met her. Not once. Or at least not that I can remember.'

Caroline felt a twinge of anxiety. Her question had been a prying one but she had not expected to uncover something quite as uncomfortable as this.

'You needn't talk about it if you don't want to, James,' she said.

He looked at her again. 'All right,' he said. 'I won't.'

19. Unknown Boys

After their truncated conversation about mothers, Caroline and James moved into the kitchen to start baking biscuits. The maternal conversation had been brief, and indeed only covered the mother of one of them. Had the conversation developed more fully, then it might have progressed to deal with Caroline's own mother, Frances Jarvis, about whom Caroline had a considerable amount to say. Had James merely asked, 'What about your own mother, Caroline?' there would have been a brief pause, as if to underline the significance of what was to follow, and then Caroline would have said, 'My mother? Oh, James, where does one start?'

James would have smiled. 'It's never a simple question, is it? You never get people saying, 'Oh yes, my mother. A very normal, integrated person. Nothing to say, really.' You don't get that, do you?'

And Caroline would have agreed. 'Never. But since you've asked about my mother, let me tell you.

'Ever since I can remember—right back—my mother has had ambitions for me. Some mothers, I suppose, bring up their sons and daughters to do great things—to play the piano well, or to become tremendously good at some stupid sport, or to get the most fantastic exam results, or whatever. With my mother, all of that energy was focused on one thing—to make sure that I met the right sort of boys.'

'No!'

'Yes. Right from the beginning, when I was at nursery school, she spent a lot of time choosing my friends. They had to be *nice*. That was the word she used. They had to be nice. And if somebody wasn't nice, then he was not allowed. That's what she said: "Not very nice. Not allowed."'

James would have sighed. 'But all parents are like that. They have very clear ideas about who their children's friends ought to be.'

Caroline would have conceded that point, but her mother, she felt, was in a different league from most parents. Her determination that Caroline should eventually marry a boy of whom she approved was single-minded and all-consuming. The teenage Caroline's social programme was strictly vetted for suitability. Invitations to parties at the houses of boys who met maternal criteria were accepted with alacrity—by Frances, on behalf of Caroline—and those from dubious boys— unknown boys, as Frances called them, the sons of unknown parents—were turned down, again by Frances on behalf of her daughter.

'I'm sorry, dear, we don't know much about that boy. In fact, we know nothing about him at all. There'll be plenty of other invitations.'

'But I do know him! He's not unknown at all. He's really nice.'

'He may well be, dear, but we don't *know* that, do we? And unknown boys—well, we don't really have to go into that, do we?'

Caroline would have indeed preferred to be able

to go into all that. What exactly was the problem with unknown boys? What did unknown boys do, if anything, that known boys did not do? In her mind one thing at least was clear: the moment maternal authority was weakened and she was in a position to run her own life, she would seek out the company, without any delay, of the most unknown, the most obscure of boys.

Of course the motives behind her mother's concern were transparent. Her ambition for Caroline was simple: marriage to a suitable boy. Anything else, in her mind, was merely preparatory to that objective. Caroline, however, thought differently. She might have sprung from a background in which a woman's ideal destiny was to marry and settle down to the task of raising children, but this was not what she wanted to do. She wanted to study the history of art. She wanted to travel. She wanted to think for herself. She wanted to move among people who stimulated her—who had something to say. The sorts of boys thrown in her path by her mother were the antithesis of all that: they were dim, rather sporty boys from boarding schools with a reputation for rugby. Not what she wanted. She wanted a boy with style, a boy with a whiff of danger about him, a witty, artistically literate boy, a boy a bit like . . . James, come to think of it.

And now, standing with James in the kitchen as he paged through *How to be a Domestic Goddess* for a suitable recipe, she found herself thinking: perhaps it's been obvious all along. Perhaps the reason why James is thinking of redefining himself is that he really wants *me*. Not girls in the abstract, but *me*.

80

It was an intriguing idea. And even more intriguing was the idea of explaining the situation to her mother. Frances had views on such matters. 'Such boys, Caroline, are fine—in their place. Which is playing the piano, like Noël Coward or somebody like that.' That is what Frances thought.

She glanced at James. He would probably make her breakfast in bed. He would even come shopping with her. They would go to lunch at Daylesford Organic round the corner and chat about the day's events. There was a lot to be said for it. But what did he feel about her? It is all very well, she thought, from my perspective, but what does he feel about me?

James had found a suitable recipe in Nigella's book. 'Lemon gems,' he said. 'Look.'

Caroline examined the large photograph of lemon biscuits sitting on a cooling rack and nodded. 'Just what we need,' she agreed. 'And we've got everything, including the ground almonds.'

'Heaven,' said James.

Once again, Caroline thought that this was a bit of an exaggeration. But then it occurred to her that in saying *heaven*, James was referring not only to the biscuits, with what Nigella herself described as their *lemoniness*, but also to the heavenliness of being there, with her, about to do some baking together.

'Are you enjoying yourself?' she suddenly asked.

He looked at her with surprise. 'Immensely. Why do you ask?'

'Because I was just wondering. The two of us . . . baking together. It just seems . . . very right.'

He looked away, out of the window. The London

afternoon light was attenuated, soft. There would be rain, he noted.

He reached out and touched her hand, gently, brushing against it.

'*Festina lente*,' he said, and smiled.

Festina Lente, thought Caroline, would be a good name for a cookery writer. Almost as good as Delia, or even Nigella.

20. *Rare Tea*

Even if there are many negative features to my job, thought Jenny, there is at least one that is unconditionally positive. Oedipus Snark might require of her that she be loyal to his highly dubious personal cause, but at least she was more or less left to her own devices every afternoon, when the oleaginous politician went to the House of Commons or enjoyed lengthy lunches with his friend, Barbara Ragg, at the Poule au Pot restaurant. He had made it clear to Jenny when he first employed her that if there was nothing still to be done in the afternoon, then she was free to go home.

'I don't know what you get up to in your spare time, darling,' he drawled, 'and I don't care too much, frankly. No offence! So if there's nothing doing here at headquarters, please toddle along and do whatever girly stuff you fancy.'

He smiled at her with the air of one conferring a favour, or even some sort of benediction.

'You mean this is a flexi-time job?'

'If you must use such terms, yes. Perk of the

position. My own job, of course, is pretty much flexi-time, as you put it, although heaven knows how much I exert myself. See?'

Jenny bit her lip. Girly stuff! She was a graduate of the London School of Economics. She was currently reading a biography of Wittgenstein. She was . . . She felt herself getting warm with resentment.

'Mr Snark, I feel that I must—'

He raised a hand to stop her. 'Please! Oedipus. We don't stand on formality here. Now then . . .'

And they had progressed to the next item of business, leaving Jenny secretly fuming and determined to correct his erroneous impression of her. But she never did; as the months wore on, she realised that she would never succeed in getting him to see her as an intellectual equal, to treat her without the condescension that he seemed to show in all his dealings with women. And the reason for that, she decided, was that Oedipus Snark was profoundly solipsistic. If he paid no attention to her feelings, it was because he did not *see* her. For one who was constantly adding 'See?' to his observations, he saw remarkably little.

That afternoon, as Caroline and James embarked on the baking of Nigella's lemon gems, Jenny found herself just a few blocks away, standing outside Daylesford Organic, debating with herself whether to go inside and treat herself to a cup of coffee, or walk up to Hatchards bookshop on Piccadilly and consult Roger Katz about what to read. It had been her birthday several days earlier and her aunt in Norfolk had sent her a book token, as she had done every year since Jenny's fifth birthday. The value of the book token had increased by two pounds each year, with the result that it was now sufficient to allow the purchase of several hardbacks.

The onset of rain decided the matter. Jenny looked up at the sky; heavy purple clouds had built up in the east and the first drops of rain were splattering on the canvas awning of Daylesford. Inside, all was light, warmth and tempting aromas.

Just inside the doorway as she went in, an elegant dark-haired woman was dispensing small cups of tea to arriving customers. Jenny took the proffered cup and sipped.

'Jasmine,' said the woman. 'Can you smell it?'

Jenny nodded, glancing at the open silver packet of tea on the table. The Rare Tea Company.

'White tea,' said the woman, 'scented with jasmine. And this is oolong. Would you care to try it? I'm Henrietta, by the way.'

Jenny sipped at the second cup. 'Very delicate,' she said.

'Proper tea,' said Henrietta. 'When one thinks of what goes into the tea bags most people make do with . . .'

Jenny agreed, and was about to say so when she noticed that a man had entered the café and was standing beside her. He reached out for the cup of oolong being offered him and it was then that she recognised him.

'Mr Wickramsinghe.'

The cup at his lips, he turned to face her. 'Oh, Miss . . . Miss . . .'

'Jenny. From upstairs at Corduroy Mansions.'

He lowered his cup. 'Of course, please forgive me. Basil Wickramsinghe.'

'Yes, I know. I've seen you, of course, and we did

84

meet in William's flat when he held that meeting about the hall carpet. Do you remember?'

Basil Wickramsinghe nodded. 'That carpet. That most regrettable carpet. It's still there—as are we.'

Jenny laughed. Something she had read last year in the biography of Wittgenstein came back to her. Wittgenstein, it seemed, had cleaned his floors by sprinkling tea leaves over them and then sweeping them up.

'Wittgenstein,' she said, 'used damp tea leaves to clean carpets. Apparently tea soaks up the dirt.'

Henrietta looked disapprovingly at Jenny. 'One would hardly use these rare teas for that.'

Basil Wickramsinghe nodded his agreement, and purchased a packet of white tea from Henrietta. He threw a shy glance at Jenny. 'Are you walking back to Corduroy Mansions?' he asked.

She explained that she had been planning to have a cup of coffee. 'The rain,' she said, looking out of the window over her shoulder.

'But I have an umbrella,' said Basil Wickramsinghe. 'Perhaps you would care to walk under my umbrella with me, and then join me for a cup of white tea in the flat.'

Jenny hesitated. She knew nothing about Mr Wickramsinghe and one had to be careful in London. But one could not go through life being suspicious of one's neighbours, and William had spoken of him with affection. She agreed; Hatchards could wait, and there was something appealing about this quiet man with his rather formal manner.

They said goodbye to Henrietta and made their way out into the street. The rain had set in now, it appeared, and puddles were forming on the edge of the road, their surfaces speckled with circles created by the raindrops. They made their way quickly down the road, sheltering under Basil Wickramsinghe's generous umbrella. A wind had blown up to accompany the rain, and the branches of the trees in the small square were bending, the canopy of the umbrella straining at its moorings. By the time they reached the front door of Corduroy Mansions, both had wet ankles and Jenny felt a trickle of cold water running down her neck.

'Most inclement,' said Basil Wickramsinghe, shaking the water off his umbrella. He had a pedantic, rather old-fashioned way of speaking, as if he were following a script. Jenny had encountered this before in actors, and wondered whether acting was her neighbour's profession. Had she seen him on the stage perhaps?

'You aren't an actor, are you, Mr Wickramsinghe?' she asked as he fumbled with the key to his door.

He shook his head. 'No more so than anybody else,' he replied.

21. In Mr Wickramsinghe's Kitchen

'I hope that you don't get too much noise from our flat,' said Jenny. 'We're immediately above you and I suppose we do walk about a bit. And Jo—she's one of my flatmates—sometimes plays music a bit loudly.'

'It is no trouble at all,' said Basil Wickramsinghe as he slit open the newly purchased packet of white tea. 'I sometimes hear a bit of noise, but nothing serious. And it reminds me that I do not live all by myself in this building.'

'One is always aware of other people in London,' said Jenny. 'The problem is that one doesn't necessarily know who they are. I suppose there are people who live in this city and yet don't know a soul. Strange, isn't it?'

It occurred to her as she spoke that Basil Wickramsinghe himself might fit into this category for all she knew, and she wondered whether she had perhaps unwittingly offended him. But he did not appear to mind and simply nodded his agreement.

'Big cities can be impersonal, but I never feel that about London,' he said. 'When I first came here, I was worried I would be very lonely, but it hasn't been the case. I came from a very friendly place, you see.'

'Which was?'

'Galle, in Sri Lanka. Have you heard of it?'

'No. I'm sorry. I'm sure that I should have, but I haven't.'

He smiled. 'There is no need to apologise for never having heard of Galle. It is not like Colombo or Kandy or places like that. It is quite small. It has a harbour and an old fort and some very nice old Dutch houses. You would like it.'

They were standing in his kitchen, waiting for the kettle to boil. Jenny looked around; it was very neat, and far cleaner than their kitchen upstairs. Containers marked Rice and Beans and Flour were neatly lined up on the shelves alongside pots, chopping boards and various cooking implements.

Basil Wickramsinghe took two cups out of a

cupboard. 'Living in a place like this, one wonders who the other people in the building are. I have often thought about all you people upstairs. William, I know what he does—he is a wine merchant— and that son of his is nothing, I believe. I do not think that he works. But when it comes to the four of you, I have no idea at all.'

Jenny laughed, and told him what she and the others did. 'I would never have guessed any of that,' said Basil Wickramsinghe. 'Never.'

'And you, Mr Wickramsinghe?'

'I am Basil, please. Me? I am an accountant. It is very ordinary. But there we are. That is what I do.'

He poured two cups of tea and passed one to her. There was silence as they both sipped the scented brew. Then Basil Wickramsinghe glanced at his watch.

'I mustn't keep you,' said Jenny.

'I beg your pardon,' he said. 'It's rude to look at one's watch. But I have remembered that I am expecting somebody.'

Jenny drained her teacup. 'You must come and have tea with us some time,' she said.

He thanked her and went to show her out. Just as they reached the door, the bell sounded.

'My guest,' said Basil Wickramsinghe, almost apologetically.

He opened the door and Jenny saw a thin woman standing outside, holding a dripping umbrella. It may have been the rain or it may have been her dress, but the overriding impression she gave was of dowdiness. When the woman saw Jenny, she gave a start.

'My neighbour,' said Basil Wickramsinghe quickly.

She's jealous, thought Jenny.

The woman glanced at Jenny and then looked away. 'Am I early?' she said.

Basil Wickramsinghe's glance darted to Jenny and then quickly back to the other woman.

'This is Miss Oiseau,' he said, in introduction.

Jenny took the other woman's hand and shook it. It was wet, and had a clammy, lifeless feel to it. She smiled at Basil.

'Thank you for the tea.'

'I'm glad that you enjoyed it.'

She slipped past Miss Oiseau and out into the hall as the other woman went into the flat, and the door closed behind her. Miss Oiseau had left her umbrella in the hall, propped up against the jamb of Basil Wickramsinghe's door, and a small puddle was growing at its tip. Jenny was about to climb the stairs when she heard voices from inside the flat.

Miss Oiseau had a thin, reedy voice, with the quality of an old gramophone record. 'Who's that?'

'As I said, she's one of the neighbours. There's a flat full of girls upstairs. She's one of them.'

'Is she a sympathiser?'

Jenny could not help but incline her head closer to the door; who would not act thus in such circumstances? She heard Basil Wickramsinghe laugh. 'But how am I to know that? We didn't discuss anything like that. I only met her in that organic place. We hadn't talked about anything very much.'

'But do you think she might be?'

'It's impossible to tell. You can't ask people outright, can you? You have to be circumspect. There are signals. You know that.'

Something else was said that Jenny did not catch.

Then the sound of the voices faded; they had moved away from the door. Jenny, thoughtful—and guilty—set off up the stairs. She was trying to make sense of the conversation she had overheard, and not getting very far. All she knew was that the anaemic Miss Oiseau and Basil Wickramsinghe had some cause in common—a cause which attracted sympathisers, of whom she, for all she knew, might be one. And signals came into it—although exactly how rather taxed the imagination. Were they . . .? No, it seemed absurd. Were Basil Wickramsinghe and Miss Oiseau involved in something illicit? And was all this happening in Corduroy Mansions, of all buildings, in Pimlico, of all places?

Don't be absurd, she said to herself. The quiet accountant and his dowdy friend were not very likely co-conspirators. But were co-conspirators ever likely? The newspapers were full of instances of unlikely offenders, who had to live somewhere, after all. Jenny was not of a suspicious nature, but it was difficult to interpret the conversation she had overheard as anything but . . . intriguing, perhaps.

A sympathiser? Was she?

22. Master of Wine (Failed)

'So,' said Manfred James, putting down his mug of tea. 'I think that we've pretty much reached agreement, wouldn't you say?'

William would not have said that, but there was something about the columnist's manner that

brooked no discussion. It was not exactly peremptory, but it was certainly high-handed—the manner of one who *knew*. That always irritated William; he was aware of the fact that there were people who *knew*, but he had always felt it incumbent upon them to keep their knowledge to themselves unless asked to reveal it. In which case they could—with all due modesty—reveal that they knew what they were talking about, while still remaining conscious of the fact that for most people it was extremely trying to listen to somebody who knew more than they did.

This was, of course, a major problem in the world of wine, the world in which William spent his professional life. Wine was a subject on which there was a great deal of expert knowledge to be acquired; for some it was a lifetime's work, requiring prolonged and diligent study. This was rewarded, in some cases at least, by the Master of Wine qualification, which entitled one to put the letters MW after one's name.

Five years earlier, William had attempted the examination of the Institute of Masters of Wine, but had failed the written part. He was not alone in this; the success rate for that particular examination was one in four, so rigorous and demanding were the tests. Naturally he had been disappointed, since he had been looking forward to putting MW after his name, which currently had no letters at all, unless one counted Esq, which some business correspondents kindly put on their correspondence with him. But Esq was meaningless, since anybody could call themselves that, whatever their status in life.

'Don't worry,' a friend had consoled him. 'At least you got as far as the examination. Why not call yourself MW (Failed)? Like the BA (Calcutta) (Failed) that people used to use to show that they had been intelligent enough to get into the university, even if they didn't pass the degree.'

'Did they really?' asked William.

'Probably not,' said his friend. 'It was always said that you encountered the odd BA (Failed) in Kipling's day, but I don't think there's any hard evidence. Sellars and Yeatman made a joke of it in *1066 and All That*. But I think anybody has yet to meet a genuine BA (Failed). Mind you, I did hear of somebody going to see a dentist somewhere abroad and spotting a plate outside saying BDS (Failed).'

'Not a dentist one would necessarily wish to consult,' said William.

'Perhaps not.'

But even though he had failed the MW examination, still William knew a great deal about wine and would share his knowledge, tactfully and discretely, with his customers. Some of them, of course, were not quite as reticent and took pleasure in parading their considerably shakier knowledge in front of William, who refrained from correcting them, except gently, and even then only in respect of the most egregious errors. ('If I may say so, Rioja is not *quite* Italian. In fact, it's Spanish—but I agree, it's so easy to mix the two up . . .')

Manfred James had opinions on everything, and these were delivered, as if *ex cathedra*, with a certainty that carried all before it. And on the subject of dogs, as became apparent to William, he was as opinionated as he was on politics and social policy. 'Diet is the key,' he said. 'The canine diet, as you know, is both physically and psychologically determined. Physically there is a taste for meat; psychologically there is a desire to hunt. There's little point in tackling one without addressing the other—as you'll appreciate.'

William wondered about the psychological aspect. Was a disposition to hunt genetically or environmentally determined? 'Is there—?' he began.

'So,' Manfred James continued, 'with a view to breeding characteristics out of the breed, we have tried to reduce the psychological urge to hunt, which will therefore lead to a reduction in the desire to eat meat—with all its environmental consequences. One cannot eradicate deep-rooted behavioural-genetic traits, but their impact can be changed.'

'Changed,' said William simply.

'Exactly. Ever since he came to us—after his retrenchment from the airport—Freddie de la Hay has been brought up to respond positively to other creatures, not to see them as a potential source of

93

food. And I must say, it's worked very well.'

'Oh.' That was all that William felt he could manage, and there seemed to be no point in saying much more. Manfred's interventions, he thought, had all the characteristics of radio jamming, designed to stop anybody else talking.

'It's been remarkably successful,' the columnist went on. 'We used straightforward behavioural techniques. Pavlov would have understood. We gave him rewards when he remained calm even in the presence of a stimulus that would normally have provoked an aggressive response. So you'll notice something very interesting about him now.'

'Oh yes?'

Manfred James looked at William with the air of one about to announce a major scientific breakthrough. 'Freddie de la Hay,' he proclaimed, 'likes cats.'

William's eyes narrowed. 'Really?'

'Yes,' said Manfred James. 'And now I think that we should agree on the details of the sharing. I suggest that you take him right now and be his carer for, what, a couple of months? Then we'll take him back for a few weeks—depending on whether I'm around—and then you take him back for another stay. Agreed? Good.'

The columnist rose to his feet and gestured to the door. 'I suggest we go and see Freddie,' he said. 'Then I'll call a cab, if you like. You'll need to take his bed and a supply of carrot sticks—I can tell you where to get more of those. And his certificates.'

'Certificates?'

'From the canine lifestyle course,' said Manfred. 'The paperwork.'

94

William nodded.

They left the study and made their way into the kitchen at the back of the house. There was Freddie de la Hay, sitting obediently in the middle of the floor—like a sentry, thought William.

'Freddie,' said Manfred. 'This is Mr French. He's your new *carer*. Say hello, Freddie.'

Freddie de la Hay looked at William with his dark, mournful eyes, eyes so liquid that they might conceal the presence of tears, might break the very heart.

23. Nice Dog

William French MW (Failed) climbed into the cab called by the celebrated columnist, Manfred James. He was accompanied by Freddie de la Hay, a Pimlico Terrier, a 'new dog', whose small canine life was now beginning an important and challenging phase. Not much happens to dogs; they lead their lives around our feet, in the interstices of more complex doings, from which perspective they look up at the busier human world, eager to participate, eager to understand, but for ever limited by biology and the vagaries of evolution to being small-part players in the drama. Every so often a particular dog might rise above this limited destiny, might perform some act of loyalty that attracts human recognition and praise. But for most dogs such saliences are rare, their lives being punctuated by nothing more significant than the discovery of an intriguing smell or the sight of a rabbit or a rat—usually frustratingly

95

inaccessible—or by some minor territorial challenge that requires a bark. Nothing much, really, but for dogs, their lot, their allocation.

'Pimlico,' said William to the taxi driver, and gave the address of Corduroy Mansions.

The driver nodded. 'Nice dog,' he said. 'Got one myself. A bit like that but smaller. What make is he, guv?'

'He's a Pimlico Terrier,' William replied.

They were moving off now, and he waved to Manfred James, standing at his gate. There was a look of relief on the columnist's face, which irritated William. One does not wave goodbye to one's dog with a broad smile on one's face.

'Pimlico Terrier?' repeated the taxi driver, craning his neck to look into the mirror. 'Bit big for a terrier, if you ask me. Are you sure?'

Freddie de la Hay was sitting at William's feet, looking up at his new carer (as Manfred James had described the relationship). The dog seemed anxious. Understandable, perhaps, in the circumstances: being passed from one carer to another is a traumatic experience for any dog, even the strongest and most secure. To them, we are God incarnate, and to have one god exchanged for another is as stressful as any change of religion can be in the human world.

'Never heard of a Pimlico Terrier,' continued the taxi driver. 'You get it by mixing something up? Crossing one breed with another?'

William found his irritation increasing in the face of this close examination by the driver. While he was as prepared as anybody to enter into conversation with a taxi driver, he felt that there were circumstances in which a driver should be able to detect reticence on the part of a fare. It should be part of the famous *knowledge* that taxi drivers went on about. It was all very well knowing the quickest way from an obscure street in one part of London to an equally obscure street in another, but it was important, too, to understand the mood of the person in the back of the cab and to know when an atmosphere of Trappist silence would be appreciated. Not all taxi drivers shared that insight.

For his part, William had devised a good way of avoiding talking, if one wanted to do so, a way that prompted the taxi driver himself either to talk at great length—to deliver a monologue, in fact—or to become quite silent. This was to ask, at an early stage of the journey, 'What do you think of the government?'

It is well known that taxi drivers have a low opinion of governments—of any government—but almost without exception take a particularly dim view of their own. This question tends, therefore, to offer them the maximum opportunity to express themselves in monologue, or alternatively it gives them the impression that the fare is a secret sympathiser with the Government and therefore not to be engaged in conversation.

This technique of asking just the right question to inhibit further conversation was a useful one, and was used by William in other social circumstances when small talk needed to be avoided. At cocktail parties, where one might quite reasonably simply wish to stand, or sit, and not be pestered by other guests seeking to make small talk, the use of a discreet lapel badge was sometimes to be recommended. This badge might state one's religious position in unequivocal terms, and invite discussion on it. Thus a small badge saying 'Please talk to me about Salvation' usually had the effect of ensuring a peaceful time at any party, leaving one untroubled by other guests coming up to engage one in unwanted conversation. Similarly a badge saying 'No longer infectious' could usually be calculated to ensure physical space, another commodity in short supply at the more popular cocktail parties.

Nevertheless, on this occasion William would have attempted to answer the taxi driver's questions had Freddie de la Hay not started to whine.

'Sounds a bit unhappy,' remarked the driver. 'Wants up on the seat, I'd say. You can let him up as long as his paws are clean.'

William thought that the taxi driver was right. Freddie de la Hay, who was still shivering with anxiety, now had his gaze fixed firmly on the seat next to his new carer.

'Want up, old chap?' William asked, patting the seat beside him. 'Up, Freddie de la Hay! Up!'

Freddie de la Hay hesitated for a few moments, and then, as the taxi slowed down to turn a corner, he leapt up onto the seat beside William.

'Good boy,' said William, patting the dog on the head. 'Clever boy.'

Freddie looked appreciatively at William, but then turned and stared pointedly at the back of the seat he was occupying.

'Something wrong?' asked William. 'Do you see something?'

Freddie de la Hay responded to this question by moving further back in his seat and nuzzling at the seatbelt. William, observing this, was puzzled. The dog appeared to be objecting to the seatbelt; perhaps he thought it was a leash of some sort.

Freddie started to whine again, pressing his snout behind the belt, trying to lift it off the seat.

'He wants you to belt him in, mate,' said the taxi driver, who had observed all this in his rear-view mirror. 'Smart dogs, these Pimlico Terriers, obviously.'

At first William could not believe this, but then, when he reached over to put the belt over Freddie de la Hay and the dog barked encouragingly, he knew that the driver was right.

Freddie de la Hay had been trained to belt up in the back of a car.

24. Lemon Gems

James and Caroline sat on the sofa and ate the lemon gems they had just baked. The biscuits were, they felt, a success, although James was of the view that Nigella could have recommended just a touch more lemon. Caroline disagreed. 'She never makes a mistake,' she said. 'She's the domestic goddess, remember.'

'I'm not saying that she's wrong,' James reassured her. 'Heaven forfend that I would ever disagree with Nigella or Delia.' He bowed his head respectfully, an unexpected gesture, but touching, thought Caroline. 'Or Jamie, for that matter,' he continued. 'You have to *trust* these people, you know, Caroline. If we started to *argue* with our cookery writers, then where would it end . . .?'

James, Caroline noticed, had a tendency to

99

emphasise certain strategic words, to italicise them, a habit that gave particular weight to his pronouncements. Impressed with this, as with many of the things James said or did, she had tried to do the same, but found that she ended up emphasising the wrong words, thus adding opacity *rather* than clarity to what she *said*.

She looked at James. Since that moment of accidental, shared intimacy in the kitchen, she had been wondering whether the conversation would revert to the subject they had been discussing over coffee earlier that day. James had said nothing further about that, and she found herself somewhat relieved. Perhaps the whole matter had been set aside; it was a delicate topic, and the baking of the lemon gems had changed the atmosphere to one of comfortable collaboration. James returned her gaze, but not in a way which gave any indication of his intentions.

'What about you?' he said.

'Me?'

James picked up another lemon gem. 'I know so little about you. We're friends, of course, and we know one another well. But there's a difference between knowing somebody and *knowing* them. You know what I mean?'

Caroline was not sure, but decided that perhaps she did. James sometimes left her a bit behind, she felt, and she was eager that he should not think that she did not understand. 'Yeah,' she said.

James wiped a crumb from his lips. 'So, I know a bit about your past, about Cheltenham and all that.' He waved a hand in the air to indicate a whole hinterland of personal history—a county, a family, a set of social expectations—Caroline's whole family history. 'I know the sort of background you've had to *endure*. Your old man being a land agent and all that sort of thing. And your mother. I'm surprised they didn't put your photograph in the front of *Rural Living*.'

Caroline froze. She was on the point of popping a lemon gem into her mouth, but now her hand fell to her lap. The lemon gem, held between nervous fingers, cracked slightly, but Nigella's mixture held and it escaped being reduced to crumbs.

'What?' Her voice was small.

'*Rural Living*,' said James. 'I can just see it, can't you? Caroline, only daughter of Mr and Mrs Whatever Jarvis of Bin End, or wherever, is pictured here—in *pearls*. Caroline is reading Art History at Oxford (almost) and hopes to work at Sotheby's.' He laughed. 'I can just see it.'

Caroline laughed, but her laugh came out strangled, prompting James to enquire whether she was all right.

'I'm fine,' said Caroline, offering him another lemon gem. That would distract him, she hoped, and perhaps steer the conversation into less dangerous waters.

'Of course, you can't help it,' James went on. 'Nobody can help their background. Although you can *correct* things later on, once you've got away from family influences. Not everybody does, of course. Some people remain clones of their parents all the way to the grave.'

'I quite like my parents,' said Caroline. And she did. They loved her; for all their fuddy-duddy ways and their outdated notions, they loved her, and she knew that she would never encounter such unconditional love again. Never.

101

'Of course,' said James quickly. 'Sorry. I wasn't picking on them in particular. I was just thinking of what parents can do to their children—often with the best intentions in the world. You know Larkin's poem?'

Caroline was not sure.

James smiled patiently. 'It's the one with the rather—how shall we put it?—*forceful* first line about what parents do to their kids. It was in a poetry book we had at school and I remember that when we got to it, the English teacher went pale and moved very quickly to the next poem, some frightfully dull thing by Cecil Day Lewis. Of course that meant we all went and looked very closely at what Larkin had to say. But it's mild stuff, really, compared with what everybody writes today. It must be frustrating being a poet—or any sort of artist—and not being able to offend anyone any more.' Or were people still as readily offended, and all that had changed was the nature of what was permissible and what was interdicted?

He reached for another lemon gem—his sixth. 'Sugar craving,' he said apologetically. 'Your fault, Caroline, for suggesting that we bake these things.'

'Oh well . . .'

James licked his fingers. 'Last one. That's it.' He stared at Caroline intently. 'What would you have done, by the way, if your parents had tried to get your photograph into *Rural Living*? What would you have said?'

She looked away. James was proving persistent, and she would have to change the subject. 'Let's not talk about all that,' she said. 'My parents are my parents. I'm me. Same as you, really. You don't sign up to everything your paren— your father stands for, do you?'

James shook his head 'No. But if I'm honest, I can see my father in me. Some of the things I do.'

'Well, that's natural enough.'

'Maybe. But look, we were talking about you.' He paused, as if unsure about continuing. 'Are you still seeing him?' he asked. 'What's he called again?'

Caroline was on the point of answering, but stopped herself. Had she replied spontaneously, she would have confirmed that she was still seeing Tom. That was true, but she was *only just* still seeing him, and she had already decided that there was no future in the relationship. Her friendship with James was, she thought, on the cusp of change, and there was a chance that he might become more than a mere friend. Stranger things have happened, she said to herself—a banal phrase, a cliché, but one that nonetheless expressed the sense of opening out, of possibility, that she now experienced. Identity was not as simple a matter as many people believed: the old idea of clearly delineated male and female characteristics was distinctly passé, as old-fashioned as vanilla ice cream. Now there were new men, men in touch with their feminine side, and the intriguing category of metrosexuals, too— sensitive men, men who used male cosmetics such as 'man-liner', men who would enjoy baking Nigella's lemon gems. These men could be more than adequate lovers and husbands, she believed; much better than the one-dimensional macho types who might score ten out of ten on the heterosexuality scale but who were somewhat boring in their conversation and *hopeless* in the kitchen. Men like Tom.

103

25. Paris

'He's called Tom,' said Caroline.

James nodded. She had spoken about Tom before but he had not really been paying attention. 'Of course. Tom. I remember—you told me. And . . .'

She looked at him enquiringly. 'And what?'

'Are you and Tom still *together*?'

She wanted to choose her words carefully. It was not that she was prepared to be untruthful, it was just that she was not entirely sure about her feelings, which were changing anyway. Togetherness was not a word she would ever have used to describe her relationship with Tom. They might have been together in the most general sense of the term, but they were not *together* in the way in which James pronounced it—they were certainly not italicised. 'I still see him,' she said, and added, 'now and then.'

He was watching her. No, she thought then. Whatever happened in the future between Tom and her, this incipient thing with James, this fantasy, would never work. Not James, her wonderful, sympathetic, companionable James. She had a friend who had wasted three years in pursuing a man who was not in the slightest bit interested. At the time she had warned this friend that one could not expect to change something so fundamental, but her warning had been ignored. She must not do the same thing herself. Some men were destined to be good friends and nothing more. James was like that; it was so obvious. She should accept him for what he was and not encourage him to be something that he so clearly was not. He was fine as he was. He was perfect. Why nudge him into a relationship that would be inauthentic to him?

James was smiling. 'You don't sound enthusiastic. You see him. That sounds really passionate, Caroline.'

She looked away. James was right: it was not a passionate relationship.

James continued. 'Tell me this: how do you feel when you've got a date with him coming up? Do you count the minutes until you see him? Feel breathless? Fluttery?' He rubbed a hand across his stomach. 'You know the feeling. Like that?'

'I like him.'

He shook his head. 'That was not the question I asked. I want to know whether you feel anticipation when you are about to see him. That really is the test, you know. Excitement. Anticipation.'

It was difficult for her to answer, and she was not sure whether she wanted to do so anyway. He had guided their conversation into a realm of intimacy that she had explored with nobody else, not even her close girlfriends. It was strange to be talking this way to a man, even as comfortable a man as James. And yet that very strangeness had a strong appeal. One should be able to talk about these things; one should be able to share them.

'It's hard for me to know,' she said. 'It's not that I don't feel something for Tom—I do. It's just that . . .'

'You don't feel it, do you?' He spoke gently, as if guiding her to a source of pain, a tender spot.

'No.'

She realised that he had brought her to an understanding of her feelings she would not have achieved by herself, and she felt grateful as a result. That single word—that single cathartic 'No'—had revealed a truth that had been there all along but which she had simply never confronted.

He made a gesture with his hands—a gesture she interpreted as saying, well, there you are. And he was right. There she was: it was the end of Tom.

And the beginning of James? The thought refused to go away.

'It's not all that easy, you know,' she said. 'Ending something. It's messy, isn't it?'

She waited for an answer, but James was staring silently at the ceiling.

'You do understand that?' she pressed. 'You must know how hard it is to end a relationship. There are all sorts of connections and ties and associations. Bits of lives meshed together. You have to cut through all of that, as a surgeon cuts

106

through living tissue.'

He nodded. 'I suppose so.'

'You *suppose* so?'

'Yes.'

'You must have done it yourself.'

He continued to stare at the ceiling as he answered. 'Not really. No, I haven't. At least, not quite like this.'

'Well, it would have been a bit different in your case.'

He looked at her coolly. 'Why do you say that?'

She blushed. 'Sorry, I wasn't thinking. Of course it's the same for everyone.'

The coolness he had shown vanished. When she looked at him, she suddenly saw only regret.

'I've never been there,' he said quietly. 'I've never had what you'd call a love affair.'

'But . . .'

'No, I mean it. People think that everybody has been involved with somebody else, whatever their nature. They find it inconceivable that one might go through life never finding anybody. But you know something, Caroline? I think that's far more common than you would ever imagine. There are plenty of people in that position.'

Impulsively, she reached out and took his hand. It seemed the most natural, the easiest thing to do, and it seemed easy for him too.

'Poor James,' she whispered.

He smiled at her weakly. 'Yes, poor James.'

For a few minutes they sat there, not speaking, and not really looking at one another either. Their hands remained together, though, and when she squeezed his gently, in sympathy, he returned the pressure. It was as if signals were being exchanged

107

in the night, in a time of war, perhaps—flashes of light in the darkness, one in answer to the other, messages that confirmed the presence of human sentiment, as feeling responded to feeling.

After a while, she gently relinquished her grip. She leaned over towards him and whispered, although there was nobody else in the flat, nobody who would hear, 'Why don't we go to Paris together?'

His eyes widened. *'Paris?'* The italicised emphasis was perfect, she thought; just right.

She had no idea why she had said this. 'Sorry,' she whispered. 'Very cheesy.'

'Cheesy! It's not cheesy.' He paused. 'It's exactly the *right* thing to do, Caroline. Paris! Of course.'

'We could go on the Eurostar,' she said.

It was a lame thing to say, enough to shatter the magic of the moment, but James was not deterred: there was nothing wrong with the Eurostar.

'There are some Bonnards I want to see there,' he said. 'We could look at them together.'

She nodded her agreement; the Bonnards would be nice. But as she stood up and went to look out of the window, she thought: that's the problem—that's exactly the problem! Paris was more than Bonnard, at least for most young couples planning *un week-end*. Far more.

26. Applied Ethics

When James left Corduroy Mansions that afternoon he did not notice the taxi drawing up a few yards away. There was no particular reason to notice it; London taxis are ubiquitous, barely noticeable other than when sought out, and often becoming completely invisible then. And his mind was on other things, preoccupied with thoughts of Paris and Bonnard, and—although not to the same degree—of the time he had spent with Caroline. There was also, of course, the memory of the lemon gems; those delicacies had left a lingering taste in his mouth, a vaguely lemony sensation that reminded him of a childhood holiday in Cyprus, where the hotel had a lemon grove in its grounds, and . . . No, he would not revisit the lemon grove.

So James did not see a middle-aged man struggling to get out of the cab while holding what seemed to be a dog's bed under one arm and the end of a leash in the other hand. The man, William French MW (Failed), succeeded in getting himself out of the taxi and then, laying the dog's bed down on the pavement, began to tug on the leash. The dog at the other end seemed reluctant to move, but eventually, after a few increasingly firm tugs, jumped out of the cab and sat obediently at the man's feet. The fare was paid and the cab moved off into the traffic.

From his position on the pavement, seated at the feet of a human being whom he had only just met but instinctively liked, Freddie de la Hay, Pimlico Terrier, sniffed at the air. He had a very good nose—a trained nose, in fact, because before he had been acquired by the opinionated columnist, Manfred James, he had been employed as a sniffer dog at Heathrow airport. He had been good at his job, but had been dismissed as part of an affirmative action programme when it had been discovered that all the dogs at the airport were male. After this matter had been raised by a local politician, it was announced that there would be a policy of equal opportunity for female sniffer dogs—an absurd notion that had provoked outraged rants in those newspapers given to such things. But for some, at least, the point raised by this exercise was a valid one. Should one treat animals fairly?

The question was a serious one. The Heathrow issue had caught the attention of at least one moral philosopher concerned with the rights of animals— a weighty matter that was increasingly, and deservedly, the subject of philosophical discussion. Most of this writing was of one view: causing pain or distress to an animal was wrong—as even the *Struwwelpeter*, that none-too-gentle children's classic, recognised in its story of Cruel Frederick. Frederick, the taunter of the good dog Tray, was bitten for his gratuitous cruelty, to the delight of all; a fate that could have been so much worse, bearing in mind what happened to Augustus in the same book, and to the digit-deprived victims of that thinly disguised castration-figure, the tailor with his large scissors, the bane of those who sucked their thumb.

But if the inflicting of physical pain was generally, if not universally, disapproved of, then what of wrongs of a lower order, such as unfairness in treatment? The moral philosopher who seized on Freddie de la Hay's case as an illustration for his paper, 'Justice and Injustice Between Species', suggested an example of two dogs and one biscuit. It was typical of the dilemmas beloved of moral philosophers, being set in a world which is recognisably our own, but not quite. Mother

110

Hubbard, the owner of two dogs, has only one dog biscuit in her cupboard. Her two dogs, whom she does not love equally, are at her feet, eagerly anticipating the treat. What should she do? Should she break the biscuit into two equal parts and give each dog a morsel, or may she give the biscuit to the dog she prefers?

The author of 'Justice and Injustice Between Species' began his analysis of the case by changing the dogs into children, a trick that would normally challenge even the most skilled stage magician, but which, for a philosopher conducting a thought experiment, is as easily done as said. A parent would be making a grave mistake were she to give a whole biscuit to a favoured child and none to another, but does the same rule apply to the owner of an animal? The answer will obviously depend, the author—a consequentialist—said, on the consequences of this act of preference. The favoured dog will be happy enough, but his unlucky companion will surely feel disappointment at not being given his share; that is, of course, if he has a notion of sharing, which, being a dog, he will not. So one must avoid, the author pointed out, any suggestion that the less fortunate dog will feel that he has been the victim of injustice. There is no such thing in the mind of a dog.

Or is there? A distinguished legal philosopher, making a point about the difference between the unintentional and intentional causing of harm, once said that even a dog could tell whether a kick from its owner was intended or unintended. If this is the case, then surely it suggests that there is in the canine mind some notion of desert, which has some connection with fairness.

111

The debate continued over several issues of a learned journal until the editor drew a line beneath it, with a masterly summing up of the unresolved issues raised by the case. Freddie de la Hay was, of course, quite unaware of his celebrity. Philosophers were, to him, the same as all humans: luminous higher beings, dispensers of favours and makers of rules, guardians of the cupboard in which he knew his own dog biscuits were stored. When he lost his job at Heathrow, it meant a shrinking of his universe, from one of suitcases and noise to one of a house in Highgate with a master who seemed bent on making him do things that he had no wish to do. But he did them, for he was an obedient dog—he had been taught to comply at the airport—and he wanted only to please. So when he was instructed to treat cats with respect by the distinguished columnist, he did as he was bade.

Now, on the pavement outside Corduroy Mansions, he looked up at his new master and awaited his instructions. And when he spotted a movement on the other side of the road, he took no notice. That it was a cat was neither here nor there. He would not try to chase it, nor even growl. That was in the past, somewhere in the scheme of things of the old Freddie de la Hay. He would not growl. He would not.

27. On the Train

At the same moment that William stood outside Corduroy Mansions with Freddie de la Hay at his side, Berthea Snark, psychoanalyst and near-neighbour of Corduroy Mansions, was arriving at Cheltenham station on the 3.15 from Paddington. It had not been a peaceful journey, thanks to a person opposite her who was engaged in a lengthy telephone call, oblivious of the fact that she was imposing her conversation on others. Berthea had struggled in vain to shut out the banalities this conversation inflicted upon her—the one-sided discussion of social events and the affairs of others. She had glared at the noisy passenger but had been greeted with a cool stare in response. Eventually she had moved seats, to what she hoped would be the quieter end of the carriage, only to find herself faced with a man whose false teeth were loose, and who sucked air through puckered lips, occasionally opening his mouth to allow the top set of teeth to fall forward before being pushed back into position with his tongue.

She closed her eyes. The carriage was full on this popular Friday afternoon train and she would not find another seat. By shutting out the sight of the man opposite, she was at least spared his unfortunate dentures. But that meant that she could not read, and closing one's eyes was unquestionably a form of denial, something she was committed to criticising in others. No, one could not go through life with one's eyes closed, tempting though such a solution might be.

She thought of a paper she might write for one of the journals, a paper she would call 'The Eyes-closed Society'. It would be about the way in which bad behaviour in others was increasingly forcing people to pretend that parts of reality did not exist. It was an interesting theme, and she could develop it by exploring its social and political ramifications.

As we became more burdened with distressing information—global warming, growing material need, the inevitability of a major flu epidemic and so on—the temptation simply to turn away became greater and greater. And so we denied the uncomfortable, the distressing—like those people who denied global warming. And so . . . She stopped. The observation was hardly original. People had always denied unpalatable truths. T. S. Eliot had written something about that, had he not? 'Go, go, go, said the bird: human kind / Cannot bear very much reality.' To say something original, she must come up with a prescription. Such books—and her article had now become a book—had to have some neat conclusion, some observation or insight that made people say Ah! when they read it. That man who wrote *The Tipping Point* knew all about it. People said Ah! when they read about tipping points. And presumably he, too, had experienced a tipping point when his tipping point book reached its tipping point.

But Berthea could not conceive of what she would say about denial, beyond pointing out that it happened. She could emphasise that one should not deny, but everybody knew that anyway. Could she say, then, that denial was a *good thing*? That would be original at least. And then, when challenged in interviews—she would be invited onto all the best chat shows—she could simply deny that she said it in the first place, thereby making a very vivid point about denial.

The daydream ended, and so, eventually, did the journey. The man with the ill-fitting teeth had dozed off and remained asleep until shortly before

114

Cheltenham. Berthea looked out of the window at the passing countryside. London seemed so far away, almost a different country from this world of fields and narrow lanes and slower lives. She thought: what if I packed everything up and came to live out here, perhaps sharing with Terence? She was on her way to spend the weekend with her brother, Terence Moongrove, who had more than once suggested that she would care to share his house in Cheltenham. It was easily large enough for two, he said, and she could even have a separate entrance if she wished. She had declined his offer, although it distressed her to do so. Terence was lonely—he was one of the loneliest men she knew—and it would have meant so much to him to have her living with him.

But she could not. She was a psychoanalyst, and she imagined that it would take time to build up a practice in a place like Cheltenham. She knew that there was an Institute of Psychotherapy in the West Country—she had met some of its members at conferences—but was there enough neurosis to keep them all going? Human unhappiness, of course, was universal, but somehow she imagined that it did not occur with quite the same intensity in the little villages that the train was flashing past. What was there to be anxious about out here? Why feel inadequate or troubled when nobody was paying much attention to you because the hay had to be got in or the cows milked, or whatever it was that people did in such places? *If* they did any of that any more, she reflected; or were they all plugged into the web, running hedge funds from the ends of these little lanes?

Of course, Cheltenham was slightly different. It

was a place where people went to the races or retired to or came to make and sell pottery. And not all of these people would be free of the neuroses they had brought with them from somewhere else. So perhaps she might not be completely without something to do after all.

But no, she could not share with poor Terence. And if she sold up in London and bought her own house here, then Terence would simply be in and out of her door every day. And he had a habit of just sitting there, going on and on about Nepal or his collection of amulets or whatever it was that he was enthusing over at the time. Sacred dance, she remembered, was his current interest. He had got hold of a book by a Bulgarian mystic called Peter Deunov, who had developed a system of dance called paneurhythmy. He had gone to Bulgaria, she believed, and danced on a mountain there; she had received a postcard which simply said 'Love in the morning', and, beneath that, 'Terence'.

She smiled as she alighted from the train. Dear Terence. For all his faults, he was her brother, and he meant well, even if it was sometimes rather difficult to work out exactly what it was that he meant.

28. Beings of Light

Terence Moongrove, searcher after truth—and self—had parked his Morris 1000 Traveller in the spot where he always collected his sister, Berthea Snark, when she came down to Cheltenham to visit him. She knew where to look, and spotted him

116

immediately and waved to him as he sat in the car, his large round spectacles catching the light. Her wave was the signal for him to sound the horn of the ancient vehicle.

'I've had a *very* difficult trip down,' she said as she eased herself into the passenger seat of the half-timbered car. 'The woman opposite me insisted on conducting a conversation on her mobile phone in a very loud voice, as per usual.'

'Very tiresome,' said Terence, reaching forward to turn the key in the ignition. 'Such people really are the end, aren't they?'

'And then I changed seats and found myself opposite a man who sucked air through his false teeth,' Berthea went on. 'He did that until blessedly he fell asleep.'

'Terribly tiresome,' said Terence. 'Still, here you are, and you can put your old feet up and *nobody* is going to talk on a mobile or suck air through his teeth. I promise.'

Berthea reached out and touched her brother appreciatively on the arm. 'Thank you, dear. You are an oasis, you know. A real oasis.'

He may have been an oasis, but she was not entirely sure whether she approved of the reference to her *old feet*. Chronologically, her feet might have been slightly older than his, she being a few years his senior. But even if her feet were in their early sixties, they were, she felt, in rather good shape for their age. The problem with Terence, she thought, was that he had not aged along with everybody else. He imagined that life was yet to happen, whereas in fact it had already largely happened for him.

These thoughts were nothing new to Berthea.

And that, she reflected, was the central stumbling block in her relationship with her brother. They were exactly where they had always been—as siblings often tended to be in their relations with one another. She saw it so often in her professional life—people came to her with the emotional baggage of family relationships and, on analysis, this was found to be baggage they had been bearing all their lives. They thought the same things about their brothers or sisters that they had thought when they were ten, twelve, eighteen, twenty-six, forty—and so on. Nothing changed.

The Morris moved off, its tiny engine labouring as Terence moved through the gears.

'I've made a leek pie for tonight,' he said. 'And we can have a glass of my latest batch of elderflower wine. Very tasty.'

'Perfect,' said Berthea.

'And then tomorrow morning you might care to join me for my paneurhythmy,' he continued. 'Forty-five minutes. That's all.'

Berthea looked steadily ahead. 'Your sacred dancing? This Bulgarian stuff?'

'Precisely,' said Terence. 'I have looked up what time dawn may be expected tomorrow, and we must be ready to align the meridians and chakras. The Beings of Light will be in attendance.'

Berthea looked out of the window. She was not sure who the Beings of Light were. Were they residents of Cheltenham or were they, as Terence himself might put it, resident on some other plane not immediately visible to us?

'I shall do my best,' she said. 'Although you will have to explain things to me, Terence. My rather literal mind, I'm afraid, precludes my full

118

participation.'

Terence smiled benignly. 'Peter Deunov met many who felt the same way,' he said. 'They inevitably stayed to dance. Many of them danced until they could dance no more, and were absorbed by Spirit.'

They drove on in silence as Berthea digested this information. I must not let this *distress* me, she told herself. The fact that my brother thinks about the world very differently from me is no reflection on my own *Weltanschauung*. It simply is not. But that, of course, is a difficult thing to accept, and I must remain calm.

They turned off the main road and onto a smaller road that meandered gently downhill, and it was here that the engine of the old Morris, which had been running quietly enough until then, gave a loud cough, expressed in the form of a backfire, and then became silent. Slowly the car came to a halt at the side of the road.

For a short time, Terence sat glumly behind the wheel, his eyes fixed on the road ahead. Then he turned to his sister.

'The car has stopped,' he said. 'I'm terribly sorry about this. It really has stopped.'

Berthea looked at her brother. 'So it appears.'

There was another silence. From the engine there came a slight ticking sound, and Berthea briefly thought that this might be a sign of life, but it was merely the sound of cooling metal. Above them, sitting on the branch of a tree, a large blackbird looked down and uttered a few notes of song.

'That's so beautiful,' said Terence, looking up. 'Birdsong is so pure.'

'It is,' said Berthea. 'Very pure.'

Terence drummed his fingers on the steering wheel. 'I should perhaps get out and take a look at the engine,' he said.

Berthea took a deep breath. 'Is there much point?'

But Terence had already opened his door and walked round to stand in front of the bonnet. Berthea joined him.

'It's extraordinary,' said Terence, gazing at the bull nose of the vehicle. 'It's extraordinary how an engine can be humming along in a spirit of perfect contentment one moment and then the next it is silent. As if the energy fields have all suddenly dissipated. Cars, you see, have chakras, just as people do.'

Berthea spoke quietly. 'How about calling the AA?'

Terence shook his head. 'I don't think so,' he said. 'I've called them rather a lot, you see. They know my car. They are quite pure beings, but I don't know if I should bother them again.'

'When did you call them last?' asked Berthea.

Terence hesitated. 'Not all that long ago, I'm afraid.' He sighed. 'Well, to be precise, I called them on the way to the station. We had a little episode just a little bit further down the road. Not far from here, in fact.'

'Not far from here?' repeated Berthea.

Terence nodded.

'Do you think,' Berthea began, 'that it may be something to do with the energy fields round here? Perhaps we're on a ley line.'

Terence looked at her with sudden interest. 'Do you really think so? They said something about

120

petrol, you know, but I wonder . . .'

29. Berthea's Project

By the time her brother's leek pie was ready,
Berthea had largely recovered from the irritation
she had felt during the longish walk from the
collapsed Morris 1000 Traveller to Terence's
Queen Anne house just outside the bounds of the
town. He had helped her with her luggage—a
small overnight case—but she had been obliged to
carry her own briefcase, which was stuffed with
papers and books for weekend perusal. Terence's
library, although extensive, was full of books that
she found vague and unsatisfactory, gaseous
indeed—there would be no intellectual meat for
her *there*.

'And what are you going to do about your car?'
Berthea asked as they began their walk. 'Are you
proposing to get a new one?'

Terence, who was oblivious of irony, replied, 'Oh
no, certainly not. That car is not all that old.
Thirty-nine years, or thereabouts, I think. There's
still a lot of energy left in it. It's amazing. It's as if
the energy fields of the men who made it are
lodged in its soul.'

'I assume that it will start again when you put
some petrol in,' observed Berthea.

Terence nodded. 'Quite possibly. Indeed, I might
go so far as to say that's probable.'

'Because cars do *require* petrol,' Berthea
continued. 'They need it for . . . for their energy
fields.'

121

'Yes,' said Terence, simply. 'That's largely true.'

'No, Terence,' hissed Berthea. 'It's not just largely true, it's absolutely and completely true. It's a truth which is verifiable in the physical world. It is the actual case.'

Terence looked at her in surprise. 'No need to get shirty,' he said. 'It'll only take us half an hour or so to walk to the house, and I *am* carrying your bag for you.' He paused. 'Do you remember *A Town Like Alice*? We saw it when we were small and we went to stay at Uncle Ted's. He took us to the cinema and that's what we saw.'

'Vaguely.'

'Well, I remember it very well. They had a long march after the Japanese captured them. Remember? All those British ladies had to march along the roads and jungle paths. It was frightfully hard work and the Japanese guards kept shouting at them if they slowed down. It must have been jolly hot, too.'

Berthea frowned. 'And what has that got to do . . . ?'

'What I'm suggesting,' said Terence, 'is that you treat this in the same spirit. Those ladies didn't complain all that much—they just got on with it. Imagine that you're in Malaysia and I'm a Japanese soldier and—'

'No, thank you,' said Berthea grimly. 'It might be better, you know, to walk in silence.'

'Oh, surely not,' said Terence. 'You should know that, as a psychologist.'

'Psychoanalyst.'

'Of course. You should know that there are little mood-changing tricks you can use if you want to make an unpleasant experience more bearable.

122

You could try whistling. Remember that popular song, the one about whenever you feel afraid, whistling a happy tune? And then there's Maria. Remember? Remember how she sang to the children when they all came and jumped on her bed, about her favourite things?'

Berthea bit her lip. 'I really don't think that we need to do any of that, Terence. As you yourself observed, the walk should not take long. Perhaps we should just walk it in silence. That, I suspect, is what any Beings of Light in the immediate vicinity would really appreciate.'

Terence had looked at her dubiously but said nothing and they completed the walk in silence. Once at the house, Berthea took a long bath; Terence's bathroom was well stocked with bath crystals of various types, and she luxuriated for almost half an hour in a deep tub of lavender-scented water. After that she felt in a better humour, and joined her brother in the kitchen where he was preparing a plate of snacks to precede the leek pie.

It was then that Berthea chose to reveal her project.

'I'm writing a book,' she said with a flourish. 'I feel you should know.'

'What a good idea,' said Terence. 'Writing a book is a very good way of getting to know oneself.'

'That is not the reason why I'm doing it,' said Berthea. 'This book is not being written as some sort of self-analysis. This book is being written as a form of public service.'

Terence snipped at a bunch of chives. 'Do tell,' he said. 'Terence is very interested.'

He had an occasional habit of referring to himself in the third person—a habit which Berthea disliked intensely, but she said nothing about it now. Terence had to know about her book because he could be called upon to help.

'I'm glad to hear that Terence takes that view,' she said. 'Yes. I have decided to write a biography of my son, and indeed I have already embarked on the task.'

Terence put down the chives and turned to his sister. 'Oedipus?'

'He is, I believe, the only son I have,' said Berthea drily. 'Yes. The biography of Oedipus Snark, MP.'

Terence exhaled, a long drawn-out sound that was half-way between a whistle and a sigh. 'By his mother,' he said. And then added, 'Sensational!'

Berthea raised an eyebrow. 'I wouldn't overstate its impact,' she said. 'I might not call it sensational myself, but I expect there will be a certain level of interest in it. After all, Oedipus is reasonably well known these days.'

'I read about him in the paper recently,' said Terence. 'He had been somewhere and made some speech or other. About something.'

Berthea smiled. 'That's the sort of detail that I need,' she said.

Terence showed no sign of having understood the barb. 'I'm sure that you'll do him justice,' he said.

Berthea nodded. 'It would be useful to have your perspective,' she said. 'After all, you are his uncle, and he did spend a lot of time with you as a schoolboy when he was on his summer holidays. Remember? You were very good to him.'

Terence sighed. 'Berthea, dear, we're both adults, aren't we? Which means that I really should be able to speak to you frankly.'

'I would expect nothing less,' said Berthea.

'In that case, dear sister, I really must confess to you that I've always had problems with Oedipus. I've tried to like him, I really have—he has an immortal soul like the rest of us. But, I don't know, my dear. The truth of the matter is . . . Well, to put it bluntly, I really can't stand him.'

'But, my dear,' whispered Berthea. 'Neither can I. And that's why I'm writing his biography. I want the world to know what my son is like. This is an act of expiation on my part. In writing this book, I am atoning for Oedipus. Do you understand that?'

'Perfectly,' said Terence. 'And now let's have some of this lovely leek pie. Smell it. Beautiful. Pure.'

Berthea sat down at the kitchen table. 'Fit for the Beings of Light themselves?'

'They love it!' said Terence.

30. Rye

Berthea Snark was not the only person to head out of London that weekend in search of the peace that the English countryside, and at least some of the towns that nestle in its folding hills, can bring. Oedipus Snark MP, the son whose distinctly non-hagiographical biography Berthea had begun to pen, was also in the country, although at a different end of it, in his case, in Rye.

The idea of going to Rye for the weekend had

not been his, but had been suggested by his lover, Barbara Ragg, the literary agent and author of the moderately successful *Ragg's Guide to the Year's Best Reads*.

'Rye,' she had said, a few weeks earlier. 'If the weather holds, it could be gorgeous.'

Oedipus Snark, who disliked being trapped with Barbara for a whole weekend, searched his mind quickly for an excuse. 'Sorry,' he said. 'I've got a constituency do, see? A long-term commitment, I'm afraid. You go by yourself. Send me a postcard.'

Barbara was prepared for this. 'But I checked with Jenny,' she said. 'She confirmed that both Saturday and Sunday are completely clear. She looked in both of your diaries and there's nothing. Friday night too. We could go down late on Friday afternoon.'

He frowned. That girl. She had no business telling any person who asked whether or not he had anything on. She was getting above herself. Going on about the LSE and the books she had read. Glorified secretary. She would need taking down a peg or two. Maybe a written warning; one had to be so careful with employment tribunals now. Best to give a written warning or two before you show somebody the door.

'She sometimes misses things,' he said. 'She's far from papal in her infallibility. Hah!'

'Not this time,' said Barbara. 'I asked her to double-check. She said that there had been something in the diary for Saturday—something to do with a development charity—but you had begged off. So, she said, it was quite free.'

Oedipus Snark fiddled with his tie. It was, his mother had once pointed out, a displacement activity, an *Übersprungbewegung*, and it occurred when he felt cornered.

'Why Rye?' he asked peevishly. 'What's so special about Rye?'

'There's a lovely old hotel there,' said Barbara. 'The Mermaid Inn. On Mermaid Street, not surprisingly. I went there years ago and loved it. Low ceilings and four-poster beds, and tremendously ancient into the bargain.'

'Well, we can't sit in the hotel all day,' said Oedipus, 'however ancient it may be.'

'We won't have to. There's a lot to see. There's Henry James's house, which was also lived in by E. F. Benson—you know, the Mapp and Lucia man— and they're having a concert in one of the churches. A young Canadian pianist. We could go to that.' She fixed Oedipus with a steely look. 'There's plenty to do.'

Oedipus had been out-manoeuvred by the combined forces of Jenny and Barbara Ragg and had no choice but to agree. So it was that they checked in to the Mermaid Inn shortly before dinner on Friday evening, having driven down in Barbara's open-topped MG in British Racing Green. The evening was warm, one of long shadows and no breeze to speak of. The air was heavy, and had that quality to it that comes at the end of the day—a comfortable, used quality.

Oedipus, who had been grumpy at the beginning of the journey, was positively ebullient by the time they arrived at the Mermaid Inn and immediately ordered them large gin and tonics in the bar.

'Not a bad choice,' he said, looking about appreciatively.

He paid her so few compliments that for a few moments Barbara was quite taken aback. She wanted him to be happy. She wanted him to stop rushing around and looking anxious, and instead have some time for her, to talk about her day, her concerns—just now and then. She wanted to marry Oedipus Snark and make him happy, not just over the occasional weekend, but for years. That is what Barbara Ragg wanted.

She was realistic, of course. One did not get where she had got in a difficult and competitive field without being astute. And she knew full well that Oedipus had no intention of settling down—at least not for the time being. That meant that she could either try to trap him into matrimony, by getting him to believe, for example, that it would help his political career to get married, a conclusion that often strikes politicians when they are just on the verge of achieving high office. Or she could simply enjoy what she already had: a relationship of convenience (for him) where they spent some time together, but not very much, and where certain subjects of conversation (marriage,

128

children, joint establishments and so on) were no-go areas, fenced about with electricity and warning bells.

Her friends, hostile almost without exception to Oedipus and, in the case of one or two of them, even given to shuddering involuntarily when his name was mentioned, spoke with one voice on the subject, even if their exact words varied.

'Give him up.'

'Show him the door.'

'Find a decent man, for heaven's sake.'

All of this was sage advice, intended to be helpful, and Barbara might have acted upon it if she felt that there was the slightest chance of getting somebody to replace her unsatisfactory political lover. But there was not. For some reason, possibly one connected with her manner, which was somewhat overpowering from the male point of view, men steered well clear of her. She was one of those women who inhibited men because of what some people described as her briskness. And she knew this. She knew it because she had once heard the nickname that some spiteful person had pinned on her and which had acquired wide currency. The Head Prefect.

I am not like that, she said to herself. I am not.

But in the eyes of others, she must have been. And when she attempted to be more feminine and to eschew any sign of high-handedness, it did not help at all. Then somebody made matters worse by coining a new nickname, again one which stuck, and travelled. Mrs Thatcher.

Who among us wants anything more than to be appreciated by some and loved, we hope, by a few? Why is the world so constructed that some find this modest goal easy to achieve and others find that it for ever eludes them? The essential unfairness of the world? Yes. Its heartlessness? Yes. Its unkindness to a certain sort of brisk and competent woman? Yes again.

31. Dinner at the Mermaid

At dinner at the Mermaid Inn, Oedipus Snark chose scallops as his first course. The waiter who took his order, a young man with neatly barbered hair who had just completed a degree in English at the University of Sussex, asked, 'Scallops, sir?' Oedipus nodded, and Barbara Ragg, looking up from her scrutiny of the menu, said, 'Oh, scallops. Yes, I'll have those too.'

The waiter scribbled on his notepad. 'And for your main course, sir?'

'Lamb cutlets, please.'

'Such a wise choice,' said the waiter, before turning to Barbara. 'And your main course, madam?'

'I'll take lamb cutlets too,' replied Barbara Ragg. She looked up at the young man with ill-concealed irritation. She did not think there was any need for a waiter to compliment one on one's choice of food, and yet so many of them did. They should be neutral, equally impassive in the face of good and bad choices, as impressed by Mr Sprat's opting for lean as by his wife's preference for fat. But there was more: he had taken Oedipus's order first, she noticed. Were waiters no longer trained to take the woman's order first, or did they now feel they had to give the man precedence, purely to make the point that they had risen above the old sexist courtesies? For a few moments she mused on the implications of social change for the strict rules of etiquette. What, for example, was the position when dealing with same-sex couples? If two women in such a relationship were dining together, and if the waiter normally observed the rule of asking women first, should he then take the order of the more feminine partner before that of the more masculine one—if such a distinction were obvious? And would such a policy be welcome or would it provoke hostility? People could be touchy, and it might not be a good idea to do anything but leave it to chance. But if the waiter turned first to an overtly masculine-looking partner, he might be suspected of doing so solely in order to avoid being thought to attend to the feminine partner first. And that would reveal that he had secretly made a judgement of roles. So only one course of action remained—for the waiter to look at neither diner while he said, dispassionately staring into the air above their heads, 'Now which of you two is first?' That would perhaps be the most tactful way of addressing the matter. Perhaps.

Oedipus Snark also looked irritated. He had no objection to the waiter's taking his order first—indeed he rather expected it, being an MP and being in the public eye. What he objected to was Barbara's choosing exactly the same courses as he had. Had she no imagination? Or was she trying to *be* like him? That really annoyed him. He could understand, of course, why somebody should wish to imitate him, but he did not like it to be so obvious. I shall have to get rid of her, he thought;

she's going to have to go.

'I read something interesting about scallops the other day,' Barbara remarked. 'Did you know that the best scallops are those that are hand-picked by divers? Apparently the other ones are sucked up by great vacuum cleaners and that bruises the scallop—ruins it, they say.'

Oedipus nodded. He was thinking of a new research assistant he had met in the House of Commons library. She had certainly been hand-picked, he thought, as opposed to being sucked up by a vacuum cleaner. She was currently working for another MP but that little difficulty could be dealt with easily enough. And if she came to work for him, then he could get rid of Jenny and Barbara at one stroke, neatly inserting this new girl into the roles occupied by both of them. It would be a perfect solution—not only more convenient and entertaining, but cheaper too.

'I think perhaps we should ask them where they get their scallops from,' Barbara said.

Oedipus waved a hand in the air. 'The fishmonger, I expect.' He looked at her. 'You're not turning into one of these people who bang on about food miles, are you?'

Barbara frowned. 'I don't bang on about anything, Oedipus. But there is some point to the food miles argument. Doesn't it strike you as odd that the fresh beans in our local supermarket should come from East Africa?'

'Not really,' he said. 'Farmers there have to sell their produce. And if we didn't buy it, then we'd be taking the food out of their mouths rather than putting it into ours. If you see what I mean.'

'I'm all for free trade,' said Barbara. 'But think of

132

the fuel it takes to airlift a sack of beans from Kenya to London.'

Oedipus shrugged. 'Everything's wrong,' he said. 'The whole way we order our affairs is wrong.'

Barbara reached for a piece of bread. 'At least you can do something about it,' she said. 'You're in Parliament.'

Oedipus erupted into sudden laughter. 'Parliament? What's Parliament got to do with it?'

'Everything, I would have thought.'

'Oh, Barbara, my dear,' said Oedipus Snark. 'Parliament decides nothing. I have no illusions about that. We're voting fodder—a sort of press conference audience for the Prime Minister at Question Time. We're more or less instructed to boo or shout. Parliament controls nobody. We're thrown a few scraps of symbolic power from time to time, but the Government, in the shape of the Prime Minister and his close allies, decides everything. Look at the way our constitution has been changed. Just like that—no real consultation. Nothing.'

'I thought—' began Barbara.

'And then there's Brussels,' Oedipus went on. 'Brussels decides our fate to a very large extent. But do we actually vote for the people who make the decisions over there? Answer: no. And are they accountable to us? Again the answer is no.'

Barbara absorbed all this. 'So why are you in politics if you can't do anything?'

Oedipus fingered his tie. 'It's an agreeable career,' he said. 'And it gives most of the people in it a sense of belonging, and purpose too, I suppose. But let's not delude ourselves as to what one person can do. Even somebody like me.'

Barbara decided to change the subject. 'I've had a very trying week,' she said. 'A lot of stress.'

Oedipus smiled blandly. He did not really care very much what sort of week Barbara had had; in fact, he did not care at all. But if she wanted to talk, then he supposed that he could at least provide an ear for her to pour her troubles into. Silly woman.

'Do tell me,' he said. 'Difficult colleagues again? Un-reasonable publishers refusing to publish your pet authors?'

'No,' she said. 'Nothing like that. Rather the opposite, in fact. You see, I've had somebody come to see me with a sure-fire, copper-bottomed bestseller. Fabulous story. Great pace. A tour de force if ever there was one.'

She saw a flicker of interest cross Oedipus's face. At least he *sees* me now, she thought.

'And?' he asked.

'I don't know what to do with it,' said Barbara. 'The author is difficult—but then so are all authors, without exception. He has his notions and he only wants to place it with the publisher of his choice. Our author is determined to try to get this particular publisher—he seems to care nothing for the suggestions I've made. He wants to go for this completely unsuitable high-end literary publisher.'

'So what are you going to do?' asked Oedipus.

'I'm going to have to sit tight for six months,' said Barbara. 'The author is off on retreat somewhere and doesn't want me to do anything until he comes back. So I sit on this fabulous idea and watch it gather dust.'

Oedipus watched her; he was thinking. 'Tell me about this idea,' he said. 'I'll let you know whether

134

it'll run the way you say it will.'

32. The Yeti Writes

'Well, it's what you might call a biographical thriller,' said Barbara Ragg. 'It's a new category. But it's going to be big. As big as *The Da Vinci Code* was. Ever since *The Da Vinci Code* was so successful, publishers have been looking out for something that will do the same thing. Code books. The uncovering of secrets. Masons. Rosicrucians. And so on.'

'No accounting for taste,' said Oedipus Snark.

'You read *The Da Vinci Code*?'

He shook his head. 'Far too busy,' he said, and then added, 'constituency business, you see.'

Barbara Ragg broke off a piece of her bread roll and buttered it carefully. 'I'm not saying that it was great literature. But it kept enough people riveted. And from our point of view as agents—not that we were the agents in question—it did the trick. It made millions of pounds. Millions. Even for the agents.'

'I can understand why you're looking for the next thing,' said Oedipus Snark. Millions of pounds: what would I do with millions of pounds? he wondered. Well, I wouldn't be here. I wouldn't be here in the Mermaid Inn in Rye talking to poor old Barbara Ragg. Paris perhaps. An agreeable little pied-à-terre on the Île de la Cité, perhaps, or near the Parc Monceau. Or an apartment in Manhattan, upper seventies, perhaps, East Side. Friends to match. Live in London, of course, but hop over to

135

New York once a month for a few days. See what's on at the Met. Take a few friends. Perfect.

'Of course,' said Barbara, 'you can't repeat things. Lightning doesn't strike twice in the same place. So all those 'me too' manuscripts that followed the *Code* ended up doing pretty miserably.'

She was warming to her theme. 'And the same goes for authors. Some of them have one book in them—just one—and they're never going to be able to write anything else.'

'Like God,' said Oedipus.

She looked at him quizzically.

'He wrote the Bible, didn't he? But he never really followed up with anything quite so successful.'

'I was being serious.'

He smiled. 'So was I. But tell me about this author of yours. I'm intrigued.'

Barbara buttered the rest of her bread roll. 'He's a first-time author,' she said. 'He came to us out of the blue. We get all sorts of manuscripts sent to us. The vast majority are impossible, of course, but every so often you get something really good. It's like mining diamonds. You go through thousands of tons of kimberlite for one little diamond. And every so often, among millions of tons of the stuff, along comes a great big stone that gets De Beers jumping up and down with excitement. Well, that's what it's like with manuscripts. One beautiful idea among the tons of dross.'

Oedipus Snark had left his roll untouched. Although he was trying not to show it, he was fascinated by what Barbara was saying. This was the sort of thing that he liked: better—surer—than

136

looking for the next high performers on the alternative stock markets. You could waste months of your time doing that and at the end of the day find that you simply could not compete with the young men in the City, with their access to whispers and rumours.

'Go on,' he said evenly. 'This person from out of the blue.'

'It landed on my desk,' said Barbara. 'We have somebody who gives things a preliminary read. She sends most of the stuff right back, or at least sends it back after we've let it sit in the office for three weeks or so. One wouldn't want the authors to think that we'd rejected them out of hand.'

Oedipus raised an eyebrow. 'So she said it had the makings?'

'She did. In fact, she said that this was the one. I remember her precise words. 'We must write to him and say thank you.' That's what she said. Do you realise how rarely that happens in publishing? The last author who got anything like that was Wilbur Smith—you know, the man who writes about deeds of derring-do in Africa. Elephants and ancient treasure. Very exciting stuff. People love reading him. Sells millions. When he sent his first manuscript off to the publishers he was a complete unknown. He parcelled it up and sent it off—this was still the days of typewriters, of course, and it was maybe the only copy. Back came a telegram in no time at all: "Thank you for this wonderful book. Letter follows."'

'Nice,' said Oedipus Snark.

Barbara agreed. 'Most of the time, when an author writes to an agent or a publisher to find out about the fate of a manuscript, he gets a reply saying, 'Your manuscript is under active consideration.' You know what that means, Oedipus? It means: we're actively looking for it.'

Oedipus said nothing. It was a useful phrase, and he would have to use it himself in his own letters. 'The point you raised with me is under active consideration.' It was very nice.

Barbara continued her story. 'Well, I took this manuscript home with me. I didn't look forward to reading it, I'm afraid—I *hate* reading manuscripts but I had to do it. So I made myself a stiff gin and tonic and sat down with this great pile of paper. I hadn't even read the title at that stage. All I had seen was the name of the author. Errol Greatorex. Not a good start. Names are important in the book business, you know. You can have one author called Stan Jones, or whatever, who writes exactly the same sort of book as, shall we say, somebody called Jodi de Balzac. Whose book makes its mark? Not Stan Jones's, I'm afraid. So we had a bit of a problem with Errol Greatorex. It was the Errol, of course—the Greatorex bit was fine. Full of literary possibilities.

'I sat down with my gin and Mr Greatorex's manuscript and looked at the title. *The Autobiography of a Yeti.*'

Oedipus Snark's eyes widened. 'The Abominable Snowman?'

'The very same. The yeti who lives up in the high forests of the Himalayas. On the edge of the treeline. That yeti.'

It was at this point that the waiter returned with the scallops. But neither of the diners paid much attention to the plate of elegantly served seafood that was placed before them. Barbara's eyes were bright with the memory of the moment when she first began to read the manuscript. And Oedipus, for his part, was thinking: what if I took over this amazing story? What if I was the one to reveal this to the world? Me. Oedipus Snark. And something else crossed his mind too. Money.

33. 'An hairy man' (sic)

Oedipus was not one to show an overt interest in anything very much but Barbara Ragg could tell that he was acutely interested in Errol Greatorex's manuscript. This pleased her; indeed, she basked in his attention, a rare experience for her. At least now he's taking me seriously, she said to herself as she tackled the last scraps of scallop.

'The scallops were just perfect,' she commented, dabbing at her mouth with her table napkin. 'They must have been hand-picked rather than sucked up, don't you think?'

'Very possibly,' said Oedipus. 'Perhaps some brave Scottish diver went down into the waters off Mull or somewhere like that. Tremendously cold, no doubt. But tell me, this Errol Greatorex . . .'

Barbara was enjoying herself. 'I wonder if they dive with air tanks?' she mused. 'Or do they just hold their breath and swim down? There's something called free-diving, you know. I read about it.'

'Maybe. But tell me, this manuscript . . .'

Barbara ignored the incipient question. 'They go down to an amazing depth, you know, these free-divers. Two hundred feet and more in some cases.

All with one lungful of air.'

'Yes, yes. But I don't think that these scallop divers . . .'

'There's something called the mammalian diving reflex,' Barbara continued. She had listened to him for so long; now he could listen to her for a change. 'It makes it easier for your system to work on very little oxygen. You can get better and better at it if you train yourself. It's quite amazing.'

Oedipus pushed his plate aside. 'I'm not really all that interested in free-diving, Barbara,' he said. 'This novel of yours: that's what I want to discuss.'

'But there's not much to discuss,' said Barbara calmly. 'It's just the story of a yeti's life.' She paused. 'And it's not fiction, you know.'

She watched Oedipus's expression. He looked mocking. 'You mean he claims to be a yeti?'

'No, of course not. Greatorex is not a yeti name. I would have thought that you would know that.' She paused. I have just said something extremely witty, she said to herself. But Oedipus Snark just stared at her. 'He's called it an autobiography,' she continued, 'because the yeti told him his story. It's an 'as told to' book. You know, the sort that pop singers and footballers write. They're just like yetis, in their way. Everybody knows that they can't do it themselves and use ghost writers. Hence the 'as told to' books.'

Oedipus shook his head. 'Don't be ridiculous. The yeti doesn't exist.'

Barbara leaned forward slightly. 'How do you know, Oedipus? How do you know the yeti doesn't exist?'

'For the same reason I know that Father Christmas doesn't exist,' he said. 'Or the Tooth

140

Fairy.'

'Or Higgs's boson?'

Oedipus Snark's eyes flashed. If Barbara imagines she can pull particle physics on me, he thought, she's in for a surprise.

'Higgs boson?' he snapped. 'There's mathematics for that. Where is the mathematics for the Tooth Fairy? And anyway, what about the W and Z bosons?'

Barbara wondered whether she could ask for more scallops. 'The W and Z bosons?' she repeated.

Oedipus held her gaze. 'Yes.'

'I haven't got the first clue,' she said. 'I'm not a physicist, Oedipus. You tell me about them. What are they, these bosons?'

Oedipus waved a hand in the air. 'Some other time,' he said. 'But where's the evidence for the existence of yetis?'

Barbara looked at her empty plate. She would buy some scallops when she got back to London and eat them privately in her kitchen, with a glass of white wine and Mozart playing in the background. It would be nice to be married, but could married people do that sort of thing? 'There's some evidence,' she said. 'Sightings. Big footprints in the snow. Quite a bit of this comes from perfectly level-headed people.'

Oedipus laughed. 'Listen, light can play tricks. People see all sorts of things—ghosts, UFOs, the face of Elvis in their pizzas and so on. If you believed half of what people claim to have seen, you'd be very badly informed.' He paused. 'And as for footprints in the snow, an ordinary footprint gets much bigger as the snow melts around the edges. See?'

Barbara shrugged. 'Well, you can believe what you will. I shall remain agnostic on the subject. All that I know is that Errol's book is absolutely riveting. And it will sell. In fact, I'm prepared to bet that it will be pretty much number one on the lists. It's absolutely compelling.'

Oedipus became placatory. 'I'm sorry,' he said. 'I didn't mean to rubbish your book. It's just I doubt if it can be true. I'm sure that it's a great read—as fiction. Look, why don't you tell me a bit about it? How did he meet the yeti?'

Barbara sat back while the waiter served the second course. 'Errol Greatorex is an American travel writer. He mostly writes for magazines but was working on a coffee-table book on the Himalayas when all this happened.'

'What happened?' asked Oedipus.

'His encounter,' said Barbara. 'He had an encounter.'

Oedipus rolled his eyes upwards. 'The effect of thin air,' he said. 'The oxygen-starved brain hallucinates.'

'Not when you're acclimatised,' snapped Barbara. 'Errol had been there for several weeks. He would be unlikely to be hallucinating at that stage.'

'All right,' said Oedipus grudgingly. 'So he had an encounter. What exactly happened?'

Barbara sat back in her chair. 'He was staying in a Buddhist monastery up in Nepal. It was a very remote place. Can you picture it? Prayer flags fluttering in the wind. Bare green pastures ringed by mountains. Grey rocky outcrops. The chant of monks hanging in the air.'

142

She waited for him to respond. He nodded.

'One of the monks came to him one morning and said that he wanted to show him something very unusual. Most of the monks spoke no English, but this one had a few words and was able to make himself understood. He said that it was not something that he would show to anybody; Errol Greatorex had been kind to him, he explained, and he trusted him.

'This monk led him off to the back of the monastery. They had a whole lot of buildings—it was all rather higgledy-piggledy. One of these buildings was a sort of classroom; he had walked past it once or twice and had seen a class of boys being instructed in religious texts. There were no schoolboys there at the time, but Greatorex saw the teacher sitting at a desk apparently marking a pile of little school notebooks. For a while the teacher did not appear to notice his visitors, but then he looked up from his task and Greatorex saw his face for the first time.'

Barbara paused. Oedipus Snark was watching her intently. 'And?' he prompted. 'What was he like?'

'He was hairy,' said Barbara. 'Like Esau. An hairy man.'

'*A* hairy man,' corrected Oedipus.

'An,' she said. 'Esau was *an* hairy man.'

He looked irritated. 'What are you going on about?' he asked.

34. William Plans a Soufflé

While Barbara Ragg regaled Oedipus Snark with her account of Errol Greatorex's manuscript, William French, wine merchant and now part-owner of the dog known as Freddie de la Hay, was in his flat in Corduroy Mansions, waiting for the return of his son, Eddie. Eddie spent Friday evenings in the pub with his friends, but would usually come home first; however, he had not done so that day. William wondered if he had gone straight to the pub, in which case he might not see his son until well after midnight—if he had the stamina to wait up for him.

He felt distinctly disappointed. Now that he had taken the plunge and acquired Freddie de la Hay, he was eager to get the inevitable confrontation with Eddie out of the way. It would not be easy—he knew that—because Eddie had a temper and was given to emotional outbursts. He would not take the presence of Freddie de la Hay lying down.

Which, as it happened, was what Freddie de la Hay himself was doing at that moment. He had found a spot on the rug in front of the drawing-room fireplace and had curled up there, his eyes just sufficiently open to watch William as he moved about the room.

When William had first taken him upstairs, the dog had rushed around the flat, sniffing at the furniture. Once he had completed his inspection, he had gazed up at William, as if awaiting instructions.

'Well,' said William, looking down at his new

144

companion, 'that's about it, Freddie, old chap. I suppose it's not all that exciting from the canine point of view, but you should be comfortable enough.'

Freddie cocked his head to the side, as if to elicit a further remark from William. The dog was aware that something had changed in his life but he was not quite sure what. His inspection of the flat had yielded nothing significant—there were none of the smells he had been trained to detect at the airport, and so there was no need to bark. But he was puzzled: he had picked up the smell of two people in the flat, yet as far as he could see, there was only one. That was about as far as Freddie's limited reasoning powers could go. Two smells, one person. All he knew, then, was that there was somebody missing.

William went into the kitchen to prepare himself something to eat. Since the death of his wife some years earlier he had become an accomplished cook, at least in respect of the twenty or so recipes that he had written out in a small Moleskine notebook that Eddie had given him for Christmas. These recipes he had numbered from one to twenty, and he worked through them one by one, in numerical order. Tonight was number seventeen, which was an easily prepared cheese soufflé served with broccoli and Puy lentils.

He started to grate the small block of Gruyère that he had bought the day before. That done, he helped himself to a glass of Chablis from an open bottle in the fridge. The Chablis, he thought, would go well with the Gruyère, the flinty taste of the wine providing a sharpness that would sit well against the cheese. Then he began working on the

145

roux for the soufflé while the lentils boiled on the stove. How comfortable, he thought; how nice to be in the flat by myself without music drifting down the corridor from Eddie's room. He has such appalling taste in music, thought William. All that insistent, throbbing bass rhythm—what can he possibly find to like in it?

William had once asked Eddie what his music actually *meant*. His son had looked at him blankly.

'What do you mean what does it mean?' Eddie asked. 'It's music. That's all.'

'But music means something,' William pointed out. 'It has structure. It tells you something. It creates a mood, doesn't it?'

'No, it just sounds good,' said Eddie. 'You like old music because you're old. I like something more lively because I'm not past it like you.'

William was used to such comments. 'I wasn't talking about our individual preferences,' he said mildly. 'I was just wondering what your music—that thudding stuff you play—what it actually says about . . .'—he searched for the right words—'about anything at all. Does it say anything?'

'It's random,' said Eddie.

William sighed. And now, appreciating the silence, he thought about how much of Eddie's random music he had been obliged to endure. He, who liked Mozart and Gregorian chant, had put up with the filling of his personal space with the very antithesis of all that. Well, now was the time to do something about it, and he would; it was *his music* that would be heard in the flat from now on.

He was thinking about this, relishing the thought, when he heard the key turn in the lock. He put down the bowl in which he had been whisking the

146

eggs for the soufflé. Eddie was his son; he had no reason to be afraid of him. And yet his breath came quickly and his mouth felt curiously dry as he made his way from the kitchen into the hall. He would have to tell Eddie about Freddie de la Hay before his son saw the dog. He needed to get the upper hand right away so that he would have the advantage in the confrontation that would inevitably ensue.

Eddie opened the door and came into the hall.

'I've got some interesting news,' William blurted out.

'Oh yeah?' said Eddie.

'Yeah,' said William. 'I've acquired a pet.'

Eddie frowned. 'You?' he asked. 'You've acquired a what?'

'A pet,' William repeated.

Eddie burst out laughing. 'A hamster?' he said. 'That's pretty tragic, Dad. 'Elderly Wine Merchant Acquires Hamster for Company'.' Eddie liked to talk in newspaper headlines—another habit that irritated William.

William shook his head. 'No,' he said. "Middle-aged Wine Merchant Gets Dog".'

Eddie, who had been walking across the hall towards his room, stopped where he was. 'Dog?' he whispered.

'Yes. A very agreeable dog,' confirmed William. 'He's called Freddie de la Hay. He's through there in the drawing room. Go and take a look, if you like.'

The deed was done, and William felt a surge of relief. He had presented Eddie with the clearest ultimatum, and it had been much easier than he had expected.

147

Eddie glared at his father. 'Have you gone out of your mind?' he hissed. 'You . . . you know I can't be near a dog. You know that.'

William spread his hands in a gesture of helplessness. 'But you said you were going to move out. I've always assumed that you were going to do that. So the fact that you don't like dogs shouldn't be a problem, should it?'

35. Eddie is Cool

For a few moments Eddie said nothing, but stared intensely at his father in frank astonishment. Then, his disbelief changing to horror, he brushed past William and strode into the drawing room.

Freddie de la Hay, half asleep on the Baluchi rug in front of the fireplace, content to doze in this new, agreeable place, lazily opened first one eye and then the other. Raising his nose from the rug, he sniffed at the air: yes, this was the other person he had smelled on his earlier rounds of the flat. So this was the second occupant of the house. One could not, as a dog, expect that most perfect of arrangements from the canine perspective: one human and one dog. Such dispositions existed but were rare, and were not to be, it seemed, for Freddie de la Hay.

He stared at Eddie for a few moments and then lowered his head back onto the rug to continue his doze. There was nothing he needed to do; any instructions, he imagined, would come from William, who was clearly now his master, and not from this new arrival.

Eddie spun round and stormed back into the hall. William saw his expression and winced, his resolve not to be intimidated by his son seeming a small thing now in the face of this towering filial wrath.

'Is this your idea of a joke, Dad?' Eddie shouted. And then, before William could answer, he added, 'Whose dog is it? Get them to come and fetch it.'

William swallowed. He belonged to a generation that had missed the two great conflicts of the twentieth century and he had a profound distaste for any manifestation of anger. Seeing his son in this mood shocked him, and he was for a moment uncertain what to do. His instinct was to agree, to assure Eddie that the dog was only a visitor and that he had indeed been joking. But he managed to steel himself sufficiently to reply, 'Sorry, Eddie, but it's not a joke. I've always wanted a dog. And you did say that you were going to get your own place. That place with Stevie.'

Eddie had been about to shout out something more but this stopped him. He frowned. He had said nothing to his father about Stevie's proposal,

149

or had he? No, he had only discussed it on the phone, when his friend had rung him. His father, then, must have been listening; it was the only explanation for his knowing anything about it.

'So now you're listening in to my telephone conversations, are you?' It was as if he were adding another outrage to a long list of grievances.

William lowered his gaze. He had never been able to lie, and he could not lie now. 'I picked up the telephone at the moment you answered it yourself. I didn't intend to listen in.'

'But you did.'

He nodded. 'I did. And perhaps it taught me the lesson that Polonius learned—you know, in *Hamlet*—that it doesn't pay to eavesdrop, particularly when people are talking about you. You'll never hear anything but ill of yourself. It's the same with Googling yourself. Don't Google yourself lest you read something you'd rather not read.'

He was rather proud of the analogy, which struck him as being bang up to date, but it seemed lost on Eddie, who simply stared at him blankly, still cross, of course, but now blank too. William decided to press his advantage. 'Oh yes,' he continued. 'You hardly defended me when Stevie suggested that you were fed up with me, did you? What did he say? 'Fed up with your old man? Blah, blah.' Weren't those the words he used?'

'Stevie's just Stevie,' Eddie mumbled. 'You know how he is. He doesn't mean it most of the time.'

'Oh no?' said William. 'Yet you went along with him quickly enough, didn't you, Eddie?'

Eddie shifted on his feet. 'You're trying to change the subject, Dad.'

William's voice rose as he replied. 'Really? Well, let's get back to the subject then, which is my life. I want to lead a life. I want to lead a life on my terms in my own flat. I want to listen to my music, not yours. I want to spend as long as I like in the bathroom in the morning, washing my own face. I want to have a dog. Maybe even two dogs. More, even. I want to have friends. I want everything that parents give up when they have children, especially children like you. I want quiet. I want to spend my own money on myself and not on you. That's what I want, Eddie. That's what I want.'

William's words were delivered with all the dignity and force of the Gettysburg Address. And the effect was extraordinary. Eddie suddenly stepped forward and put an arm around William's shoulder. Then he leaned forward so that his face brushed against his father's cheek, briefly, before he drew back and stared directly into William's eyes.

'All right, Dad,' he said. 'It's fine to cry. It really is.'

'I'm not crying,' said William.

'Sure, sure,' soothed Eddie. 'Don't hold it in.'

'I have no desire to cry,' repeated William, emphasising each word. 'I don't know why you're going on about it. I have no desire to cry. I'm in perfect control of my emotions, as I'm sure you can see.'

'But that's the trouble, Dad,' said Eddie. 'That's the trouble that all men have with their emotions. Particularly middle-class men like you. Elderly middle-class men. They can't let go. It all builds up and then . . . out it comes, and they flip.'

William now raised his voice. 'I have *not* flipped,'

151

he said.

'No, not yet,' said Eddie. 'But that's the way it happens. Everything looks fine on the surface, but just below there are all those churning emotions—all of them without an outlet. It's unnatural.'

William tried to pull himself away from his son, who still had an arm around his shoulder. But Eddie hung on. 'I'm with you, Dad,' he said. 'We can get through this thing together.'

'What thing?' asked William.

'This whole mid-life crisis thing that you're experiencing. This dog thing. It's nothing to be ashamed of. A powerful car. A dog. A younger woman. Same thing. Lots of men do exactly that during their MLC.' He paused. 'So don't you worry any more—it's going to be all right. If it helps you, then I can live with a dog. I'm cool with that. *Hakuna matata*. You know what that means? No problems, in Swahili. *Hakuna matata*, Dad!'

36. I Find You Attractive

On Saturday morning it was Jo who was up first in the shared flat in Corduroy Mansions. She was an early riser and always had been, a result of her upbringing in Perth. Her architect parents, Gavin and Madge Partlin, were believers in a healthy outdoor existence, which had been one of the reasons why they had moved from Sydney to Perth shortly after Jo's birth. It was not that their lifestyle in Sydney had been particularly unhealthy—it had not—but neither had enjoyed the constraints of the flat in which they lived, nor the chilled,

conditioned air of the tall city building they both worked in. In Perth they could live near the beach and work from home; in the mornings they could go running together along the beach, just below the high-tide mark, where the sand was firm enough for pounding feet, carrying Jo in her special baby-backpack. At weekends, if they wished, they could go camping near Margaret River, where the air that wafted in from the coast blew straight from the southern oceans; scented with the eucalyptus of the forests, it seemed to fill the lungs with life and energy.

Coming from such a background, Jo might have expected to find the transition to a life in London a difficult one. But she had not. London was for her something of a promised land—not a place where she could see herself staying for ever, but *the* place to be for that stage of one's life at which one yearned after something different, even if one might not come right out and say that one wanted *adventure*. Which is what she did want, in fact; but where might one find such experiences when the world had contracted so much? When Base Camp at Everest itself could be reached in two days rather than two weeks? When even space flight was about to become a commodity which one might pay for on a credit card and book online? Like so many of her peers, she had gone travelling for a year after completing her course in physical education at the University of Western Australia. She had gone to Thailand, where she had spent four months working her way up from Krabi to Chiang Mai, staying in hostels and cheap guest houses. But the life of a lotus-eater, to which the existence of staying in Thai resorts proved to be so similar, became boring and eventually palled. Travel was all very well, but it needed a sense of purpose—something which a journey without a terminus always lacked. After Thailand there were Vietnam and Cambodia, but she was impatient and beginning to run out of money. It was time to go to London.

The flat in Corduroy Mansions was the first one she looked at, seeing Jenny's advertisement by chance a few minutes after it had gone live on Gumtree. She had arrived two hours later, been interviewed by Jenny and agreed to move in the next day.

Dee had been interviewed the day after that, with Jo being co-opted onto the vetting committee. She and Jo had taken to one another immediately, although both of them had been less sure about Caroline when it was her turn to be assessed as the final member of the flat. 'I'm not too sure,' Dee whispered to Jo as Jenny took Caroline out of the room to show her the bedroom she would have.

'No? What's the problem?'

'She's a bit . . . you know.'

Jo had her doubts too, but was it because Caroline was a bit . . . you know? And what was 'you know' anyway?

'I don't know actually,' she said. Was 'you know' the same as being a *whinger*? English people were said to whinge a bit but perhaps in England itself they could be allowed to do so. After all, it was their country, even if it was run by Scots.

'Posh,' said Dee simply.

'Oh.' That was different from being a whinger, although one might have, of course, a posh whinger.

But Jo's fundamental sense of fairness, her Australian heritage, came to the fore. She remembered her father once remarking, 'You can't help the bed you're born in, you know.' She had been a teenager when he said that, and the observation had stuck in her memory. Of course you can't help who you are. That is something that people forgot, she felt. They forgot it when they were unkind to people because of where they came from, or because they were different, or because they had greasy skin. Her father was right. 'She can't help that, you know,' she pointed out. 'She can't help the way she talks, can she? None of us can.'

Dee had found herself unable to argue with that, although she mumbled something about Sloane Rangers. But they both decided that they would not object to Caroline's admission to the flat, which was just as well because Jenny announced when she came back into the room that Caroline would be moving in.

'Why did she ask us to interview her if she was going to make up her mind by herself?' Jo later

155

complained to Dee.

Dee thought for a moment. 'Because that's what we call consultation in this country,' she said. 'It's the same with government. Look at how they have all these consultation exercises. But they decide policy in advance, before they have the consultation exercise, and then they announce what they're going to do—which is exactly what they were always going to do anyway. That's the way it works.'

'But that's very hypocritical,' said Jo.

Dee laughed. 'Oh yes, it's hypocritical all right. But there's an awful lot of hypocrisy in this country. Isn't it the same in Australia?'

That question required more than a few moments of thought. Then Jo replied, 'I think we're more direct speakers,' she said. 'We say things to people's faces.'

Dee was intrigued. 'Such as?'

Again Jo hesitated. 'That I find you very attractive.'

37. Dee Meets Freddie de la Hay

Dee had not known what to say. For a few moments she stared at her flatmate, not in the way that one stares at something that interests one, but with the sort of stare used when one is looking at somebody and is suddenly too embarrassed to look away. If such a stare lingers, it lingers because it can do nothing else.

'Oh,' she said. And then, again, 'Oh.'

Then it was Jo's turn to show embarrassment.

She, too, said, 'Oh.'

Dee tore her gaze away and looked at the floor. They were standing in the kitchen, and she was looking down at cork tiles, which had been pitted over the years by stiletto heels. It was like the surface of a brown planet somewhere, she thought, the indentations being tiny hits by ancient meteorites.

'Oh,' repeated Jo. 'I didn't mean it like *that*. You didn't think . . . ?'

Dee looked up with relief, and laughed. 'Of course not.'

She was lying. Of course she had.

'You see,' Jo went on, 'that shows the truth of what I said about us Australians. We really do speak our minds. I was thinking that you look really good in that top. It suits you. Suits your colouring. Green.'

Dee reached up to touch her blouse. 'Thanks. I've had it for ages.' All her clothes were old; second-hand, mostly, bought from charity shops or passed on by more affluent friends. There was a woman who came into the vitamin agency who had taken to giving Dee the clothes that she no longer needed. This top came from her, she remembered.

'You've got good skin too,' Jo went on. 'High cheekbones. My face is going to sag when I'm forty. God, I'm going to sag.'

'Not necessarily,' said Dee. 'And your skin's fine. I don't see anything wrong with it.'

'That's because you don't live in it,' Jo retorted. 'I know. You should see my mother. I'm going to be like her.'

'We're all going to be like our mothers,' said Dee. 'And we're going to say the same things, too.'

157

Jo shook her head. 'Never.'
'We'll see.'

*   *   *

Now, almost a year later, Dee found herself in the kitchen making herself a pot of green tea when Jo came into the room, already dressed in the grey tracksuit that she donned for her regular morning runs.

Jo looked out of the window. 'Nice day,' she said. 'I'm on duty at the wine bar this evening, worse luck. But the day's free. I'm going to do ten miles this morning. Then I think I'll have a picnic with some friends. One of the parks.'

Dee thought that this was a good idea. She approved of exercise and took it herself, in theory at least. But exercise without a good diet was not enough. What was the use of pounding the pavements if one was deficient in selenium, or magnesium for that matter?

She poured green tea into her cup. 'I'm working,' she said. 'Saturday morning's always busy for us.' They would be so busy that she would not have very much time to talk to Martin. But she hoped that she would be able to sit him down after lunch and discuss his colonic irrigation. She had planted the seed in his mind, and she wanted to get back to it because she thought that he was on the point of agreeing to it. If he did agree, then she was going to suggest that they did it the following day. Doing it on a Sunday would give him time to take the salts in advance and it could be done in a leisurely way. Their flat would be best—she did not fancy going all the way out to Martin's house in

158

Wimbledon or wherever it was that he lived with his parents, carrying all the necessary equipment. And what would his parents think? People were sensitive about colonic irrigation, largely because they had no idea, Dee thought, about what it involved and what the benefits were. If only they knew, if only they could see what could be flushed out of the system. She had heard recently of a man who had swallowed a marble as a child and had only now, at the age of thirty, had it flushed out of his system. Imagine having a marble in one's digestive tract for over twenty years! She would have to tell Martin about that. Perhaps it would persuade him.

She was thinking about this when she suddenly heard an unfamiliar sound on the landing outside. 'Is that a dog barking?' she said to Jo.

Jo frowned. 'Sounded like it. But inside?'

There was another bark—louder this time.

'I'm going to take a look,' said Dee. 'Perhaps a stray has come in. Eddie often doesn't shut the front door. I've asked him. But he doesn't care.'

She left the kitchen and went into the hall to open the front door. When she looked outside, it was to see William beginning to descend the final flight of stairs. At his side, attached to a leash, was Freddie de la Hay.

William, hearing the door open, looked over his shoulder.

'Yes,' he said, smiling. 'Meet your new neighbour, Freddie de la Hay.'

Dee stared at Freddie. How very strange. A dog with a surname. But it was Pimlico, after all, and one might expect anything to happen in Pimlico.

'How do you do?' she said.

159

Freddie looked at her. Was this woman addressing him? Perhaps he should sit, just to be on the safe side. People were always asking dogs to sit, even when there was clearly no need to. Freddie sighed, and sat. Life was complicated. And he had just picked up an interesting scent, too. It came from downstairs. Very interesting.

38. At Breakfast

Down in Rye, Barbara Ragg sat with Oedipus Snark awaiting breakfast in the dining room of the Mermaid Inn. They were at the same table at which they had eaten dinner the previous night. That had hardly been the romantic evening she had been looking forward to; she rather regretted, in fact, mentioning the Greatorex manuscript at all, as Oedipus had harped on about it for the entire meal, eager for every detail she could provide. It was an extraordinary story, she agreed, but not *that* extraordinary, particularly since she had a very strong suspicion that Greatorex had made the whole thing up. Of course there was no yeti, even if there were some puzzling unexplained sightings of creatures that *could* be the yeti. But there was always a rational explanation for these things: a trick of light, an error of the human brain, a misinterpreted shadow.

She found it strange that she should have argued for the existence of the yeti when faced with Oedipus's scepticism; normally she would be the first to agree that we need evidence for our beliefs; she had no time for paranormal speculation, for

160

wishful thinking. But in the face of his doubting—even if his doubt had rapidly turned to interest—she had defended Greatorex. Why? Because he was her author and that was what an agent should do? No, it was more than simple knee-jerk loyalty. It was something to do with the carapace of certainty that Oedipus Snark had about him. He was just so *right*, especially in his own eyes, and she wanted to puncture that. She had had enough.

The word *enough* can be potent. It can begin as a statement of dissatisfaction and rapidly become a call to arms. In the minds, or the mouths, of the oppressed it becomes the trigger of resistance, the rallying cry which signals the turning of the worm. *Henry VI*, Part 3, Barbara Ragg's thoughts now turned to: 'The smallest worm will turn, being trodden on / And doves will peck in safeguard of their brood.' Well, she thought, I have had enough.

She looked over the table at Oedipus Snark, who was reading the newspaper. Then she glanced at other tables where other couples, husband and wife, lover and lover, friend and friend, were sitting over their own Saturday morning breakfasts. None of them had a newspaper, but sat facing one another, talking. In one corner, near the window, a couple actually laughed at something one of them had said, their eyes bright with mirth.

Enough.

She made the observation casually. 'Something interesting in the paper?'

Oedipus shrugged. 'Not really.'

Barbara felt her heart beating faster. She was fully aware of what she was doing. Her relationship with Oedipus Snark had lasted for two years. She had hoped for something out of it. She had hoped that he would give some indication that he was at least thinking of something permanent, something publicly acknowledged. She had hoped that they might get invitations headed 'Oedipus and Barbara'. She had hoped that he might remember her birthday without being prodded; she had hoped for a few signs that she was important to him. But I am not, she thought. I am a casual companion, that is all; an incidental adjunct.

She drew in her breath. 'Do you know that game that children play? Where they say, would you rather be eaten by a lion or a shark? Or would you rather . . .'

Oedipus did not glance up from the paper. 'What?'

'I said that there's a game that children play,' she said quietly. 'My nephew played it when he was ten. He kept asking me which of two options I would like.'

'Your nephew? The one who liked cricket?'

At least he remembered, she thought. Louis liked cricket, and Oedipus had talked to him about it. He had promised to take him to Lords one day because he knew somebody there and the boy's eyes had lit up. Of course he had never taken him.

'Yes. Louis. Remember?'

'I remember him. Lewis.'

'Louis.'

'That's what I said.'

There was a short silence. Then Barbara continued. 'So,' she said, 'would you rather be with me or in the House of Commons? Do you prefer me or the House of Commons? Or how about this: would you rather be on a slow boat to China with me or be elected leader of the Liberal Democrats?

162

Or . . .'

Oedipus lowered his newspaper. 'What's all this?' he said.

Barbara reached for a spoon. She did not know why, but she reached for a spoon and held it firmly in her right hand, as if it were a weapon. *With this spoon, I shall . . .*

'I've had enough, Oedipus.'

The newspaper was now lying on the table, the corner of one of its pages dipped in the butter, which was soft. Oedipus frowned.

'Is there something biting you?' he asked, glancing over at the table nearest them. Women were impossible, he felt. They wanted attention. Attention, attention, attention—all the time. One could not even read the paper without them wanting you to talk to them instead. They were fundamentally unstable creatures, Oedipus Snark thought: demanding, critical, quick to take offence because one was doing something as innocent as reading the paper.

Barbara looked at him, trying to get him to look her in the eye. But he would not. His gaze moved away to the neighbouring table, to the ceiling, to the newspaper in the butter.

'I don't think that there's much point in our continuing to see one another,' she said. 'I really don't. You show no interest in me, you see? You don't really care for me.'

She tried to keep her voice even, but it faltered as she spoke the words she had not spoken to him before. I only want to be loved, she thought. I only want what other people get, which is somebody who loves them. And I thought it might be you, and I was so wrong. I'm convenient to you, that's

163

all. You want somebody around you because you don't want to be by yourself. But you don't really mind who it is, do you? You don't.'

She stood up, nudging the table as she did so and causing Oedipus's coffee to spill. It made a large brown stain on the tablecloth.

'Look what you've done,' he muttered. 'What a mess.'

'You can get a train back,' she said. 'You can get a train back or stay here all weekend and read the papers. I don't care either way.'

He looked at her through narrowed eyes. 'You do, you know. You do care,' he said, adding, 'see?'

39. Barbara Ragg Acts

She packed through her tears. She thought that Oedipus would come up to the room, would follow her, would plead. And she might relent—might—if he at least apologised for his indifference. If he had said, 'Oh, I'm so sorry, Barbara, I've been under such pressure and you know how it is . . .' she would have dropped whatever it was that she was holding at the time and gone to look out of the window. And he would have come up behind her and put his arms around her and said, 'Sorry. Really sorry. I think the world of you, you know that, don't you? See?' And she would have turned and said, 'All right. I know that you work very hard and that there's a lot on your mind, but please try to think of me from time to time. Just a little.' And that would have been that; she would have stayed. But none of this happened, and Oedipus remained

164

downstairs, indifferent, it would seem, to her leaving. Perhaps he had been in the middle of reading an article and needed to get to the end. Or perhaps he had not yet finished scouring the paper for a mention of his name; he did that, she knew—he did that a lot.

Her suitcase ready, she left the room, bumping her head on the low ceiling of the corridor outside. The Mermaid Inn had been in business for five hundred years—five centuries of providing for guests, through the rise and fall of an Empire, through poverty and plenty. Through all those years people had slept in these rooms, had bumped their heads on these very beams. The bumps had been less frequent in the past, she thought—through her sorrow—because people had been shorter then due to their nutrition, or lack of it. Although if you looked at the accounts of what they ate—when they were in a position to eat—you would have thought that at least some of them might have been taller. The groaning tables, of course, were not for everybody, and tallness in a population depended on an improvement in general nutrition.

She negotiated her way down a tiny staircase—too narrow, it occurred to her, for some of the better-nourished visitors from those countries where obesity had now become an issue. Not that we were ones to talk, she thought, with our couch-potato children fed on crisps and convenience food, children to whom a bicycle or a football were quite foreign, objects from a real world barely glimpsed, a world parallel to their virtual one. That young chef, the naked one, would be our salvation, if only people would listen to him. But the public

165

was too narcissistic now to listen to anything but flattery, she reflected.

All these thoughts went through her mind because she did not want to think about what she had just done. She had walked out on Oedipus; she had brought their relationship to an end. And now, at the high desk in the hall, she encountered the quizzical look of the hotel receptionist. There was the bill to consider. Normally she and Oedipus shared the cost of their trips away, although he never offered to pay for petrol, instead remaining seated in her car while she went to the cashier. For a moment she was flustered, uncertain whether to ask the receptionist to split the bill in half. But the bill wasn't yet finalised. If Oedipus stayed a further night, then there would be the cost of his dinner to add to it. And if he did not stay, would they still be expected to pay for Saturday night because they had booked it in advance?

'I have to get back to London,' she said. 'My . . .' She faltered. What was he? Could she say, 'My ex will decide whether to stay'? Or should she say, 'My friend may have to leave early too'? She did not like the term *ex*, but it had its uses, and this might be one of them. She settled for Mr Snark. 'Mr Snark might stay, or he might not.'

The receptionist looked at her sympathetically. She knows, thought Barbara. She has obviously seen this sort of thing before.

'That's fine,' said the receptionist.

'About the bill,' Barbara continued, 'I'd like to pay . . .' She was about to say 'half', but then she decided against it. 'I'd like to pay for everything. Can I leave the number of my credit card? Put everything on that.'

166

The receptionist nodded. 'Of course. No problem.' It was said—and done—with discretion and courtesy, as one would expect of a professional.

'I suppose you see everything in your job,' said Barbara, handing over the card.

The receptionist smiled. 'Almost. And nothing surprises me, frankly.' She paused. 'Are you sure you're all right?'

Barbara nodded. She felt gratitude for this kindness—a kindness between women, who understood, of course. This was the true meaning of sisterhood—something that men did not have. One man would not say to another 'Are you all right?' A man would not.

'I'm all right,' Barbara replied. 'I just decided that it was not for me. I just decided to take control of my future.'

'Good for you,' said the receptionist.

'It's a strange feeling,' Barbara went on.

'Independence always feels strange at first,' said the receptionist. 'These things can be difficult, can't they? It would be nice not to have to worry about them, but . . . but they're all around us, men. And we keep going back for more, don't we?'

Barbara smiled ruefully. 'Not me,' she said.

She said goodbye to the receptionist and went out into the small alleyway that led to the hotel car park. The sun was bright and already warm. She would drive back with the top of her sports car down. She would let the rush of air blow away old memories. Men. Yes, they were all around one. But she would certainly not go back for more. This was it.

In the car park, as she turned the car, she hit the

wing mirror on a small hitching post that she had not seen. The glass of the mirror tumbled out and shattered on the cobbles below. She switched off the engine, got out of the car, and stooped to pick up the pieces.

'Bad luck,' said a voice. 'Let me help.'

She looked up. A young man was standing at her side, amused, certainly, but concerned too.

She straightened, dusting down the knees of her jeans.

'I didn't see it.'

He bent down to start picking up the glass. She noticed the trim shape of his back. She noticed the nape of his neck.

'You aren't by any chance going to London?' he asked.

40. Remember Mateus Rosé?

Although Saturday was the wine shop's busiest day, it did not become so until lunchtime. From then on until William closed the door at six, ushering out the last-minute purchasers of a bottle of wine for the evening's dinner party, there was barely time for a cup of tea. The late-afternoon customers sometimes sought his advice not only on what wine to choose but as to whether or not to take a bottle to their hosts at all. The issue was a delicate one, and William had toyed with the idea of printing a small leaflet that would explain the etiquette of such matters—at least as he understood it.

'The most important thing,' he would say, 'is to

do whatever you do with *good grace*. If you take a bottle with you, never present it apologetically. There is nothing worse than people who hand over a bottle of wine to their hosts with a look bordering on resentment—as if they were paying the taxman his dues.

'But, of course,' he would go on, 'the real issue is whether you have to take a bottle of wine with you or not. There is no strict ruling on this matter—as indeed on any issue of etiquette; what counts is *attitude*. The most terrible apparent breach of etiquette can be carried off by one who means well and is charming about it. But for most of us, charm will not suffice—in that we don't have enough of it—and we therefore need rules. Here are some:

'If you are a student and you are invited to a meal or a party at another student's flat, there is absolutely no doubt that you must take a bottle of wine with you. If you do not do so, then the host is perfectly within his or her rights not to let you in. This is an absolute rule and cannot be avoided by saying that your friend, who is coming later, will be bringing a bottle for you. Most hosts have heard that line before and will not believe you.

'Students should not bring good quality wine with them as to do so will be seen as elitist and arrogant, and will imply that you do not approve of whatever your host will provide. This rule does not apply if you can explain that you took the wine in question from your parents' stocks while they were away. That is perfectly acceptable in today's dishonest climate.

'In my own day, the correct thing for students to take to a party was a cheap Spanish wine or, if flush with funds, Mateus Rosé, distinguished by its squat oval bottle, which can later be turned into a lamp stand or candleholder. This wine can occasionally be found in the back of parental cupboards and may be circulated at dinner parties without ever being drunk, in the same way as boxes of out-of-date After Eights do the rounds, like bankers' negotiable instruments never presented for payment.

'If you are no longer a student, you should nevertheless continue to take a bottle of wine when invited for dinner unless the invitation comes from people who are much older than you. As far as friends of equal age are concerned, you should take a bottle of wine with you until you have all celebrated your fortieth birthday. After that, you must assume that your hosts will be in a position to entertain you without assistance.

'It is never wrong to take a bottle of champagne, even to a host who is well off. If the host is not on the breadline, this should be in a presentation case; it should never be taken chilled, as that implies that his own supplies of champagne will be exhausted and recourse may need to be made to the bottle you brought with you.

'In no circumstances is it polite to take away with you the bottle that you brought if it has not been consumed at the table. It is also impolite to say at the end of a meal, 'I hope that you enjoy the wine we brought.' That is not a friendly comment, and will be interpreted accordingly. Nor, as a host, is it polite to examine the label of a bottle brought by your guests. If you do, always misread the vintage, saying, for example, of a 2007 Bordeaux, "Ah, 2001. What a treat."'

That is the advice that William would have put in his leaflet had he written it. He thought about it now as he made his way downstairs with Freddie de la Hay, his newly acquired Pimlico Terrier. He would take Freddie for a walk—that is what dog-owners do—and then he would make his way to the shop at eleven or even half past eleven, before the busy period started. Paul, his assistant, always opened up the premises on Saturday mornings and so it did not really matter when William arrived.

As they stepped out of the building, Freddie de la Hay looked up at William appreciatively, as if to endorse the decision to bring him out. He raised his nose into the air, sniffed, and began to tug at the leash. As they walked down the street, he stopped at each lamp post, inspected it and then walked on. There was a jaunty spring in his step; it was, thought William, the gait of a dog who had been released from durance vile and was now enjoying the increased freedom of his new circumstances.

'We're going to get along just fine,' said William. 'Wouldn't you agree?'

171

He was pleased that Freddie seemed comfortable with the new arrangement, although he was worried about Eddie. His son's initial reaction to the arrival of Freddie had been more or less what he had expected, but then had come that rapid and curious acceptance of the dog's presence. William wondered whether this meant that he now had a dog *and* a son living with him. The freedom that he had dreamed of seemed to be receding rapidly; perhaps *he* should move out, or . . . It occurred to him that if Eddie would not be displaced by a dog, then perhaps he might be displaced by a person. Marcia. Eddie hated Marcia, and if she were to come and live in the flat it would be unbearable from Eddie's point of view. Yes, he would invite Marcia to stay. If Eddie thought that he was having a mid-life crisis, then a mid-life crisis was what he would give him.

He crossed the street. He was now at the corner occupied by an elegant interior decorator's shop. And there in the window of the shop he saw the sign: *Belgian Shoes*. He had often wondered what these Belgian Shoes were, and now, on impulse, he went in, taking Freddie de la Hay with him.

If one was going to have a mid-life crisis, William thought, then one might as well have it in Belgian Shoes. They sounded like ideal footwear for a mid-life crisis.

41. Belgian Shoes

William went into the shop and looked about him. He had walked past this shop many a time—almost every day—but had never paid much attention to it, beyond the *Belgian Shoes* sign in the window, of course. William felt that he had reasonable taste and was artistically as sensitive as the next person, but he did not take a great interest in interior decoration. There was something rather unworthy, he thought, about interior decoration; he knew that there were men who were interested in curtains and *bibelots*, but he was not one of them. In his view, curtains should be functional: keeping the light out, or in, and that was it. Chairs and tables should similarly be functional: allowing one to sit down when necessary and to eat, or write, or stack copies of *Decanter* magazine, also when necessary. William had no time for all the fussy bits and pieces which decorators seemed to go in for; the bronze horses' heads, the casually displayed old glass fishing floats, the *objets trouvés* that covered every surface of a fashionable living room. What was the point? he asked himself. What was the point of all this ridiculously expensive *clutter*?

But now he saw that this particular shop was not like that—it had attractive things: an imposing smoked glass table, for example, that would do very well in his sitting room, he thought, and a small bookcase that would look good in the spare bedroom, once he got Eddie out of it. And there was a rug, too, which he rather liked, and which Freddie de la Hay now sat upon in a gesture of canine approbation.

'Are you looking for something in particular?'

William turned round to see that a tall, extremely attractive young woman had appeared at his side, smiling as she spoke—and she spoke to him. Where was she from? he wondered. She was

173

Italian, he decided. Milanese, perhaps; Milan was the design capital of the world, was it not?

Taken by surprise, William needed a moment to gather his thoughts. 'Belgian Shoes?' he asked eventually. 'I saw the sign in the window, and . . .'

'Of course,' said the assistant. 'Belgian Shoes. The men's shoes are over here on the table.' She led him to a table on the other side of the room.

'May I leave my dog on the rug?' William asked. 'He's very well behaved. A very good dog.'

It occurred to him that he did not know this. Was Freddie de la Hay well behaved in all circumstances? William realised that he simply did not know whether Freddie de la Hay could really be described as a good dog. That was not an appellation that should be conferred automatically; good dogs should earn it, thought William, in the same way as soldiers earned their medals. Soldiers did not get the MC for nothing— or at least British soldiers did not. Some countries gave their soldiers a medal the moment they received the slightest injury: William had heard of a medal (a foreign one) awarded to any soldier who cut himself while shaving, but he could not believe that. It simply could not be true. Surely one had to do far more than that to get a particular medal? One had to get one's finger jammed in the door of a tank *at the very least*.

'Your dog may certainly stay on the rug,' said the assistant. 'He seems to be a very fine dog.'

Standing in front of the shoe table, William looked at the selection. He had had no idea what Belgian Shoes would look like; now he gazed upon a selection of about twenty exemplars of the footwear, ranging from black patent-leather

174

dancing pumps to brown ostrich-skin casual loafers.

'Very nice,' he said, picking up one of the shoes. It was feather-light.

'They are very comfortable,' said the assistant, 'because they are so light. The sole has horsehair in it.'

She turned one of the shoes over and showed it to William. The underside of the sole was thin leather—not a conventional sole, but rather the smooth leather that one might find on an expensive pair of slippers.

'They're not really outside shoes,' said William. 'These soles wouldn't last long outside.'

He wondered whether Belgians spent an inordinate amount of time indoors; in restaurants, perhaps, enjoying their distinguished cuisine.

'They are designed for wear inside the house,' said the assistant. 'However, you can have a thin rubber sole applied, which will protect the shoe if you take it outside. But they are not for the rain.'

William picked up the ostrich-skin loafers and looked at the inner sole. Like the rest of the shoe it was of soft, light leather, and had imprinted on it a picture of a cobbler's sewing needle and thread and the words 'Belgian Shoes'.

They then discussed his size and the assistant went off to get an appropriate pair of the ostrich-skin loafers. William realised that he had not asked the price, but it was too late now to do so. He had to have a pair of Belgian Shoes. He simply had to.

'They look very good on you,' said the assistant when William put on the shoes and stood up to admire them. 'You must have them.'

William nodded. There are some shoes that say

to us: 'Buy us and we shall change your life.' That is what these shoes now said to him—quite unequivocally. And William knew that the claim was true: his life would change once he had a pair of shoes like this. He knew it.

Of course, it all seemed so unlikely. Belgian Shoes! Nobody would associate elegant footwear with the Belgians of all people; the Italians, yes—they were *destined* to design and make elegant, life-changing shoes. But the Belgians? What were they best at making? Regulations?

He turned to the assistant. 'Why are they called Belgian Shoes?' he asked.

She smiled. 'They are made in Belgium,' she said. 'And the Belgians are a great people for comfort. Belgians do not like to be uncomfortable.'

William thought about this. Did anybody wish to be uncomfortable? The British certainly lived in conditions of great discomfort, with their cold, draughty homes and their admiration for a culture of cold showers. But did they actually *like* to be uncomfortable, or did they accept discomfort as a constant factor in British life, like bad weather and run-down trains?

'So the Belgians are hedonists, are they?' he remarked.

He had not thought he would get an answer to this, and he did not. But what he did get was a sudden chilling of the atmosphere.

'You're not . . . you're not Belgian?' William stuttered.

The assistant shook her head. 'I am Italian,' she said. 'But I have nothing but admiration for the Belgians.'

She placed the Belgian Shoes in a dark green

shoe bag and passed it over to William.

'These shoes will make a difference,' she said. 'They will bring you a great deal of happiness. It is very clear.'

William paid—one hundred and seventy pounds—and then, collecting Freddie, he left. As he made his way back to the flat, he considered how his life had changed dramatically within a couple of days. He had acquired a dog. He had begun to resist his son. And he had acquired a pair of potentially life-changing Belgian Shoes. And . . . He was about to add: 'And I've embarked upon my mid-life crisis,' but he stopped himself. It was not a crisis he had initiated, it was a rebellion—a full-blooded post-teenage rebellion. I am rebelling, he thought. I have never rebelled in my life—not once. Not as a teenager, when I was entirely compliant; nor as a young adult. Never. Now, at long last, I have started to rebel.

It was an intensely satisfying feeling.

42. *The Morning Sun was in Her Eyes*

When asked whether she was driving back to London, Barbara Ragg hesitated before replying. She looked at the young man standing beside her: what business of his was her destination? She appreciated his materialising from nowhere and helping to pick up the shattered glass from her wing mirror, but she did not think that it gave him the right to ask where she was going. She looked at him coolly—or in a manner she hoped would give the impression of coolness—but even as she stared

at him she knew that the effect of her gaze was probably quite different from what she wanted. She felt flushed, rather than composed; suddenly unsettled, rather than determined. Only a few minutes ago she had walked out of the Mermaid Inn filled with resolve and firmness—a free agent once again after deciding that no longer would she endure the humiliation of being a mere adjunct to Oedipus Snark's life. And here, within the space of a few minutes, she found that a pair of green male eyes fixed on hers had reduced her to a state of vulnerability and indecision. How she answered this simple question, she vaguely sensed, would in some way determine the course of her life.

That, of course, was absurd. The pattern of one's life could not be changed by a chance encounter in the parking place of the Mermaid Inn. And yet, it could—lives, even our own, could be changed by such apparently insignificant events, and Barbara knew it. An apparently throwaway remark by one person could send another in a direction that would have profound consequences for what they did. 'Why don't you write poetry?' one young schoolboy had said to another young schoolboy—the sort of thing that boys used to say to one another in more literate days, and the sort of remark that might have no effect on the world unless . . . unless the boy to whom the suggestion was made was none other than the young Wystan Auden. Perhaps a similar boy had said to another small boy called Horatio, 'Why don't you go to sea?', and the juvenile Nelson had replied, 'Yes, why not?'

So, in less elevated circles, we might toss a coin as to whether or not to go to a party, decide to go, and there meet the person whom we are to marry and spend our lives with. And if that person came, say, from New Zealand, and wanted to return, then we might find ourselves spending our life in Christchurch. Not that spending one's lifetime in Christchurch is anything less than very satisfactory—who among us would not be happy living in a city of well-behaved people, within reach of mountains, where the civic virtues ensure courtesy and comfort and where the major problems of the world are an ocean away? But had the coin fallen the other way—as coins occasionally do—then that wholly different prospect might never have opened up and one might spend the rest of one's days in the place where one started out. Or one might pick up a newspaper abandoned in a train by a person not well trained in those same civic virtues, open it and chance to see an advertisement for a job that one would not otherwise have seen. And that same job might take one into the path of risk, and that very risk may materialise and end one's life prematurely. Again the act of picking up the paper has consequences unglimpsed at the time, but profound nonetheless.

Barbara knew this, and knew that how she answered would have consequences for her. It would be safest to say, 'No, I'm not going to London,' but that would mean that she would never know why he had asked, and it would, in addition, be a lie, and she was a truthful person. Oedipus lied; he lied all the time, she thought, but somehow *lies suited him*. He was a natural liar—he had a gift for meretricious speech that would be the envy of any snake-oil salesman or politician in a tight corner, a facility based on the fact that he actually believed his lies. It was a great gift, as it had immense transformative powers: if everything that one said was true, then what power one had over the world. Bad weather could be changed at a stroke to good; a downturn of fortune could simply by misdescription become something quite different. But Barbara could do none of that, not even mislead a stranger as to her destination.

So she said, 'Yes, I am going to London, as it happens.'

The young man holding the shards of glass looked over his shoulder. 'One sec,' he said. 'I need to go and put these in the bin.'

He turned round and walked over to a small rubbish bin beside the hotel's back door. She watched him. The morning sun was in her eyes and she used a hand to shade them. She watched the young man, and did not see Oedipus at the window of the hotel dining room, looking down at her. *He* was watching her.

The young man dropped the glass in the bin and came back to join her. She saw his face now, for those few seconds that are crucial—so psychologists say—for the forming of an opinion one way or the other about another person.

He dusted his hands on the side of his jeans. 'I was wondering . . .' he began.

'Do you need a lift up there?'

She had not intended to say this; it just came out.

He smiled. 'Well, I wouldn't mind. I was going to catch a train, but I'd have to walk down to the station and get a ticket . . .' He shrugged, and smiled in a self-consciously helpless way. 'And I'd far rather travel in a car like yours than in a train.'

'Why not?'

'That's great.'

She glanced into the open-top car. 'Have you got a suitcase? There's not all that much room, but I can shift my things a bit.'

He had only a small bag, which he went into the hotel to retrieve. While he did that, Barbara moved the car to the side of the parking place and took stock of her situation. One should not give lifts to a stranger; that was now an elementary precaution, which anybody would be considered very unwise to ignore. The days of hitchhikers standing by the roadside seemed to be well and truly over, such was the distrust that prevailed. Everybody was a potential assailant; nobody spoke to one another for fear of being misinterpreted; nobody comforted another, put an arm around a shoulder—to do so would be to invite accusation. And yet here I am, thought Barbara, picking up a man whose name I don't even know, allowing him to get into the car, and driving off to London. Anything could happen.

She reached for the key in the ignition. The

simplest thing to do, the safest thing, would be to start the engine and drive out while he was fetching his bag. She turned the key and the engine sprang to life.

43. Terence's Battery has a Near-death Experience

'I can't start it,' said Terence Moongrove, coming back into the kitchen where his sister, Berthea Snark, was reading a newspaper.

Terence's Morris Traveller had been towed back to the house the previous evening by the proprietor of a local garage, who, knowing the car well, had encountered it on the roadside and returned it to its home while Terence and Berthea were having dinner. He had refused payment, an act of kindness that had deeply impressed Berthea.

'That sort of thing would never happen in London,' she said. 'Nobody would be that kind.'

'Oh, I'm sure that people in London are as kind

as anywhere else,' said Terence. 'They just don't have the time to show it.'

'I doubt it,' said Berthea. 'Too many people. It changes one's attitude to others. Simple social psychology. Put a whole lot of rats in a cage and they fight. Put one or two in and they get along reasonably well.'

Terence looked doubtful. 'Are you sure about that? I mean, about people? I can understand about rats—nasty, long-tailed creatures. And those teeth! Have you seen their teeth, Berthy? They've got long, slightly curved teeth, like that. Jolly sharp, I imagine.' He paused. 'But people? Do they really fight just because there's a lot of them in the same space? Look at the Japanese. Their cities are jolly full of people. Have you seen the pictures of their train stations? They have these men who wear white gloves and push people into the carriages so that the doors can close. What a horrible job, Berthy—I wouldn't do it for a hundred pounds. I really wouldn't.

'Yet the Japanese don't fight with one another,' Terence went on. 'They behave terribly well. Japanese cities are not like our cities at night—with all that shouting and heaven knows what. And—'

'That's alcohol,' Berthea interjected. 'And the Japanese have manners. They're very particular about how to behave and that means that everybody gets on very well with one another even in a confined space. Manners, Terence. Something we're losing sight of. We laugh at people who bow to one another but the bow is an act of respect, and respect leads to considerate behaviour. We could learn a lot from the Japanese. In particular, we

183

could learn how to live harmoniously in crowded spaces. We could learn about territory.'

Terence thought about this. 'We must rise above the territorial,' he said. 'Obviously our territory is finite, and we will find ourselves contesting it. But if we project ourselves onto another, altogether higher plane, then physical territory will matter much less.'

Berthea pursed her lips. 'Not everyone,' she said, 'can exist on a higher plane. I, for example—'

'But you could!' interrupted Terence. 'You really could, Berthy! You need to try, that's all.'

Berthea sighed. 'What you describe as a higher plane, Terence, is probably just a slightly altered mental state. A dissociative state, I'd say. Anybody can experience that.'

Terence looked out of the window. 'You can't say that. You're just reducing it to a matter of brain chemistry. It's more than that.'

'You're wrong,' said Berthea. 'I am not a reductionist in that way. If I were, I can assure you that I would not be a psychoanalyst. All I'm pointing out to you is that there are dissociative states of mind that can be mistaken for something else. A state of religious ecstasy might involve dissociation. Or even the state of mind that one is in when one is driving and suddenly realises that one has covered quite some distance and not really been aware of it.'

She realised that the motoring example might be a sensitive one. Did Terence drive, she wondered, while he was on a higher plane? Or did he come down from the higher plane before he started to drive, and then return to it later on? Either way, she was not sure whether she would be at all confident making any car journey with him other than the relatively direct one from the railway station to his house. That took them along quiet residential roads, where nobody would be held up by the Morris Traveller's customary speed of twenty miles per hour or Terence's habit of driving in the middle of the road.

Now, seated in Terence's kitchen on Saturday morning, with the newspaper in front of her and a cup of coffee at her side, Berthea listened while Terence described his efforts to start the Morris Traveller.

'Mr Marchbanks told me that he had put some petrol in,' he said. 'He had a can of petrol in his truck and he realised that I might have run out, so he put it in. But it still won't start.'

Berthea frowned. 'Does it make any noise at all?'

'No,' said Terence. 'It's as quiet as anything. Nothing happens. Nothing at all. It's as if it's in one of your dissociative states.'

'Battery,' said Berthea simply. 'If nothing happens when you turn the key, it means that your battery's dead.'

Terence digested this. 'Dead?'

'Well, batteries don't necessarily die with such finality,' said Berthea. 'They have what I suppose you, Terence dear, might call a near-death experience.'

The metaphor was exactly what Terence needed to grasp the state of his battery. 'Ah! I see. So a battery that has a near-death experience comes back? Its life isn't entirely over?'

'Precisely,' said Berthea. 'And what you can do is you can give the battery more . . . more life force.'

'More electricity?'

'Yes. You charge it, you see. You take electricity from the mains and you put it in the battery. Then the starter motor will—or may—work. I think perhaps that is what you should do.'

Terence nodded. He had seen where the battery of the Morris Traveller was, and although he was not sure how to remove it, he knew that he had a long extension cord in the garage. Mr Jones, the man who came to cut the lawn, used it to enable him to take the electric lawn mower to the far end of the garden. Now, if Terence simply removed the plug socket from the end of the extension cable he could then separate the two wires, strip them at the ends, and wind them round the terminals of the battery. Then he could turn on the switch at the wall and revitalise the battery in that way.

It seemed simple, and he decided that he would do it while Berthea finished reading her newspaper and drinking her coffee. She thought he was impractical—oh, he knew that, all right. Well, he would show her.

44. Don't Try This at Home

Terence Moongrove left Berthea in the kitchen and made his way to the garage off to one side of the house. Mr Marchbanks, who had rescued Terence's Morris Traveller, had pushed the car into the garage with its nose facing outward, pending some resolution of its mechanical plight. He had rescued Terence on many occasions before and knew the car well; indeed, he had fixed it several times over the last few months.

'They make new cars, Mr Moongrove,' he had observed to Terence the last time that the car had been in his garage. 'Have you ever thought of getting something a bit more up to date? Not that I've got anything against Morris Travellers, of course. Just asking.'

Terence frowned. 'But should we be rushing around replacing our cars all the time?' he asked.

'How long have you had this Morris?'

'Oh, not all that long. Thirty years—something like that.'

Mr Marchbanks sighed. 'I wouldn't call it rushing around replacing a car if you got a new one now. Some people change their car every three years, you know. Alfie Bismarck down the road gets a new Jag every year. Regular as clockwork.'

Terence shook his head. He disapproved of Alfie Bismarck. 'I would certainly not get a new Traveller every year,' he said. 'Out of the question.'

'You couldn't, Mr Moongrove. They don't make Travellers any more.'

Terence expressed surprise. 'But they're such good cars,' he said. 'With this wood and everything.'

Mr Marchbanks explained that very few cars were made of wood now; only the Morgan, which had a chassis made of Belgian ash. But it was no use trying to talk to Terence Moongrove about Morgans, Mr Marchbanks thought: he was dangerous enough in a Morris Traveller and would be lethal in anything more powerful.

Now, as he stood in front of the static Morris Traveller, Terence wondered whether he should telephone Mr Marchbanks and ask for advice on how to charge the battery. He almost did, but in the end decided not to; he was looking forward to announcing to Berthea that he had fixed the car himself. He was fond of his sister but she tended to condescend to him, and he felt it was about time that it was brought home to her that there was something he could do.

He went inside the garage. He had seen Mr Jones hang the extension cable on a hook at the back. He was another one, he thought; he also believed that Terence Moongrove was incapable, in this case of looking after his own garden tools. Ever since that incident with the rake—which was *not* my fault, Terence muttered to himself—Mr Jones had stacked the tools away somewhere and wouldn't tell him where they were. He had thought of inviting the gardener to join in the sacred dance, but was not going to do so now—not after the language he used. Such a person would certainly not fit in with the other adherents of paneurhythmy. What if somebody inadvertently trod on his toes and he said some of the things that Terence Moongrove had heard him say? Perhaps the Beings of Light would not understand the words and would therefore not be distressed; one could never tell.

The cable was where he had thought. Unhooking it, Terence examined the end and saw that there was a square plastic box attached to it. He knew what that was: those holes received the plug, obviously, but the whole thing could be taken off if one simply removed the screws. He made short work of it, using a screwdriver that had been left lying around by Mr Jones, or Mr Marchbanks, or possibly that boy from down the road who always

188

seemed to be fiddling about in his garage.

It was now a simple enough business to strip off a small amount of outer cable covering and end up with a reasonable length of separated wires, one black and one red, it being an old-fashioned cable. Terence now plugged the other end of the cable into the mains. He knew exactly where the battery was, and how to open the bonnet of the car; he had watched Mr Marchbanks do this often enough and it took only a small amount of fumbling with the catch to reveal what he was looking for.

Terence remembered what his sister had said: the electricity from the mains would run into the battery and charge it. He was not sure how long this would take, but he would err on the side of caution and give it at least two minutes. That should do it.

He attached the black wire to one of the terminals and the red wire to the other. Then he surveyed his handiwork. It was quite an interesting business, he thought. Perhaps he could enrol for one of those courses that taught you home mechanics. That would mean that he would have to trouble Mr Marchbanks a bit less frequently. He could even have conversations with him about mechanical matters. He had heard Mr Marchbanks talking about big ends and he would be able to discuss them with him. Big ends were a problem, he knew, judging from Mr Marchbanks's grave expression when he spoke of them, and there was obviously a lot to be said about them. But that could come later; for the moment there was the issue of the charging of the battery.

The socket into which the plug end of the cable had been inserted was on the garage wall immediately beside the car. This meant that when Terence turned it on with his right hand, his left hand was touching the side of the Morris Traveller. So when, with a flash, the entire car went live, Terence received the current through his left hand.

There was an explosive sound. There was a small wisp of smoke. There was a slightly acrid smell, as of burned rubber. Terence, half thrown from the side of the car, half felled, slumped over the front mudguard. Then he rolled sideways, cutting himself on the bumper as he did so and ending up on the concrete floor of the garage. There his face came to rest on the oily patch where the Morris Traveller had, while undergoing surgery from Mr Marchbanks, discharged half its oil; the blood of the car and the blood of its owner for a moment mixed.

45. *In the Ambulance*

Berthea Snark, having finished her coffee and been depressed by the newspapers, had left the kitchen and gone into the drawing room at the front of the house. She had been cast into gloom by what she had read in the newspapers about the banking difficulties that the country was experiencing. It was not that she feared for her own situation—she made a reasonable income from her psychotherapeutic practice and had also received, as had Terence, a half-share of their father's estate on his death. That was more than enough for anybody, since Walter Moongrove had been a successful London stockbroker of the old

type—upright and financially righteous in every respect. How he would have disapproved of these people who had got us into this trouble—the reckless bankers who invented money, just *invented* it, she thought.

She mused on the Freudian view of the banking crisis. Financial systems were not abstract entities dreamed up by dispassionate architects: they were human working practices caught up in the messy real world. That meant that the psychopathology of those people running such systems would determine the operation of the system; Berthea was sure of it. And therein lay the problem: banks had been taken over by the wrong types.

The real key to the crisis, then, was this: if banks were run by hoarders, then they would be slow to lend money they did not have. They would accumulate rather than dispose of money, and they would never risk funds they did not have. So what one wanted, then, was a class of bankers who were predominantly *retentives*—people who had not moved from an early stage of infantile sexuality to the more mature stage. In other words, a good banker would be one who had moved on from the oral stage of early infancy but had not progressed beyond the next stage. They were the ones. But recruitment might be difficult. She could determine if they were at that stage of course, but she was not sure whether the sort of questions one had to ask would be easy to ask in a job interview.

She was thinking of this—and smiling to herself—as she entered the drawing room. That was the wonderful thing about Freudian theory, she thought: it gave one an acute insight into all aspects of human behaviour, including history and, as she had just imagined, economics; even mechanics, even Morris Travellers . . .

She looked out of the window towards the garage. What on earth was Terence up to? Looking at his Morris. That would not do much good. She would have to speak to him about a new car—indeed, she wondered whether she should not have a word with Mr Marchbanks and get him to arrange it. She could easily fund it—not that Terence was short of funds, but he had difficulty in spending money on himself; retentive in that respect, she decided, but not in others. He was very generous when it came to presents and sharing.

What *was* he doing? Terence sometimes talked about resolving problems through meditation. One could summon up great energy, he claimed, simply by thinking hard about something. He even hinted that he had seen objects levitated by this method, but declined to give concrete instances. 'You'll see, Berthy,' he said. 'One day you'll see.'

And now she did. Now she saw Terence suddenly slump forward and fall across the front of the car. Then she saw him drop to the ground, where he remained, motionless. For a moment Berthea was unable to do anything. Then, with remarkable clarity of purpose, she suppressed the urge to run out to her brother's side and instead spun round, snatched up the telephone and called for an ambulance. That coolness of purpose, which resulted in the arrival of the ambulance within minutes, saved the life of Terence Moongrove.

The telephone call made, Berthea ran out to the garage. She moved the inert form of her brother away from the side of the car. She saw the oil on the side of his face, and the blood. She bent down and tried to establish whether he was breathing; he was not. She let out a wail and pounded on his chest; she positioned his head to ensure unblocked airways. A stroke, she thought. A stroke.

Before she knew it she heard the sound of the ambulance's siren, and then it was pulling up right there.

'My brother,' she said. 'My brother . . .'

There was an ambulance man and an ambulance woman. They crouched beside Terence and moved him gently onto a stretcher. Then they whisked the stretcher into the back of the ambulance.

'I want to be with him. He's my brother . . .'

'All right, dear,' said the ambulance man. 'Sit with Holly in the back.'

Berthea was to have only a vague recollection of what happened in the ambulance on its breakneck journey to the hospital. Holly, the ambulance woman, worked on Terence's chest. She applied an instrument that looked like some sort of iron. Terence shuddered. She felt his pulse; she did something else. Berthea wept. My brother, my only brother.

She closed her eyes and she saw Terence, not as a man, but as a little boy. She saw him standing with his teddy bear and then bending down and putting the limbs of the teddy bear through the motions of dance. Had it begun that early? she wondered. Were those the seeds of all this, of the sacred dance? Watch children playing, she had always advised; see them enact their inner dramas with their toys.

Poor Terence. Poor, dear, gentle Terence. He had been searching for something all his life—he said as much himself—and he had never found it. And that thing, of course, was love, although he never saw it that way. He said that he was looking for enlightenment, for beauty; he said that he was looking for the sacred principle that informed the world. And all the time he was looking for that simple thing that all of us look for; that we yearn for throughout our lives. Just to be loved. That was all.

She took her brother's hand and held it lightly. There was oil on it, or blood, she was not sure which. When had she last held his hand? When had she last held anybody's hand? That simple gesture of fellow feeling, which expresses ordinary human solidarity, which says: *you are not alone, I am with you. I am here.*

46. *Terence Moongrove has a Near-death Experience*

At some point on the journey between the Moongrove Queen Anne house and the Accident and Emergency Department at Cheltenham General Hospital, Terence's heart, which had stopped as a result of his coming into contact with an electrically live Morris Traveller, began to beat again. It had been still for a very few minutes, not long enough for the memories and attitudes stored somewhere in his brain to fade as their supporting cells died. But it was a close-run thing, and the ambulance lost no time in its journey to hospital, nor did anybody linger as Terence was wheeled in on a trolley and rushed into the care of his doctors.

Berthea had no time to reflect on the fact that she had saved her brother's life. She sat fretting outside the ward where the doctors first assessed and then stabilised his condition, and when a nurse came out and whispered to her, 'He's coming round just fine—a few little burns on his hand but nothing much else,' Berthea wept with relief. Not long after, she was ushered into the ward to stand at his bedside and find him looking at her with an expression of slight puzzlement.

'What happened?' Berthea asked. It was a trite thing to say to one who had just returned from the dead, and an insensitive thing too, even if not quite as tactless, perhaps, as asking, 'What on earth did you do?'—which is, of course, what she meant.

'The Morris's battery must have been faulty,' said Terence. 'I was charging it and I think that it exploded, or something like that.' He waved a hand in the air to demonstrate the vagaries of car batteries.

Berthea frowned. 'I didn't know you had a battery charger,' she said.

This remark was greeted by another expression of puzzlement from Terence. 'Battery charger . . .?' He did not complete his sentence: Berthea was staring at him with a look that he knew well, a

195

look made up of a mixture of incredulity and irritation. She began to say something, but thought better of it; a reunion with a brother saved from death was hardly the time to comment on a lack of technical understanding. There would be time for that later on. Or perhaps not; he would not change. All she could hope was that the divinity that hedges about those whose concerns run to sacred dance and Beings of Light would somehow be kind to him and protect him from the worst dangers of this world. And lightning, she reflected, tended not to strike in the same place twice. Could one say that same thing, though, of electricity? Somehow she thought not.

'The important thing,' Berthea muttered, 'is that you did not die.'

Terence thought about this for a moment. 'But I did,' he said. 'I died. The ambulance man told the doctor that my heart had stopped when they picked me up. And I saw them trying to start it in the ambulance with that pad thing. A battery charger perhaps.'

Berthea looked doubtful. 'You saw that? But your eyes were quite closed, Terence. I was there, remember? I was in the ambulance with you.'

Terence nodded. 'Yes, I saw you. I saw you sitting . . .' He hesitated for a moment as he clarified his recollection. 'You were sitting at the back, at my left side. You were holding a handkerchief in your hand and twisting it round and round. I saw you. I also saw you take my hand and look at the blood that was on it. Here, you see, where the bandage is.'

Berthea said nothing. She had the handkerchief in her pocket, and she remembered that she had twisted it so tightly that the fabric had torn.

'You see,' Terence continued, 'I had died and I was hovering—that's the only word for it—hovering at the top of the ambulance, looking down. I saw everything—you and the ambulance man and my own body lying there. It was very clear.

'And then I was called away for a few minutes. I was led through a tunnel of some sort, a tunnel that had light at the end. Very bright, lovely light. And there were people there—very gentle people—who took my hand and said that I was forgiven. They said that they understood and I was not to worry about anything. And the AA was there too—some AA men in their uniforms, but with a light behind them, shining. They said I was not to worry about the Morris—they were very kind.'

Berthea could not contain her surprise. 'AA men?'

'Yes,' said Terence. 'They were not the usual AA men who come to help me with the car in Cheltenham. I did not know who these ones were. But one of them said, 'Don't imagine that there are no AA men in heaven. We're here too. We're ready.'

'And then somebody came to my side and said to me, "It is not your time yet; you must go back. There is work for you to do."' Terence paused and looked at his sister. 'Do you believe me, Berthy? Or do you think I'm making all this up?'

Berthea thought for a moment. She had read of near-death experiences and knew their general shape. People who had died—at least in the sense of their heart having stopped—upon recovery sometimes reported going through a tunnel and

197

being ushered into the presence of light. They were sincere in these accounts, and often withheld them from others because they feared ridicule. She had put all this down to the last flickerings of oxygen-deprived consciousness, although the common features of these experiences were puzzling; if all this was entirely subjective, then surely accounts of these experiences would differ widely? Of course, Terence had introduced precisely such a subjective factor: AA men. That was ludicrous really, unless the AA men were symbolic of something—of care and attention and kindness to those in need. And why should they not be such symbols? In the iconography of European painting it was St Christopher who performed such a role; in the iconography of a society in which saints and their doings were becoming a distant memory, meaningless to so many, perhaps it was appropriate that AA men should fulfil the role saints had previously had.

She looked at Terence. 'Oh, Terence,' she began, but did not finish her sentence. Terence's eyes had closed.

'Eh?' he muttered sleepily. 'Eh, eh?'

She took his hand and stroked it; his frail, foolish, human hand. He was still talking about the AA; dear Terence, dear constantly searching but never finding Terence.

47. Your Shoes, Your Sad Shoes

As William began to make his way back to Corduroy Mansions, he became aware that

Freddie de la Hay was trying to tell him something. The dog, who had been trotting happily at his side, circled round and sat down pointedly in front of him, all the while looking up with an expression that seemed to be a mixture of concern and anticipation. It occurred to William that Freddie merely wanted to prolong his walk, which was perfectly understandable: just as a walker might wish to draw out the pleasure of a stroll in bucolic surroundings, so might a dog wish to put off the moment of going back inside. Outside was a world of fascinating smells—a whole map, a palimpsest of the comings and goings of people, of other dogs, of cats, even the trace here and there of a wily urban fox; how could a dog be indifferent to all that? Inside, by contrast, was very much the same thing all the time and quickly exhausted from the olfactory point of view. That must be it: Freddie de la Hay was simply not ready to come in.

'More walks?' enquired William. 'Is that it, Freddie?'

Freddie de la Hay stared at his new owner, his head moving slightly in what William thought might be a shaking motion; but surely no dog would shake his head to convey disagreement? I shall not be anthropomorphic, thought William; I am not going to imagine that this dog understands English.

He bent down to get closer. 'What is it, Freddie? I can't spend all my time taking you for walks, much as I'd like to. You do know that, don't you, my boy?'

Freddie de la Hay stared into William's eyes. Very brown, thought William, you have very brown, liquid eyes. And what lies behind them?

What emotions? What canine thoughts?

Freddie answered the question with a whine. It was not a large sound, just a whimper really. And then, glancing quickly at William, the dog stood up and took the bag containing the Belgian Shoes in his jaws. Carrying the bag jauntily, he moved to William's side, ready to continue the journey back to the flat.

William chuckled. 'Oh, I see. That's what you want. Thanks, Freddie.'

They made their way up the staircase in Corduroy Mansions, man and dog, Freddie de la Hay carrying the Belgian Shoes with the air of a gundog bringing back a pheasant—and this, William thought, was the urban equivalent. London dogs might not be able to bring pheasants back to their owners but they could at least retrieve Belgian Shoes.

William's amusement over Freddie's desire to be useful meant that he did not dwell on the question of Eddie until he was taking off Freddie's leash in the hall of the flat. Eddie was not an early riser on a Saturday—nor on any day, William reminded himself—but now there were sounds, and the smell, of freshly ground coffee coming from the kitchen. Eddie always ground coffee with careless abandon, putting far too much into the grinder and then throwing out the surplus. I paid for that, William thought; I pay for every single coffee bean that my son grinds and then throws out.

Leaving Freddie de la Hay in the hall, William walked into the kitchen. Eddie was standing at the kettle, filling the coffee jug with water. He had just got out of bed by the look of things and was wearing only a pair of red boxer shorts. William looked at his son with distaste; he looked at the small mole on his back, at the line of hairs at the top of his spine, and . . . there was a tattoo just above the beginning of the natal cleft.

Eddie, continuing with his coffee-making, did not turn round. 'Morning, Dad. Taken your new friend for a walk? Or the other way round? 'Dog Makes Fat Owner Lose Weight'.'

It was another of Eddie's headlines. William clenched his teeth. It helped, he found, to do this when Eddie said something particularly annoying. "Idle Son Wastes Father's Hard-earned Coffee",' he replied. 'And I am not fat, by the way.'

Eddie laughed. 'Come on, Dad. No need to be so sensitive. So you're thin. Feel better now?'

William found himself staring at his son's tattoo. 'You've got a tattoo,' he muttered.

Eddie looked over his shoulder nonchalantly. 'Oh, that. Yeah, I've got a tattoo. So? You want one too? I know this guy who does really good work. Not cheap, but you have to pay for quality. You could have 'wine merchant' tattooed on your arm if you like. Or 'Pimlico' maybe. Anything you like—he's really artistic. Calls himself Da Vinci Tattoos. How about that? Da Vinci Tattoos.'

'I wouldn't dream . . .' began William. But he was now peering more closely at his son's back, straining to make out the details of the somewhat indistinct tattoo. There were words underneath the picture and he read these now—and then recoiled sharply. 'Eddie, why on earth would you have that put on . . . put on your back?'

Eddie shrugged. 'Because it says it all, doesn't it?'

William sighed. 'And what if you decide that you

201

don't want it any longer? What then?'

Eddie moved across the room to pour the coffee. 'Oh, people always say that about tattoos,' he replied. 'But that argument could be used against doing anything. Any building, for example. The Dome. The new terminal at Heathrow. Anything.' He paused, sniffing at the jug of coffee he had just made. 'You need to get more of that Jamaican stuff, Dad. I don't like those big bags of Colombian that you get cheap. Anyway, where's our dog?'

'Our dog?'

'Yes. Freddie de la Whatever. The dog you got us.'

William looked out of the window. 'I thought that you didn't like . . . ?'

'Exactly, Dad—didn't. Past tense. I've been thinking, and I think Freddie and me are going to get on fine.'

'Freddie and I.'

'Yes, you too.'

William felt himself getting warm at the back of his neck. He looked at the red boxer shorts. Disgusting. My own flesh and blood. Disgusting.

'I thought I might take Freddie down the pub,' Eddie remarked. 'I'm meeting Stevie. He's keen on dogs.'

William said nothing. His plan had failed. *He* had failed.

Then Eddie saw the Belgian Shoes, which his father had retrieved from Freddie de la Hay in the hall. For a moment his eyes narrowed, then he looked up at William. 'You're going to *wear* those, Dad? You're going to wear *them*?' He reached forward and snatched one of the shoes from William's hand. ''Man Buys Sad Shoes'',' he said.

202

48. A Golden Parachute

By the time he left for the shop that Saturday, William was in a thoroughly bad mood. Exchanges with Eddie were difficult at the best of times but that morning's conversation with his son—if one could really be said to converse with someone who spoke in newspaper headlines—had made him feel quite bereft of hope. Eddie, it seemed, was the cross that he was destined to bear in life, the reluctant, work-shy fledgling who would never leave the nest. The prospect of years of his company was grim indeed, and what if—awful thought—Freddie de la Hay were to decide to side with Eddie? It was too appalling to contemplate. 'Man Pushed Out,' he thought, 'By Son and Dog.'

He stopped. He could not allow himself to catch Eddie's dreadful headline habit; like all linguistic short cuts, it was so seductive, so easy to slip into. No, he would take command of the situation and act decisively . . . He would . . . he would . . . he would move out. No, he would not. That would be capitulation. He would give an ultimatum to Eddie. He would throw him out. He would tell him . . . No, he would speak to Marcia. She would tell him what to do.

When William arrived at the shop he found Paul serving a small queue of customers. His assistant threw him a reproving sideways glance, muttering under his breath, 'Look at the time.'

William smiled at the customers and then turned to glower at Paul. 'Did you say something?'

Paul counted out a customer's change. 'I said, look at the time,' he repeated out of the corner of his mouth.

William drew in his breath. 'That's what I thought you said. And what, may I ask, do you mean by that?'

Paul now turned away from the customers and addressed William. He spoke quietly but his voice became louder as his indignation increased. 'I meant that you're always criticising me for being late and then where are you when all these people need to be served? I had to get up on the ladder twice this morning to get those stupid Californian wines off the top shelf. Twice. Almost broke my neck. And people waiting to be served.'

William smiled again at the customers. 'I'll speak to you later,' he whispered to Paul. 'And remember it's *California* wine, Paul. Not *Californian*. A Californian is a *person*, not a wine. They're very fussy about that. And that, if I may remind you, is how we tell those who know what they're talking about from those who don't.'

'I don't care,' said Paul. 'I'm going over to Oddbins.'

'Then we'll have a little chat when you come back. And don't be long, please.'

Paul laughed. 'You didn't get it, Mr French. I said I'm going over to Oddbins. Not to buy anything. I'm going to go and ask for a job. The manager said that any time I needed a job I should speak to him. So I'm going. Right now. This morning.'

William stood in silence. He reached out to place a hand on his assistant's shoulder—a gesture half of apology, half of restraint. 'Now listen, Paul—'

'No, I've just had enough. Sorry. You don't pay me enough. You never have.'

William felt the same warm feeling that came to him when he argued with Eddie. It was exactly the same: inter-generational-generated subcutaneous warmth.

'I'll pay you more—'

'That's not the point.'

'Then why did you raise it?'

'Dunno. Just did.'

The customers had now drifted away in embarrassment. One had gone to examine a shelf of special promotions; a couple had left the shop altogether; another, thought William, had been carrying a bottle of unpaid-for wine when he walked out of the door.

William rubbed the back of his neck. 'Look, Paul, if you've been unhappy here you should have said something. We could still sort this out. You've got a great future ahead of you in the wine trade.'

'Thanks. With Oddbins. I've got a great future with them.'

William sighed. 'I can't stop you, can I?'

'No.'

William sensed that there was no point in prolonging the discussion. 'All right. But you don't think that you should work your notice? A week at least?'

Paul looked surprised. 'Notice?'

William stared at his assistant. 'No?'

'I said that I'd get over there this morning,' said Paul. 'Saturday's busy for them. They'll need me.'

William stretched out a hand. The young man hesitated, then took it, limply. Nobody, thought William, has taught him to give a proper handshake. Where was his father? And then it occurred to him: have I taught Eddie how to shake hands properly? Where have I been?

William gripped Paul's hand. The young man winced. 'Ow. Let go.'

William smiled apologetically. 'Sorry. It's just that when you shake hands you should give a little bit of pressure—just a little bit, to show that you mean it.'

'Mean what?'

'Mean what a handshake is meant to mean. In this case . . . well, I suppose I'm wishing you good luck and also . . . well, I'm saying thank you.'

William looked down on his assistant; he was appreciably taller, and better built, too. And he had everything, he thought, while this young man seemed to have nothing: a rather dim girlfriend somewhere, an mp3 player that he was always fiddling with, not many clothes—the scraps of a life. He slept on somebody's floor, William remembered him once saying; slept on the floor of a shared flat because he could not afford to rent his own room.

Paul hesitated. 'Yeah, well, thank you too. You

taught me a lot.'

William frowned. Had he?

'Yeah, you did. You always explained things really well. You did.'

'I'm glad.'

'And you were kind to me too.' Paul paused. 'I'm not really leaving because I don't like you or because you didn't pay me enough. I'm leaving because I want a new job . . . You know how it is.'

William reached out again and put an arm on the young man's shoulder. It was bony. He wanted to embrace him, but could not. He wanted to say sorry. 'There's something I want to give you before you go.'

'What?'

William walked through to the office and took his cheque book out of the drawer. Then he sat down and wrote out a cheque for one thousand pounds. Returning to the counter, he passed the cheque over to Paul, who stared at it with wide eyes.

'That's what they call a golden parachute,' said William. 'Ever heard of it?'

49. A Confession of Loneliness

'That was generous of you,' Marcia said. 'One thousand pounds. And he didn't give you any notice at all?'

'Ten minutes,' said William. 'Maybe fifteen.'

It was Saturday evening, and Marcia was sitting on William's sofa, her favourite seat in his flat. She wished that he would join her there, and occasionally she patted a cushion, not too overtly, she hoped, but in a way that could be interpreted either as an adjustment of the upholstery or as an invitation. But William, if he was aware of the gesture, ignored it and remained firmly seated in the place that he preferred, a single armchair on which it would have been impossible for Marcia to perch, had she decided to try.

Marcia had come round to the flat in response to William's quietly desperate telephone call earlier that day. He had called at about five, an hour before the shop was due to close. 'I've had it,' he said. 'I've been single-handed all day. I'm finished.'

Marcia had immediately offered to come to his aid. 'Poor darling,' she said. 'Would you like me—?'

He did not let her finish her question. 'To cook supper? Yes, I would. You're an angel.'

The compliment thrilled her. He had occasionally called her an angel before, and the term had given her cause to debate with herself the precise implications of the compliment. Just how warmly did one have to feel about somebody before angelic status was conferred? Did one have to feel actual affection?

Now, however, there was no time to consider nuances. 'I need to talk to you about something,' she heard William say. 'A problem.'

'Oh . . .' There were so many things she would have loved to talk to William about other than problems. In a rare moment of realism she thought, I'm a sympathetic ear for him, nothing more.

And now, sitting with Marcia, and with a restorative gin and tonic on the table beside him,

208

William unburdened himself of the day's trials. He told her about Paul's sudden decision to leave; he told her about the hectically busy day; he told her about the sheaf of unfilled orders that he would have dispatched had Paul been there to assist him with the customers. And he told her about Eddie's Damascene conversion to liking Freddie de la Hay and the resultant failure of his plan. Marcia listened attentively, making sympathetic faces as each hammer blow was described.

'I feel so frustrated,' said William at last. 'I feel that I just allow events to wash over me. Where is my life going?'

'Make a list,' said Marcia. 'Make a list of the things that are wrong, and then write a solution. Look, come over here. I've got a pen. Get some paper.'

Once again, she patted the cushion beside her. William hesitated, but decided that it would be churlish to remain where he was. They were going to make a list, that was all. He rose to his feet and crossed the room.

'Now,' said Marcia, folding the piece of paper he handed her. 'Let's write down the big thing, the worst thing in your life.' Her pen was poised over the paper. 'Begins with a capital E, I'd say.'

William sighed. 'I suppose so.'

Marcia wrote down: *Eddie. Won't grow up. Won't go.*

'All right. Now number two. 'Being short-handed at the shop. Need to replace Paul.''

William nodded. 'That's a serious one.'

'All right. Serious, but still number two.' Marcia lowered her gaze. 'On to number three.'

William looked up at the ceiling. 'I can't really

think of a third thing,' he said. 'I suppose . . .'

'Loneliness?' Marcia spoke softly, almost seductively. 'I'd say loneliness must be number three. Here, I'll write it down. "Loneliness."'

'I don't know—' William began.

'Of course you're lonely,' Marcia interrupted. 'You're all on your own.'

'But that's exactly what I'm not,' protested William. 'I'd like to be on my own, but there's Eddie. And now there's Freddie de la Hay. I'm not really on my own.'

Marcia smiled, tolerantly, with the air of one who has an insight that others lack. Men often had no idea how lonely they were, how much they needed women; she was convinced of it. Masculine independence? Nonsense. That was an oxymoron.

'What do they say about big cities, William? That they're the loneliest places on earth. Full of people, millions of people, but how many of those are by themselves, really lonely? How many do you think?'

William shrugged. 'Four hundred and seventy-five thousand,' he said.

She frowned. 'I didn't mean it like that. And it's not a joke.'

'Sorry.'

'Well?'

'Well what?'

'How many people in London are lonely?' She did not give him the chance of another flippant answer. 'I'll tell you. Lots and lots. Including you.'

He decided not to argue. 'All right. I'm lonely.'

'There!' exclaimed Marcia. 'I knew you were.'

'But I don't really see what I could do about it anyway. Ever since Mary died I've been by

210

myself—lonely, if you insist. That's the lot of widows and widowers. They're lonely.'

Marcia shook her head. 'Widows may be,' she said. 'But not widowers. Men can do something about it. It's easy for them to . . . remarry.'

'I don't see why it should be any different,' said William. 'Men and women these days—either can make the first move.'

Marcia was silent, and William knew immediately, almost as soon as he had finished speaking, that he had said something very dangerous. Like a diplomat who makes an inadvertent confession of state perfidy or a negotiator who gives away a strategy in a careless phrase, he sought to repair the damage. 'That is,' he said, 'where both want the move to be made. Where it's *right* for something to happen.'

Marcia was thinking. 'So a woman can—?'

And at that point, almost on cue, Freddie de la Hay, who had been sleeping in the kitchen, chose to enter the room. The dog looked about him, and then, seeing William, bounded across the room to hurl himself onto the sofa between William and Marcia.

William greeted him with undisguised affection—and relief. Marcia, however, was cooler. Freddie had been her idea, but she had not anticipated *this*.

'Can Freddie not go back to the kitchen?' she asked pointedly.

'I don't think so,' said William. 'I think he wants to go out. I'll take him. Why don't you start cooking dinner? I'll take Freddie outside for a few minutes. Freddie,' he said, once they were out on the landing. 'Good boy!'

Freddie looked up. It was as if he understood.

50. The Dignity of Distance

William took Freddie downstairs, relieved that the corner into which he had inadvertently painted himself had proved to have this escape route. He liked Marcia and, if he was honest with himself, he was very slightly dependent on her—if one can be slightly dependent on anything, he thought. Dependence was surely something that was there or was not: a boat was either tied to the jetty or it was not. Would it matter to him if Marcia were to take it into her head to leave London? Would it make any real difference to his life? No, it would not. But then people are extremely resilient; most of us could lose somebody from our lives and not feel that the resulting gap could never be filled. Of course it could. Most of us know how to bounce back.

He looked down at Freddie de la Hay as they went out into the street. Dogs were an example to us all: they made the most of their current circumstances, whatever hand of cards they were dealt. Of course dogs, unlike humans, did not look back; what interested them was what lay ahead. So Freddie, he imagined, did not think back to his former career as a sniffer dog, but was instead more interested in the possibilities of Corduroy Mansions, such as they were.

'I'll do my best by you, Freddie,' he said. 'Starting with a change in diet. Would you like that? Meat?'

Freddie, aware of the fact that he was being addressed, looked up and wagged his tail. He liked William, indeed he loved him. He would have died for William, even after only two days, because that was his job, his calling as a dog. That was what dogs did.

William turned the corner. Freddie de la Hay had business with lamp posts but was quick and considerate, and did not linger. Their walk round the block completed, William found himself approaching Corduroy Mansions just as one of the young women from the flat below was returning from the shops, laden with bags of groceries.

'I'll open the door for you,' he called out.

The young woman turned round and William saw that it was Jenny. He liked her, although he had on occasion found himself slightly intimidated by her conversation and her tendency to litter her remarks with references to the works of obscure writers. And even when she referred to somebody of whom he had heard, he felt that he had little to add.

'Don't you think that modern transport rather

213

diminishes the world?' she had once observed to him when they had found themselves standing at the same bus stop.

He had thought quickly. How is the world diminished by modern transport? In one sense, surely, it opens up the world, makes it available. Could that be construed as a diminution in that it shows the world not to be the grand place we fondly thought it to be? Or did she mean that it shrinks the world? That made more sense, perhaps.

He did not have time to answer because Jenny, peering down the road for the arrival of the bus, expanded upon the theme. 'As you'll probably know,' she went on, 'Proust said that steamships insult the dignity of distance. I think he was right. But just imagine what he'd say about the Airbus 380.'

William laughed. 'Of course. Just imagine!' And then he added, just to be on the safe side, 'Proust.'

Jenny looked at him expectantly. She seemed pleased to have discovered a neighbour who could discuss Proust; so few neighbours could.

William looked down the road. There was no sign of the bus.

'Proust wasn't a great one for buses,' he said. It was a wild remark: he had no idea whether Proust had views on buses, or even whether there were buses in Proust's time. When had Proust lived? Eighteen something? In which case a reference to buses was inappropriate. 'Not that he saw many buses,' he added quickly, and laughed. That would cover the possible non-invention of buses in Proust's time.

Jenny smiled. 'Proust would not have liked all

214

the germs you find on buses,' she said. 'He was a frightful hypochondriac. Most of his time he spent in bed—and when he did go out, he worried about draughts.'

'Of course,' said William. 'He was always going on about that sort of thing, wasn't he?'

'And remember when they held that wonderful dinner party?' Jenny said. 'It was the biggest event of the nineteen-twenties.'

So there were buses, thought William. 'Vaguely.'

'And Proust came along and met Joyce and Diaghilev. He had had his maid call up ten times in advance to ensure that there would be tea for him on arrival. And he enquired about draughts.'

'Hah! His famous draughts!'

The bus had lumbered into view and the conversation had stopped at that point, but William had remembered it and had been slightly wary of Jenny since then. But now, burdened with shopping bags, she could hardly start talking about Proust.

'Here,' he said, 'I've got my key. And then I'll give you a hand with the bags once we're in.'

She nodded gratefully, and he opened the door. Once inside, he released Freddie de la Hay from his leash and reached out to relieve Jenny of one of her bags. And it was then that he noticed that she was crying.

'My dear . . .' He was about to place his hand on her shoulder but stopped himself. He would have done so a few years ago, would have put his arms about her to comfort her, but he realised now that the times discouraged such gestures. We did not touch one another any more.

'My dear . . . what is it?'

215

She looked away. 'It's nothing. I'm all right.'

'But you're not! You're not.'

He waited, and then she turned to look at him. She was wearing mascara, which had smudged. There was a black streak down her cheek. He felt in his pocket for his handkerchief, which he used to dab at the smudge. One could surely do that these days: one could unsmudge somebody.

She looked into his eyes. 'I've been . . . been fired,' she said. 'I've lost my job.'

William frowned. 'Your job with that MP? What's his name? Snarp?'

She shivered as she uttered the name. 'Snark.'

'Oh dear, I'm very sorry.'

'He did it by text message,' she said. 'He fired me by text.'

51. A Very Good Risotto

By the time William eventually got back to his flat, Marcia had prepared the risotto and was becoming anxious.

'You took your time,' she said, glancing at her watch. 'That was a long walk. Did Freddie de la Hay run off or something?'

William shook his head. 'No. Freddie de la Hay was a model dog—as always. No, our walk was not all that long. It was that young woman.'

Marcia arched an eyebrow. 'You met a young woman?' It was her constant fear: William would meet somebody and go off with her. It was her nightmare.

'One of the downstairs girls. You know, the tall,

216

good-looking one.'

Marcia did not like to hear William use the term 'good-looking', especially in relation to young women. She remained silent.

'Yes,' William went on. 'Jenny. She worked for that oleaginous MP, Snark. Apparently he sacked her today. Sent her a text telling her. Can you believe it?'

Marcia relaxed. 'Oh, I can believe anything of politicians,' she said. 'I cater for them from time to time. You should see them! Quite a few of them exist entirely on free food, you know. They go to meetings and presentations and the like where there's free food and they stuff themselves with whatever's available. They're real shockers.'

'I can well believe it,' said William. 'And free drink too. I provide the wine for a lobbyist. Gets through *gallons*.'

'So he sacked her? Just like that? Can you do that these days?'

'If you have grounds,' said William. 'Or if somebody's not worked long enough for the legislation to apply. Your people—those students you take on—have no protection. They're casuals.'

'I wouldn't sack even one of them by text,' said Marcia. 'It's really unkind.'

William nodded. 'Of course you wouldn't. No decent person would. This chap Snark must be a real shocker. She was in floods of tears, poor girl. Her mascara had run all the way down her cheek. She looked so . . . so vulnerable.'

Marcia stiffened. 'I'm sure she did.'

'I did my best to comfort her,' William continued.

Marcia's eyes narrowed. 'Good,' she said. 'That

217

was kind of you.'

'Well, I could hardly do anything but,' said William. 'And Freddie de la Hay was marvellous. I swear he knew that she was upset. He went up on his back legs to try to lick her face. And he nuzzled her as if he was trying to make it better for her.'

'Dogs can tell,' said Marcia. 'They can always tell. And so . . . what happened?'

'Well, I spent about fifteen minutes with her in the flat. I saw her in—*we* saw her in, Freddie and I. Her flatmates were out, but I managed to see that she was all right. And then . . . well, then I had a brilliant idea.'

Maria looked puzzled. 'A way of getting her job back?'

William said no. That would not have been a good idea at all, he explained. 'She said that she had no desire to go back to Snark. She seemed determined, in fact, to get her own back in some way. But I didn't go into that. No, it suddenly occurred to me that she would be the ideal stop-gap for Paul. She's just lost her job and I've just lost my assistant. Perfect match.'

Marcia was not at all sure that she welcomed this. A male assistant would have been better, she thought, but she felt she could hardly make that point.

'Has she got any experience?'

William shrugged. 'I doubt it. Or at least no experience of working in a wine shop. But it's hardly rocket science, Marcia. She won't have to advise anybody—she can refer them to me for that. She'll just have to open up the shop and do the till and so on.'

'And did she accept?'

William told her how Jenny had been doubtful at first, but had thought about it and accepted—for a month or two. 'I don't see myself doing this for ever,' she had said, adding apologetically, 'not that there's anything wrong with the wine trade.'

He had not taken offence. She knew about Proust and Wittgenstein and the like; she could not be expected to operate a till for too long.

'So,' he said to Marcia, 'that's all fixed up. And what started as a terrible day has turned into something much better. Much better.'

Marcia smiled. She was pleased that his mood had changed, because she had decided that she would simply have to act. She had placed a bottle of champagne in the fridge and it would be nicely chilled by now. She would serve the risotto, which she was confident would also help matters. It was a magnificent risotto, reverse-engineered from a dish she had eaten in her favourite restaurant, Semplice: Milanese risotto with small pieces of grouse worked into the rice. William would not be able to resist, especially after a glass or two of champagne.

'Bibbly,' she said, using her idiosyncratic pronunciation. 'This calls for bibbly, which I have fortunately put on ice.'

William rubbed his hands together. 'Perfect,' he said. 'Bibbly. Just perfect.'

Marcia went into the kitchen and poured two glasses of champagne. When she came back into the drawing room, William was doing something with his shoes. What was it? Changing into . . .

He stood up. 'Look,' he said. 'Do you like my new Belgian Shoes?'

She looked down at the ostrich-skin slip-ons.

219

'Oh, William!' she said. 'They're beautiful! Absolutely beautiful! Belgian, you say! Who would have thought?'

William accepted the glass of champagne that she held out to him. 'You like them, Marcia? You really do?'

'I *love* them,' said Marcia. 'And they look perfect on you.'

They raised glasses to one another. It was going very well. And in front of the fireplace, Freddie de la Hay watched them somnolently. The world of humans was a strange one—quite unintelligible to a dog. But Freddie could tell that things were going well, and he liked the smell of risotto. Would they leave some for him? One never knew, but for Freddie de la Hay, even the smell of such a risotto was enough.

52. Eddie's Wardrobe

By nine o'clock it was agreed. William would later reflect on the actual process of agreement and ask himself how it came about. At no point, he thought, did Marcia come right out and ask him whether she could move in, and yet there was no room for misunderstanding or ambivalence: she would pack up Eddie's things for him and move them into the hall; then she would move her own possessions into his room and arrange for the lock on the flat door to be changed. It was a bold move, but, as she pointed out to William, Eddie had failed to take hints and had ignored a succession of direct requests. In the circumstances what else could they do?

The delicate issue of Marcia's taking up residence was glossed over. 'I'll take his room,' she said. 'It won't be any trouble. And this place could do with a woman's touch. Nothing dramatic, of course—just a bit of sprucing up.'

Nothing was said about any of the other normal concomitants of moving in with somebody. Was she merely going to be a flatmate, sharing in the same way as the girls downstairs shared? Or was she planning to *live with* William, in the sense in which most men and women live with one another? Had it not been for the champagne, William would have resisted. He liked Marcia, but he had not yet decided whether they would be lovers. He knew that was what she wanted, but he was unsure whether she was quite right for him and he realised that if he made a move in that direction, it would not be easy to extricate himself should he wish to do so. And now she was moving in . . .

'Let's go and take a look at his room,' Marcia suggested as she cleared the plates from the table.

William frowned. 'Well, I don't know . . . He could come back.'

'We'll hear him,' she said. 'And anyway it's far too early for Eddie to come back. I thought he stayed out all night on Saturdays. You said so yourself.'

'Did I? Well, maybe.'

She took him by the arm. 'So . . . let's go and take a look. I need to see what's what, if I'm going to be living in that room.' She looked at him sideways as she made this last remark, but he did not take up the invitation to say that she would be in his room. It's my life, he thought, my room. Nobody has the right to force their way into other people's rooms.

221

Bedrooms require an *invitation*—it was basic etiquette.

Half propelled by Marcia, William led the way into Eddie's bedroom. As they entered, he became aware that Freddie de la Hay was at their heels and was looking about the room, his nose twitching with interest. Did Eddie *indulge*? He thought not: Eddie had shown no interest in such matters and indeed had often expressed a hostile view of drugs. Stevie, he had once said, had taken something that made him see double for three days. 'It's stupid,' Eddie said. 'What's the point?' So if Freddie de la Hay was picking up a scent it was probably no more than the minute traces which might have stuck to Eddie's clothing during his visits to those clubs of his. The air in those places must be laden with the sort of thing that pressed an olfactory button with Freddie de la Hay.

'What a pit,' Marcia said, poking with her foot at a pile of dirty washing on the floor. 'He's such a—' She stopped herself. Eddie was William's son after all and she should be careful.

'I tried to bring him up to be tidy,' William sighed. 'But you know how it is.'

'Oh, it's not your fault that Eddie's like he is,' Marcia soothed. 'It's the . . . It's the . . .' She searched for the right object of blame. 'It's the Government's fault. They've done nothing to stop the rot. They've undermined the authority of teachers. They've—'

'Yes,' said William. He had heard Marcia on the subject before; it was all very familiar.

Marcia crossed the room to the desk, which Eddie had positioned under the window. A number of unopened letters lay on the top.

'A red bill,' she said, picking up one of the envelopes. 'And this one is for jury service—you can tell.'

'I don't think Eddie would be a particularly good juror,' William said.

'Well, I'll pack all these up for him,' said Marcia, moving the letters into a pile. She bent down and opened the top drawer of the desk. Old chocolate wrappers had been stuffed inside and now cascaded out.

'Eddie always had a sweet tooth,' said William.

Marcia pursed her lips. 'I see.'

While Marcia had been busying herself with the desk, Freddie de la Hay had moved across to the wardrobe at the other end of the room and seated himself in front of it. Then, turning towards William, he gave him an intense stare.

'He's found something,' said Marcia. 'Look.'

William sighed. He did not want Freddie to find something. Life was complicated enough without having to think about Eddie's possible use of drugs.

'They all do it,' he muttered. 'But perhaps he doesn't inhale . . .'

Freddie was now scratching at the wardrobe door and whining.

'We can't ignore him,' Marcia said firmly. 'I'm going to have a look.'

'I wish you wouldn't,' muttered William. 'It's Eddie's wardrobe, you know. We should respect his privacy.'

But Marcia was not listening; she was now at Freddie de la Hay's side. The dog looked up at her briefly and then glanced over at William, as if to confirm Marcia's authority. William nodded.

223

The catch on the wardrobe was stiff and it took Marcia a minute or so to twist it in such a way that the door would open. William came and stood behind her, craning his neck to see what the wardrobe would contain. Chocolate wrappers? A cache of dirty laundry? Or would it, as he feared, contain something considerably worse?

53. Freddie de la Hay Points to Something

William and Marcia found themselves staring into Eddie's wardrobe, each noticing something different about the clothes hanging from the rail. In contrast to the rest of Eddie's room, the inside of the wardrobe was at least a corner of order, with jackets at one end of the rail and trousers, belts and ties at the other. Marcia's eyes were fixed on a tie: ghastly, she thought, but just right for Eddie. For his part, William spotted several garments that he recognised but had not seen for a long time, including a suede jacket fringed in the cowboy style. This had been a favourite of the teenage Eddie—his mother had bought it for him for his fourteenth birthday and he had cherished it. And here it was, still loved, perhaps a reminder to Eddie of the mother he had lost, or of his earlier years, when he had been happier. William swallowed and looked away. Eddie had been an affectionate boy, enthusiastic, friendly in a puppyish way; William had been so proud of him, had loved him, and then something had gone wrong. Eddie had changed, had grown surly and distant. At first he had thought that it was the normal teenage change—that mutation which transforms likeable children into odious beings. But the teenage years had passed and the old (young) Eddie had not returned, and it seemed to William that he never would. But should he be throwing him out now—because that was what Marcia had somehow engineered? Was that what a father should do?

'I wonder . . .' began William, but he did not finish. Marcia had seized his arm and was pointing down at Freddie de la Hay. The hairs on the back of Freddie's neck seemed to be standing up and he was pointing with his left paw towards a small pile of sweaters on the floor of the wardrobe.

'He's seen something,' whispered Marcia. 'Look. Freddie's seen something.'

His heart cold within him, William bent down and felt around under the pile of sweaters. As he did so, Freddie de la Hay growled softly.

'That's all right, Freddie boy,' William muttered. 'I'll handle this.'

But Freddie de la Hay remained on duty as he had been taught to do at Heathrow Airport, and when William extracted the item that had been concealed under the sweaters, he gave an eager bark and pointed more energetically at the object in William's hand.

'All right, Freddie,' said William. 'You've made your point. You can sit down now.'

Freddie immediately sat back and looked up at William, an expression of satisfaction on his face.

William straightened up. He had in his hands a rectangular parcel about twelve inches by eight, wrapped neatly in brown paper and tied about with waxed string.

'A book?' Marcia suggested. 'Or . . .'

William waited for her to make an alternative suggestion, but none came.

'I wonder why Freddie was so interested?' he mused. 'This doesn't look like anything . . . anything illegal.'

'Then open it,' said Marcia. 'Or give it to me. I'll unwrap it.'

William frowned. 'I don't know,' he said. 'This is Eddie's property. I don't know whether we should be . . .'

'Oh, nonsense,' said Marcia. 'It's your flat and you can look at anything you like in your flat.' She reached out and snatched the parcel from William's hands.

'I really don't know,' William said. 'When I was Eddie's age, I don't think I would have liked my father to open my private parcels.'

Marcia was dismissive. That was the trouble with William: he was frightened of Eddie. Eddie! That complete waste of space! William needed stiffening up—needed more *backbone*. Or bottom. That's what people said, was it not, when they talked about courage? Bottom. He needed more *bottom*.

'Come on, William,' she said. 'Bottom. More bottom.'

William looked at her in astonishment. He blushed. 'I beg your pardon?' he stuttered.

'In the sense of courage,' Marcia said coolly. "Bottom" means courage.'

'Oh.'

'Yes,' said Marcia, beginning to unwrap the parcel. 'You have a perfect right to see what's in here. What if it's something . . . ?'

She did not finish. Released from its string binding, the brown paper wrapping fell away to reveal a small, exquisitely executed painting.

Now Marcia finished her sentence. 'Stolen,' she half whispered. 'What if it's stolen . . .'

It was more of a statement than a question. And when William took the painting from her and began to examine it, he knew that what Marcia feared was surely correct. Eddie had never expressed any interest in art and it was inconceivable that he would have bought a painting, especially a painting so beautiful and so obviously expensive as this.

'Oh no,' he groaned, staring at the tiny scene depicted in the painting: the expulsion from Paradise. God, stern as a righteous magistrate, pointed the way; Adam and Eve, chastened and aware now of their nudity, looked back over their shoulders at what they were leaving behind them. It looked a little like the private gardens near a friend's house in Notting Hill, thought William, but without the signs telling you what the committee decreed you should not do. And we were all expelled, he thought, from something.

'It must be stolen,' said Marcia. 'Why else would Eddie hide it under a pile of sweaters in his wardrobe? And why else would Freddie de la Hay . . . ?'

The tension that had been building up within William now came flooding out. 'Oh don't be ridiculous, Marcia,' he snapped. 'How could Freddie know that a painting was stolen? He's only a dog, for heaven's sake!'

Marcia was not one to be put down in this way. 'Oh yes?' she challenged. 'Then why did he point

227

to it? You saw him—he pointed to it.'

'He must have smelled something,' said William. 'Maybe there's something on one of those sweaters. Eddie spends time with a young man called Stevie. I'm sure that Stevie smokes all sorts of things. In fact, I'd be highly surprised if he didn't.'

Marcia's response to this was to bend down and pick up the pile of sweaters. Separating them, she passed each in turn under Freddie de la Hay's nose. Each time, the dog sniffed briefly at the wool and then, after appearing to think for a moment, shook his head.

'There!' said Marcia triumphantly. 'You see? Freddie has given the sweaters a clean bill of health.'

'This is ridiculous,' said William. 'Absurd.'

'I don't think so,' said Marcia. And with that, she snatched the painting from William and bent down again to hold it in front of Freddie de la Hay's snout. Almost immediately, the dog stiffened and began to growl. Finally he lifted a paw and pointed at the painting.

'There!' said Marcia. 'That proves it.'

William was perplexed. Freddie de la Hay had certainly reacted to the painting, but what could that mean? Perhaps he had had another job before he had been posted to the sniffer-dog unit at Heathrow airport—perhaps he had worked with the Metropolitan Police's art squad. Anything, he mused, was possible.

'I need to think,' he said. 'This is getting very confusing. I really need to think.'

'Of course you do,' said Marcia soothingly. 'Of course you do, darling.'

William looked down at Freddie, who gazed back up at him with unambiguous affection. The possibility occurred to him that Freddie de la Hay was merely trying to please; after all, that was what dogs did, and it really was the only possible explanation for Freddie's behaviour. He turned to Marcia and suggested this, but she discounted it out of hand.

'Highly unlikely,' she said.

William said nothing, but thought, what does Marcia know about dogs? The answer, of course, was that Marcia knew nothing. And now she was going to be living with him.

I have a criminal son. I have lost my assistant. My domestic arrangements have been turned upside down. My future, he thought, is markedly crepuscular.

54. Polar Bears and Vitamin A

Dee's Saturday was busy, even if it was not as hectic as William's single-handed ordeal at the wine shop. The Pimlico Vitamin and Supplement Agency always took a close interest in the latest vitamin stories to appear in the press, since the effect of these was inevitably felt during the week following publication. That Thursday had seen the announcement of the results of a study into vitamin D deprivation in Scotland and she knew that it would result in a run on vitamin D in Pimlico.

This proved to be correct.

'Three bottles of cod liver oil capsules left,' said

229

Martin. '*Everybody* wants it now.'

'So they should,' said Dee. 'But I do wish they'd send us a circular before they made these announcements. Then we could meet demand.' She paused. 'Are you taking it yourself?'

Martin shook his head. 'Should I be?'

Dee looked at him. 'Your skin's quite pale,' she said. 'Pallid, even. Are you getting enough sunlight?'

'I thought we shouldn't,' said Martin. 'My dad plays golf with a dermatologist. He says that people shouldn't be going to Spain and sitting in the sun.'

'That's true, but you need some sunlight to manufacture vitamin D. That's the trouble with people in Scotland. They don't get enough sunlight what with all that mist. And their diet's awful too. Look at Glasgow.'

Martin nodded. He was uncertain about Glasgow. The previous week he had been on a train with some Glaswegian football supporters on their way to a friendly. Perhaps their problem had been vitamin D deficiency.

'Of course, you can get too many vitamins,' Dee went on. 'Do you know that if you ate a polar bear's liver you would die? Did you know that, Martin?' She made the statement with the air of one giving a warning.

'Really?'

'Yes. Their livers contain lethal doses of vitamin A. They're very efficient at making it, polar bears are. They need to be, up there. Poor things. Their ice floes are melting.'

'And people shoot them,' Martin observed.

Dee was puzzled. 'Do they? Or do they just shoot

grizzly bears?'

Martin adjusted the position of one of the remaining bottles of cod liver oil on the shelf. 'I don't know. But could you sleep at night, if you were a bear, in the knowledge that people were out there, prowling around, hoping to shoot you?'

'Why do they do it?' Dee mused. 'Why does anybody shoot anything for pleasure, Martin? Do you understand it? You, being a man, does it make more sense to you?'

It did not. 'Of course not,' he said. 'But it's not just men, Dee. There are some women who shoot too. They approve of shooting creatures to death. Ending their lives, which is all they've got. Even if they're just bears, their lives are all they've got.'

It was a defence of men that Martin felt he needed to make. Many of the shop's customers assumed that men did not understand, and Martin resented this. He understood.

Dee did too. 'No,' she said, 'you're right. Women can be as bad as men, I suppose. Not normally, of course, but sometimes. They have fewer toxins than men, you know. That makes a big difference to behaviour.'

Martin shifted on his feet. He was not sure that he wanted the conversation to drift onto toxins, but now it was too late. Dee was looking at him with renewed interest.

'On the subject,' she said, 'have you thought about what I said yesterday? About colonic irrigation?'

'Not really,' he mumbled. This was not true, however; he had thought about it a great deal and had even looked the matter up on the Internet, where he had found numerous descriptions of the process, complete with diagrams.

'Well, you should think very seriously about it,' said Dee. 'In fact, why don't I do it tomorrow?'

Martin suppressed a shudder. 'Do what?'

'Give you colonic irrigation,' said Dee. 'You really need it, you know. When I gave you the iridological analysis it was sticking out a mile. You really need it. All those toxins . . .'

'I don't think I'm particularly toxic,' Martin said.

'But you are, Martin! You are!' She reached out and took his arm. 'Listen, Martin. Tomorrow's Sunday. Come round to my place. Come round to Corduroy Mansions tomorrow morning. Eleven o'clock, maybe. Round about then. And I'll do it for you. I've got all the stuff there. All right?'

He looked about him wildly. 'I don't know—'

Dee cut him off. 'You're in denial, you know, Martin.'

'I'm not—'

'There you are—denying.'

'I'm denying that I'm in denial. That's not denial.'

'Well, if it isn't denial, then what is it?' asked Dee. She did not wait for an answer. 'So that's settled then. Eleven tomorrow. Sunday's a very good day to do it.'

Martin seemed defeated. He found it difficult to stand up to Dee and this, in spite of the intimacy of the subject, was no exception. Even if he did need colonic irrigation—and he had nothing against it in principle—he was not sure that it was something that one should have at the hands of somebody one *knew*.

'I'm sorry, Dee,' he said. 'I know that I might need it but why don't I go and get it from . . . from a colonic irrigation place? From somebody I don't know.'

She stared at him. 'And pay for it? Why? Why pay for it? I'm helping you to save money. You didn't think I was going to charge you, did you?' She laughed at the sheer absurdity of charging a friend or, in this case, an employee, for colonic irrigation. Colonic irrigation could be a gift between friends; surely he knew that?

'It's not the money,' Martin protested. 'Money's got nothing to do with it.'

Dee seemed puzzled. 'Well, what is it then?' She paused, searching his expression for some clue. 'You aren't embarrassed, are you, Martin? Surely you aren't embarrassed?' She smiled playfully. 'It's that, isn't it?'

'Well . . .'

'Oh come on,' she said. 'You won't find it in the slightest bit embarrassing. Not after we start. I promise you. So don't think twice about it. Really, don't.' She looked at him. 'Feeling better about it? Good. Tomorrow then. Eleven.'

55. *The Late Isadora Duncan*

As this conversation was taking place between Dee and a reluctant and embarrassed Martin, Barbara Ragg's thoughts could not have been further removed from vitamin D, polar bears, or indeed colonic irrigation. She was driving at the time, sweeping along the winding road from Rye in her British Racing Green sports car, with a young man in the passenger seat beside her. A cynic, standing

233

by the roadside, contemplating the passing traffic, would have had no difficulty in describing the situation. He would have said, with all the snide innuendo that cynics so effortlessly muster, that here was a woman in her early thirties, prosperous—driving the fruit of last year's bonus—accompanied by a trophy man a good few years younger. And the cynic would have observed that Barbara was driving, which underlined the status of the young man, who was nonetheless enjoying the trip greatly, a scarf trailing from his neck.

At the beginning of their journey, noticing the scarf, Barbara had warned him of the fate of Isadora Duncan.

'Remember Isadora Duncan,' she said as they drove out of the Mermaid Inn's car park.

He looked at her blankly. 'No, I don't know her, I'm afraid.'

The car started down the cobbled street. 'You wouldn't,' said Barbara. 'She died in 1927. In tragic circumstances that are brought to mind, I'm afraid, by your scarf.'

The young man frowned. 'You've lost me,' he said.

Barbara explained. 'The reason I know all about this is because I represented an author who wrote about Gertrude Stein. I'm a literary agent, you see. Anyway, Gertrude Stein, who was an American with a literary and artistic salon in Paris, said 'affectations can be dangerous'. She said it when she heard about the death of Isadora Duncan, who was a famous dancer and femme fatale.'

The young man was watching her as she spoke. There was a light in his eyes—the light of discovery that ignites when one encounters for the first time an intellectually stimulating companion. Barbara noticed this light, and responded. Oedipus Snark never listened to her—she could say the wittiest things and he would just ignore her. This young man, by contrast, appeared to be appreciating her, and she felt glad; one might *sparkle* before such an audience, and she had him to herself all the way to London, and after that . . . Well, it was possible. These things happened in fiction, and if they happened in fiction, then they might just happen in real life; just . . .

She turned the car at the bottom of Mermaid Street, noticing as she did so their reflection in a shop window nearby. Seeing one's reflection in a window is a reminder of what one is; this is what one is in the eyes of others. And she was a woman in an expensive sports car with an attractive young man at her side. How satisfying.

'It's rather a sad story,' Barbara went on. 'Isadora was given a lovely long scarf by a Russian artist. She was taken for a ride in Nice in an Amilcar GS—a very nice little sports car of the

235

time—by a very glamorous Italian mechanic, Benoît Falchetto.'

Barbara thought: what it would be to be invited to drive off with a glamorous young mechanic, and an Italian to boot! And one called Benoît Falchetto . . .

'Anyway,' she continued, 'as they drove off, the scarf which Isadora had been wearing got caught in the back wheel of the sports car. It was made—the scarf—of very strong silk and when it wound round the wheel it tightened round Isadora Duncan's neck. She was pulled out of the car and bumped along behind until the Italian mechanic stopped. But by then it was too late.'

She glanced at the young man. I haven't even asked his name, she thought. I've picked him up in the hotel car park and I have no idea what he's called. Bruce? Andrew? Mark? . . .

The young man felt gingerly at his neck, loosening the scarf slightly. 'Not a nice way to go.'

'No indeed. Even if it immortalises one.' Hugging the side of the road, Barbara put her foot down on the accelerator. 'You know, I've always thought that immortality comes at a price. If you look at the career of anybody who's achieved enough to be immortal, there's a cost. Neglected family, a relentlessly demanding muse, deep, driving unhappiness—it's all on the balance sheet.'

'I wouldn't want it,' said the young man.

'No. *Moi non plus.*'

They were breasting a blind rise in the road. To the east, the land dropped away into a valley; cattle grazed, a tractor moved slowly across an as yet unploughed field. As Auden observed in his 'Musée des Beaux Arts', disaster always took place

236

against a background of very ordinary life: Icarus fell from the sky while a ship went innocently on its way, while a farmer tilled his fields. So too, against a backdrop of the quotidian, did the knot of the scarf now suddenly fall apart, releasing a yard of tightly knitted wool in colourful stripes; and, while these ordinary country things were happening in the nearby field, the scarf snaked out backwards, too quickly for any movement of the hand to arrest it, and, by dint of aerodynamics and gravity, found its way to the revolving hub of the sports car's near-side rear wheel.

It happened so quickly, just as it had happened in Nice all those years ago: the scarf was caught in the hub and wound up immediately, tugging with sudden and brutal force at the young man's neck. Feeling the unexpected pressure, he opened his mouth to shout, but the sound was blocked by the immediate occlusion of airways as the scarf tightened around his throat. Not that a cry of alarm was necessary: Barbara had seen it happen and immediately slammed on the brakes, bringing the car to a halt in a squeal of burning rubber. For a moment she could not believe that it had happened, that the accident she had described had come to pass, as if in neat illustration of some safety lesson.

She grabbed at the scarf around the young man's neck, struggling to insert her fingers into the tightly wound loops. But she could not get purchase and he was turning red, his face suddenly puffed up. She almost panicked, but did not, because the idea came to her of reversing the car, which she now did, crashing the gears.

It was the right thing to do, even if the right thing

may sometimes come too late. To reverse the car is not the solution to an ordinary accident; one cannot just drive backwards, and in doing so bring a broken vehicle to wholeness again. But in such an accident as this, one can reverse and unwind that which is wound up; in theory, at least.

56. *O, Venus*

'I'm terribly sorry.'

It sounded trite, almost a parody of an inhibited apology; but what does one say to somebody whom one has almost strangled, even if it is largely the fault of the victim for wearing too long a scarf and ignoring a cautionary tale? And the situation was made all the more difficult by the fact that Barbara did not know the name of the young man who was sitting in her now static car, gingerly touching his neck. She should have asked him at the beginning, she thought; introductions become more embarrassing the further one gets from the initial encounter.

'And I don't even know your name,' she blurted out.

He managed a smile. 'Hugh.'

She peered at his neck. 'I'm Barbara. Barbara Ragg. And I'm really sorry about this. Especially after our conversation about Isadora Duncan. I should have . . .'

He began to shake his head, but the movement obviously caused him pain because he winced. 'It was my fault. I should have taken my scarf off. You warned me.'

She reached out to touch the angry red patch of skin in a line round his neck. 'That looks a bit nasty,' she said. 'I think we should get you to a doctor.'

'No need. It's just like one of those rope burns. It's a bit sore but I don't think that the skin is too bad. It'll get better.'

Barbara looked doubtful. 'It might be better just to have it checked. What if something's crushed inside—inside your throat?'

Hugh smiled. 'I wouldn't be able to talk,' he said. 'And it feels fine inside—it really does.'

'Well, at least let me put something on it,' she said. 'I've got something back at the flat that is really good for skin things. Zinc ointment. It really works. Would you like me to . . . ?'

He said that he would and they set off again, the scarf now tucked away behind the passenger seat. Barbara drove slowly; she was shocked by the experience and was imagining what would have happened if she had not braked so quickly, or had not reversed to loosen the scarf. She shuddered.

'Where's your place?' Hugh asked.

She told him about her flat in Notting Hill and they discovered that he lived within walking distance. That was handy, she said, and he threw her a glance. She had spoken without thinking. Why was it handy? Did she seriously think that something was going to come of this chance encounter?

She wanted to ask him how old he was. She often found it difficult to judge men's ages; women were easier because she was used to sizing them up as competition. Once one was past thirty, whether or not another woman was still in her twenties could be a matter of intense interest. They were the ones who were the real competition—the ones who could attract a man just by *being* the age they were, whereas after thirty . . . Well, it was just so unfair. One had to really work at it.

She decided to ask what had taken him to Rye. 'I just wanted to get away somewhere,' he said. 'I couldn't bear the thought of going on one of these cheap weekends in Amsterdam or Prague or wherever. All those drunken hen and stag parties. It makes me really ashamed to be British, just to see them.'

Barbara knew what he meant. 'Yes,' she said. 'It's not an edifying sight. I suppose there are no hen parties in Rye.'

'None at all.'

There was a brief silence. Then she asked, 'By yourself? Or did you go with somebody?'

He hesitated for a moment before answering. 'By myself. Which was the point, really. I wanted to be by myself.'

'Why?'

He looked at her in a way that suggested that it was a painful topic. 'End of a relationship,' he said.

She was thrilled, but said, 'I'm so sorry.'

He shrugged. 'They end. That's what relationships do: they end.'

'Me too.'

'What?'

'I'm just out of one too.' She glanced at her watch. 'Just over an hour ago.'

He let out a whistle. 'That's very recent.'

She smiled. 'I suppose so. But it had been building up. I suddenly wanted to be . . .' She paused. She had intended to say 'to be free' but it occurred to her that if she did, it would suggest that she did not want to meet somebody else. And that was not true. She wanted desperately to meet somebody else. And he would do; oh, he would do just fine.

He looked thoughtful. 'I remember being told—years ago—by somebody or other that the best cure for a broken heart is another lover. Have you heard that?'

It was ridiculously trite—but she had heard it. And perhaps it was true, as trite remarks often can be. *What goes round comes round*—another trite saying if ever there was one, but nonetheless completely true. And if there was anybody who deserved to contemplate that particular aphorism, it was Oedipus Snark. There were many things that would be coming round to him, she thought—not without satisfaction.

'You're smiling.'

She nodded. 'I was thinking of a saying that I think is probably true. "What goes round comes round."'

241

He raised an eyebrow. 'Do you think so?'

'Yes, I do. I'm thinking of the man I used to be involved with. He's got it coming to him—he really has.' She paused. 'And you? Did she get rid of you or did you get rid of her?'

'She got rid of me.'

Barbara marvelled at this. How could any woman let go of him—with his looks and his manner? How could she?

'I'm sorry,' she said. 'I'm sure you didn't deserve it.'

He laughed at this. 'I don't know about that. I suppose I have my irritating ways. And you never know—sometimes the chemistry just isn't right, or it's one-sided.'

'That's true,' she said. 'But when it's right, you can tell, can't you? You just know.'

He nodded. And then he looked at her sideways and their eyes met—just briefly, but they met.

Barbara said to herself: Oh, please, please, please! Please let nothing go wrong with this—this wildly improbable, impossible, but gorgeous thing. She was not sure to whom to address this invocation. To Venus, perhaps? If the goddess of love were listening, she would surely cherish such an invocation and understand the urgency, the yearning, that lay behind it.

57. Barbara Ragg Writes a Letter

On Monday, Barbara Ragg went into her office in Soho, the Ragg Porter Literary Agency (founded 1974, by her father, Gregory Ragg, and his friend,

Fatty Porter). She was usually the first to arrive in the morning, coming in even before the cleaning lady, who emptied the wastepaper bins and vacuumed the floor, and then, her duties done, was to be found in the waiting room reading unsolicited manuscripts over a cup of tea. She had a good eye for a promising script, Barbara and her colleagues had found, and they encouraged her to note down her verdict on a piece of paper and pin it to the front page of the manuscript. 'Promising', a note might read, or 'A bit sentimental, I think', or simply 'Rubbish'. And sometimes these notes would be accompanied by a request for fresh cleaning supplies, as in: 'A good romance—credible characters—and please order more liquid soap for the toilets.'

The Ragg Porter Literary Agency did not reveal to the world that some of its reading was done by the cleaning lady; such an admission would be misunderstood by those who did not know the cleaning lady in question and her record of spotting a good literary prospect. It was as reliable a system, the agents felt, as any other, and certainly more truthful than the practice of sending manuscripts back completely unread but accompanied by a letter which implied that the manuscript had been carefully considered. The statement 'Your manuscript has been carefully considered by our reader' did not reveal that the reader in question was the cleaning lady. And why reveal this? asked Barbara. What difference does it make?

That Monday morning, when the cleaning lady came in and began her cheerful rounds of the various cubicles that made up the office, she noticed that Barbara's light was on. A glance

243

through the open door revealed Barbara at her desk, writing a letter.

'Early start, Barbara!' she said.

Barbara looked up. 'I'm writing a letter, Maggie. I woke up very early this morning.'

The cleaning lady nodded. She liked Barbara and she was pleased to see her looking bright. That awful man of hers, that MP, she thought, the horrible one, he's the one who makes her miserable. It's always a man—always. If there's an unhappy-looking woman, then there's an awful man somewhere. Always.

Barbara returned to her letter. She was writing to her friend James Holloway in Edinburgh, telling him about her weekend.

'I know you don't mind my burdening you with the details of my life, James, and that's why I'm writing to you this morning about something really, really important that has occurred. No, don't worry—this is not something difficult or challenging. Far from it. Something really remarkable has happened to me and I wanted you to know about it. I'm not looking for any advice—I am utterly sure of what I'm doing and I think it's the right thing for me. I just want to tell somebody about it. You know how it is when something good happens—when you read a book that strikes a chord, or see a picture that really speaks to you— you want to share it with a friend. You just have to. That's how I feel.

'The first thing I have to tell you is this: I've left Oedipus. Now I know that you'll be pleased by this because I always knew your view of him—and you were right. Do you remember how you said to me, 'Sorry, but he's *not* for you, Barbara'? Those were

244

your exact words, as I recall. You had come down to London for some meeting or other, and we went for lunch at the Poule au Pot and Oedipus was with us to begin with and then had to dash off to the House. At first you didn't want to give a view, and then, when I pressed you, you did. Well, you were right. As the saying goes, Oedipus is now history— or history to an extent. I still have a score to settle with him and will do it. I know, I know, one shouldn't be vengeful, but that's the way I feel and he deserves it. He's used me, and I'm going to make sure he knows it.

'But that's not what I'm writing to you about, James. It's something that happened almost immediately after I left Oedipus. I met the most wonderful, kind, handsome, considerate, soft-spoken, gentle, sympathetic, interesting man. How can a man be all that? Well, he can, and I've found him.

'And now, James, the bombshells. One: he's six years younger than me. Twenty-five; but so what? Two: I found him in a car park in Rye. Yes! And I took him back to London in the British Racing Green car—remember I drove you to Oxford in it once?—and, anyway, we drove back together and, apart from an Isadora Duncan moment, it was a blissful trip. And then one thing led to another and . . . well, he's moved into the flat. Last night he made me scrambled eggs and we watched *To Kill a Mockingbird* together. I cried; I just cried. And he didn't say that I shouldn't cry; he just held my hand and let me do it.

'And how do I feel? Well, I feel happy. That's the only way I can describe the way I feel: happy. Do you know that anthem, 'I Was Glad'—the Parry one? That's what I feel like singing at the top of my voice, the first line of it, announcing to everybody that I feel today that I am the most fortunate woman in London, by far. That's how I feel, James, and I know that happiness doesn't last for ever, but when you're truly happy, you think it will. That's what I think. I really do.

'Bless you for listening, James, and love from your friend, Barbara Ragg, who feels today the most blessed of women: ecstatic, fulfilled, and wanting for nothing.'

58. *Dee Makes Tea for Jenny*

For Jenny, Monday was the first day of her new job as assistant to William in his wine shop. The shock of her dismissal by Oedipus Snark had dominated her weekend and had left her with that curious numb feeling that we feel when we encounter a real setback. Of course she knew that she did not deserve to lose her job—and certainly did not deserve to be dismissed as Oedipus had done, by text message—but this knowledge could not protect her from the smarting sense of rejection that the dismissal brought with it. She had worked hard in her job; she had done everything Oedipus had asked of her, including the constant sending of made-up excuses when he broke his word to do one thing or another. I colluded in his lies, she thought, and I am ashamed.

On Sunday, lying in bed in her flat in Corduroy Mansions, she had been too dispirited to get up and had instead lain there rehearsing all the possible reasons for her dismissal. She could think of nothing, other than that Oedipus had simply grown tired of her and wanted a change. And when Dee had knocked at her door to see if she was all right, she had simply burst into tears, unable for a few minutes to say anything cogent. Nice, patient Dee; they had held hands, with Dee sitting at the edge of the bed comforting her as best she could.

'He *what?*' asked Dee. 'He sacked you? Snark did?'

'Yes. He sacked me. I've lost my job.'

'But that's ridiculous! You must be the most efficient assistant or whatever that there is. We all know that. Are you sure?'

Jenny nodded miserably. 'Look, here's the text.'

She reached for her mobile phone and brought up the text message she had received from Oedipus the previous day:

SORRY. JOB OVER. ☹ WILL PAY ONE WEEK'S SALARY IN LIEU. ☺THANKS FOR EVERYTHING. OEDIPUS.

Dee read the message, her astonishment giving way to outrage. 'Is he serious?' she said. 'How can anyone . . . ?'

'It's the sort of thing he does,' said Jenny, taking the phone from her friend. 'He's horrible. He doesn't care about anybody. He doesn't care about me. He doesn't care about the leader of his party, about the constituents, about the people who work for him in his constituency office. Nobody. We're just disposable.'

'But why would he sack you? What's he got to gain?'

Jenny shrugged. 'He's bored with me, I imagine. He thinks . . . well, I don't like to say this, but he thinks that I show him up. He thinks that he knows everything and then he discovers that I've read books he's never even heard of. Some men can't take that.'

Dee nodded. 'I knew somebody like that. He couldn't bear the thought that a woman could have her own ideas and that these ideas could be better than his. There are a lot of men like that. We make them feel insecure if we show signs of knowing more than they do.' She paused. 'Did he ever . . . did he ever make any moves? You know . . .'

Jenny frowned. 'Moves?'

Dee explained further. 'Did he ever make a pass at you?'

Jenny looked up at the ceiling. She could not recall Oedipus ever doing anything like that; he had shown no interest in her, she thought, as a woman. She had assumed that this was because he had that girlfriend of his, Barbara Ragg, but it could equally well have been because he was so narcissistic that he could only think of making a pass at himself. What had somebody said of him in a newspaper column somewhere? 'If Snark were to be found covered in love bites they would surely be self-inflicted.'

She told Dee about this and they both laughed. Then she explained about her temporary job with William, starting the next day.

'Mr French upstairs?' asked Dee. 'But he's lovely, Jenny. He's the nicest man there is. You'll be far happier with him.'

Dee went off to make them both a cup of tea and when she came back she discovered that Jenny was sitting up in bed and although her face was still puffy around the eyes from her tears, she was looking more cheerful.

'So, let's not talk about him any more,' said Jenny. 'I'll get my own back some day.'

'Great,' said Dee. 'And I'll help you. Any ideas?'

'I'll think.'

They drifted into pleasant, companionable conversation. Jenny was going to buy a new blouse that she had seen in a shop off Oxford Street. Dee approved. Jenny was going to book a holiday to Tunisia online, for about three months' time. Dee approved of that too.

'And you?' asked Jenny. 'What about you, Dee?'

Dee looked at her watch. It was already half past eleven and there was no sign of Martin. They had agreed on eleven o'clock and everything was ready for the colonic irrigation session but he had simply not arrived.

'I was going to do colonic irrigation for somebody,' she said. 'But he hasn't turned up. He promised. It's my assistant at the vitamin shop, Martin. You met him when you came in that day.

249

Remember? That rather nice-looking boy.'

Jenny sipped at her tea and looked at her flatmate. 'You were going to give Martin colonic irrigation?'

Dee nodded. 'Yes. You see, when I looked at his eyes I saw flecks, which indicated toxins. You can always tell. He needs it.'

Jenny grimaced. 'But . . . but do you think it's a good idea to give colonic irrigation to somebody you work with? Especially if he's a young man and you're . . . well, you're you. Don't you think that . . . ?'

'I don't see what the problem is,' Dee retorted. 'You know, people treat colonic irrigation with such suspicion—as if it were open heart surgery or something. It really isn't. It's simple, you know, you just—'

Jenny raised a hand. 'I really don't want to hear about it, Dee. Frankly, I don't think it's the sort of thing you should talk about. Vitamins, OK. Echinacea, OK. But colonic irrigation, that's another thing altogether.'

'I don't think so.'

'No, you obviously don't. But think of it from the point of view of that poor young man. Here's his boss—his boss, remember, even if it's you—saying to him that she wants to take down his trousers and—'

'It's not like that at all,' Dee said. 'Colonic irrigation is not like that at all.'

'Well, he's not here, is he?' snapped Jenny. 'You've scared the poor boy, haven't you? And who can blame him?'

'He'll be grateful,' said Dee. 'You'll see. He just needs a bit of time, that's all.'

59. *Something to Do With Justice*

William was delighted with his new assistant.

'Our customers are quite sophisticated,' he explained to her as he showed her round the shop. 'Buying wine is not like buying groceries. The enjoyment of wine is an aesthetic experience, you know. Wine is about place and the culture of place.'

Jenny looked at him anxiously. 'I don't really know much about wine, you know.'

'You don't have to,' he said. 'If somebody asks for a recommendation and you feel out of your depth, then simply say so. Refer them to me. And if I'm not here, suggest to them that they try something new, something that looks interesting to them. Say something like, 'Well, you're going to be the one who's drinking it. What do you think?' Something like that. Of course there are a few tried and tested expressions you can use. You can always talk about nose. Most wines can be said to have an interesting nose.' He smiled encouragingly. 'Shall we have a little practice before the first customer comes in? I'll be the customer and you be you. But you'll be me, if you see what I mean.'

He adjusted his tie. 'All right. Here we go. You say to me: 'Can I help you with anything?' Go on—you say that.'

Jenny took a deep breath. 'Can I help you with anything?'

'Well, good morning. Yes, you can actually. I'm looking for something for a dinner party I'm going to be having. Can you recommend anything?'

She looked flustered. 'Well . . .'

'Ask what I'm having,' whispered William.

Jenny complied. 'What are you having?'

'I was thinking of a venison stew,' said William. 'And maybe smoked salmon to begin with.'

Jenny thought quickly. 'You'll want white for the fish and . . . er, red for the venison.'

'Good, good,' whispered William. 'But you need to be a bit more specific. Ask what sort of white I like.'

'What sort of white do you like?'

'Something clean.'

She stared at him.

'New Zealand,' he whispered. 'You can't go wrong with New Zealand.'

'I don't think you can go wrong with New Zealand,' said Jenny.

William nodded. 'Good, good. So you show me the New Zealand section over here. See? And then you wave a hand at the whites and you say: 'Would you care to look over some of these?' And I do, like that. And I choose this one, let's say, and you say, 'That's very nice.' Because it is. All the wines I stock are nice—so you won't be telling a lie. And then you say, 'As for the red, you'll need something big for venison, don't you think?' And I'll say 'Big? Yes, that would be nice.' So you take me to the Bordeaux section over there and you wave your hand at that shelf—those are all big wines—and I choose one and, again, you say, 'That's very nice.' You see how it is. Simple, isn't it?'

He showed her the till and the way the credit card machine was operated. 'Always turn your face away when customers put in their PIN,' said

William. 'Thus. You see? You must never watch them putting in their PIN.'

That was the end of her training, and she was launched. When the first customer came in, William deliberately held back and gave her a nod of encouragement. It was not difficult and by the time that William made her a mid-morning cup of coffee, she had competently attended to over ten customers, all of whom seemed pleased enough with her service.

Then, while she was drinking her coffee with William in the back office, her mobile phone rang. She glanced at the number on the screen just in case it was Oedipus—in which case she would not answer. But she did not recognise the number, so she answered.

'Jenny?'

She knew the voice immediately. Barbara Ragg—his girlfriend, poor woman. She saw her from time to time and sometimes took calls and messages for Oedipus from her. She quite liked Barbara, who could surely do far better, she thought, than Oedipus.

'Before you go any further, Barbara,' she said, 'I don't know if Oedipus has told you—I'm not working for him any longer.'

There was silence at the other end of the line. Eventually Barbara spoke. 'Oh.'

Jenny debated with herself whether to say anything about the circumstances of her dismissal. Why not? It was nothing to do with Barbara, she knew, but perhaps it would be a good idea for her to know how her lover behaved.

'Yes. Oedipus sacked me over the weekend. On Saturday. He sent me a text. He sacked me by text message.'

There was a further silence at the other end of the line. Then: 'By text? My God, Jenny! That's . . . that's hateful.' There was a pause. 'And to think . . . Saturday. That's the day I walked out on him. You didn't know that, did you? I was phoning to tell you because I thought that you might get a very different version from you-know-who. I thought I'd set the record straight.'

Jenny's heart gave a leap. 'You dumped him? You dumped Oedipus?'

'Yes. You know we went down to Rye?'

'Yes, I put it in the diary.'

'Well, we were down there and the scales fell from my eyes. Over breakfast, to be precise. I was sitting there at the table and the scales fell from my eyes.'

'Well done.'

'And I feel much better. I can't tell you how much better I feel. I've already met somebody else, by the way, but that's another story. Now, look . . .'

William, listening to one side of the conversation but pretending not to, stared at the inside of his coffee cup. He had problems of his own—with Eddie, and, to an extent, with Marcia. And here were these two women talking about their own problems with that nasty Snark character. Was anybody's life straightforward, he wondered, or did one have to go into a monastery for that? To be a monk and keep bees and make wine for the abbot and lead a life of quiet order and contemplation. Was it still possible, he wondered, or had the world become too complicated, too frantic, to allow such peace of mind?

Jenny and Barbara finished their conversation.

254

They would meet for lunch the following week. Barbara had a proposition that she wanted to put to Jenny. Something to do with Oedipus. Something to do with justice, she said.

60. Going Home

The hospital authorities in Cheltenham were doubtful at first, but there was pressure on beds and Terence Moongrove seemed to have made a remarkable recovery from his near-death experience.

'Ideally, we'd like to keep you under observation, Mr Moongrove,' said the doctor who had attended him, 'but you seem to be pretty bright and breezy. How would you feel about going home?'

'It'd suit me very well,' said Terence, sitting up in bed. 'I feel fully restored, both in karma and in body.'

The doctor smiled. 'I gather that your sister is staying with you at present. She told me that she'd see that everything is all right.'

'She's very helpful,' said Terence. He could not think of any way in which Berthea was particularly helpful, but she had saved his life, he had to concede, and that was helpful, he supposed.

'Well then,' said the doctor. 'I think we can probably discharge you. But you will be careful, won't you? Electricity is very dangerous.'

'Oh, I know that,' said Terence. 'What happened was . . . Well, it was an accident really. I think that there was something wrong with my car battery. I'll get my garage man to get me a new one.'

255

The doctor frowned. 'You tried to charge it, your sister said. Was the charger faulty?'

Terence looked away. 'Perhaps,' he said.

'You have to be terribly careful with these things,' said the doctor.

'Oh, I am, doctor. I'm very careful. But . . . Well, thank you so much for bringing me back from the other side.'

The doctor smiled. 'That's what we're here for. We try to keep people from . . . going to the other side before their time.' He laughed. 'I suppose that's our job.'

Terence looked thoughtful. 'It was very peaceful over there,' he said. 'It was exactly the way I had seen it described.'

The doctor looked at his watch and excused himself while a nurse helped Terence out of bed and took him to a small compartment where his clothes had been stored. Shortly afterwards, Berthea appeared and accompanied Terence to the car park, where a taxi was waiting for them. In less than fifteen minutes they were on the driveway of Terence's house. There, in the open garage, was the Morris Traveller, with the fatal cable leading away from it. While Terence went into the house, Berthea coiled the cable away. The incident had thrown the fuse switch and everything was quite safe, but she handled the cable with evident distaste: this, after all, was the instrument of her brother's near-demise. He really was useless, poor Terence; imagine connecting the mains directly to the battery! What could he have been thinking? And would she ever be able to leave him now without worrying that he would do something really stupid?

She sighed. She could not take Terence back to London—there was not enough room in the house, unless she gave up her study, and it would be impossible having him mooching around, going on about sacred dance and such matters. There were plenty of *soi-disant* visionaries in London, of course, and he would doubtless fall in with others who shared his interest in Bulgarian mystics and the like, but she had her own life to lead and she just could not look after her brother too. No, Terence would have to stay in Cheltenham.

As she walked up to the front door, an idea occurred to her. If she could get to know some of Terence's friends—the sacred dance crowd—then perhaps she would be able to find somebody who would agree to keep an eye on him. There were women in the sacred dance group, no doubt, and one of these might be taken aside, woman to woman, and asked to help see that he came to no harm. England was full of helpful women, Berthea was convinced: there were legions of them, all anxious to help in some way and many of them feeling quite frustrated that there were not quite enough men—for demographic reasons—in need of their help. One of these women would be the solution and, with any luck, it might even turn into a romance. That would be the best possible outcome—to get Terence settled with a suitable woman who would look after him and make sure that he did not try to do anything unwise with electricity.

Berthea sighed. It was something of a pipe dream. What woman in her right mind would take on somebody like Terence? What would be the point? He had no conversation to speak of, other than sentimental memories of things that no woman would be remotely interested in. He read nothing of any consequence, apart from peculiar tomes from small, mystically minded publishing houses, and even then he rapidly forgot both the titles and the contents of these books. He could not cook; he was inclined to asthma; and if sacred dance required any deftness of foot, then Terence would almost certainly be no good at it. And when it came to the romantic side of things—oh, dear, poor Terence with his square glasses and his untidy hair and his cardigans that always had buttons missing . . .

But she could try; it was the least she could do.

'Terence,' Berthea said as she came into the dining room, 'I've decided to extend my stay a little, if I may.'

Terence, who had seated himself at the small bureau, where he was going through mail, seemed pleased. 'You're always welcome, Berthy. We could sort out some of those old photographs together. There are Daddy's pictures of Malta—all those photies—and maybe we could even stick them in an album.'

Berthea nodded. She could think of nothing worse than going through the several boxes of old photographs of Malta that she knew Terence had in the attic, but he was her brother and she had to do something. 'I thought that I might also come along to one of your sacred dance meetings,' she said. 'If you don't mind, that is.'

Terence looked up from his letters. He beamed. 'But that's wonderful, Berthy. You'd be very, very welcome. You know that. And I could give you one of Peter Deunov's books to read first. You could then see what the objectives are, and understand.'

'That would be very nice.'

'Good.' He pushed the mail to the side of his desk. 'And you know what, Berthy? You know what? I've decided to do something about my car.'

Berthea looked at him through narrowed eyes. 'Oh yes?'

'Yes,' said Terence. 'I'm going to get rid of it. I shall phone Mr Marchbanks immediately and ask him to find me a new one.'

61. A Suitable Car

Lennie Marchbanks, patient *garagiste* to Terence Moongrove and the proprietor of Marchbanks Motors, drove round in his truck and parked before the stranded Morris Traveller. Terence, who had seen the truck coming up the drive, went out to meet him, while Berthea watched discreetly from an upstairs window.

'So what's the trouble now, Mr Moongrove?' asked Lennie. 'Old Morris not starting? I put petrol in for you, remember? Should go now.'

'I've decided to sell it,' said Terence. 'That's why I asked you to come out, Mr Marchbanks. I want to get rid of it and get a new car.'

Lennie stared at him in frank disbelief. 'You want to sell the Morris? Did I hear you correctly, Mr Moongrove?'

'You heard perfectly correctly, Mr Marchbanks. I think the time has come.'

Lennie whistled. 'Well, I've been saying that for a good long while, you know. But you always said

259

you were fond of the old bus and didn't see the need. Remember, Mr Moongrove?'

'That's as may be, Mr Marchbanks. But things move on. I've moved on now and need a new car, I think.'

Lennie moved round to the front of the car. 'Bonnet's open, I see,' he said. 'You been fiddling around with the engine, Mr Moongrove?'

Terence looked shifty. 'The battery wasn't working properly. I decided to charge it.'

Lennie peered into the engine compartment. 'Oh yes?' He reached in and touched something, and then wiped his hand on his overalls. 'Battery looks as if it's been a little bit stressed, Mr Moongrove. Your charger all right? Can I take a look at it?'

Terence cleared his throat. 'I didn't exactly use a charger,' he said. 'Perhaps . . .'

Lennie stared at him. 'You didn't use a charger? You . . .' He glanced around the garage and saw the cable lying coiled on the floor where Berthea had placed it. 'You connected it directly to the mains, Mr Moongrove? Is that right?'

'Possibly,' said Terence.

Lennie's mouth opened as if he was about to say something; then it closed again.

'So I wondered whether you would like to buy the car off me,' Terence went on. 'What do you think it's worth?'

Lennie had now regained his composure. 'What's it worth? Well, that's a difficult question, Mr Moongrove. There are people who like these old cars and do them up. We might find somebody like that. But, you see, if you connected the battery to the mains, then the whole electric system will have been live, I suppose, and these wires . . . you know? Well, maybe you don't know. But a car's wires are like its nerves, you see, and if your nerves get a big jolt like that, then . . .'

Terence frowned impatiently. Mr Marchbanks had a tendency to become rather too technical, he felt. 'Well, perhaps you could tow it away, Mr Marchbanks. And then we can talk about a new one. Get what you can for the Morris. A hundred pounds, maybe. I really don't mind very much.'

Lennie nodded. 'Fair enough,' he said. 'And what sort of car would you like in its place, Mr Moongrove?'

'I thought something greyish-green,' said Terence. 'The same colour as this.'

Lennie stared at him. 'A greyish-green car, you say?'

Terence confirmed this. 'And not very big, please. I don't want a large car. Two seats would be quite sufficient, I think.'

Lennie inclined his head. He was thinking. 'A two-seater? That sounds rather . . . How should I put it, Mr Moongrove? A bit sporty, perhaps?'

Terence laughed. 'Oh, I wouldn't mind

261

something sporty, Mr Marchbanks. I'm not exactly Toad of Toad Hall, you know. But a nice little sports car would be fine.' He paused. 'What would the AA think?'

Lennie answered quickly. 'I think they'd be very happy to hear that you'd bought a new car.'

Terence patted the bodywork of the Morris. 'This has been a very fine car, Mr Marchbanks. It represents British engineering at its finest, don't you think?'

Lennie also gave the Morris a pat. 'Some may say that. Of course things have come on a bit since then, but they were grand little cars—no doubt about that.'

Terence looked thoughtful. 'Have you seen the car that Alfie Bismarck's son drives? You know, the son who runs their racehorses? Have you seen his car?'

'Monty Bismarck's car? You talking about Monty Bismarck?'

'Yes. I must say that I thought it was rather nice. Nice and small.' Terence paused. 'Do you think you could get me one of those, Mr Marchbanks?'

Lennie moved away from the Morris and stared into Terence's eyes. 'That's a Porsche, Mr Moongrove. Alfie Bismarck's son drives a Porsche.'

'Is that what it's called? Well, I thought it was very nice. I like small cars, you see.'

'Nice?' echoed Lennie. 'Oh, it's nice all right, Mr Moongrove. A Porsche is a very nice car altogether. But it's very fast, you know.'

'I wouldn't have to drive it fast though, would I?'

Lennie made a face. 'No, you wouldn't have to. But you'd have to be very careful, you know. If you put your foot down hard, you'd take off.'

'But I'd never put my foot down hard,' said Terence. 'You know me. I don't drive very fast.'

'That's true.'

'So can you get me one, Mr Marchbanks? It doesn't matter if it's a little bit expensive—I've got plenty of money, you know.'

'I'm not sure I'd recommend it, Mr Moongrove. Perhaps you should talk to your sister about it?'

It was the wrong tactic, and Terence pursed his lips in determination. 'No,' he snapped. 'I shall not talk to my sister about it. Cars are things for men, Mr Marchbanks. We men can make up our own minds about these things without bossy women coming and poking their long noses into our cars. My car is not a matter for my sister at all.'

Lennie shrugged. He was very reluctant to acquire a Porsche for Terence, but could he stop him? And if he did not do this for him, then somebody else—some unscrupulous person— would sell him some dreadful Porsche that had been driven to death and would just prove a headache for everybody: for him, for Terence and for the AA.

'All right,' he said. 'I'll get you a Porsche, Mr Moongrove. But only if you promise to drive it very, very carefully.'

'Thank you,' said Terence. 'And you must promise not to tell my sister until the new car is safely in the garage. She can be very bossy, you know.'

Lennie nodded. He knew.

62. Eddie Shows His True Colours

Marcia came round to the wine shop shortly after two on Monday afternoon. It was a good time to call, as the midday rush, when people took advantage of their lunch-break to do a bit of shopping, was over. If Marcia was in the area—as she often was—she would call and share a cup of tea and an apple with William in the back office. In the days of Paul—before his sudden defection to Oddbins—he would be left in charge while William chatted to Marcia. Now, of course, it was Jenny who took over, even though it was her first day in the shop and everything was very new to her.

'She's doing remarkably well,' said William, gesturing in the direction of the till, where his new assistant was attending to a smiling customer. 'Her first day, but it's very much a case of being to the manner born. A natural.'

Marcia looked through the open door of the office and took a thoughtful bite of her apple. She had been prepared to dislike Jenny on the grounds—and they were perfectly adequate ones, she thought—that she was a younger woman and she was now working in close proximity to William. But the welcome she had received from Jenny when she had come into the shop had been a warm one and clearly quite genuine, and that had taken the edge off her hostility. Then there was the matter of her own rather stronger position. For Marcia had that morning moved at least some of her possessions into Corduroy Mansions and was officially living in William's flat. From such heights of advantage, the threat posed by other women, even young and attractive women like Jenny, was perhaps not so acute. She could afford to be generous.

Looking back on it, she marvelled at the smoothness with which the whole move had been accomplished. William had shown little resistance, a passivity that she attributed to his utter weariness of Eddie's perverse refusal to move out. When, on Sunday morning, she had telephoned William and been told that Eddie had not come home the previous night, she had decided to take decisive action.

'Right. We go ahead.'

William had hesitated. 'I'm not sure that—'

But Marcia had pressed on. 'I'll come round,' she said. 'I'll finish what we started yesterday. I'll clear his room and dump his clothes in the hall.'

William had been privately appalled. He had never imagined that it would come to this, that he would effectively throw his own son out of the flat, but what were the alternatives? Every attempt at discussion, every offer of help with the purchase of a flat, every hint or offer of pastures green— elsewhere—had been ignored. Had Eddie been more considerate, had he made the slightest effort to recognise that his father also lived in the flat, it might have been different. But he had not, and William had reached the reluctant conclusion that Eddie wanted *him* out. And once he had come to that realisation, then the only thing to do was to assert himself by acting first. Had we been cavemen, he thought, it would have been a battle with old animal jawbones or whatever it was that cavemen used to settle family disputes. And the outcome, in those days, would have been clear: he would have been lying on the floor of the cave while his son took over as the dominant male.

Eddie had returned late on Sunday afternoon.

At first there had been an ominous silence. Sitting in the living room, a newspaper on his lap, William had glanced nervously at Marcia. 'He's back,' he whispered.

Marcia raised a finger to her lips. 'Wait.'

The silence ended. 'What's my stuff doing in the hall?'

Marcia indicated that there should be no reply.

'I said: what's my stuff doing in the hall? Are you deaf, Dad?'

A few moments later, Eddie burst into the living room. The presence of Marcia took him by surprise and he stood quite still for a moment while he took in the scene. In the corner of the room, Freddie de la Hay, who had been dozing on his rug, raised his head to sniff at the air.

'Your dad and I have decided to live together,' Marcia said calmly. 'So you'll have to move out, I'm afraid.'

Eddie stared at her in blunt incomprehension. 'I live here,' he said. 'This is my place.'

'No, it isn't, Eddie,' said Marcia, throwing William a discouraging glance. She would handle this. 'You see, it's normal for kids to move out . . . eventually. Your dad has tried and tried to help you to move on but you've never done anything about it. Now he's decided that enough is enough.' She paused. 'And if you look on the top of the pile of clothes in the hall there's a piece of paper with an address. That's a landlady who's agreed to give you a room for two weeks while you find somewhere yourself. Your dad has paid for that.'

Eddie, who had been glaring at Marcia, now turned to his father. 'Dad . . . ?'

'I really did try, Eddie,' said William. 'Remember the flat I found for you—the one that I offered the deposit for? And the housing association place . . . And . . .' He had tried; it was true. He had tried on numerous occasions, taking Eddie to letting agents, dictating advertisements for him—advertisements that attracted offers his son had no intention of replying to—in short, doing everything that a parent could possibly do to help his son get started by himself. And it had all been to no avail, which had made him wonder whether this was his sentence in life: to be saddled indefinitely with a dependent, layabout son. Did he really have to accept that? Was that a concomitant of parenthood, an inescapable moral burden of the act of reproduction?

He looked at Eddie hopelessly, but Eddie had turned to Marcia and was pointing a finger at her. '—,' he said. '—, —, —!'

'It's no good using that language, Eddie,' said William.

Marcia smiled. 'I've heard all that before, Eddie.'

'—,' screamed Eddie. '—!'

It was at this point that Freddie de la Hay, disturbed by the human conflict he was witnessing, rose from his rug and lifted his snout in the air. '—,' he howled. '—!'

'Look,' said William reproachfully, 'you've upset Freddie de la Hay.'

Eddie turned and stared at the dog. Then, walking swiftly across the room, he kicked him.

63. My Door is Always Open

Now, sitting in the office on Monday afternoon, Marcia and William could look back, if they wished, on that moment of truth and reflect on the efficacy of direct, unambiguous action. And it had been effective: Eddie had stormed out, taking, significantly, his sponge bag and his well-used duffel bag. The note with the address of the landlady had been torn up and thrown on the floor, but, curiously, it had been replaced with another note, this time in Eddie's hand, saying: 'Thanks a lot, Dad! After all those years, this is what I get! Anyway, when you eventually succeed in chucking that woman out of your life—and I feel really sorry for you, Dad—then get in touch with me at Stevie's place. I've written the address below. My door is always open, Dad. You know that. Blood is thicker than water, Dad!'

For William, the whole situation had become so painful that he preferred not to think about it. But at least the strategy had worked: Eddie had moved out and the lines of communication between them still appeared to be open. He would contact his son in a week or two. He would continue to pay the money that he transferred into Eddie's account each month. That would cover his rent and give him a bit left over. He had to do that; he could not cut him off altogether.

But now, in the office with Marcia, William found himself reflecting on the fact that the Eddie problem was by no means fully resolved. Even if Eddie settled in Stevie's flat, even if he found a reasonable job and stopped being a drain on the family finances, even if Eddie were to meet some respectable girl . . . Yes, respectable, thought William, and why should I be *ashamed* to use the word? What was wrong with being respectable? How had it become virtually a term of abuse, employed, if at all, with a snigger? It was time for respectable people to *strike back*, he felt. After years of being ridiculed and mocked, they would strike back and say . . . What would they say? We told you so? We told you that things would get like this and did you listen? You did not. You did not . . . He took a deep breath and returned to his original line of thought. Even if Eddie met a respectable girl and settled down with her, there was still the issue of his past and of the parcel that William and Marcia had found in his wardrobe.

'What are we going to do?' he asked Marcia as she passed him another cup of tea.

'About?'

'About the picture we found in Eddie's wardrobe.' He stared gloomily into his teacup. It was not easy to acknowledge that one's son was an art thief.

Marcia shrugged. 'Do we have to do anything?'

William watched her sip her tea. She was an attractive woman—in a slightly blowsy sort of way—and he enjoyed her company. But he was not entirely sure about her, and the answer she had just given caused him some concern. He wanted a soulmate—not just a flatmate—and he wondered how close he could be to somebody who thought that the presence of a stolen painting under one's roof was not a matter for immediate anxiety. Did women think about moral issues in a different way? Were they simply more pragmatic?

'I don't think we can just leave it,' said William. 'It must belong to somebody. There must be an owner somewhere who's missing it.'

Marcia thought about this. After a while she put down her cup and looked at William. 'So the painting's stolen—it's not our fault. Eddie's stolen it or is looking after it for somebody who stole it. But we didn't do any of that.'

William shook his head. 'No, Marcia, you're wrong. If you hold on to something that's been stolen, you're in trouble. It amounts to being in possession of stolen property. You can be prosecuted.'

Marcia seemed unconcerned. 'I still say that it's nothing to do with us. Return it to Eddie. Get rid of it. What else can we do?' She paused. 'Unless we go to the police. You could always do that, I suppose.'

It was not what William wanted to hear. He had, of course, considered the possibility, and in normal circumstances he would not have hesitated to hand in stolen property. But this was different. This was property that had been stolen by his own flesh and blood.

'I can't do that,' he said, his voice taking on a stressed, almost agonised tone. 'I can't turn in my own son.'

Marcia understood. 'Of course you can't.'

William rose to his feet and began to pace about the room. 'And yet . . . and yet there must be cases where you have to report a member of your family. What if you know that somebody in the family is a serial killer, for example? You don't keep quiet about that, do you?'

270

'It can't be very easy,' said Marcia. 'But Eddie's not a murderer, is he? Eddie's just a . . . well, Eddie's just a bit of a naughty boy. That's all.'

William did not seem to have heard her. He had stopped in front of the small window at the back of the office and was looking out of it. 'Of course, I could get the painting back to its owner,' he muttered.

He turned round and smiled at Marcia. 'That's the solution, Marcia. We return the painting. Discreetly. We set things right that way. Then I'm spared the duty of handing my own son over to the police.'

William waited while Marcia considered this. She looked doubtful. 'Maybe.'

'Just maybe? Don't you think it's the obvious thing to do?'

Marcia looked at her watch. She had an appointment with one of her suppliers and she needed to get going. 'The problem is,' she said, 'that we don't know the first thing about it. Whose is it? Where did Eddie get it?'

'We ask,' said William.

Marcia looked at William dubiously. 'Ask Eddie?'

That was not necessary, William explained. 'Something I read came back to me,' he said. 'I think I know where to go.'

Marcia looked at her watch again. Her seafood man, whom she was due to meet, always insisted on punctuality—which was a good thing, she thought, in a man who dealt in perishables. 'Where?' she asked. 'Where do we go?'

William waved a hand in the air, indicating the ether, the world of www.

64. Requin Trouvé

At the same time as William and Marcia were agonising, or William, at least, was agonising, over what to do about their awkward discovery in Eddie's wardrobe—their *damnosa hereditas*, as Roman lawyers might put it—Caroline and James, feeling the need for a late lunch, were peering into the window of a small bistro behind the British Museum. It was on a street of book and antique shops; to one side was a dusty dealership in antiquarian maps, and to the other a shop that specialised in Greek and Roman antiquities.

'That's what I really like about this area,' mused James. 'If somebody from the past slipped through a time warp and ended up standing on this street, he would not feel lost. Not at all. He'd look into that window next door and think: oh, a new lamp shop. Of course, the lamps are several thousand years old. And if he didn't know where he was, he could pop into that map shop and pick up a map of the Roman Empire. Or a map of Londinium.'

Caroline gazed at the menu displayed in the bistro window. Her mind was on quiche. Quiche could be dodgy: it was often soggy and very unappetising. Was she in a pasta mood? she asked herself. Perhaps. 'What are you talking about, James?'

'I'm talking about people who might find themselves in the wrong time. Through some quirk of physics.'

'Oh. Is pizziccata hot? I don't like those really hot chillies. I never have.'

'Not sure,' said James. 'Of course, nobody ever does, you know. Nobody wakes up and finds themselves in the wrong century. Mind you, some people just seem to have been in the wrong century from the beginning. Young fogeys, for instance. Do you know any young fogeys?'

Caroline kept her eyes on the menu. Reading menus always made her hungry and she heard her stomach growl softly. 'Young fogeys?' she said. 'You?'

'Very funny, Caroline,' said James. 'You don't listen to me, do you?'

Caroline prodded him playfully. 'Sometimes. But look, I'm really hungry and we can get quite a good lunch in here for . . . Well, look at the menu.'

'Poor dears,' said James. 'Restaurants are really struggling, aren't they?'

They went in. The restaurant was busy enough—what with the special promotions—but a table was just being vacated by another customer and they got that.

'Well then,' said James after they had given their order. 'Caravaggio.'

273

They had just attended a lecture on the artist given by a passionate lecturer whom James had described as 'a bit like Caravaggio himself, except, one assumes, for the violence'.

'One can hardly imagine,' he said, 'that a shrinking violet would be drawn to lecture on Caravaggio.' He paused. 'What do you think of Caravaggio, Caroline?'

'Too dramatic for me,' she said. 'I can't imagine that people of the time *writhed* quite as much as they do in his paintings.'

'Oh, I don't know,' said James. 'They were very expressive. It's just that we've become so cool. They would probably consider us very stiff.'

Caroline knew what he meant. 'It's very sad that people feel they have to be cool,' she said. 'They have to suppress all sense of joy and excitement.'

'Precisely,' said James. 'And colours too. All those blacks and greys. Everything is toned down— muted really. Imagine finding a Caravaggio. Imagine how the Queen felt when she discovered that what she thought was a copy was the real thing.'

'I suppose she's used to it,' said Caroline. 'But what about those Jesuits in Dublin who discovered a Caravaggio in their sitting room . . . ?'

'Their *parlour*,' corrected James. 'Jesuits have parlours, not sitting rooms. There's a difference, you know.'

'Which is?'

'A parlour is more formal. It's the place where you receive people. You don't sit around in a parlour; you do that in a sitting room or a living room—a drawing room if you're a bit grander.'

'Well, whatever. Just imagine it, though. You

have a rather dark old picture in your parlour, a picture that you think is a mere Honthorst.'

James corrected her again. 'Honthorst is not mere. He was a very important painter, one of the major Caravaggisti of his time. He was—'

'But he was not Caravaggio,' interrupted Caroline. 'And if you had a choice: Honthorst or Caravaggio? If the chips were really down and you had to choose.'

It was not a difficult choice. 'Caravaggio out of sheer avarice,' said James. 'Well, one has to eat, you know, and a Caravaggio would bring in millions. And he was a better painter too. That's always convenient. Choose somebody on aesthetic grounds but make sure that he's also the most expensive.'

'Yet value isn't the sole consideration,' argued Caroline. 'You can have artists fetching stratospheric prices and yet their work may be trite, banal even. Those people who do installations, for example. They fetch millions, but what are the people who buy such things actually getting?'

'A take on the world,' offered James. 'A fresh perspective on things. A new understanding of the everyday world. Visual surprise.'

Caroline was doubtful. 'Sometimes,' she said. 'But it's not real value we're talking about here. It's an inflated sense of value—like tulips in the Dutch tulip frenzy. Everybody thought they were worth millions until somebody said, 'Aren't those just common-or-garden tulip bulbs?' And that was the end of that.'

James toyed with his fork. 'You think contemporary art will go the same way?'

275

'I do. Of course it will. When people wake up.'

'So if I said, 'This fork is by you know who,' you might say, 'It's just a fork.' Right?'

Caroline said that she would.

'And the shark?' James asked.

'It's just a shark,' said Caroline. 'And whoever bought it must surely be sweating over the day that somebody stands up and says, "It's just a shark, for heaven's sake!"'

James smiled. 'I think they've already said it. And yet people still pay those prices at auction for that stuff.'

'They have to,' said Caroline. 'If they didn't, then what they already had would be worthless. You can't really sell sharks, you know. Particularly dead ones.'

'But I think you can,' said James, 'as long as you get people to believe it's an *important* dead shark.' He paused. 'That shark, you see, has been canonised.'

65. *Caravaggio as a Role Model for Boys*

James chose sparkling mineral water and a glass of house white. 'I shouldn't drink at lunchtime,' he said. 'And I normally don't. But all that Caravaggio, you know—what else can one do?'

'Did you see the film about him?' asked Caroline. 'The Derek Jarman film?'

James nodded. 'Caravaggio doesn't exactly come out of it very well. He had a penchant for knives. And that awful scene where he murders his model by slitting his throat.' He shuddered, and reached

276

for the sparkling mineral water. 'Do you think artists have to lead intense lives? Do you think that you can be a great artist and be bourgeois? Or does it all have to be very gritty? Caravaggiesque.'

Caroline considered this. 'Let's try to think of artists who were straightforward, conventional types. Can you think of any?'

James looked up at the ceiling. 'Difficult. It seems that the artistic personality has a certain contrariness to it. If you're conventional, then perhaps there's no impulse to create.'

Caroline helped herself to a small amount of James's water. 'So creativity comes from conflict? Inner conflict? You have to be *hurt* into making art?'

James thought that this was probably true. 'Art comes from a desire to make sense of the world and one's experience in it,' he intoned. 'It's intended to make up for the separation that we feel between us as humans and beauty. The artist tries to recreate beauty—to make it whole again.'

'If the artist is really concerned with beauty,' said Caroline.

James thought this self-evident. 'Surely he is?'

Caroline shook her head. 'No. I don't think so. Look at the sort of art we've just been discussing— installation art, the unmade beds and so on. Where's the beauty in that?'

James grinned. 'In an unmade bed?'

'Yes. How can that have anything to do with beauty?'

James thought for a moment. 'Ugliness can be beautiful,' he said. 'Anything can be beautiful. And maybe that's what a certain sort of artist is trying to do: he—or she, of course—is trying to open our

277

eyes to a beauty we would not otherwise see.'

Their plates arrived and were placed before them. Caroline looked at her pasta—all twisted shapes and beauty, an *installation* perhaps. She felt that she should say something about it, but the topic of generalised beauty took precedence over the particular, and certainly over the beauty to be found in pasta. James's last remark interested her; it was right in one way, but she thought that in another way it was wrong. If everything was beautiful—as he appeared to be suggesting—did that not deprive beauty of all its aesthetic, and indeed moral, force?

'How can everything be beautiful?' she asked. 'Human suffering, for example? Is that beautiful? A scene of carnage? A place where suffering has occurred?'

'Some things are horrible,' James said. 'Some things are hateful. What you've just mentioned is horrible, and hateful too, but surely it can be beautiful in the sense that it's part of our world, and our world, in its totality, is beautiful?'

'Rubbish,' said Caroline. And then added, 'What about a discordance in music? Is that beautiful?'

James looked at her reproachfully. 'You're being very aggressive,' he said. 'Why don't you eat your lunch instead of attacking me and everything I say? Go on, eat your lunch, you horrid girl!'

He laughed, and she laughed too. Dear James: he was so unlike . . . so unlike Caravaggio. She reached out and put her hand on his, just for a moment. The contact was brief, fleeting, but she noticed that he tensed; she could tell. She cast her eyes down to her plate. 'Don't you like to be touched?' she asked.

His manner was one of affected nonchalance. 'I don't mind,' he said.

'But you flinched just then, when I put my hand on yours. You did, you know.'

He frowned. 'Maybe I did. It's just that I'm not used to being touched. I like to think of myself as quite tactile, but only when *I'm* in control, when I'm the one doing the touching. I suppose I'm just not used to not being in control.'

Caroline sighed. 'That's sad. It really is.'

James looked up. 'I know. But it's difficult, sometimes, to deal with something you know you want to change. You can't just do it like that.' He clicked his fingers. 'You have to understand why it is that you feel the way you do and then you have to tackle it.'

Caroline was silent. 'Did something unsettling happen to you, James?' she asked. 'Is that why . . .?'

James met her gaze. I love his eyes, she thought. Nobody I know has such sensitive eyes. Like the eyes of a Botticelli model. Wide. Light brown.

'There was something,' said James. 'Something I saw a long time ago. I don't really like to talk about it, though.'

'Then you don't need to,' said Caroline.

He seemed to mull this over for a few moments. 'No, maybe I do. Maybe that's what I really have to do. Think about it. Talk about it.' He took a sip from his wine glass. 'I read somewhere that this is exactly what you should do. You should talk about the thing that frightens you and in that way you deprive it of its power.'

Caroline listened carefully. She had suspected ever since their conversation over homemade

279

lemon gems that there was something that had to be dealt with in James's past and now she knew that it was so. He was undoubtedly right: one had to confront these things if one wanted to lance the boil that they represented. In her own case, there had been the incident at the pony club, which she had brooded over for years, until somebody—somebody quite unconnected with the pony club—had casually mentioned it and it had all come pouring out. That was when she had discovered that what had seemed large was, in fact, small—ridiculously so—and suddenly she was able to talk about the pony club again without feeling guilty. I did not cheat, she said to herself. I did not. But although she was convinced of the liberating power of revelation, she was not sure that this bistro, over lunch, was quite the right place and time to encourage James to talk.

'Perhaps we should talk about it some other time,' she said gently. 'I don't want you to think that I'm not willing to listen—I am, I really am. It's just that . . .'

James looked at her imploringly. 'I want to talk, Caroline. I want to tell you about what I saw behind the cricket pavilion . . .'

'Of course you can . . . But couldn't we go back to the flat? Go back to Corduroy Mansions and talk there?'

James shook his head. 'The moment is sometimes right,' he said. 'And . . . Well, I feel *secure* here. Do you understand?'

She reached out to take his hand again but stopped herself in time. He saw this and smiled. 'No, please go ahead. It seems right. Please go ahead. I'll talk. You hold my hand. I'll talk.'

But she did not have the opportunity. Two men at a neighbouring table had just paid their bill and one of them now stood up and looked intently in her direction.

66. Tim Something Sits Down

'It is you, isn't it?' said Tim Something.

Caroline looked up at the man who had come across to their table and was standing before them. He had been lunching with somebody—a man with a moustache—who was obviously in a hurry because he was already at the door and waving perfunctorily to his erstwhile companion.

The thought occurred to her that the answer to this question of whether one is one must always be yes. If somebody says 'It is you, isn't it?' then what else can one answer? No? That would only be possible if one read into the question a proper noun—implicit and unspecified—immediately after the pronoun. Of course it was her, but perhaps not the *her* this man had in mind. And then she realised. Tim Something!

'Tim,' she said weakly. 'It is *you*, isn't it?'

Tim laughed. 'Of course it is. Well, I hope it is. It's me.'

Caroline felt warm with embarrassment. Tim Something was not somebody she wanted to meet—or not with James. She remembered the conversation she had had with James in which he had made light of those pictures of young women in the front of that country magazine, and she had said nothing, had failed to confess to him that she

281

herself had in fact been one of those young women. Now here was Tim Something, the very photographer who had taken the photograph, and he would be bound to mention that fact. James would look at her and remember that he had made a joke about it and realise that all the time she must have been squirming. And then he would feel guilty about not having known how cruel his words must have seemed to her.

Tim looked at James. 'I'm Tim Something,' he said, extending a hand.

Caroline almost blurted out: *But he doesn't like to be touched!* Here was James, coming for a quiet lunch after a lecture on Caravaggio, and suddenly everybody was touching him.

But James did not seem to mind. He reached up and took Tim's proffered hand and shook it. Yet he dropped it quite quickly, thought Caroline; it had not been a lingering handshake.

'Tim what?' asked James. 'I didn't quite get your name.'

'Something,' said Tim.

James glanced at Caroline. 'Tim Something,' she muttered.

James looked increasingly puzzled.

Caroline decided to take the initiative. 'How are things, Tim? Are you working in London?'

Before Tim Something could answer, Caroline turned to James and said, 'I know Tim from Oxford.'

'Yes,' said Tim, 'I took a—'

'When was it, Tim?' Caroline interrupted. 'Over two years ago now, wasn't it?'

'What?' asked James.

'I haven't seen Tim for a couple of years, I think,'

Caroline went on. 'And now, well . . . London. What are you doing, Tim?'

There was a third, unoccupied chair at their table, which Tim now lowered himself into. 'Do you mind?'

Caroline wanted to say, yes, I mind a lot. I was talking to my friend James and he was about to say something important, something really important to him, and maybe to me . . . And then you came along and sat down at our table *uninvited* and . . .

'Yes,' said Tim, leaning his elbows on the table. 'I do a bit of work over in Oxford and thereabouts from time to time—I've still got a flat there, you know—but most of the time I'm in London. More work here. And I must say that I got a bit fed up with taking those photographs of village fetes and . . .' He paused, and smiled at Caroline. 'County-ish girls for the inside page of the mag. Sorry, Caroline!'

'What mag?' asked James.

'You should ask her,' said Tim with a grin. He nodded in Caroline's direction. 'There's this mag that county types read and they love having—'

'What sort of work do you get in London?' Caroline blurted out.

Tim turned back to face her. 'This and that. Some social stuff, quite a lot of business-related work. The City. Men in suits sitting in boardrooms or behind desks. I do them really well, you know. You have to make them look solid and reliable but not too dull. Apparently there's a look that's just right. You see the photo and you think: that chap's got ideas. And sometimes I photograph the odd actor or author. That chap who bought me lunch— you probably saw him leaving the restaurant—

283

Christopher Catherwood, I've just taken his photograph for a magazine.'

Caroline wondered whether James was getting annoyed with Tim and his interruption of their conversation. But if he was, he did not show it. In fact, he seemed quite pleased that Tim had sat down at their table. Perhaps, she thought, James did not really want to speak about whatever it was that he had been going to speak about—in which case he probably welcomed Tim's arrival.

'So you were at Oxford Brookes with Caroline?' James asked Tim. 'Did you study art history too?'

Tim shook his head. 'No. I was at Bath Spa University. They have a degree course in photography. I did that.'

Caroline saw her opportunity to navigate the conversation away from perilous shoals. 'Bath Spa is terrific,' she said. 'I had a friend who did design there. She had a great time.'

'When?' asked Tim.

'When she was there. She had a great time when she was there.'

'No, I didn't mean that,' said Tim. 'I meant: when was she at Bath Spa?'

'Oh, same time that I was at Oxford Brookes.'

'Then I wouldn't have known her. When you were at Oxford Brookes was when I took that—'

Caroline interrupted again. 'She was called Stella.'

Tim looked interested. 'I knew a Stella. What was her name again? Her surname? You know, you forget these things. Stella . . .'

'Stella Something,' suggested James.

Tim looked at him. He opened his mouth to say something—or something other than Something—

284

but Caroline seized the initiative again. They needed to talk about anything but photographs and country magazines. Anything.

'I think she's no longer with us,' she said. 'The Stella I knew, that is.'

James looked puzzled. 'What do you mean? She died?'

Caroline looked away. Stella did not exist. She never had. And now she was proposing to kill her off. No, she could not do that.

'She went to France,' she said wildly.

'Why?' asked James.

Tim Something looked amused. 'I can think of plenty of reasons to go to France! Where do you start?'

'She met this French boy,' muttered Caroline.

'That's a good enough reason to go to France,' said Tim, glancing at James.

'I didn't like him,' Caroline went on; how easily were the lives of others invented. 'But she did. They went to live in Paris. And then . . .' She trailed off.

Both Tim and James were looking at her expectantly.

'Then what?' asked James. 'You know, it's a fascinating story. This Stella person! You've simply got to tell us more, Caroline. I've got to know!'

'Then she found out that he wasn't French at all,' she said. 'He was Italian.'

James snorted. 'Is that it?'

'I've remembered the name of the Stella I knew,' said Tim Something. 'Stella Lachfield. An unusual name. I took her photograph for the mag.' He looked up at the ceiling. 'Quite soon after I took yours, Caroline.'

67. Where's Freddie de la Hay?

Marcia told William that after she had seen her seafood supplier she would go back to Corduroy Mansions to carry on with the task of sorting out Eddie's room.

'I hope that he's picked up the rest of his clothes,' she said, 'because if he hasn't, I'm going to give them to a charity shop.'

This brought a sharp intake of breath from William. It was one thing to bundle Eddie's clothes out of his room; it was quite another to give them away. Did they have the right to do that? Could anybody give away somebody else's clothes, or was it simple theft? Marcia was showing a fairly cavalier attitude to the law, what with her apparent indifference to the presence of the stolen painting and now her willingness to dispose of Eddie's property. He would have to watch this and, if necessary, start educating her as to the requirements of the law-abiding life.

'I really don't think we can give his stuff away,' he protested. 'It doesn't belong to us, you know.'

Marcia had no time for such niceties. 'It's in your flat, isn't it? Surely you've got the right to dispose of things from your flat?'

William was doubtful. 'I don't think so.'

'But you must have,' said Marcia. 'Otherwise it would be ridiculous. Listen, if I came and dumped something in your flat without your permission—just dumped it in the hall, let's say—surely you have every right to put it out on the street? After all, you didn't ask me to bring it, whatever it is.'

William thought about this. People obviously could not land their property on others but Eddie had not done that anyway; his property was in the flat because he lived there. That, William felt, made a big difference.

'I'm still not sure,' he said. 'Look, here's an example. Let's say that I go and stay in a hotel.'

Marcia smiled sweetly. 'All right. Let's say that you and I go and stay in a hotel.'

William froze. He had not said *you and I*, he was sure of it. He would have to correct her; he could not let it pass.

'I go and stay in a hotel—' he continued pointedly.

Marcia interrupted him. 'You know, that's what Eddie has taken you for all these years. A hotel. He's treated you as if you were a hotel.'

'All children treat their parents like that,' William mused. 'It's the way they think of home. Anyway, let's say that I go and stay in a hotel but leave my pyjamas behind. Can the hotel—?'

He did not complete the question. 'Of course, some people don't wear pyjamas,' Marcia muttered.

William faltered. What was this? A comment? A confession? A come-on? He raised his voice to prevent further interruptions. 'I leave something behind. A tie, then. Can the hotel just give it away?'

Marcia looked thoughtful. 'Well, it depends, doesn't it? A tie is nothing very much. So I think they could probably get rid of it. They can't send on everything their guests leave. Where would you draw the line?'

'So they hold on to anything of any value?'

Marcia shrugged. 'I suspect that's what they do. Although I don't really know. I imagine that the staff just pocket most things.'

William sighed. He had brought up the hotel analogy but he did not feel that it had helped. 'Well, I don't think that Eddie's stuff is in quite the same category,' he said. 'And I also don't think that you should give it away. We'll find room in a cupboard somewhere, or I'll take it over to Stevie's place in the car.'

The matter was left there, and when William went home after work he discovered that Marcia, having arrived a few minutes before, had bundled some of Eddie's clothes into a cupboard. Although he said nothing, William was pleased that she had heeded his advice; he had never been sure whether Marcia listened to anything he said, but at least in this case she appeared to have done so.

He stood in the hall, watching her push the last of Eddie's possessions into the cupboard. 'Is Freddie de la Hay sleeping?' he asked.

'I suppose so,' said Marcia. 'I haven't looked for him. He must be in that smelly dog bed of his.'

William raised an eyebrow. He did not like Freddie's bed to be described as smelly; it was not. At least, it was no smellier than any other dog bed. Of course it smelled of dog, which was what Freddie de la Hay was. Did Marcia expect it to smell of anything different?

He left the hall and went into the living room. There was the bed, but there was no sign of Freddie. He now felt a twinge of alarm.

'He didn't slip out when you came back, did he?' he shouted to Marcia.

And she called back from the hall, 'No. I didn't

see him at all.'

William looked about the room. A cat might conceal itself in some odd place and bide its time before announcing its presence. A dog would never do that. Dogs were *transparent*, he thought; you knew where you stood with a dog.

He called Freddie's name and went into the kitchen to see if he was there. He was not. Nor was he in the bathroom or any of the other rooms in the flat.

'Freddie de la Hay's missing,' he said to Marcia. 'He's not here.'

Marcia groaned. 'Eddie,' she said.

'What about Eddie?'

'Eddie's stolen Freddie de la Hay,' she said.

William closed his eyes. 'Why on earth would he do that?'

The answer was clear—to Marcia at least. 'To get at you,' she said. 'Eddie has decided to punish you and so he's taken your dog.'

William sat down. 'Oh no,' he said. 'Do you really think so?'

'It's obvious,' said Marcia. 'You know what Eddie's like. He'll have said to himself: 'Son Liberates Dog from Mean Father'. You know how he talks.'

William was silent.

68. The Dog House

William had put up with a great deal from Eddie but this was too much. He was not given to displays of anger but now, watched by Marcia, who very much approved of the change in her friend's demeanour, his cheeks and brow flushed choleric.

'That's it!' he shouted. 'That's it!'

'Yes,' said Marcia. 'It is. It's it all right!'

She waited for William to say something more but he just stood there, looking red in the face.

'Well?' said Marcia.

'I'm going over to Stevie's place. I'm going to fetch my dog.'

Marcia got up and reached for her coat. 'I'm coming too,' she said. She was secretly pleased that Eddie had taken Freddie de la Hay, not because she had anything against Freddie, whom she was nevertheless planning to get rid of sooner rather than later, but because she relished the thought of a further confrontation between William and Eddie. It would firm up matters in her direction, she thought: the more that William was freed of his son, the more he would come to rely on her. And that, at the end of the day, was exactly what she wanted.

As for Freddie de la Hay, the beginnings of a plan had already been made. Being aware of the dog's background, she had made a discreet enquiry of a friend who occupied a senior position in catering at Heathrow airport. Did this friend know if the sniffer-dog department was short of dogs? Would a former sniffer dog be at all welcome if there were any vacancies?

The friend reported back within a few hours. She had spoken to somebody who knew about these things and the answer was an enthusiastic yes.

'It's been a disaster,' Marcia's friend said over the telephone. 'You know that they sacked half of the dogs in order to make vacancies for female dogs? It was something to do with equal opportunities and gender balance.'

Yes, Marcia had heard about it. William had told her about Freddie's background and about his sacrifice on the altar of equal rights.

'Well, it hasn't worked,' said the friend. 'The female dogs are all over the place. Apparently they keep sniffing out perfume in people's bags. And then, to make matters worse, all the male dogs proved to be more interested in the female dogs than in suitcases. So all hell broke loose, with the male dogs going after the female dogs and carrying on like nobody's business. Now they want to try to

291

get the male dogs back.'

This information was exactly what Marcia had wanted to hear and she filed it away in her mind. Freddie de la Hay could be quietly relocated in the fullness of time—back to Heathrow, where he belonged and where he obviously had a brilliant career awaiting him. And as for William, well, her recent victory at insinuating herself into the flat—taking her rightful place, as she preferred to call it—had demonstrated that there was no difficulty there. William could be managed.

They drove over to Stevie's flat in Marcia's van. William calmed down on the way but was clearly still angry. Marcia listened sympathetically, nodding her agreement at appropriate points.

'I've given him everything,' said William. 'Everything. And now he steals my dog.'

'Yes,' said Marcia. 'Typical.'

'And Freddie,' said William. 'What will he be thinking? He hardly knows Eddie and I suspect that he doesn't like him very much after Eddie kicked him. Dogs don't forget that sort of thing, you know.'

'No, they don't,' said Marcia. Although in fact she thought that they did. Lots of dogs were ill-treated and then appeared to forgive the humans who had subjected them to all sorts of cruelties. Dogs were like that.

They parked outside the address that Eddie had written down, a shabby terrace house in wedding-cake white, now divided into flats. William had been told that the flat was on the first floor, and he looked up to see if there were any lights on. There were not; the windows were in darkness.

They got out of the van and walked up to the

292

front door. William saw Stevie's name on a button: *Potts*. He pressed it.

They waited a minute, and then William pressed the button again.

'The pub,' Marcia muttered.

William agreed that this was the most likely place. 'The Dog House,' he said. 'That's the pub they go to. How appropriate.'

He knew the way. Eddie took him there on his birthday each year—William paying, of course—so he knew where it was. Stevie went there as well, and on one occasion William had paid for his drinks too, and for the drinks of Stevie's girlfriend, Poosie. He had ended up paying for everybody, in fact, and Eddie had said at the end of the evening, when he, William, had thanked him, 'My pleasure, Dad. Any time.'

Marcia parked the van in a nearby street and they made their way to where the Dog House, with its large, welcoming windows, dominated a street corner. William glanced through the windows hoping to catch a glimpse of Eddie but the pub was busy and he could not see him.

'Now listen,' said Marcia as they went through the door, 'don't let him sweet-talk you in any way. He's in the wrong, remember.'

William nodded grimly. But righteous anger is all very well when one is on one's home ground; here at the Dog House he was on Eddie's turf.

'See him?' asked Marcia, peering about the dimly lit bar.

William shook his head. 'I'll ask somebody,' he said.

He looked about him. Immediately to his left, a small group of people around a table had the air of being locals. He tapped one gently on the shoulder and the man looked up at him.

'You don't know Eddie French, do you?'

'Yup. I know him.'

'Has he been in?'

The man looked at his fellow drinkers. 'Anybody seen Eddie?'

'Yes,' said one. 'He was in when I turned up. He went off a few minutes ago. Him and Stevie and that girl who hangs around with Stevie. They went off with that geezer who owns Diesel. I saw them going up the lane there—over there. See? That one. Few minutes ago.'

William turned to Marcia upon hearing this information. Diesel? Who, or what, was Diesel? And what would be going on in the lane?

69. *Freddie de la Hay in Peril*

'I don't like the sound of this,' said Marcia.

'Nor do I,' muttered William. He wondered how well he knew his own son. Not very well, it appeared, what with the discovery of stolen property in his wardrobe and now finding him consorting in the pub with somebody who owned something called Diesel.

They walked swiftly and in silence a short distance up the road to the small lane that the man in the pub had indicated. It was a narrow one-way street, barely large enough to allow the passage of a vehicle, and not a very wide vehicle at that. On either side were shop windows—a barber's, a cramped newsagent, an Indian restaurant from which an enticing smell of spices drifted.

'No sign of them,' said William, peering through the window of the restaurant to see if he could see Eddie and his friends within. 'Is this the right place, do you think?'

Marcia had spotted an entrance further up to the right—the mouth of a close or a small courtyard, she thought. 'Let's take a look up there,' she said.

The entrance, a gangway between two buildings, was little more than a passage, dark even on this summer evening and slightly malodorous in an indefinable way. But as they entered it they heard sounds coming from the far end, and William stopped when he recognised Eddie's laugh. He caught Marcia by the sleeve and pointed ahead.

'That's them,' he whispered. 'That was Eddie's laugh.'

'Right,' Marcia whispered back. 'Let's go and see what they're up to.' She had an idea already but hardly dared utter it. Now a barking sound drifted up the passage and she knew that she was right.

At the end of the passage, tucked away to one side, was something midway between a courtyard and a postage stamp of waste ground. As they came upon it, they saw Eddie to one side of the space, next to Stevie and Poosie, and on the other side was a thick-set man with a shaved head and a tattooed neck. And there was Freddie de la Hay, held at the collar by Stevie and facing a large white bull terrier that was, like its owner, extensively tattooed. As they came upon this scene, the bull terrier had just been released by his owner and was glaring at Freddie de la Hay, his teeth exposed in hostile rictus, emitting a low growling sound.

It was what Marcia had suspected—an organised

dog fight.

'Eddie!' shouted William. 'What on earth are you doing?'

Eddie spun round to face his father, staring at him speechlessly.

'What does it look like, mate?' shouted the thick-set man. 'This is private business, innit? Get lost.'

The bull terrier looked briefly at William and snarled. This was Diesel.

'I said get lost!' shouted Diesel's owner again. 'Or shut up and watch.'

Stevie was busy with Freddie's leash and collar, while Freddie stared in dread at Diesel and growled defensively.

'Eddie!' cried William again.

'Go back to the pub,' Eddie said. 'We'll come and see you later. We're having some private fun.'

'Fun!' exclaimed William.

Stevie chose to intervene. 'Yeah, fun, Mr French,' he said. 'A bit of innocent fun.'

'This is preposterous,' said William. 'That's my dog, for a start.'

'Listen, mate,' shouted the other man, 'Diesel here is getting very irritated with you. So just shut your cake-hole . . .'

'Come on, Dad,' said Eddie. 'This is just a bit of fun. Where's your sense of humour?'

Poosie now looked at William. 'Yes, don't be so old!'

'Old!' exploded William. 'Who's old?'

'You,' said Poosie. 'You're acting seriously old.'

'Tart,' said Marcia.

Diesel now took a few steps forward. He was an extremely muscular dog and he walked a little as a drunken sailor might walk—swaying slightly from side to side. William looked in alarm at Freddie de la Hay, who had now been released by Stevie. 'Chew him up, Freddie boy,' said Stevie. 'Go for the jugular.'

In a moment of great clarity, William realised that anybody who got between the dogs would be in danger of being badly mauled—not by Freddie, of course, but by the mesomorphic Diesel. Yet he was in no doubt that if he did not intervene, this would be the end of Freddie de la Hay. Valiant though Freddie undoubtedly was, he would be no match for the steroid-fed Diesel, the worst sort of dog in terms of attitude.

William took a deep breath. Then, directing himself towards Diesel, he shouted in as stern a voice as he could manage, 'Diesel!'

Diesel hesitated and looked towards William.

'Diesel!' William continued in stentorian tones. 'Diesel, sit! Sit!'

For a moment Diesel looked confused, and then sat down firmly. He was well trained, like a Royal Marine, and when told to sit, he sat.

Diesel's owner looked on in astonishment while William stepped firmly forward and snatched Freddie de la Hay's leash from Stevie's hand. Attaching it quickly to Freddie's collar, he led the relieved dog back to Marcia, took her by the arm and walked at a fast pace down the passage.

Eddie shouted out something, as did Diesel's owner, but neither William nor Marcia heard what it was, nor bothered to listen.

'Chutzpah!' said Marcia as they turned onto the lane. 'William, you're brilliant!'

'Oh, I don't know,' said William. 'It seemed the obvious thing to do.' He spoke casually but inside he was shaking with a mixture of relief, fear and sheer astonishment at his own performance. It could have ended quite differently, he thought. What if Diesel had ignored him or possibly not understood the way he spoke? Freddie could be dead by now if that had happened.

They went back to the van and Freddie de la Hay hopped into the back while William sat in the passenger seat, wiped his brow with his handkerchief and closed his eyes. Marcia could detect a state of shock when she saw it, and she held William's hand gently before she started the car.

'We'll go home and have a nice dinner,' she said. 'I've got some scallops. And we'll give Freddie de la Hay a steak.'

William opened his eyes. 'He's a vegetarian,' he said. 'Remember?'

'Was,' said Marcia.

70. At the Ragg Porter Agency

That Monday was not proving to be a particularly busy day at the Ragg Porter Literary Agency, and the three directors—Barbara (non-fiction), Sheila Stevens (films and other media) and Rupert Porter (fiction)—had taken the opportunity to have their quarterly planning meeting somewhat in advance of its normal date. The agency was doing well, having recently taken over the administration of the estate of a deceased novelist who had suddenly—and posthumously—become immensely successful. They were now looking at the list of

298

their existing authors with a view to guessing which of them might be expected to die in the short rather than the long term, and which of these might enjoy a sudden burst of posthumous popularity.

'It seems such a pity that some people have to pass on in order to be widely read,' said Sheila.

Barbara winced. 'For heaven's sake don't use that term,' she said. 'Passing on! What a euphemism. Call it what it is. You die when you die, you don't pass on. Where do you pass on to, may I ask?'

Rupert came to his colleague's defence. 'Oh, I don't know,' he said. 'Passing on sounds very reassuring. Rather stately, in fact. And who knows where we go after this mortal vale? My housemaster at Uppingham used to talk about the Elysian Fields as if they really existed. I think he may have believed in them. Probably did.'

Barbara gave him a glance. They heard a great deal from Rupert about Uppingham.

'Well, that's very nice,' she said.

Rupert did not pick up her sarcasm. 'Yes, indeed

299

it was. He used to give us little talks and, do you know, everybody listened. Even the chaps who were not very academic. They sat there and listened. He explained that the Elysian Fields were probably restricted to those connected with the gods in some way; ordinary people had to go to the Fields of Asphodel, if I remember correctly. Not quite so comfortable.'

'Like standard class on the trains,' suggested Sheila.

Rupert nodded. 'Yes, I suppose so. That's quite a good analogy, in fact. Indeed, one might expand it and apply it to Christian notions of the afterlife. First class would be heaven, while standard class would be hell, or purgatory.'

'That depends on the line,' said Sheila. 'Some lines are all right, the others, well . . . Why do we tolerate it? Why do we tolerate having the worst train service in western Europe? And one of the most expensive ones in the whole world?'

'Because we privatised the railways,' Barbara said. 'The French and the Germans warned us. They said: 'It's not going to work.' And we ignored them, and look at us now. Dirty trains. Not enough seats. Nowhere to put your luggage. When you get into the train in France, for example, there's always bags of room to stow your suitcase. They assume, you see, that people are going to travel with a suitcase. Radical assumption!'

'So what are we going to do about it?' asked Rupert.

They looked at one another. 'Well, frankly,' said Barbara, 'I don't see that there's much that Ragg Porter can do about it. So I suggest that we get on with our meeting.'

'All right,' said Rupert. And then, with the air of one who had just remembered something, 'Oh, I took a call for you, Barbara, while you were out for lunch.'

'Yes?'

'Yes,' said Rupert. 'It was a journalist. I noted his number down somewhere. He wanted to know about that Greatorex manuscript of yours.'

Rupert now had Barbara's full attention. 'Greatorex?' How had the press got to hear of this?

'Yes. That's the yeti biography, isn't it?' said Rupert. 'Not that I believe it for one moment. At Uppingham we had a chap who had climbed quite a few of those mountains in Nepal. He said that the yeti was complete nonsense.'

Barbara gave him a withering look. 'That is a matter of opinion. Errol Greatorex is a highly regarded travel writer.' She held Rupert's gaze. 'And may I remind you of the advance we're going to be getting for this particular manuscript? And serialisation rights sold to the *Sunday Telegraph*. So don't talk this thing down, Rupert.'

Rupert put up his hands in mock defence. 'All right.'

Barbara still looked at him severely. 'Who was this person, anyway?' she asked.

'Somebody from *The Times*,' he said. 'He said that he had been talking to an MP he knows who told him that you had this manuscript and that you could arrange an interview for him.'

Barbara's eyes glinted. 'Which MP, may I ask?' She knew the answer, of course.

Rupert laughed. 'Your boyfriend. Oedipus Snark.' He paused. 'Pillow talk getting out of hand,

Barbara?'

Barbara ignored this and they moved on to the next topic on the meeting agenda. But immediately after the meeting she got the journalist's telephone number from Rupert. She would have to handle this carefully, she thought. If the story broke prematurely, then the large advance that she was confident of securing for her author might be compromised. The point about the yeti book was that it would have impact, and the leaking of the story beforehand could substantially diminish that.

The journalist was available and took Barbara's call.

'So what's the story?' he asked. 'Is it true that you've got the biography of the abominable snowman?'

Barbara laughed. 'Who on earth told you that?'

'Somebody. You know that we don't reveal our sources.'

'Well, I know exactly who it was: Oedipus Snark. And yes, it's true that I spoke to him about this. But it was a joke. A complete joke. I didn't expect Oedipus to take it any further. I assumed that he'd know that the whole thing was absurd.'

The journalist was silent. 'You mean there's no yeti?'

Barbara laughed. 'Of course there's no yeti. Sorry about that. And no Father Christmas either.'

The journalist sounded disappointed. 'Oh well,' he said. 'The best-laid scoops of mice and men . . .'

'Well put,' said Barbara, and rang off.

She stood at the window and thought. Oedipus Snark could spoil everything unless he were stopped. But how did you stop somebody like that? Threaten him with something? But what could she threaten Oedipus Snark with? Unless . . .

71. On the Nature of Friendship

She was still thinking of the yeti—and Oedipus Snark—when she reached the door of her building in Chepstow Villas. Like William French, Barbara Ragg lived on the top floor, but that was where the similarities between his and her domestic arrangements ended. Corduroy Mansions was nowhere near as well appointed as Sydney Villa, the house in which Barbara had lived for the last twelve years. Her flat in Sydney Villa, a four-floor building of generously sized apartments—one to each floor—had belonged to Fatty Porter, the business partner of Barbara's late father, Gregory Ragg. When Fatty had stopped working and moved to Norfolk, he had sold the flat to Gregory, who had lived in it for little more than a year before he too retired and took up residence in Kent. Gregory had given the flat to Barbara, much to the annoyance of Rupert Porter, who thought that his father would not have sold the flat to Gregory had he known that Gregory intended it for his daughter.

'I would have loved to live there, Dad,' Rupert had complained to his father. 'Gregory knew all along that Barbara wanted it. Why should she be there and I'm stuck in my smelly old place?' His smelly old place was in fact a rather pleasant flat in Holland Park, not far away from Sydney Villa. What really rankled Rupert was that the transaction had meant that he could not fulfil his

303

ambition to have two flats rather than one.

Not that Rupert and Barbara did not get on—they sparred a little, as colleagues will do, but beneath there were the strong bonds that bind those who are members of families that have run a business together over more than one generation. And Fatty and Gregory themselves had been very close friends—both members of the Savile Club, where they dined together once a week and where Fatty had for many years sat on the catering committee. Rupert and Barbara were not quite as close, because Barbara had never really got on with any of Rupert's girlfriends, nor, after he married, with his wife, Gloria.

'She doesn't like me,' said Gloria. 'I can sense it. You know how you can sense dislike. You just feel it.'

'Negative waves,' said Rupert. 'You can pick up negative waves. But do you think Barbara really doesn't like you? She seems civil enough.'

'Yes, civil,' said Gloria. 'But have you noticed that when she's talking to us, she always looks at you? Have you noticed that? Even if she's saying something to me, she looks at you.'

'There was a chap like that at Uppingham,' mused Rupert. 'He always looked at somebody else when he spoke to you. Strange chap.' He paused. 'Maybe she looks at me just because she's used to my face. She sees it at the office all the time and so she's used to it.'

Gloria shook her head. 'I think it's because she's jealous. Deep down, she's jealous of me. You were her friend—ever since you were small. You went to each other's birthday parties, didn't you? Right from the beginning.'

Rupert smiled. 'She's not jealous,' he said. 'She's just a friend. There's never been anything more than that between us.'

Gloria did not doubt that—at least from Rupert's point of view. But she was a woman, after all, and she had views on how women felt about their male friends. No male friend, she believed, was ever just a friend. His potential for being something else was always, even if only subconsciously, evaluated, thought about.

'And anyway,' Rupert went on, 'she's got that awful boyfriend of hers. That Snark. Oedipus Snark, no less. I was at Uppingham with him, you know. What on earth was a mother doing calling her son Oedipus? What can she have been thinking of?'

'I can't stand him,' said Gloria. 'Remember when Barbara managed to persuade him to come and open the Elizabethan Fair in the gardens and he turned up twenty minutes late and left after five minutes? Ghastly man. Insincere. Untrustworthy. Strange that he should be a Liberal Democrat. Not a trace of sandals.'

'I don't care for him a great deal,' said Rupert. 'It's funny, when we were at school there was another boy and the two of them looked quite alike. Not alike in any other way, just their looks. A chap called Ratty Mason, poor fellow. None of us knew, or even suspected.'

Gloria frowned. She had not heard of Ratty Mason before and felt that she needed to find out more. But not now; now she was thinking of friendship between men and women. She was wondering how possible it was for a woman to form a friendship with another woman who was

305

principally a friend of her husband or her lover. Could one do that, or were there always going to be tensions underneath the surface? And in her particular, difficult case, was the problem hers or was it Barbara's? Barbara might not be jealous of her being married to Rupert; it might be she who was jealous of Barbara. Was that the way it was?

'Do you think that a woman can have a friendship—a strong friendship—with a man?' she asked.

'Depends on what sort of friendship you're talking about,' said Rupert. 'If you're talking about the type of friendship that D. H. Lawrence goes on about, then . . . well, I'm not sure. I suppose man–woman friendships are different.'

'Different from what?'

'From the friendships that men have.'

Gloria looked at her husband. He was always talking about a whole cast of friends, but she very rarely saw any of them; nor, she thought, did he. 'David and Jonathan?' she asked. 'That sort of friendship?'

'Not many men have that,' said Rupert. 'Most men have rather distant relations with their male friends. Whereas women are much more emotionally engaged with their female friends. They love their friends. They're much better at that than we men are.'

Gloria thought that Rupert was generalising rather too much: there were some men with a great talent for friendship; there were some, too, who were emotionally engaged with their friends to the same extent as were women. But then there were so many men who were, quite simply, lonely; who did not seem to know how to conduct a friendship.

There were legions and legions of those.

But now she came back to the other question that was troubling her: who was Ratty Mason? Wives believe they know their husbands, but often do not—not really—she now realised. There are whole hinterlands that they do not see: old friends never mentioned, private sorrows, worries about virility, doubts and disappointments. And men go through life bearing all these in the name of masculinity and manliness, until it all becomes too much and they dissolve into tears.

'Who was Ratty Mason? Tell me about him.'

Rupert shook his head. 'No,' he said. 'Can't.'

72. *Rupert's Insecurities*

Barbara Ragg, of course, had not been troubled by Rupert's feelings over her flat for the simple reason that he had never expressed them within her hearing. There had been the occasional comment that was mildly suggestive of envy, but nothing unambiguous. That would have been difficult; one person could hardly say to another that he considered her house to be his by right. Although there were cases where that was said—at an international level—by those who eyed with intent the land and dwellings of others. Such claims are made here and there in our troubled world by bullies and expansionists of every stripe. But Rupert was not one of these—not by the remotest stretch of the imagination—and so he never revealed to Barbara the views he discussed with Gloria. 'They stole that flat,' he remarked to his wife. 'Her father did *not* pay a full market price. Dad thought that Gregory wanted to live in it himself. And all the time he was planning to give it to Barbara! If Dad had known that it was for her, he would have passed it on to me instead. They stole it—it's as simple as that.'

Gloria was not so sure. She was a fair-minded person and although she thought that Barbara, in Rupert's words, directed negative waves towards her, she was not prepared to leap to conclusions about her involvement in this particular historical injustice—if that was what it was.

'But they did buy it, didn't they? Fatty sold it willingly. 'Willing seller, willing buyer'—isn't that what they say?'

This annoyed Rupert. 'Who says? Who is this *they* that people talk about?'

'Oh, don't be ridiculous,' snapped Gloria. 'It's an expression, that's all. It's a way of saying "I've heard it said".'

'Well, you should be more exact,' said Rupert peevishly. 'At Uppingham we had this really good housemaster. He used to fine you a penny if you made any statement that couldn't be supported. He collected all the fines and then used the money to buy books for the house library.'

Gloria stared at him. 'The point is, it's no good raking over old coals. Even if Gregory induced your father to sell on the understanding that he would live in the flat himself, you can't go back and re-open all that. It's old business. You have to move on.'

Rupert looked irritated. 'I have moved on,' he said. 'I moved on ages ago. I wouldn't dream of taking this up with Barbara—it's just that I do

308

occasionally think of it, and it makes me really cross. It's like when you hear of some great injustice—it rankles, even on an individual level. You may know that you can't do anything about it, but it's there—it's there in the room with you and you can't ignore it.'

'Such as?'

'A great injustice?' Rupert asked. 'Oh, there are bags of those. Which one do you want me to name? The Poles?'

'What about the Poles?'

Rupert spread his hands in a gesture of despair. 'We let them down. The whole world let them down. We put them into the hands of the Soviet Union—into Stalin's bloody hands. Ireland. The Kurds. The list is a very long one.'

Gloria nodded. 'We were bullies, I suppose. We broke our promises. We stole people's land on an epic scale. But so did everybody else.'

'We were bullies?' repeated Rupert. 'We jolly well were. And have we said sorry?'

Gloria thought for a moment. 'On one or two occasions,' she said. 'Mr Blair said sorry to Ireland, but he was the first British leader to find it possible to do that. Nobody else bothered. Mr Clinton also said sorry to quite a few people. And remember when that German Chancellor—it was Willy Brandt, I think—went to Warsaw and fell to his knees, and people were so moved by his contrition? That was a very profound moment, a moment of utter apology. Yet it's strange how hard it is to say sorry.'

Rupert agreed. 'Sometimes politicians dress it up in the language of regret. They say that they *regret* what happened.'

'That's not the same as saying sorry,' said Gloria. 'Look at Mr Nixon. What did he say? He said that *mistakes* had been made. That's very different from admitting that you have done something terrible.'

'That's not always easy,' said Rupert. 'What you can do, though, is do things that make up for the past. That's maybe even more important. You can show that you mean business. You can do things.'

For a moment they were both silent as they contemplated historical injustice. Then Gloria said, 'There comes a point at which one has to forgive. One has to forgive others—and also forgive oneself.'

'Oh yes?'

Gloria's reply was emphatic. '*Yes*. Because if we continue to think about historical wrongs, then nobody can get on with life. The memory of old wrongs poisons relations—freezes them too. *Those people are our enemies because of something that they did fifty, one hundred years ago*—that sort of thinking is fatal. It clutters everything up. We can't get on with life if we allow all sorts of unfinished business to distort our dealings with others. So we draw a line and say, "That's the past. The past is dead."'

'Except that the past is never dead,' Rupert said quietly.

'Are you thinking about that flat again?'

Rupert looked away, ashamed. He was.

'Listen, Rupert,' said Gloria, 'you really have to do something about this. You need to sort yourself out. No, don't make that face. You're going to have to listen to me. And what I want to say to you is this: you live far too much in the past. No, listen to me—don't look like that. Listen. You need to get your past sorted out. You need to tackle all the *baggage* you carry with you. Barbara Ragg's flat, for instance. No, I called it that deliberately. It's *her* flat. It's *her* flat, Rupert! We've got a perfectly good flat of our own. What? You think it's smelly. Don't be so ridiculous. Our flat doesn't smell. Where? Nonsense! And the other thing you have to sort out is Uppingham—you really do. Uppingham is in the *past*, Rupert. You're thirty-six. You left Uppingham *eighteen* years ago. I know that it's a wonderful school. I know that you were very happy there. But it's *past business*, Rupert. You haven't got a housemaster any more. We have a bedroom, Rupert, not a *dorm*. And I am *not* your housemistress.' She paused. 'Who was Ratty Mason, Rupert? Let's start there.'

Rupert looked at her sullenly. 'Ratty Mason is also in the *past*, Gloria. He's gone.'

Gloria was not one to allow herself to be hoist with her own petard. 'Well, maybe that's one of the things you need to look at. Some of the past is still inside us. You need to talk to somebody about all that.'

'Who?'

'There's a therapist I've heard of. Apparently she's really good.'

'Who?'

'She's called Berthea Snark.' She paused, and then added, 'I think.'

Rupert frowned. 'Snark? Do you think she's related to Oedipus?'

'Must be. His mother maybe?'

Rupert nodded. His manner seemed distant; he was pondering something. Schooldays. Oedipus

311

Snark. Ratty Mason. It was all coming back.

73. Free at Last!

Still outside her flat, Barbara Ragg now put all thoughts of yetis and their amanuenses out of her mind. She had been thinking about Errol Greatorex and his manuscript and about the damage that would have been done had the story found its way into the press prematurely. It was Oedipus who had alerted *The Times*, she was sure of it; he would have done it out of spite or even for gain. In fact, the more she dwelled on it the more convinced she became that money was his motivation. Oedipus was greedy: in spite of all his political rhetoric about sharing, he meant sharing only *after* he had helped himself to his own, somewhat larger share. I am finally free of him, she thought; *I am free.* And freedom had been so easy—as it often is. The step is taken, the resolution made, and the shackles fall away.

In her case, all that was required was for her to assert herself, to tell him what she thought of him, and he was deprived of all his power over her, as a muttered prayer or spell breaks the hold of some ghastly demon. No need for garlic or a sword of ice; merely a few words and Oedipus was . . . She asked herself what Oedipus was. History. That was it: Oedipus was history. The cliché, so easily uttered, nonetheless seemed to fit so perfectly, even if describing somebody as history was a very unkind thing to do. Well, he was unkind to me, thought Barbara, and if I have to be unkind to him

312

in order to free myself, then so be it.

But this was no time to be thinking of Oedipus Snark because within the flat, she reminded herself as the key slipped into the lock, was a young man *sent from heaven*. She could still hardly believe what had happened. Never would she have imagined that she, Barbara Ragg, would do something quite as precipitate as pick up a young man in a *car park*—'A handbag!'—and then, piling Pelion upon Ossa, take him back to her flat and *allow him to move in*. This last development almost took her breath away. Perhaps it was true that we all had an impulsive twin lurking beneath the surface and this twin occasionally manifested himself—or herself, in this case—and did something utterly outrageous. Perhaps her twin had done all this.

And yet why shouldn't two people decide that they were suited to one another and embark, perhaps rather quickly, on a relationship? There were many occasions in this life, she thought, when the impulsive decision proved to be exactly the right one. Too much hemming and hawing could result in the missing of an opportunity. It would be too late. Had Robert Graves not written about this? she asked herself. Yes, he had. She had read a poem of his, 'Dream Bird', in which he said that once one had the dream bird in one's grasp one should close one's fist about it and hold it tightly—one should never let it go. She had done no more than follow this advice—to grasp at something that had presented itself suddenly and without warning, a romance with a young man who seemed as smitten by her as she was by him. Why wait? Why let the dream bird fly away? Graves certainly said you should not.

She closed the front door behind her. The light in her hall was on and there were sounds coming from the direction of the kitchen. She noticed that the mail had been retrieved from downstairs and neatly stacked on the hall table, bills to one side and personal letters to the other. Junk mail—those desperate Technicolor exhortations to avail oneself of take-out restaurants or invitations to send away photographs for printing—had been put at the back, neatly rolled and secured by an elastic band, ready for disposal. And a vase of flowers, which had not been there that morning, had been placed on the low shelf above the table: a small arrangement of roses and delicate supporting fern. For a moment she stood still and stared at the roses. Oedipus had bought her flowers on how many occasions? None. Not once.

She smiled. Further sounds emanated from the kitchen: running water, the sound of a knife on a chopping board. She made her way across the hall and pushed open the kitchen door.

Hugh had his back to her, but heard her come in and spun round in surprise. 'You said that you were going to be late.'

'Well, actually it is quite late,' she said. 'I'm normally back shortly after six.'

He picked up a tea towel, wiped his hands and then looked at his watch. 'Oh, it's seven already.'

'You've obviously been busy,' said Barbara, looking around. 'You lose track of time when you've got lots to do.'

He tossed the towel down on the kitchen table. Then he crossed the room and kissed her lightly on the cheek. She felt herself blushing.

314

'I wanted to surprise you with a meal that was already prepared,' he said. 'There's a bottle of Chablis in the fridge and I thought we'd sit down and have a glass before we eat.'

'We can still do that.'

'Yes, I suppose we can. It's just that I've still got some stuff to do. I have to clean some mussels.'

'Mussels!'

'Yes. And then we're having . . . Well, I want it to be a surprise.'

Barbara beamed with pleasure. When had Oedipus last surprised her? 'You're terrific,' she said.

'Not really. I just like cooking.'

She moved over to the sink and looked at the mussels. They were large and succulent-looking. 'I love mussels,' she said. 'I love all seafood.'

'I know a place where one can get the most wonderful seafood,' Hugh said. 'Absolutely fresh. Clams. Lobsters. Octopi.'

'Octopodes,' muttered Barbara.

She regretted it the moment she said it.

'Octopodes?'

She had to explain. 'Sorry, I didn't mean to be pedantic. Octopi as a plural form suggests a Latin origin. But the word octopus is Greek and the plural should not be the Latin –*i* form but *octopodes*. I didn't mean . . .'

He had turned round and resumed his work at the sink. Oh, she thought, and then, again, oh. I've hurt his feelings. Already.

'Why don't you go and have a bath?' he said over his shoulder. 'Then dinner will be ready when you are.'

She went into the bathroom. I must be so careful,

315

she thought.

Then she saw the box of bath oils, tiny flasks in a row, placed beside the taps. He had somehow found out her favourite and had bought it: Jo Malone. And next to that, Clinique's Sparkle Skin—another favourite. How did he know? How would any man know?

74. Sparkle Skin

It's very strange, thought Barbara Ragg, how we can be transformed by the small luxuries of life. A new item of clothing, an impractical but glamorous pair of shoes, a well-made pen with a gold nib— any of these things is capable of making us feel so much better about ourselves. Now, stepping out of her bath with its pampering Jo Malone bath oil, exfoliated by Sparkle Skin, she felt herself filled with energy, lit by an exhilarating *glow*.

It was just the right feeling to accompany the glass of chilled Chablis that Hugh presented her with when she returned to the kitchen. Taking the glass, she raised it to him in a toast. 'You're spoiling me,' she said. 'What a lovely surprise through there . . .' She gave a toss of the head in the direction of the bathroom.

He smiled self-deprecatingly. 'Oh that. Just a couple of little presents.'

'But how did you know?'

'How did I know that you liked those particular things?'

'Yes.'

He tapped the side of his nose. 'Intuition.'

She stared at him in disbelief. Surely it would be impossible to find out a person's tastes purely on intuition. 'I don't believe . . .' She stopped herself. She should not contradict him. She had already corrected him over the plural of octopus; it would not do to disagree with him again. So she said instead, 'You're very clever.'

He laughed modestly. 'Not really.'

'What else can you tell about me on the basis of intuition?' she asked.

'That you like France.'

She nodded. 'Yes.' But everybody liked France.

'And Jane Austen.'

He was right once more but then, again, everyone liked Jane Austen. 'What else?'

'That your favourite colour is a sort of russet brown.'

That was a little bit more impressive, but then it occurred to her that he had enjoyed the run of the flat and must have seen all the russet brown in the rugs and elsewhere. And he must have seen the volumes of Jane Austen on the bookshelves too. And the empty tube of Clinique Sparkle Skin in

317

her bedroom drawer . . . If he had looked in the drawer, that is.

She took a sip of wine. A cold hand had touched her, somewhere inside, and she imagined him prowling around the flat while she was at work. She did not like the thought of his looking into things; he could examine things on the walls and on the shelves but he should not poke about in drawers.

She tried to sound light-hearted. 'You seem to know a lot about me,' she said, giving a short, nervous laugh. 'But what do I know about you?'

He looked at her over the top of his wine glass, his expression one of bemusement. 'You'd have to tell me that yourself.'

She thought for a moment. What did she know about him? That he was called Hugh. That he had been in a relationship but was out of it now. That he . . .

'I really don't know much about you, Hugh,' she confessed. 'I suppose you told me a little. But it wasn't very much.'

As she waited for his response, she thought how foolish she would look if he did something terrible. People would say, 'She picked him up in Rye and brought him home, *just like that*.' And others would shake their heads and say, 'Well, what did she expect?'

Hugh put down his wine glass. 'Would you like me to tell you?'

'Yes. We should know a bit about each other, don't you think? I mean, rather more than what our favourite colours are and so on. About who we are. About where we come from. About what we do. That sort of thing.'

It was as if her answer had disappointed him. 'All right,' he said. 'But it's a pity, isn't it, that we can't just be . . . well, just ourselves to each other? Not the social self, the self that other people have created for us, but the real inner soul, stripped of all the trappings of social identity. I think that's a pity.'

'I know what you mean,' she said. 'But I'd still like to know.'

Hugh reached for the bottle of Chablis and topped up her glass. 'You know the Hugh part of my name,' he began. 'The second part is Macpherson.'

'You're Scottish?'

'Yes, I'm Scottish. And don't say, *'But you don't sound Scottish.'* I really hate that. Not everyone in Scotland sounds like Rob Roy.'

She defended herself. 'I wasn't going to say that. I know that there are plenty of . . .' She was about to say posh people in Scotland, but she stopped herself in time. 'I know that there are plenty of people in Scotland who . . .'

He saved her. 'Who went to school in England, as I did. I was sent off to school at twelve. I went to a boarding school in Norfolk. Not a very well-known one—in fact, hardly anybody's ever heard of it.'

'Unlike Uppingham.'

He looked surprised. 'Yes, unlike Uppingham. How do you know about Uppingham, by the way?'

'Rupert Porter, my partner—my business partner, as one has to say these days—went there. He still talks about it. I think he was a prefect and has never grown out of it. I once gave him a prefect's badge that I found on a stall on the

Portobello Road. I told him that if he was going to dictate to me then he might as well have a prefect's badge. He didn't find it funny.'

'Well, the place I was at was distinctly downmarket of that. But it wasn't too bad, I suppose.'

Barbara had never been able to understand why anybody would send their child to a boarding school. Why have children in the first place unless you wanted them to spend their childhood with you? She asked Hugh why he was sent away, and he thought for a few moments before answering. 'It was complicated,' he said. 'We had a farm in Argyll and I would have had to go away to school anyway, or travel for hours every day to get to Fort William. It was a very remote place. And my mother, you see, was English and she wanted me to have a bit of both cultures—my father's and hers—of Scotland and England. So they decided to send me to boarding school in England. The place I went to was quite cheap and that suited them too. We did not have all that much money.'

'And then?'

'And then what?'

'Then what did you do?'

He looked up at the ceiling. 'I had a gap year. Sixteen months in fact.'

'Where?'

'South America, for the most part.'

'Whereabouts in South America?'

It was not, she thought, an intrusive question and she was quite unprepared for his reaction—which was to start to weep.

75. Terence Moongrove Confesses

Over in Cheltenham, that particular day had proved an eventful one for Terence Moongrove and his sister, Berthea Snark. Berthea had decided to extend her stay in Cheltenham by a few weeks, and had spent several hours on the telephone cancelling and rearranging her patients. (She refused to call them clients. 'They are under my care,' she explained. 'If somebody is under your care, then they are the patient, in the old-fashioned sense of being one to whom something is done. A client is not under your care. That is a totally different transaction. You do not care for clients in the same way that you care for patients.')

It happened that her diary over the following month was not particularly full, so it was not too difficult to find alternative appointments for everybody. Had her patients not been loquacious, the task of arranging these appointments would have been the work of half an hour at the most. But many of her patients were given to long-windedness and took the opportunity of the telephone call to unburden themselves of doubts and anxieties that they had felt since they last saw Berthea. They knew, too, that telephone time was free—at least to them—and anything they said to her on the telephone was therefore very much cheaper than what they said to her in their hour-long sessions in her consulting room.

'Phew!' Berthea exclaimed, as she replaced the telephone receiver in its cradle. 'You wouldn't imagine that it would take quite so long to arrange

321

something so insignificant as a change of appointment.'

'Poor dears,' said Terence. 'They do so need to talk. All those horrid worries and doubts bottled up inside! They must be bursting to tell you all about it.'

'There's a time and place for that,' said Berthea briskly.

'Mind you, Berthy,' Terence went on, 'I can understand why the poor souls want to talk to you. You're such a good listener, you really are. And you aren't bossy at all. Not really.'

Berthea looked at him with surprise. 'Who said I was bossy?'

Terence spoke sheepishly. 'Well, I'm afraid I have a teeny confession to make,' he said. 'I called you bossy when I was talking to Mr Marchbanks. I said that you were bossy and you stuck your long nose into my business. And I'm terribly sorry that I said it. It was the electricity, I think. I really don't think that way.'

Berthea looked at him reproachfully. She had saved his life by her prompt action and in return he had called her bossy. Well, if she had not stuck her long nose into his business—and her nose was not long at all, she told herself—then Terence would be no more. He should remember that, perhaps.

'I know,' said Terence, holding up a hand, 'you must think me utterly beastly for saying something like that. I really am sorry, Berthy. But at least I've got it off my chest now and I can see the forgiveness in your eyes. It's like a great light, you know, from where I'm sitting. It's like the Great Lighthouse of Alexandria—a beam of forgiveness piercing the encircling gloom.'

322

Berthea looked at her brother. If anybody's nose was long, she thought, it's his. But there was no point in saying it; one of the things she knew, both as an analyst and as a person, was that remarks about the nose of another would never be anything but the cause of misunderstanding or annoyance. The only thing anybody ever wanted to hear about their nose was that it was a very fine and attractive one; that was the only acceptable thing to say. You could not say to somebody, 'Your nose is average,' or 'Nobody will notice your nose.' You had to be positive.

'Well, at least you've told me,' she said. 'And you're right, I don't think you were yourself for a little while after the accident.' She paused. 'But how are you feeling now?'

'I feel extremely well,' said Terence. 'Quite optimistic, in fact, especially since I made my decision to replace the Morris.'

'Good,' said Berthea. 'Well, I shall stay, if I may, for another couple of weeks, just to make sure everything's settled. Sometimes accidents like that can leave one feeling a bit vulnerable for a while. I'll stay until you're absolutely sure that you've recovered from the experience. You don't mind, do you?'

'Not at all,' said Terence. 'We can go to sacred dance together, and do those photies I mentioned—the ones that Daddy took in Malta.'

'Maybe,' said Berthea quickly. 'I was also hoping to get some of my book done—the biography of Oedipus that I mentioned. I've got as far as his schooldays at Uppingham. I don't have much information about that part of his life, but I'm hoping that I'll hear from people who spent more time with him than I did in those days. I've written to one or two of his contemporaries and I've already had a couple of replies.'

'Oh,' said Terence. 'From his school friends?'

'Yes.'

'And what did they say?'

Berthea looked evasive. 'Nothing very much, I'm afraid. In fact, now that you ask, they weren't very helpful. One of them wrote and asked for Oedipus's address because he had something to discuss with him. I didn't like the letter and so I didn't send Oedipus's address. I didn't fancy the way that the handwriting became shakier and shakier as the letter progressed—as if the writer were under acute emotional stress.'

'Oh dear,' said Terence. 'Perhaps the writer was a lunatic. Did he write in green ink, by any chance?'

'What's the significance of green ink?'

Terence nonchalantly waved a hand in the air. 'It's well known,' he said. 'Lunatics choose to write in green ink. Everybody knows that.'

'Nonsense!' exclaimed Berthea. 'To begin with, the term lunatic is frightfully old-fashioned.'

'Nutters, then,' said Terence.

'Even worse,' said Berthea. '*Differently rationaled* is the term, you know.'

Terence raised an eyebrow. 'Whatever you say. Anyway, I'm jolly glad that you're going to stay, because I really appreciate you, Berthy. I don't think I've ever told you that, but I really do appreciate you. So you can stay as long as you like—and we can even go on some trips in my new car. How would you like that?'

'That would be fine, Terence,' Berthea said. 'But

listen, what sort of car will it be?'

Terence's brow knit with concentration. 'I think
. . . I think it's something beginning with a P. Yes,
I'm pretty sure of it. I can't remember the exact
name though. Mr Marchbanks is going to get me
one—he's promised.'

'A Peugeot,' said Berthea. 'That'll be very
suitable, Terence.'

'Yes, I believe it's a Peugeot. Are they good cars?
It's the sort that Monty Bismarck drives.'

'I don't know Monty Bismarck,' said Berthea.
'But I wouldn't be surprised if he drives a Peugeot.'
Monty Bismarck drew up in his Peugeot. Yes, that
sounded very appropriate.

She rubbed her hands in satisfaction. Two weeks
in the country, away from the demands of her
patients and the noise and crush of London, was
exactly what she needed. And yes, she would like
to go for drives with Terence in his Peugeot, out
along the rural roads that led through little valleys,
deep into England, into the country that everybody
took for granted but which was so beautiful, and
fragile, and threatened.

76. Lennie Marchbanks Calls

It was at three o'clock in the afternoon that the
doorbell rang. Berthea was sitting in the small
morning room at the back of the house—the sunny
side—reading a rather slow-moving autobiography
when she heard the bell. She laid the book on the
table with some relief and decided, at that
moment, that she would pick it up again only to

replace it on the shelf in her brother's study. Terence's house was replete with books but very few of them were to her taste. She had seized on the autobiography—which was by a minor literary figure of the nineteen-thirties—hoping that the claim on the back cover would prove true. 'A gripping account of a life of passionate involvement,' the publisher enthused, 'a life lived to the full in turbulent and trying times.'

The book, unfortunately, failed to live up to this promise. After eighty pages, the author had done nothing more exciting than contemplate going to Spain to visit a friend who was cooking for the Republican forces. However, he had developed a heavy cold and had cancelled his passage on grounds of ill health. That was the high point of a narrative that was otherwise mostly concerned with the minutiae of a very modest existence, that of an assistant editor of a literary magazine. Names were bandied about, of course, but it seemed that the author had never had any conversations with the well-known writers of the day, although MacNeice wrote to him once and he spoke to Spender on the telephone when the poet called the magazine office. The call, however, had been a mistake. Spender had been given the wrong number and had really wanted to speak to somebody else. Nonetheless, he had commented on the weather before hanging up, and the author had made a note of the exact words he used, observing that the sentence in question was undeniably an iambic pentameter.

'That's a frightfully exciting book,' Terence had said when he saw his sister reading it. 'I must say they had a jolly lively time, those writers of the thirties. I wouldn't have minded being alive then.'

Berthea looked doubtful. 'Nothing much seems to have happened so far,' she said. 'He's just got to Oxford and had a letter from a friend in Florence.'

'Jolly exciting,' said Terence. 'I remember that bit—I think. Does he write back?'

Berthea ran an eye down the page she was reading. 'He doesn't say.'

'Well, I bet he did,' said Terence. 'They were good correspondents in those days, always writing letters to one another, full of interesting observations on the world. You wait until you get to the bit where he's turned down for the Navy during the war and goes to teach in Bristol.'

And now, of course, she would never get to that part, since she was abandoning the book altogether. How narcissistic these people were, she thought as she went to answer the doorbell. How special they thought themselves to be. Whereas in reality they led rather uneventful lives—much like everybody else. Nothing really remarkable happened to most of us, she thought; we grew up, we got a job, we fell in love—if we were lucky—and then we went into decline and eventually disappeared. And at the end of the day, what did we achieve? Well, perhaps it was an achievement just to get through life without any conspicuous disasters. If we did that, then we were pulling off at least something.

It was Lennie Marchbanks at the door. She had met him once or twice before and rather liked him; mechanics struck her as being such easy, agreeable people. And, she noticed, as a psychotherapist, one never had a mechanic for a patient. Why was that? Were they invariably balanced people, free of the neuroses that afflicted non-mechanically-minded others?

Lennie smiled at Berthea. She noticed that he had false teeth and that they were not a very natural colour, being rather too white; ill-fitting, too.

'Is your brother in?' asked Lennie.

Berthea went to fetch Terence, who had been taking an afternoon nap in his room upstairs.

'That electricity has done me no good at all,' he said as he sat up and rubbed his eyes. 'It's got all my ions going in the wrong direction. I can tell, you know. I need to be re-polarised.'

The mention of Lennie Marchbanks seemed to cheer him up though, and he was very talkative as they made their way downstairs. 'I suspect he's found me that new car,' said Terence. 'If he has, then we could go for a spin later on. That is, if you'd like to. I don't believe in forcing people to do things they don't want to, you know. There's far too much coercion in the world today. They should just leave us to get on with our lives rather than telling us to do all sorts of things. Have you seen those signs, Berthy? Those signs on the road? They have big messages in lights telling you to put on your safety belt and do this and do that and not do the other thing. It's really very, very cross-making. These government people sit there in their offices and think up things they can tell us to do. Did you see that they actually issued a code of practice on how to look after your cat? What a cheek.'

'Yes, yes,' said Berthea.

'And there's another thing . . .' Terence continued. But he did not finish because they had arrived in the front hall, where Lennie was waiting.

'Afternoon, Mr Moongrove,' said the mechanic. 'I hope that you're fully recovered.'

Terence nodded. 'Thank you, Mr Marchbanks. I expect I shall be fine—in due course.' He looked past the mechanic through the open front door. 'You haven't . . .'

'Yes, I have. Your new car. Or, rather, one that I reckon you might like. You can take a look at it and see what you think.'

Terence rubbed his hands together gleefully. 'One of those small cars we talked about?'

Lennie nodded. 'The very one.' He glanced anxiously at Berthea as he spoke.

'It's all right,' Terence reassured him. 'My sister knows about this car and gives it her blessing.'

77. Terence Moongrove, Porsche Owner

Berthea had no real interest in cars and left Terence and Lennie to get on with their transaction while she returned to the morning room. There could be no question of taking up the autobiography again, so she picked up the newspaper and began to tackle the crossword. 1 across: He conquers all? A nubile tram. This old clue required only a moment's thought. Tamburlaine! Of course. And 1 down? This for two and two for this (3 letters). Well really! Who did they imagine would be doing these crosswords—children?

Outside, Lennie led Terence to the garage, where he had parked the Porsche.

'I took you at your word,' the mechanic said. 'At first I thought you were joking. But then I realised that you really did want one of these jobs. So I had a word with our mutual friend. Not a fancy price. Good motor. Nice and clean.'

'Our mutual friend?'

Lennie chuckled. 'Yes. Monty Bismarck. As it happens, he was ready for a new model and he'll be happy for you to take this one off his hands—through me, of course.'

Terence stood before the Porsche. He reached down and touched the bodywork, gently, with a single finger, as if to confirm the car's existence.

'So this is the car I've seen Monty Bismarck driving,' he said. 'The very car. Isn't it lovely, Mr Marchbanks?'

'It's a nice motor all right, Mr Moongrove. I wouldn't have thought of you as driving one of these, you know, but where there's life there's hope, I suppose . . .'

Terence laughed. 'I could cut a bit of a figure in this, couldn't I?' He moved round to the side of the car. 'And I see there are two seats. One for me and one for my sister.'

Lennie reached forward to open the driver's door. 'Exactly. And you might even find that other women would fancy getting into that passenger seat.' He turned and winked at Terence.

Terence looked surprised. 'What do you mean, Mr Marchbanks? Two women wouldn't fit in there. Berthy's quite large, and I don't think she'd want another woman to sit on her lap.'

The mechanic looked at him conspiratorially. 'Truth is, Mr Moongrove, women like these cars. A Porsche does something for a woman. I was

330

thinking of . . . well, other women. You know. Hey?'

Terence frowned. 'We'll see.'

'Monty Bismarck told me . . .' Lennie checked himself. 'Well, maybe not. Perhaps I should show you what's what and then we can take a little test drive down the road.'

'Oh, I'd like that,' said Terence appreciatively, stooping to get into the low-slung car. 'My goodness, this is not a car for very tall people. Oops! My poor old head. Do you think they build these cars for short men, Mr Marchbanks?'

Lennie thought about this. Unintentionally, Terence had displayed a real insight into the psychology of car manufacture. Who drove these very flashy, sporty cars? Short men. Yes, Terence was right. It took a tall man to drive a Morris Traveller.

Lennie showed him the instruments. 'That's a rev counter,' he said. 'You don't want the engine to strain too much. So you keep it low.'

Terence peered at the dial. 'I see. And this thing here?'

'The speedometer. The one on your Morris went up to 80, I think. Which was a bit optimistic. I think that nobody ever got more than 72 miles per hour out of a Morris.'

Terence pointed. 'This one goes up to 160, I see, Mr Marchbanks. That's jolly fast. Do you think we might . . . ?'

'No,' said the mechanic firmly. 'Listen, Mr Moongrove, I'm only going to let you have this car if you promise me—and I mean promise—that you won't go above 50 in it. That's it. You see that mark there? That's 50. No more than that, please.'

Terence looked momentarily annoyed, but then nodded his assent. 'All right. But what's the point of being able to go 160 miles per hour if you aren't allowed to?'

'That's for Germans,' said Lennie. 'These cars are made in Germany, you see, and they're allowed to do whatever speed they like on their autobahns.'

'That's very unfair,' said Terence, adjusting the rear-view mirror. 'What's the point of having a European Union if there are different rules for the Germans? Tell me, Mr Marchbanks, are there any Bulgarian cars?'

'Not that I've heard of,' said the mechanic.

'I just wondered,' said Terence. He gave the mirror a final tweak. 'But why don't we set off? I can't wait to drive this car.'

Lennie swallowed. Oh well, he thought. Here goes.

Terence turned the key in the ignition, as instructed by Lennie. Immediately there came a deep growling sound. 'My goodness!' he said. 'Is there something wrong with the exhaust pipe? You know that pipe that comes out the back? When the Traveller's exhaust pipe had a big hole in it, it made that sort of sound.'

Lennie smiled. 'That's what they call a low, throaty roar. People pay for that sort of thing. No, there's no hole.'

'Well, I must say, that will certainly warn everybody that I'm coming,' said Terence. 'Now, shall I put in the clutch?'

He engaged the car in gear and then, very slowly, they moved off. It was a very smooth start, and Lennie was impressed. 'You're doing fine, Mr Moongrove,' he said. 'Nice smooth start.'

Terence beamed with pleasure. 'She handles well—even at speed.'

Lennie glanced at the speedometer. 'Well, you're only doing 8 miles per hour,' he said. 'And we're still on the drive.'

'Very nice,' said Terence. 'I really like this car, Mr Marchbanks.'

'Good.'

'I shall go to the bank tomorrow morning and get the money. How much will I need?'

'Twenty-five grand,' said Lennie. 'Are you paying cash, Mr Moongrove?'

'Oh yes,' said Terence. 'I've got bags of money in my current account. Bags.'

Lennie looked at him sideways. He felt a very strong temptation to ask just how much money that was. Why not? Old Moongrove had no idea about anything and would not resent a question like that. Many would, but not old Terence.

'How much?' Lennie asked casually.

'In the bank?'

'Yes.'

'Six hundred and eighty thousand,' said Terence. 'Maybe a little bit more, I think.'

Lennie looked out of the passenger's window. He was worried. He could try to protect Terence when it came to cars, but he could not look after him in other departments. Terence was clearly very liquid. Was he worldly-wise enough to know that there were plenty of people who would be very happy to help him change all that?

78. Whose Home?

William felt quite elated when he returned to Corduroy Mansions with Marcia and Freddie de la Hay. He had been profoundly shocked by his experience of the narrowly averted dog fight; not only had he been appalled by Eddie's involvement, but he had been astonished that anybody—even Diesel's disagreeable owner—could find pleasure in such activities. But then, he told himself, there would appear to be plenty of people who found violence agreeable—as professional pugilists knew very well.

'Boxing,' he remarked to Marcia, as she parked her van.

'What?'

'I was thinking about boxing. It just came into my mind. I was thinking about how hypocritical we are. We don't allow dog fighting, but it's perfectly legal for *people* to knock the stuffing out of one another in the boxing ring. Doesn't that strike you as being a bit odd?'

Marcia shrugged; there was so much in life that was odd, she had stopped being surprised by anything. 'Not necessarily. Dogs don't consent to being harmed in the same way as boxers do. We push dogs into it. We don't make boxers fight, do we? Maybe that's the difference.'

It was an interesting point, and the more that William thought about it, the more intriguing it became. Boxers were not forced to fight, but did they have a truly free choice in the matter? How many of them became boxers because they were obliged to do so by poverty and restricted opportunities? He was not sure whether he knew the answer to that; it could be condescending to assume that boxers were not volunteers just because they tended to come from the lower levels of the social heap. One could get one's nose punched for that sort of assumption . . .

'And anyway,' said Marcia as they reached the landing outside William's door, 'we're funny about animals in this country. We don't approve of cruelty to animals. Not at all. So dog fighting is out—completely out.' She paused, and added, 'We're home.'

'Yes,' said William. 'We're . . .' He did not complete the sentence. *I'm home*, he thought. This is *my* home. Marcia may be staying here, but she has her own home over in Putney and she should not be saying *we're* home because that implies that this is her home too, and it isn't.

Marcia was unaware of this mental reservation on William's part and opened the door with all the assurance of a settled resident. And as she hung up her coat in the hall cupboard and patted Freddie cheerfully on the head, William felt his spirits sagging. He had made a dreadful mistake, he felt. It was like marrying somebody one did not want to marry and being unable to get out of it. He did not want to hurt Marcia—he liked her, and he found himself liking her even more after experiencing all the support she had given him that evening. She was generous; she was a character; she was easy company . . . *but he was not in love with her*. And, for William, that precluded anything but a platonic relationship. One did not enter into an affair unless one loved the other person—it was a minimum requirement of decency. It was as simple as that; or at least it was as simple as that when you were in your fif— late forties and above.

Freddie de la Hay seemed relieved to be home. Free of his leash, he rushed around the flat, careering into each room and then bursting out again, barking joyously. And when he had completed his tour of inspection, he bounded over to William and enthusiastically licked such portions of his master as he could find: hands, shoes, and, standing on his hind legs in a brief moment of exhilaration, William's face.

Marcia went into the kitchen and began to prepare dinner. Freddie's steak was cooked first— a choice cut which sizzled delectably in the frying pan. When it was done, she cut it into squares and put them on the dog's plate. Freddie, sitting obediently as he had been trained to do before tackling his dinner, stared at the plate for a few moments before he stepped forward, on Marcia's invitation, and sniffed at the steak.

'You can eat it, Freddie,' said Marcia. 'It's all right.'

Freddie looked up at William, as if to seek confirmation. 'Go ahead, my boy,' said William. 'Nice steak. Nice Freddie.'

Freddie began to eat the steak—slowly at first and then very quickly, wolfing down the small squares of meat.

'See?' said Marcia. 'So much for Freddie being a vegetarian.'

William nodded. Freddie had indeed tackled the steak with enthusiasm, but now he had taken a few steps back from the plate and was sitting with his head sunk, his gaze focused on the floor.

'Guilt,' said William. 'He feels guilty.'

'Nonsense,' said Marcia. 'Dogs don't feel guilt.'

William disagreed. He had only owned Freddie for a short time, but he knew that the dog had a broad cupboard of emotions and that it was perfectly possible that he was now feeling guilt and remorse.

'Dogs feel these things,' he said. 'They really do. They have emotional centres in their brains, same as we do.'

'But surely not one for guilt?' said Marcia.

'Why not? When a dog does something that he knows he should not, he often looks unhappy. He puts his tail between his legs. He skulks around.'

Marcia nodded. 'But that's only because they fear our displeasure. They think we're going to beat them or shout at them. It's just a reaction. They don't feel guilt deep down—not like we do.' She paused. Freddie de la Hay was looking up at her with mournful eyes. 'And there's no reason for Freddie to think that we're going to disapprove of him for eating steak. After all, we gave it to him and encouraged him.'

William was sure that there was a flaw in Marcia's argument—as there often was. 'He may not fear consequences from us—but that doesn't mean that he won't be afraid of somebody else. Somebody from his past. That Manfred character, for instance.'

Freddie growled.

'You see?' said William. 'Freddie recognised the name. He's still frightened of Manfred.'

Freddie now whimpered, looking furtively over his shoulder, as if he expected the famous columnist to enter the room and remonstrate with

337

him. Noticing this, William bent down to comfort him, putting an arm around the dog and whispering into his ear.

'Don't you worry, Freddie, old boy,' he said. 'Daddy won't let that man browbeat you any more.' It slipped out, and he thought, *Our animals make fools of us—infantilise us just as we infantilise them.* No, Freddie de la Hay, I'm not your real dad . . .

'And neither will Mummy,' added Marcia.

William caught his breath. He was going to have to talk to Marcia; he really was. And he would have to do it this evening, before things went any further.

79. Marcia Understands

'Coquilles St Jacques,' Marcia called from the kitchen. 'How about that? And then . . .'

'Perfect,' William replied from the living room. 'I love anything with cheese.'

'Sometimes I think that cheese doesn't help,' Marcia said. 'I use it if I think that whatever I'm cooking is maybe just a little bit past its best. You can get away with a lot when you use cheese.'

This elicited only silence from the living room.

'Not that these scallops aren't fresh,' Marcia added hurriedly. 'I think that they're all right, but when you consider the distance they have to travel to reach us in London . . . Quite a journey.'

William was about to say something about seafood and the case of prawns that had been discovered to have been flown out to Malaysia,

338

frozen there, and then flown back to London. That was a criminal waste of precious fuel, he thought, but once one started to think of the wastage of fuel, where would one stop? How many of the journeys we made were necessary? Twenty per cent? Possibly less. We did not *need* to go to Florida for our holidays, let alone Thailand. If there was something unnatural about transporting our food halfway round the world, the same might be said about transporting *ourselves*. And yet, if the means existed to do something, we would do it; the most cursory glance at human history confirmed that. Here and there, brave souls questioned this and were often howled down for their pains. Or people agreed with them, nodded sagely, and then did nothing. Very few people were prepared to take the first step, to deny themselves—on principle—something that was readily available.

William sighed. He would have to go and talk to Marcia, and he would have to do it before dinner. He rose to his feet, watched by Freddie de la Hay, who had settled himself on his favourite rug and was beginning to doze off, but still kept an eye half open, just in case something should happen in the inexplicable world of humans.

She was standing in front of the cooker, attending to the scallops. There was a cheese grater on the worktop beside her and a square of cheese rind.

'Marcia,' he began, 'there's something that I need to talk to you about.'

She did not turn round. 'I know,' she said.

He was momentarily taken by surprise. What did she know? That he wanted to talk—or what he wanted to say? Marcia had many talents, and perhaps prescience was one of them.

Now she turned round and he saw that there were tears in her eyes. He gasped, and took a step forward, instinctively ready to comfort her. 'Oh, my dear . . .'

She held up a hand. 'No, William. I'm all right. I'm all right.'

'You're crying.'

She put down the spoon she had been holding and wiped at her eyes. 'Not really. Not really crying.'

'But why?'

She looked at him. 'I know, you see. You don't even have to talk to me about it. You don't have to say a thing—not a thing. The whole idea of my moving in here was a mistake. I should never have done it.'

William looked down at the floor. If he had imagined at one time that he might be alone in feeling that things were not right—that he alone might have picked up on the unspoken—now he was being reminded that when an atmosphere exists, it is usually not just one person who detects it. He felt bad about Marcia; he should have been firmer, he should have made his position clearer, rather than allowing her to make unwarranted assumptions.

'Marcia,' he began, 'I . . .'

'No. You don't need to spell it out. It was all my fault—my own silly fault.'

'It was not. It was not.'

She shook her head. 'And now you're being kind to me—which is just like you. But you don't need to be.'

He drew in his breath. 'Listen,' he said, 'I like

340

you a great deal. It's just that I don't know whether it should go further. That's not to say that I don't ... that I don't find you attractive. It's just that ...'

'I know,' she said. 'You really don't have to say anything more.'

He swallowed hard. 'But I want to. Look, why don't you stay on for a while? We could be simply flatmates, like the girls downstairs. How about that?'

'Is that what you'd like?'

He nodded. It was. And when Marcia accepted, tentatively at first, but with greater warmth when after a few moments she realised he meant the invitation, he felt a surge of relief. The encounter with Diesel's owner had left him feeling raw, as can happen when one comes up against hatred, or evil, or just sheer rudeness. It was a form of moral shock and it made one yearn for reassurance. Having Marcia in the flat for a while longer would provide just that. And he was not doing it under any false pretence; she would stay there as a friend, free to come and go as she pleased, with neither of them reading anything more into the situation.

He stepped forward and took her hand. 'I'm sorry,' he said. 'This has all been my fault.'

She put a finger to her lips. 'I have to do the scallops.'

'I can't wait. Coquilles St Jacques. Do you know why they're called that?'

She shook her head. 'St Jacques?'

'St James. The scallop was his symbol. I'm not sure why. It was something to do with his having saved somebody from scallops, I think.'

Marcia laughed. 'Are they dangerous?'

'Get your fingers in a live scallop shell and see,'

he said. 'And they swim around in shoals, you know. They're quite energetic little things. They propel themselves by sucking water in and out. So I suppose if you had a whole shoal of them latching onto you . . .'

Marcia frowned. It was hard to envisage, but it was, she feared, something else to worry about. There seemed to be so much already—and now scallops.

But there were other, more pressing matters. 'That painting,' she said. 'What are we going to do?'

William thought for a moment. 'Show it to somebody,' he said. 'Caroline downstairs is doing some sort of course at Sotheby's. Shall we show it to her?'

Marcia turned to stir the white wine sauce she had been preparing. 'Can she keep her mouth shut?'

William wondered why this would be necessary. Did Marcia know—or suspect—something that he did not? Or did she have some plan that she had not yet disclosed?

He was thinking about this when Freddie de la Hay came into the room with something in his mouth. It was something that he had been chewing—a piece of old leather perhaps. William bent down to examine the plaything and Freddie dropped his tail between his legs. It was a metaphor for guilt, and it was guilt itself.

'What have you got hold of, Freddie?' William asked, taking the piece of leather from the dog's mouth.

Freddie looked up at William with his large, liquid eyes. William froze.

A Belgian Shoe—or what remained of it.

80. In Touch With His Feminine Side

Hugh did not weep for long.

'Look, I'm sorry,' he said, unfolding a handkerchief. 'I'm meant to have got over it all. But every so often it comes back.'

Barbara Ragg wanted to say, 'What comes back?' But she did not. Instead she said, 'I often have a bit of a cry myself. We all do. And it's nice when a man does. It shows . . . well, it shows he's in touch with his feminine side.' That, she thought even as she uttered the words, is a terribly trite thing to say; why should it be that weeping is feminine? We all weep, the only difference being that men often suppress their tears.

Hugh nodded. He looked grateful. 'There are different views as to how to deal with a traumatic experience,' he said. 'When I came back from South America, they said to me—or, rather, some people said to me—that I should have counselling. They said that I was suffering from post-traumatic stress disorder and that the only way I could deal with it was to talk about what had happened. So I was made to relive the whole experience, to look at it from all possible angles, with the aim of coming to terms with it. And yet I'm not so sure. There's another view, you know, that you should try to put things out of your mind and get on with life.'

He paused. 'Go on,' said Barbara, adding, 'if that's what you want.'

'Oh, I'm all right now,' Hugh reassured her. 'And

I don't mind talking about the whole thing, I really don't. I do find the question interesting, though— whether one should talk or whether one should try to forget. I read a lot about that, you know.'

'Did you?'

'Yes. I had an uncle, you see, who was a psychiatrist, and he was very interested in these things. He had dealt with mountain rescue people who had found climbers who had fallen great distances. They were encouraged to go for debriefing over what happened. It's something that employers often arrange.

'My uncle said that he was not at all convinced that debriefing helped. He said that if you looked for hard evidence—studies and so on—to show that there were benefits, you just couldn't find them. Everybody said that debriefing was a good thing, but when you asked for evidence to show that people who were debriefed suffered fewer symptoms of psychological distress in the long term than those who were not, nobody could come up with the necessary proof. The point was that debriefing had become a sort of ideology—like so much else.'

'So were you debriefed?' asked Barbara. 'After it happened . . .' But what was *it*?

'Yes,' said Hugh. 'I was sent to a very depressing woman. She was a clinical psychologist and she encouraged me to tell her every single little detail of what happened during the whole three months. Everything.'

Barbara drew in her breath. 'Three months?'

Hugh stared at her. 'Yes,' he said. 'Three whole months.'

'That was a long time,' said Barbara. But she still

344

had no idea what *it* was, and she now decided that she should ask. 'What actually happened?' she asked.

Hugh smiled at her. He had put his handkerchief away, and if he was still upset, his feelings were well concealed. 'You won't laugh, will you?'

'Of course not. I wouldn't laugh at a thing like that.' Like what? she wondered. Perhaps she would. Perhaps it was really very funny, in retrospect—as traumatic experiences can be, provided they happen to others.

'I was kidnapped,' said Hugh. 'I was kidnapped in Colombia.'

That, as Barbara knew, was not in the slightest bit funny. The victims of Colombian kidnappings could be held for much more than three months—for years, even—and if anybody deserved sympathy it was them. So she reached out and touched his arm in a gesture of sympathy. 'How terrible.'

'Well, there are plenty of people who have suffered far more than I have,' said Hugh. 'I was relatively lucky. And that, interestingly enough, was something that I think really helped me to get over what happened. If I had sat about feeling sorry for myself and bemoaning my fate, I would have been more affected by it. As it was, I managed to get over it by keeping it in perspective.'

Barbara waited for him to continue. She did not wish to replicate the role of the depressing clinical psychologist whom he had referred to, so she said nothing; he would continue when he was ready.

'It happened in a place called Barranquilla,' he said. 'It's a rather strange place on the Caribbean coast—quite a busy industrial city, but one with all

345

sorts of schools and universities. I had been travelling in South America for about eight months and I was heading for Cartagena. I had been right down in the south, in Tierra del Fuego, and had then gone up all the way to Ecuador and Colombia. When I got to Bogotá, I was beginning to run a bit short of money and somebody I met said that they could arrange a job teaching English as a foreign language at a school in Barranquilla. I had one of those very basic TEFL certificates—the sort you can get in a few weeks—and they said that this would be quite enough for the Colegio Biffi la Salle, which was the name of the school that was looking for an English conversation tutor.

'Well, I applied for the job and I got it. I went up to Barranquilla and was given a room by a family who lived near the school. They were tremendously kind and made me feel very much at home. We exchanged lessons—I spoke to them in English one day and the next day they would speak to me in Spanish. My Spanish improved greatly and I learned all the current slang. Not that I could use any slang at the Colegio—it was a very proper place. A few days after I arrived, one of the teachers came up and asked me, quite seriously and in a very correct English accent, "Is it true that in Hertford, Hereford and Hampshire, hurricanes hardly happen?"'

Barbara burst out laughing. 'And what did you reply?'

''Ardly hever,' said Hugh.

346

81. A Country House Weekend

This is hardly very traumatic, thought Barbara. She now reckoned that the moment had come to offer Hugh a further glass of Chablis, having felt until then that to mention Chablis in the midst of an encounter with past trauma would have been perhaps a little flippant.

Hugh accepted. 'I was happy enough in Barranquilla,' he went on. 'My working commitments weren't heavy and I had made a lot of new friends. It was warm and comfortable—a very easy place to be. You had to be a bit careful, of course—everywhere in Colombia has its dangers, and every so often there were items in the papers about kidnappings, and worse. As you know, in Colombia there are always guerrillas popping up and taking a swipe at the government. There were also thousands of *narcotraficantes*, who could be pretty ruthless. These people even had submarines that they ran from Barranquilla to the

US to smuggle cocaine. It was a bit of a frontier town, in a way.

'I thought, of course, that none of this would have anything to do with me. I was a very junior, insignificant teacher of a foreign language, and I didn't imagine for a moment that I would see any of these things, let alone get involved in them. How wrong can you be?'

He looked at Barbara as if expecting an answer, so she replied, 'Very wrong?'

Hugh took a sip of his Chablis. 'Yes, very.' He paused and looked at Barbara with concern. 'You promise you won't laugh?'

'Of course I promise. I wouldn't dream of laughing. I really wouldn't.'

He seemed reassured. 'Well, all right. One Friday afternoon I had a telephone call from the mother of one of my pupils at the school. These people, who were tremendously grand, did not live in Barranquilla but had an estate out in the country, some distance away. The school holidays were coming up, she said, and would I be interested in spending a couple of days on their estate? She explained that they were very isolated, but there would be plenty of opportunities to ride, if I wished, or I could just sit around and read and swim in the pool. She made it sound very attractive, and since I had nothing else to do I saw no reason not to accept the invitation. She then said that I would be picked up and flown there in their small private plane. Her husband, she explained, would send his pilot.'

Barbara Ragg watched him as the tale unfolded. He had a way of telling a story that was completely natural and quite transfixing. She could not bear

348

the thought of waiting for the outcome, although she knew in advance that it was not going to end well.

'I told the family I was staying with about the invitation, and they seemed a little bit concerned. I asked them whether they thought I should have turned it down and they said, rather enigmatically, that even if they had thought that, they would not advise me to refuse. 'There are some people in this country,' they said, 'whose invitations *cannot* be turned down. The only excuse they accept is that you're dead and can't come for that reason. Even then, they can be a bit grudging.'

'I thought this very strange but I chose not to let it prey on my mind. When the car came to collect me to take me to the plane, I decided to take with me more than just the things I would need for only a few days. I took my trip diary and my walking boots and the very long Russian novel I was reading. It was just as well.'

Hugh had reached the bottom of his glass of Chablis, and Barbara reached forward to refill it. She was attracted by the slight air of vulnerability, both touching and profoundly appealing, that settled upon him as he told this story. Oedipus Snark would never have been able to achieve an effect like this—he was always in control of the world, defeating it, proving himself, like the hero of some impossible adventure novel. What have I done, she asked herself, contemplating Hugh now, to merit a move from *that* man to *this*? The gods of mortal concupiscence had been kind—far kinder than she could ever have imagined they would be to a thirty-something literary agent with a bad record for choosing the wrong sort of man.

'Colombia is a strikingly beautiful country,' Hugh went on. 'I remember so vividly the flight in that small plane over the rich green landscape. The pilot said that we could fly low if I wished to see things: villages, colourful buses on the roads, fields, those great, towering trees they go in for. Then suddenly there was a landing strip on a sweep of land in front of a large hill, and we were down.

'We were miles from anywhere, on a landing strip cleared out of thick bush. Under the trees to one side of the strip there was a jeep—two jeeps, in fact—one with two or three men carrying small machine guns. That did not surprise me all that much—I had become used to seeing machine guns in Colombia. People had to have them to protect themselves against attack from all sorts of quarters. It would have been surprising, in fact, if my hosts had not had any machine guns—it would have been a reason to be suspicious.

'My hostess was waiting to greet me up at the main house. I had met her once before at the school when she had come to discuss her son's progress, and I had quite liked her. She had the bearing that the South American rich have—a sort of imperious confidence that comes from knowing just what their wealth confers upon them, which is immunity from the lot of everybody else, whatever that may be. And they don't hesitate to let you know that they have a lot of money. In this country the rich are discreet: 'Rich? Not us! Oh no!' In South America it's very different.

'Apolinar, their son, was standing with his mother on the veranda when I arrived. He was thirteen or thereabouts, and he hadn't made a particular impression on me at the school. I remembered his name, of course, as it was Spanish for Apollo. In fact, I found myself thinking of him as Apollo rather than Apolinar, which made things rather comic. *Has Apollo done his homework yet?* is rather a strange thing to ask yourself, don't you think?'

Barbara laughed but then stopped herself, remembering that she had promised not to. But Hugh was laughing too. Then he became grave again.

'I had no idea at the time,' he said. 'None.'

82. *Poisonous Snakes*

'My hostess,' Hugh continued, 'left Apollo to show me round. His manner was rather shy at first, which was understandable I suppose, in view of the fact that I was one of his teachers—even though there were probably only six years between us. Such a gap may be nothing later on, but at that age it seems like a whole generation.

'The house was vast, rambling off in every direction from a central courtyard, but with the comfortable intimacy that you find in Spanish colonial architecture. We don't go in for courtyards in this country, do we? I wish we did.'

Barbara frowned. Did we really have no courtyards? Hugh saw the effect of his question and pressed her on it. 'Well, just think: how many people do you know who have a courtyard in their house?'

She thought there must be some, but when she tried to list them . . .

351

'You see?' said Hugh. 'We're deprived of courtyards.'

'Well, so many people live in flats. You can't expect them to have a courtyard.'

Hugh was quick to contradict her. 'Yes, you can. If you go to a French or Italian city you'll see flats arranged around a courtyard. And there are some in Scotland. In some of those small fishing villages in Fife, quite modest houses have little courtyards. There are very few courtyards in England. Some, but not many.'

Barbara thought that there must be a reason for this. 'The weather?' she wondered. 'Why have courtyards if you have weather like ours? And space, too. We don't have much room, do we?'

Hugh was not convinced. 'A courtyard is actually rather a good thing to have in bad, blustery weather. You're sheltered from the winds. And as far as space is concerned, look at the room that is taken up by gardens. People insist on a little strip of grass and a flowerbed—but how much use do they get out of that? They would use the space much more if they had a courtyard and grew plants in tubs and troughs. I really think that.

'And there's another thing,' he went on. 'There's a book you should read. It's called *A Pattern Language* and it's by a group of architects. I think the main author's called Christopher Alexander, something like that. Anyway, they set out a whole lot of principles for humane architecture—for making rooms and houses in which people will feel comfortable. Rooms, for instance, should have light from two sources. Houses should not be built in long rows along the side of roads—that's why so much of urban Britain has been rendered sterile, you know, because people just don't feel comfortable living in long lines. They can't relate to the other people on the line. It's that simple. The same goes for American strip malls—they've killed cities. Whereas if you build everything in clusters, around what are effectively open-air courtyards, then it all feels quite different. People feel happy and secure. We feel at our most comfortable when we're living round a courtyard. It's just such a sympathetic space.'

Barbara smiled. She was enjoying the luxury of being with a young man who used the expression *sympathetic space*. That was a real treat. The expression, she felt, could be used as a shibboleth, an expression that one had to utter to establish *bona fides*—a password at the gate of the camp. But in spite of the sheer, almost physical pleasure of listening to Hugh talk about courtyards, she was keen to discover what had happened in Colombia.

'And the Colombian family's mansion had courtyards?' she asked.

'Bags of them. Small courtyards leading off bigger ones. Courtyards filled with plants—orchids grew well there. A courtyard that contained an aviary. Highly coloured South American parrots. A toucan. It was all very beautiful.

'Apollo was matter of fact about it; the children of the rich usually are. Didn't everybody have courtyards like this? That's what he probably thought. Either that, or he didn't care one way or the other. I suppose if you're called Apollo, there's a lot that's going to be beneath your notice.

'One of the servants had taken my bags to my room, which was at the back of the house, looking towards the large jungle-covered hill that dominated the property. It was a suite of rooms, actually. Leading off the bedroom was a sitting room with heavy Spanish colonial furniture and pictures of family ancestors: a fierce military type with an intimidating moustache; a rather sultry-looking woman in a blue satin dress, all ostrich feathers and bows; a couple of children dressed in uncomfortable-looking outfits, a pony standing behind them. How unhappy that pony looked— later on, during my incarceration, I used to stare at that pony's face and marvel at how well the artist had captured the state of being subservient, trapped, under the power of another. It was a look of resignation, of resigned acceptance of a fate that was not that which one would have chosen for oneself.

'Apollo took me outside to show me the swimming pool, which was reached by walking along a narrow, well-tended path through a great shrubbery of rhododendrons. The pool was at the edge of the cleared land where the house and outbuildings stood and it projected into the jungle itself. It was a large stone construction, rather like a half-sunken reservoir. To get into it, you had to mount several stone steps at the side, leading up to the rim, and there before you was the surface of the water, which was very clear but seemed black. This was because of the colour of the stone from which the basin was made. It was a sort of basalt, I think.

'The pool was fed by a stream that entered it at one end—it was really rather long. Then, at the other end, the water tumbled over rocks and became a small rivulet that disappeared into the shrubbery. Apollo explained that it was wise to

354

walk round the perimeter of the pool before diving in, because of snakes. They often became trapped, the smaller ones finding it difficult to surmount the obstacle presented by the six inches or so of sheer stone between the water and the top of the wall. There was a net on a long pole, which could be used to extract the snakes from the water and deposit them in a large urn that the gardeners had placed at the edge of the shrubbery.

'I asked him if the snakes were poisonous and he replied that many were. 'Everything is dangerous in this country,' he said. "Snakes, plants, mountain roads . . . mothers."'

83. Freddie de la Hay Forgiven

William had loved his Belgian Shoes, even if he had only had them for a very brief time. They had been so comfortable, with their lightness and their soft, horsehair-filled soles. And now, holding the piece of mangled leather he had taken from Freddie de la Hay's jaws, he reflected on how foolish, indeed how vain it was to be proud of something like an item of clothing or a pair of shoes. But that was how we were—the pride we felt in childhood when we got something new to wear never really went away. When he was six he had been given a pair of red wellington boots that had filled his heart to bursting point with pride and pleasure; he had been reminded, years later, by his mother how he refused for weeks to take the boots off, wearing them to bed, to church, everywhere.

Marcia looked at Freddie de la Hay with horror when she realised what he had done. 'You wicked, wicked dog!' she shouted. 'Bad dog!'

Freddie de la Hay hung his head. A small drop of saliva fell from his mouth to the floor; it could have been a tear.

'Smack him,' Marcia urged. 'William, you can't let him get away with it! Your lovely Belgian Shoes. Bad, bad dog!'

'I can't smack him,' said William. 'He's already suffering remorse. Look at him. He's saying sorry.'

'Rubbish,' snapped Marcia. 'He's just bad.'

William shook his head. 'He's not bad. He's had a bit of a lapse, that's all.'

He crouched down on his haunches and gently lifted up Freddie's snout so that man and dog were looking at one another eye to eye. 'Freddie, I'm very disappointed,' he said. 'Those shoes . . . well, they were very special shoes. Do you promise never to do that again?'

Freddie stared at William. He knew that he had done something terrible and that he was in disgrace. He was not quite sure what it was, but he

356

knew that there had been a sudden interruption of the current of love and affection that existed between him and William, which was, for him as it was for all dogs, the entire rationale of his existence. His theology was simple: William existed, and he, Freddie, existed to do William's bidding and to please him. William's displeasure was terrible unto him, and he could not bear it. But now his owner was patting his head and that brief, awful period of being cut off was over. He licked William's hand, grateful for the restoration, the forgiveness.

Marcia turned away. Seeing William forgive Freddie de la Hay in this way, she had become conscious of how vindictive she sounded when she had urged him to smack the dog. How mean she must have seemed in William's eyes; how cruel. William was a good man, a gentle and kind man, and she had behaved like one of those women, strangers to the case, who hammer on the side of the police van as it takes some unpopular criminal away from court and off to prison, the contemporary equivalent of the *tricoteuses* who knitted as the guillotine did its terrible revolutionary work.

This realisation amounted to more than a mere dawning of self-understanding; it made her see, too, how different they were. William was a sensitive, thoughtful man, and she admired him for that. But was she worthy of such a man? The problem was that there were depths to him that she simply could not match in herself. He was more perceptive than she was; he had read more; knew more about the world; saw things in a different, more subtly nuanced light. And while

357

she appreciated this, her appreciation was that of the amateur who gazes upon a work of beauty, a great painting perhaps: the work of art is admired, but the observer knows that it belongs to a realm of understanding that will be for ever beyond him. He may look on, but that does not mean he can *converse* with the artist.

All of this made her conscious that her decision to renounce her claim on him was the right one. And although Marcia did not know it, that very decision, in its unselfishness and realism, made her something of a great person too. She was unlikely ever to say anything profound; she would never change the way the world was; but she had taken a step in the direction of living rightly. That made Marcia great—in a tiny way.

She turned back to face William and Freddie de la Hay. 'I'm sorry,' she said. 'You're not a bad dog, Freddie de la Hay. We all fall into temptation from time to time.'

'Hear that, Freddie?' said William. 'Marcia says that you're not so bad after all.'

Freddie looked at Marcia and made to lick her from a distance—a token, virtual lick, but an important gesture nonetheless.

'I'll buy you a new pair of Belgian Shoes,' Marcia said to William. 'Tomorrow.'

'Oh, you can't do that,' protested William. 'They're very expensive.'

'How much?' asked Marcia.

'One hundred and seventy pounds,' said William.

Marcia laughed. 'That wouldn't be expensive by the standard of women's shoes. Men's shoes are obviously much cheaper.'

'Maybe,' said William. He was remembering the

358

pair of handmade shoes he had bought from John Lobb in St James's Street. 'Unless you get a pair of made-to-measure from Lobb. They're rather expensive.'

Marcia repeated her direct question. 'How much?'

William looked embarrassed. 'Two and a half thousand pounds,' he said. 'But they last a long time.'

Marcia let out a whistle. 'Imelda Marcos! You didn't, did you . . .' It was meant to be a question but it came out as an accusation.

William sighed. 'I'm afraid so. But they're extremely comfortable. At least Freddie didn't choose to chew them . . .' He stopped. A terrible possibility had occurred. And if the worst came to the worst, would he be able to forgive two and a half thousand in the same way he had forgiven one hundred and seventy?

Marcia had reached the same conclusion as William. 'You'd better go and check,' she said. 'Or would you like me to do it for you?'

William shook his head. 'I'll go.'

He went out of the kitchen. While he was away, Marcia looked down at Freddie de la Hay, who looked back at her, uncertain as to what this latest development meant. Was he in renewed disgrace? he wondered. And if so, why?

84. James Reveals His Good Eye

William returned, smiling; Freddie de la Hay's aberration had been confined to his Belgian Shoes and nothing else had been eaten. So while Marcia finished preparing the coquilles St Jacques, he went to the telephone to dial the number of the flat downstairs. Dee answered and confirmed that Caroline was in; she had a friend round, Dee said, but she was sure that she would be happy to speak.

'My friend Marcia and I need some advice on a painting,' William said to Caroline when she came to the phone. 'I wonder if you would be able to come up for a drink, or coffee, later on? Perhaps you would look at it.'

'You've bought a painting?' asked Caroline. 'How exciting.'

'Not quite bought,' said William. 'Sort of . . . sort of found, I suppose.'

'Even more exciting,' said Caroline. 'And of course I'd be happy to come up. May I bring my friend, James? He's doing the course with me but he knows much more than I do. He could be helpful.'

That, said William, would be perfect, and rang off. Then it was time for the coquilles St Jacques, which Marcia had cooked to perfection. They ate them in silent mutual enjoyment. There was no real need to say anything, at least on William's side, as he felt quite happy and replete. The new arrangement with Marcia, which removed all the threat from an otherwise tricky situation, was an unmitigated relief. Eddie was no longer living in the flat and inflicting his music on him—another cause for relief, if not outright celebration. And although he had lost a Belgian Shoe, his John Lobb shoes had escaped the attentions of Freddie de la Hay. The world, or his very small corner of it, could have been in a far worse state, and he was grateful for it. And for the scallops and Sauvignon blanc too.

When Caroline and James arrived half an hour later, William and Marcia were ensconced in the drawing room, Marcia on her sofa and William in his chair. Marcia had made no attempt to persuade William to sit on the sofa with her—a sign, he thought, of her better understanding of the relationship between them. So James was able to sit next to Marcia while Caroline occupied the small tub chair alongside William's armchair.

William asked James about his course and where it would lead. 'I'd like to work for a gallery or one of the auction houses,' James explained. 'I've been promised an internship at the end of the course, and that might help. But there are lots of people after those posts. Everybody wants to do that sort of thing. Or everybody who has a degree in the history of art, that is.'

'Well, it must be wonderful work,' said William. 'I sometimes go to the wine auctions at Sotheby's. I understand the excitement.'

'I'd like to work in the Old Masters department,' said James. 'I wish!'

'James has a very good eye,' said Caroline. 'He really does.'

'Go on,' said James modestly. 'Just because . . .'

'No, you do,' Caroline persisted. 'Remember when we saw that Brescia-school painting and everybody said that it was something else, and you said, no, it was Brescia. Even Professor Marinelli was wrong about that. And what he doesn't know . . .'

James laughed. 'Beginner's luck.'

'Well, we won't be showing you anything special,' said William.

'What will you be showing us?' asked James.

William shrugged. 'I don't know. It looks old—or it looks old to me. But I suppose that somebody could paint something today and make it look old.'

'Of course they could,' said James. 'They'd have to make their own paints, of course—you can't get modern paints to do the trick. Everything painted with modern paints—paint out of a tube—looks far too chalky and white. You need to mix pigments with varnishes and a drop of oil. That enables you to get the light effect that you find in Old Masters. You put on layer after layer and the light shines through.'

'James knows how to do it,' said Caroline. 'James could have been a great painter if he wanted.'

James blushed. 'You're really flattering me tonight, Caroline. I couldn't.'

As they spoke, Marcia looked on, bemused. She was wondering about the nature of the relationship between the two students—were they just friends or was there something more between them? It was difficult to tell. He was obviously the sensitive type, which meant that he might not be interested, but one could never tell. It was quite wrong to assume that just because a man tucked his legs underneath him, as James was doing on the sofa next to her, and lowered his eyelids when he spoke—it was wrong to assume just because he did those things that he would not be interested in Caroline. And even if he was not interested in her, it was clear to Marcia that Caroline was interested in James. Any woman could tell that.

For his part, William was wondering what Caroline saw in James. That was a very peculiar way to perch on the sofa, but then everybody was so peculiar these days, in William's view, one could not read anything into anything. Caroline was really very attractive, but William wondered whether James was even aware of it. He rather thought James was not, and he felt a momentary pang of regret. Here was an attractive, physical girl, obviously in desperate need of a boyfriend, and here was he, William—too old even to be considered by her—while this boy seemed to take her completely for granted. It was all very depressing. He thought of Eliot's poem, and of wearing the bottoms of one's trousers rolled. Prufrock, was it? Am I Mr Prufrock in the flat above? Is that what I am to her?

'Shall I get the painting?' he said.

James clapped his hands together. 'Yes, let's see it. I can't wait. Ooh!'

William smiled at the *ooh*.

'Before you get it,' said Caroline, 'tell us where you found it.'

'In a wardrobe,' said Marcia.

The two students looked at her in astonishment, while William went out of the room to fetch the painting from his study. When he came back, he held it turned away from them. 'Close your eyes,' he said.

They did, and he turned the painting round. They'll say something disparaging, he thought; a cheap nineteenth-century souvenir of the Grand Tour—something like that.

'Open your eyes now.'

James let out a gasp. Then he muttered, '*Caspita!*'

'Who was he?'

James looked up at William. 'Sorry. He wasn't an artist—*caspita* is an Italian exclamation. It expresses how I feel looking at . . . looking at this painting.'

And you? thought William, turning to gauge Caroline's reaction.

Caroline said nothing at first. Then, glancing at James, she frowned. A shadow came over her and it was as obvious to William as a thundercloud in the sky. He looked again at James, who had reached out to take the small painting from William's hands and was holding it out in front of him. There was no shadow there—just astonishment, and unmistakable, spontaneous delight.

85. *A Poussin in Pimlico*

William gazed intently at James as he studied the painting in front of him. Marcia watched him too, and even Freddie de la Hay, his disgrace forgotten, looked on with interest.

'First impressions,' said James, 'are so important. You look at a good painting and *bang*, it's there. You just *feel* it.'

'It's the same with wine,' William said. 'You know when you first experience it when it's a great wine.

364

It can change in the glass, of course, but that first encounter leaves you in no doubt. I tasted a 1961 Médoc the other day. The balance!' He paused. 'But I'm distracting you.'

James looked up and smiled. 'Not at all. I like talking about wine too. It all involves aesthetics. And isn't it amazing how things survive? There's your wine, in its fragile bottle, surviving almost fifty years, and here's this painting, in pretty much the condition it was when it left Poussin's studio . . . Except the colours in just about all Poussins have faded rather badly.'

'Poussin!' exclaimed Caroline.

James turned to her and smiled triumphantly. 'Yes, Poussin. Nicolas Poussin.'

Caroline, who had leapt to her feet in her excitement, now sat down again. 'I don't believe it,' she muttered.

'You don't?' asked Marcia. She wondered whether she should have been incredulous too. The problem, though, was that she was not sure who Poussin was. Picasso, yes. But Poussin?

It was as if James sensed Marcia's

embarrassment. 'Don't worry,' he said. 'Lots of people aren't all that familiar with Poussin. There are so many painters!'

That helped. 'Is he important?' Marcia asked.

James nodded. 'Immensely. He was a great classical painter. He disapproved of other French painters of his time and went off to Rome. He did some wonderful paintings.'

William was frowning. 'Do you really think that this is by him? And how can you tell?'

James placed the painting on the table in front of him. 'It's a question of style—principally. When you get to know an artist's work, you'll always recognise it—in much the same way as you'll recognise a face. It's just there, the flow and feel, the way of looking at the world—everything. It's like a signature.' He turned to William. 'It's the same with your wine, surely? You know where a wine comes from when you first taste it. You may not be able to put your finger on the exact reason, but you know, don't you?'

William agreed. But how could one tell, he wondered, whether something was the real thing, as opposed to an imitation or a copy? He raised this doubt now. 'What about that chap who did the Vermeers during the War? If he could churn out Vermeers, then surely there could be somebody doing Poussins—in the same convincing way?'

James reached out and touched the picture lightly with his fingertips. 'Of course you're right,' he said. 'This could be a copy by a follower of Poussin. A very good follower. It could be of the period, or it could be by a modern forger. It could be anything. But to me it looks like a Poussin—a very small Poussin. Mind you, I'm no expert . . .'

'James is only a student,' Caroline pointed out. 'Nobody will listen to a student.'

'We're listening,' said Marcia.

James smiled. 'Thank you. But Caroline's right. My opinion counts for nothing. We need to show it to somebody whose attribution will stand for something. We need to find an authority on Poussin.'

'Can you do that?' asked Marcia. 'Can you just approach somebody out of the blue like that?'

'Of course,' replied James. 'That's what these people are there for. And there's bound to be a Poussin expert in London. There was Anthony Blunt, of course, at the Courtauld . . .'

William looked up sharply. 'The Fourth Man?'

James sighed. 'That's right. He's dead now, of course. And people seem only to remember the fact that he was a spy. They don't remember what he did for Art History. Or for the Courtauld Institute. Or for all the students he helped.'

William raised an eyebrow. 'He spied for one of the greatest tyrannies the world has ever known,' he said. 'He lived in a democracy but spied for a tyranny.'

James was cautious. 'He believed in his cause, I think. People really believed in communism; they thought that it was the only possible way out. And once he was recruited—as a young man—it might have been difficult to escape. I can imagine how easy it was to find oneself on the wrong side and then . . .'

William thought for a moment. 'Yes. It's not as simple as people think it is.'

'It never is,' said Marcia.

'Yet I don't condone what he did,' added

William.

'Nor do I,' said James.

They looked at Caroline. 'He had no real excuse,' she said. 'What a mess he made of his life. And then he was publicly humiliated.'

'Even if what he did seemed unforgivable,' said William, 'perhaps we should still have forgiven him.'

'Well, we can't ask Blunt,' concluded James. 'But there's bound to be someone. So what do you want us to do, William?'

Marcia now made a suggestion. 'We've shown them the painting,' she said to William, talking as if Caroline and James were not in the room. 'I think we should tell them about how we came to have it. About whose wardrobe it was in and so on. Then we can all decide what to do.'

Caroline had already guessed. 'It was Eddie's wardrobe, wasn't it?'

William confirmed this, and added, 'I think . . . well, I have to say that I think it's stolen—how else would it be here?'

'He may have bought it in an antique shop,' ventured Caroline. 'Sometimes you see paintings hanging up in such places. They often have no idea what they've got.'

William thought this unlikely. 'Those characters—the dealers—know what's what. If they see anything remotely interesting, they show it to an expert. It's inconceivable these days that any antique dealer would let something like this slip through their fingers.' He paused. He had more to say on the subject of the painting's provenance. 'I should tell you, by the way, that I found a site on the web. It lists stolen paintings, and there was

368

nothing by Poussin, I'm sure. So—'

'If the owner knew that it was a Poussin,' James interjected. 'What if this had simply been an attractive painting hanging on his wall? He might have had no idea at all what he had. Then along comes somebody and steals it.'

William winced. That *somebody* could have been his only son.

86. *Terence and Berthea*

'It's entirely unsuitable,' said Berthea Snark. 'You told me that you were buying a Peugeot. Now look what you've gone and done. You've bought a Porsche. What am I to think, Terence? Honestly, you tell me—what am I to think?'

It was Tuesday morning, and Berthea was at breakfast in the garden room of her brother's Queen Anne house on the edge of Cheltenham. It was a fine morning and the sun was streaming through the large glass windows, making brilliant the white tablecloth, glinting off the cutlery laid at each end of the breakfast table. It was a day that made Berthea glad that she had postponed her return to London and still had two weeks to spend in the bucolic surroundings of Cheltenham, even if looking after Terence was proving to be a frustrating experience. One does not expect one's brother to have a near-death experience when one goes to spend a few days with him; nor does one expect him to buy a totally unsuitable Porsche, when up to that point he has been perfectly content to drive a Morris Traveller.

Terence, who was cutting the top off his boiled egg, seemed unconcerned. 'It's a lovely little car,' he said. 'It used to belong to Monty Bismarck. So I know it's been well looked after.'

Berthea made a face: Monty Bismarck sounded a completely unsuitable man from whom to buy a car. 'And who exactly is this Monty Bismarck? You've mentioned him before,' she said.

'Monty is Alfie Bismarck's son,' he explained. 'Alfie has racehorses. A terribly nice man. He's offered me a share in a racehorse on several occasions but I've never taken him up on it. Maybe I shall sometime in the future.'

Berthea sighed. 'I don't think so, Terence. But tell me—why did you want a car like that? Is it a . . .' She hesitated. Terence was sensitive to criticism from her, but there were some questions that just demanded to be asked. 'Is it a potency issue?'

Terence looked at her in puzzlement. 'I really don't see what a car has to do with potency, of all things. What a funny thing to say, Berthy! You really are a silly-billy!'

Berthea busied herself with the buttering of a piece of toast. 'Well,' she said briskly, 'don't say that I didn't warn you. I've had so many middle-aged male patients for whom the purchase of a car has been the first sign of something going awry. It's the new car first and then it's infidelity. New car, new girlfriend. It's all so predictable.'

Terence sighed. 'But I don't have anybody to be unfaithful to, Berthy. You know that.'

Berthea's hand was poised above the toast. Terence was not one for self-pity, and the absence of that unattractive quality made the words he had just uttered all the more poignant. Berthea looked

370

at her brother and reflected on how we allow loneliness in others to escape our attention. The lonely are often brave, putting on the pretence of being content in their condition but all the time wanting the company of another. Was that how it was for Terence? Did he sit by himself in this morning room, contemplating empty days in which there would be nobody to speak to? Did he yearn for telephone calls that he knew would never come? She realised that his telephone never rang—indeed she had had no idea where it was until she had been obliged to look for it quickly when he had had his near-death experience. Poor Terence! And here she was sniping at him over his one little extravagance, the one bit of excitement in his life, this new Porsche of his. It was like laughing at a little boy's new bicycle, like saying that it was too red, or too small, or that the girls would laugh at him as he rode it. It was every bit as mean as that.

Berthea put down her knife. 'Actually, Terence, I'm having second thoughts. Maybe it is just the car for you. It must be lovely and fast.'

Terence responded immediately. 'Oh it is, Berthy—it really is. Do you know, when I went for the test drive yesterday, Mr Marchbanks and I did over forty-five miles an hour! You just touch the accelerator and *zoom!* Before you know it you're doing forty and above.'

Berthea tried to appear impressed. 'And I bet it's got a radio and CD player,' she said. 'Surround-sound, I should think.' Berthea actually did not know what surround-sound was, but she did know that it was highly sought after and was just the thing for a Porsche.

Terence looked blank. 'Is there a radio? I'm not sure. And as for a gramophone, I expect it has one but I haven't found it yet. We'll have plenty of time to read the manual and see how to work everything. Plenty of time.'

His own mention of time made him look at his watch. He was due at sacred dance in twenty minutes and, even if he was driving there in his Porsche, he would have to leave in ten minutes or thereabouts.

'Sacred dance calls,' he said. 'Are you going to come?'

At first, Berthea's response was to feel reluctant. She did not relish the thought of mixing with Terence's peculiar friends—and they would be peculiar, because his friends had *always* been peculiar—but at the same time she felt that she owed it to her brother to go. She had pledged that she would. I must not be selfish, she told herself. I must be more supportive of poor Terence, Porsche and all.

'Very well,' she said. 'I'll come along. But what should I wear?'

'Something loose,' said Terence. 'I wear a tracksuit. But if you don't have that, choose clothes that you can dance in. Nothing too tight.'

Berthea remembered something. 'Last time I was staying with you,' she said, 'I left a tennis dress in the wardrobe. Do you think it will still be there?'

'I'm sure that it will be,' said Terence. 'And it would be ideal. We encourage white. My anorak, as you will see, is entirely white. So your tennis dress will be perfect. And I can lend you some white socks—I have plenty of those.'

They went off to their respective rooms to get

372

changed, and a short time afterwards met in the hall.

'There we are,' said Terence. 'Both of us quite white! The Beings of Light love white because that is the colour of their auras.'

Berthea said that she was sure that they did. And would the Beings of Light be in attendance on this particular morning?

'Of course they will,' said Terence. 'They are always there, even if they are on a different plane. We can reach their plane by opening ourselves mentally to their thought-realm. That can be done through sacred dance.'

'I look forward to it,' said Berthea.

She wanted to ask how long it would take but felt it would be tactless. Terence's functions always seemed to go on far too long, and she was sure that sacred dance would be no exception. She did not ask. She would be positive about this. *Think positively*, she whispered under her breath.

'What was that?' asked Terence. 'Did you say something, Berthy?'

'I said I'm positively looking forward to this, Terence.'

He beamed. 'I'm so happy, Berthy. And did I tell you? The BBC people are coming to make a programme about us. They'll be there at the dance, filming. So just think—your friends might see you! What fun!'

87. Sacred Dance

The sacred dance meeting was held on the back lawn of a large Victorian house belonging to a member of the group.

'It's the best possible place,' Terence explained to Berthea as they walked round the side of the house. 'Minnie—she lives here—has been in the group since it started. She went to Bulgaria two years ago and danced on some of the sacred mountains there. They were not far from Peter Deunov's birthplace at one point, and Minnie said that the presences were very strong. The energy fields that Peter Deunov left behind him— wherever he travelled—were just overwhelming, Berthy. You know, some people say that this happens with lots of spiritual leaders. Places are different after they've been there. They change them.'

'Highly unlikely,' said Berthea. 'That last Pope, for instance—he travelled a lot. Were all those airports somehow different after he had been through them?'

'Very possibly,' said Terence. 'I hadn't really thought about it, but very possibly they were.'

Berthea chose to say nothing. It was the best thing to do with Terence, she had decided. There was no point in trying to persuade him of anything; he was on another wavelength altogether and he simply did not take in what you said, no matter how hard you tried.

They rounded the house and found themselves at the edge of a sweeping lawn, beautifully tended, surrounded on three sides by a tall yew hedge. In the middle of the lawn a group of about twelve people, all dressed in white, were standing in a semi-circle, hands joined. Beside them, conspicuous for their dark clothes, stood two men, one with a large video camera resting on his shoulder. The cameraman was engaged in conversation with one of the dancers, who was describing circular movements with his hands.

Terence turned to Berthea. 'Oh look, Berthy! The BBC!'

Berthea had a sinking feeling in the pit of her stomach. 'I don't know if I want to dance with them looking on,' she said. 'They'll . . . they'll interfere with the flow. Spoil the karma.'

Terence was not going to be put off by this. He turned to his sister and shook a finger. 'Naughty, naughty! I see that the Devil can quote scripture for his own purposes! Naughty!'

One of the dancers, a small woman somewhere in middle age, came over to join them. She looked inquisitively at Berthea and then turned her gaze to Terence.

'I've brought my sister,' said Terence. 'Minnie, this is Berthea. And Berthea, this is Minnie.'

'Peace be with you,' said Minnie.

Terence leaned over and whispered to Berthea. 'You say: "Peace be upon your house, and in your steps."'

Berthea did as she was told. In *what* steps? she wondered. In the steps of the house? Or in the steps of the dance?

Minnie acknowledged the greeting. 'I thought perhaps you had brought a girlfriend, Terence,' she said playfully.

'I'm between girlfriends,' said Terence.

'Oh well,' said Minnie. 'Such a gay cavalier! There'll always be another time. The Beings of Light are patient. They think in centuries.'

'I would have thought that they don't think at all,' said Berthea. 'Are they not above thought?'

There was complete silence. The other dancers, who had been chatting to one another, all turned and stared at Berthea.

She gulped; there was no going back now. 'Time is meaningless,' she said. 'It is . . . without meaning.'

The silence persisted. 'Without time, we are timeless,' Berthea went on.

Now there was a buzz of excited conversation. Minnie raised a hand for people to be quiet. 'Our sister has revealed something to us today,' she said. 'And what she says is . . . Well, it's just *so true*. And now I'd like to dedicate our first dance to an interpretation of our sister's insight. This dance will be called "Without Time We Are Timeless". Our sister will stand in the middle of the circle to represent time itself. We shall weave around her, all holding hands, inviting the Beings of Light to join us. Then we'll see what happens.'

Bertha found herself pushed into the middle of the circle. From a woman standing on the edge of the circle she heard the comment, 'That's a tennis dress, you know. It is not a pure garment at all.' She did not see who said it though, and could not respond with a discouraging glare. She was conscious of the BBC camera, which was moving from one member of the group to another, its automatic telephoto lens whirring in and out as the focus adjusted.

The dancers began to move round in a circular motion, like the figures in Matisse's painting. Some of them were chanting, others were silent, but all were smiling benignly as they danced. Minnie occasionally uttered a high-pitched whistling sound.

'O Sister Time,' implored Minnie. 'Tell us about time.'

'Yes,' sang a thin woman dancing next to Minnie. 'Enlighten us, O timeless one.'

Berthea, who had been swaying slowly from side to side, more from embarrassment than conviction, looked at her wristwatch; she would have to say something.

'It's ten-thirty,' she chanted.

'Ten-thirty!' repeated one or two of the dancers.

At this point the BBC cameraman, who was standing just outside the circle, his camera trained on the dancers, began to laugh. Minnie, looking over her shoulder, frowned at him, as did the thin woman who had also been singing invocations to Sister Time.

'I'm sorry,' muttered the cameraman, trying to

control himself. But it was just too difficult, and the camera resting on his shoulder began to wobble wildly. His assistant, who was holding a powerful lamp on an extended pole, began to giggle.

'Beings of Light!' intoned Minnie.

'That's you,' muttered the cameraman to his assistant.

This brought more giggles from the lighting man.

'Stop!' shouted Minnie, clapping her hands together. 'We have some very negative forces present today.' She turned and glared at the cameraman. 'You're behaving very discourteously,' she admonished, 'and I must ask you to leave.'

The cameraman lowered his camera. 'I'm sorry,' he spluttered. 'I really am. It's just that . . . You know how it is, sometimes one gets an attack of the giggles for no reason at all. It's nothing to do with you.'

'But it is,' said Minnie, shaking a finger at him. 'It's everything to do with us. You think we're funny, don't you? Oh, there are plenty of people like you, you know—people who mock the spiritual lives of others. We admitted you to our dance and now you're laughing at us.'

The cameraman looked down at the lawn.

'I think you should leave,' said Berthea from the centre of the circle. 'It's easy to laugh, isn't it?'

The cameraman looked at her with regret. His assignment was ruined; they would never get an interview with Minnie now. He would have to explain himself to his editor. 'I'm terribly sorry,' he said. 'I really am.'

Berthea looked at him intently. She was the hard-bitten psychoanalyst now. She was angered by

378

this man and his presumptions.

'I don't think that you're really sorry,' said Berthea. 'Not really. You'll laugh at these people behind their backs, won't you? The moment you leave. Your type thinks it funny to humiliate people, to laugh at them.'

The cameraman turned to his assistant. 'We'd better pack up, Bill.'

The assistant nodded.

'We shall resume our dance in due course,' said Minnie. 'Agreed?'

The dancers all agreed.

'They're jolly rude,' said Terence, with some force. 'But then what can you expect these days? Everybody's so rude.'

88. Through the Letterbox

It had been William's idea that James should take the Poussin with him.

'There's no point my trying to find out anything more about it,' he said, pressing the painting into James's hands. 'You take it and show it to the right person.'

James looked at the painting dubiously. It was nice to hold a Poussin, but a *stolen* Poussin? He glanced uncertainly at Caroline.

'Or Caroline could hold on to it,' he suggested. 'Then it can stay safely here in Corduroy Mansions. My place . . .'

Caroline came to the rescue. 'Is less secure,' she supplied. 'James's building has had two break-ins recently. Or is it three, James?'

'One, actually,' said James. 'The flat downstairs was broken into last month. They didn't take much. Just some books. A literate burglar apparently.'

'Anyway,' Caroline continued, 'I'll look after it. Then we can work out what to do.'

The pair returned to Caroline's flat and made themselves a cup of coffee.

'Well,' said James, 'what are we going to do?'

Caroline picked up the painting and studied it closely. 'Did you look at the snake?' she asked. 'It has lovely, fluid lines. As if somebody's just taken a crayon and drawn an S. Just like that.'

'That's what makes a great painting,' said James. 'Everything looks as if it should be there. Of course, Poussin was interested in snakes. There's that famous picture in the National Gallery of the man bitten by the snake at the side of the road.'

'What are we going to do, James?'

'That's what I just asked you.'

Caroline sighed. 'Of course we could just do nothing.'

James frowned. 'You know, I rather regret agreeing to take it. What if it is stolen? We'll be in possession of stolen property. And who would believe us if we said that it had been found in a wardrobe?' He looked anxiously at Caroline. 'I think that we should take it back to William. It's his problem—not ours.'

Caroline agreed. 'I'll take it back to them right now.'

'I hope that you don't disturb them.'

Caroline looked puzzled.

'I mean, they were having some sort of romantic dinner. You know . . .'

Caroline laughed. 'But he's *ancient*,' she said. 'Fifty-something.'

'I'm just warning you,' said James. 'You might find them having a cuddle on the sofa.'

'I'll take that risk,' said Caroline. 'They're probably playing Scrabble.'

As she went upstairs, she thought about what James had said. It was all very well for him to imagine the neighbours having a love life—but where was his? They had skirted around the issue of their relationship both verbally and physically. Nothing had happened—absolutely nothing. She, of course, found James attractive, and he had said, had he not, that he found women interesting, and yet there had not been so much as a kiss or a tender gesture—he had been as chaste as a monk.

It's hopeless, she thought; it really is. Lovely, amusing James was lovely and amusing because he was above all that. If she wanted a love affair then she was wasting her time with him; they would be friends—they already were close in that sense—but it would never mature into anything else. Perhaps she should be satisfied with that—her half a glass of blessings rather than a full one.

Unless, of course, she made the first move. Perhaps that was the key to it. James was inexperienced and probably did not know what to do, or was too shy to do it. Well, she could show him. She could turn the lights down and put on a suitable piece of music, and perhaps one thing would lead to another. What music? she wondered. 'My Heart Will Go On'. That was a good choice. People had been using it as a romantic background for years.

By the time she had climbed the stairs to

William's flat she had decided that she would act. Tonight would be the night where things were decided: whether she and James would have a proper relationship, or whether it would be made finally and unambiguously clear that they were just good friends.

She looked at the fanlight above the door. It was in darkness, and she hesitated. Perhaps James was right; perhaps it would be tactless to ring the bell now. She bent down and peered through the letterbox; the dim light coming through a window picked out the shape of the hall table but there was no light from anywhere else.

She stood up again. She would have to take the Poussin back to the flat, which was irritating, unless . . . She peered through the letterbox again. It was as she had remembered: the floor was carpeted.

Very gently, taking care not to scratch the frame, she posted the painting through the letterbox. There was a dull thud as it landed on the carpet. No, it's not irresponsible, she told herself. I've merely returned it to its owners—or its sort-of-owners.

Back in the flat below, James asked her what had happened.

'It's back where it belongs,' she said. 'You can get William to take a photograph of it and you can show that to people at the Institute.'

James agreed that this was a good idea.

'Now,' said Caroline, 'there was something I wanted to talk about.'

James was sitting on the sofa, paging through a magazine. He looked up with interest. 'Paris?' he asked. 'Do you want to talk about our trip to Paris?

I'm so looking forward to that, Caroline. Aren't you?'

She nodded. 'Yes. It's going to be great.'

'Do you know the Renoirs in the Orangerie?' asked James. 'There's a whole corridor of them. They're really lovely.'

'I love Renoir,' said Caroline vaguely. She suddenly thought that it might be better to put her plan into action in Paris. Paris was far better than 'My Heart Will Go On' for seduction purposes. Seduction . . . Is that what I'm doing? she asked herself.

'Where are all the others?' James suddenly asked. 'Jenny. Dee. Jo. Where are all your flatmates?'

'They probably went to the pub,' said Caroline.

There was a sound at the front door. Caroline thought that somebody—one of her flatmates— was coming back, but then the sound became a knock.

'Somebody at the door,' said James.

'Evidently,' said Caroline.

She looked at her watch; it was a bit late for a casual caller. William? Did he want to find out why they had returned the Poussin? Or somebody else?

89. Resolution

'Tom!'

He stood before her, in black jeans and a striped jersey, fiddling with a car key in his right hand. He looked at her in a slightly bemused way.

'Pleased to see me? I was passing by.' He leaned

forward. 'Give us a kiss.'

She stepped towards him and he seized her, dropping his car key as he planted a kiss on her cheek.

'Your hair smells terrific,' he said.

She could not help but laugh. 'What?'

'Your hair. It smells terrific.'

She made an incredulous face. 'Are you serious?'

'Of course I am. I know it's a cheesy thing to say, but it does.'

She was not sure what to do, but she could hardly leave him standing in the hall. 'Come in. You can't stand out there all night.'

He followed her in. 'I was driving past,' he said. 'And I thought I'd drop in. Did you get my messages? I left them on your mobile. Three. Maybe four. You should turn it on some time.'

She winced. 'I haven't checked my messages for days. I know I should. Sorry.'

He looked at her reproachfully. 'You haven't been in touch for ages. I had to go off to Frankfurt for . . . I forget, about six days. But I did try to contact you.'

They were standing in the flat now and Tom was looking towards the living room, where she and James had been sitting. Tom had noticed the light coming from there. 'The others?' he asked. 'Dee and what's-her-name?'

'Just me,' said Caroline. 'And a friend. He's still here.'

The effect of her words was immediate; she saw Tom become tense.

'Yes?'

'Yes,' she said. 'Come and meet him. He's on the course with me.'

She was relieved that James was still there. She had intended that things should fizzle out with Tom, and they had been drifting apart, but she had not taken the final step. I should have spoken to him before this, she thought. It's always messy if things are left hanging in the air.

They went into the living room. James had picked up another magazine and was flicking through it—one of Dee's vitamin magazines, Caroline noticed. He looked up when she came in with Tom.

'James,' she said. 'This is Tom. I don't think you've met.' She was certain that they had not encountered one another before this; what she was less certain about was whether James would remember who Tom was.

Tom stepped forward and the two men shook hands. She noticed James flinch at Tom's grip. The two had completely different handshakes, James's being artistic and Tom's being somewhat firmer. She almost smiled at the sight; the handshakes, she thought, said it all.

'So,' said Tom. 'Busy?'

'How about coffee?' said Caroline. 'James and I were about to—'

'About to what?' Tom interjected.

'About to have coffee. Would you like some?'

He nodded. 'All right. Thanks.'

He and James sat down while Caroline moved off to the kitchen. This is not good, she said to herself. And once in the kitchen, which gave off the living room, she stood near the door while the kettle boiled, listening to what was being said.

'So you're doing the same course? You and Caroline.'

'Yes,' James replied. 'It's a great course.'

'Mostly women?'

There was a brief silence. 'Mostly, I suppose. Mind you, look at most courses these days. I know somebody who's a medical student and she says that most of the people in her year are women.'

'Oh. Well.'

The silence returned. Then Tom spoke again. 'Known Caroline long?'

'Just this year. On the course.'

'I see.'

Silence.

Tom cleared his throat with the air of one about to announce something portentous. 'You know that she and I are quite close? You know that?'

In the kitchen, Caroline froze.

James sounded quite calm. 'Yes, I did actually. Or used to be. I thought that you and she . . .'

'What?'

'I was about to say that I thought that you and she were . . . were drifting apart.'

'Who told you that? Caroline?'

James began to flounder. 'Well . . .'

'Well, whatever Caroline may have told you, the fact is that she and I have been seeing one another for ages. Get it?'

'Listen, this has got nothing to do with me. Caroline just said that she—'

Tom cut him short. 'Actually, I shouldn't really be worried. It doesn't seem to me that she's your type. Know what I mean?'

For a few moments nothing was said. Then, 'No, I don't know what you mean. Maybe you could explain.'

'I mean you don't look the type to me . . . to be

all that interested. Sorry, I don't want to get personal, but you just don't.'

Caroline decided that this was the point at which she would have to intervene. With the kettle almost boiling, she came out of the kitchen and caught Tom's eye. 'Tom, could I have a word in the kitchen, if you don't mind?'

Tom got up, smirking. He crossed the room and went into the kitchen, closing the door behind him. 'Yes?'

Caroline spoke through clenched teeth. 'Give me one reason, just one, why I shouldn't throw you out right now.'

'I don't know what you're talking about.'

'Oh don't you? Well, I'll tell you then. What did you say to James just now?'

Tom shrugged. 'This and that. Small talk.'

Caroline came up to him and stood up close. 'Oh yes? Well, I want you to go right now. If it wasn't quite over between us before, it is now.'

He didn't flinch. 'Are you saying that you prefer him through there to me?' He gestured with a motion of the thumb in the direction of the living room. 'That . . .'

'Don't you dare!' shouted Caroline.

'There's no accounting for taste, I suppose.'

'Get out!'

He turned and made to leave. 'So,' he said. 'This is how it ends.'

She hesitated. She had not ended it properly before this because she dreaded upset of any sort. And now, because she had failed to act, it was ending wretchedly.

She reached out to him. 'I'm sorry, Tom. I really am. I meant to talk to you and I . . . Well, I just let it drift. I like you. But it's not working any more. Sorry.'

He said nothing for a moment. It was clear to Caroline that there was some sort of internal struggle going on; she would let it. Then, after a while, he looked at her and said, 'I'm going to go through and apologise to him.'

He turned away and walked back into the living room. James had picked up the magazine again but had obviously not been concentrating on it.

'Listen,' Tom began. 'I'm sorry about what I said. I was upset. Jealous, I suppose. What I said was unkind and . . . Well, it was just stupid.'

James stood up. 'I don't mind,' he said. 'Thank you for apologising, anyway.'

Caroline watched as the two men shook hands. This time Tom tried to avoid crushing James's hand, and James made an effort to be firmer.

Later, when Tom had left, James said to Caroline, 'You know, Caroline, your hair *does* smell terrific.'

'Did you overhear that?'

'Yes. And tell me: is that what *real* men say? Is it really?'

90. *A Major Surprise (Of the Pleasant Variety)*

'You're going to have to carry on telling me about Colombia over supper,' Barbara said to Hugh. 'I can't wait to hear, but I'm absolutely starving. It's been that sort of day.'

'Of course,' said Hugh. 'How selfish of me. I've been nibbling at things while preparing them. And

you've been working hard all day.'

She smiled at this. He berated himself for selfishness but he was, in fact, as far as she could make out, completely unselfish. Ever since she had met him—although, admittedly, it was not all that long ago—she had been struck by the fact that what appeared to give him pleasure was doing things for her. He had insisted on carrying her luggage from the car; he had bought her flowers; he had cooked meals. Oedipus had done none of this. He had never even bought her a birthday present.

She looked at Hugh fondly. 'How did this happen?' she asked.

'What? The Colombian thing? I was telling you . . .'

'No. Not that. This thing between us. How did it happen?'

Hugh shrugged. 'We met. And . . .'

'And what?'

'We hit it off. I thought: here's the most interesting woman I've ever met. And then I thought: she won't even look at me.'

Barbara was astonished. '*You* thought that *I* wouldn't look at you?' She laughed at the very notion. 'Do you know that I was thinking exactly the same thing?'

James reached for her hand. 'We were both wrong. Fortunately. The planets were in alignment.'

She raised an eyebrow. 'You don't believe in all that, surely?'

He shook his head. 'Of course not. Who does?'

'Nobody I know. But I suppose there are some who do. And I suppose it's rather reassuring. All sorts of beliefs that we can't justify or prove may be reassuring.' She paused. 'I used to be so arrogant, so sure of myself, that I laughed at people who had what I wrote off as irrational beliefs. Then I realised that we all need something to cling on to. And that it's not necessarily a bad thing to have beliefs as long, of course, as they aren't positively harmful.'

He thought about this. 'I saw an advertisement on a bus yesterday,' he said. 'It was an advertisement for atheism. It said, "There's probably no God." It made me think.'

Barbara had read about these advertisements but had not herself seen one. 'I suppose everybody has the right to advertise a viewpoint. Atheists. Religious people. It's the same right they're exercising.'

'Yes,' said Hugh. 'But I wondered whether those advertisements were . . . well, were *kind*. I know that seems an odd word to use here but it's the word that came to me. Sometimes I think it's best not to voice doubts about beliefs that mean a great

390

deal to someone else.'

'Yes,' Barbara said. 'I agree. I suppose that being kind to one another includes not saying things you think may be true but which threaten to upset other people unduly. People may need their beliefs. For all I know, in their essence, in the heart of what they say, those beliefs may be expressing something that is very true—something that people really need to help them through life.'

'Such as?'

'That we need to love one another. It might be that people need to believe that they are loved by some divine being because they get precious little love on this earth. Would you set out to shatter such a belief?'

Hugh was certain he would not. 'It would be like . . .'

Barbara took over. 'Like shooting a dove. Or, as Harper Lee told us, like killing a mockingbird.'

Hugh mulled this over in silence. There was a curious intimacy about the moment, an intimacy that had been promoted by the subject of their discussion. Talking about love, and God, and what people owed to one another had brought them to a point of close spiritual communion that he had never before shared with a lover; it was a stripping away of everything, because one could not conceal anything in such a conversation. It was a conversation about essentials—the sort of conversation that mourners sometimes have after a funeral when for a few moments the reality of death brings people together in mutual appreciation of the simple gift of life.

Hugh looked at his watch. 'Dinner . . .'

'Of course.'

He touched her gently on the shoulder. 'You go and sit down. I'll bring things through from the kitchen.'

She saw that he had laid the table. There were two candles, yet to be lit, and another arrangement of flowers that she thought he must have bought from the florist's round the corner. There was a small flower, a small blue flower, on her plate, and she touched it, bruising the petals. She wanted to cry—to cry for sheer happiness.

He brought through the first course—slices of duck on a bed of salad, served with a dark red sauce. He lit the candles and took his seat opposite her, from which position he poured them both a glass of wine. He raised his glass in her direction.

'To Father Christmas,' he said.

She smiled. 'Even if it's not Christmas.'

'I know. But he must have such a difficult time. People expect him to give, give, give.'

She tasted the duck. The sauce was slightly tart, which was how she liked it. Suddenly she said without thinking, 'Don't go away, Hugh.'

He gave a start. 'Why do you say that? I never said anything about going away.'

Barbara took a sip of her wine to hide her embarrassment. She had spoken aloud, giving expression, as we sometimes do, to thoughts that she had not intended to reveal. 'I know you didn't. Sorry, I wasn't really thinking.'

Hugh was staring at her. 'About going away—of course I won't. And there's something that I need to say.'

She looked down at the table, at the small blue flower that she had put to the side of her plate.

'I'd like to marry you,' he said.

392

91. A Flower in the Air Between Two People

The next morning in Barbara Ragg's office at the Ragg Porter Literary Agency, she said to her colleague, Rupert Porter, 'I have some news for you, Rupert.'

'Ah!' said Rupert. 'Who's done a big deal then? Six figures. Dare I say it—seven?'

'It's nothing to do with advances,' said Barbara. 'It's to do with me.'

'Oh, to do with you, is it? Let me guess then. The author of your yeti book has turned up and he's covered in hair, as I said all along he would be, and you don't really know whether you can take him out to lunch or not?'

'Can't you be serious for two seconds?'

'Oh, little Miss Gravitas! All right, sorry. Some personal news.'

She waited for a few moments before she told him. 'I'm engaged.'

He had not expected this, and for a short time he seemed to lose his composure. 'You?' he asked in disbelief. And then he realised that that sounded a bit rude, and he followed it with immediate congratulations. 'Well, you and Oedipus! An MP's wife!'

She shook her head. 'Not to Oedipus. He and I haven't got back together. It's somebody else.'

'To the yeti? Is that *wise*? Such different backgrounds . . .'

'Very funny. To a young man called Hugh. I haven't known him all that long, but we became engaged last night.'

Rupert had now recovered sufficiently to congratulate her properly. He stepped forward and embraced her warmly. 'I'm very pleased to hear this, Barbara. It's very good news. Tell me about him.'

She realised that had he asked that question only a couple of days ago, she would not have been able to tell him very much. Now she knew a little more but it was still not a great deal.

'He's Scottish,' she said. 'He's lived in South America. He's . . .'

Rupert waited. 'What does he do?'

'I'm not too sure.'

Rupert's expression changed. 'You're not sure? How long have you known him?'

'Not very long,' said Barbara airily. 'But I'm sure. I'm absolutely sure.'

Rupert looked down at the floor. He had known Barbara for so long—all his life, in fact—that he almost regarded her as a sister. He had thought Oedipus was a terrible mistake, and he had been pleased to hear that they were no longer together, but was she now about to make another mistake, on a par with, or even exceeding, her Oedipal mistake?

He began nervously. 'I'm . . . I'm very pleased that you're happy, Barbara. The only thing is that this is rather . . . well, sudden, wouldn't you say? You know the old expression—"marry in haste, resent at leisure".'

'Actually it's *repent*, Rupert, although *resent* makes sense too. People do resent their partners, don't they?' She corrected herself. 'Not their *business* partners. Their spouses.'

'Of course they do—or some do. But the point is:

394

are you sure?'

She smiled serenely. 'Never more sure.'

Rupert thought for a moment. There was the question of the flat. That was always present, somewhere in the background, and now it came to the fore.

'Where are you going to live?' he asked, affecting a nonchalance that was not really there.

'Why, in London, of course. Hugh seems happy enough here.'

Rupert pursed his lips. 'I see. But what I meant was, where in London? Has Hugh got a place?'

'He's with me at the moment.'

Rupert persisted. 'But has he got his *own* place? His own flat?'

'I don't think so. He's a bit younger than me, you know. He hasn't bought anything yet.'

Rising from her desk, Barbara walked to the window and looked out over the rooftops. The office was on the top floor of a three-storey building in Soho and there was a good view of the neighbouring roofs. Directly opposite, the occupant of an attic flat had opened a window and was putting a small tub of red flowers out onto the roof to expose it to the sun. The flowers were a tiny splash of red against the grey of the roof.

'I wonder,' Rupert said. 'I would have thought that you might need a bit more room. You might move somewhere bigger.'

Barbara turned to look at him. You have this thing about my flat, she thought. You always have had. And my father bought it fair and square from your father, and that's all there is to it.

'But my flat is perfectly large enough,' she said. 'It has two bedrooms and then a study which could be used as a bedroom if one wanted. And the drawing room is really large too. It's wonderful for parties.'

Rupert received this badly. His own drawing room was far too small for entertaining and they had never had a party in the house as a result. It would have been different if the flat in Sydney Villa—Barbara's flat, or the flat she *claimed* to own—had come to him. They could have entertained on quite a scale then.

Rupert tried again. 'Well, there may be a case for starting afresh somewhere,' he said. 'A lot of people like to set up in a place that is really their own—somewhere they've chosen together. Rather romantic!'

Barbara held his gaze. 'And a lot of people don't.'

'Oh well,' said Rupert. 'I hope that you'll be very happy, Barbara. Come, let me give you a kiss.'

He kissed her on the cheek and then went back to his own office. 'You'll never guess,' he said to his wife on the telephone. 'La Ragg is engaged!' And then he said, 'She doesn't want to move, by the way. She's installed the toyboy in the flat.'

Rupert's wife sighed. 'Oh well. We must take a look at him. I wonder who on earth would have taken her on? The yeti?'

'I cracked that joke too,' said Rupert.

Seated behind her desk again, alone in her office, Barbara found it difficult to concentrate on work. There were contracts to peruse but she felt too exhilarated to get down to it. So she closed her eyes and went over in her mind the previous evening with Hugh. The little blue flower by her plate; the care he had lavished on the preparation of the meal; his gentleness and humour; the way he looked at her. Everything. Everything.

She got up from her desk and returned to the window. The man in the attic flat opposite had appeared again. He was gazing at the red flowers he had placed outside on the lead surface of the roof. He yawned and looked across in her direction.

She caught his eye. He was only thirty or forty yards away. He smiled at her. They had seen one another from time to time and had occasionally waved. Now Barbara opened the window and leaned out. The man opposite leaned out too a little way, his hand resting on the edge of his tub of flowers.

'I love your flowers,' shouted Barbara.

'Thanks,' shouted the man in return.

A gust of wind had blown up and Barbara had to raise her voice to be heard. 'I'm terribly happy.'

The man made a thumbs-up gesture.

'I've just got engaged,' Barbara continued.

The man clapped his hands together and then, reaching forward, plucked one of his red flowers and threw it across to her. It was a lovely gesture, even if the flower fell far short of bridging the gap between them and dropped, a tiny Icarus out of the sky, tumbling down to the street below.

92. Caroline Goes to Lunch Again

If Barbara was certain that morning that she had found the man with whom she wanted to share her life, the same could not be said of Caroline. The final break with Tom, which could so easily have been messy, had proved to be simplicity itself. After his initial show of jealousy and resentment, manifesting itself in an almost immediately regretted bout of incivility towards James, Tom had proved to be perfectly reasonable. She suspected that they both wanted the break, and that his reluctance to let her go was no more than a vestigial sign of the feelings he had once had for her. Now it was done, and she was free again. Or was she?

James was a problem. She was becoming very used to his company—so used to it, in fact, that she found herself feeling dissatisfied and at odds on days when she did not see him. It was worrying, because it seemed to her that some sort of dependence was building up and she was not sure that that was what she wanted. Then there was also the question of James's fundamental suitability. That he liked her was not in doubt, but could he ever be *passionate* about her? And if he could not, then what was the point of his being anything more than a friend?

That morning, James was not in the lecture room for the lecture on sixteenth-century Venetian painting. His absence was expected: he had told her that he was due to go for an interview for a position at a gallery; the interview was to be at eleven, and was to be followed by lunch.

'A bad sign,' Caroline had said. 'If you go for a job and they ask you to lunch it's a bad sign.'

James seemed surprised. 'Oh? Why's that?'

'They're wanting to look at you in social surroundings,' she explained. 'They want to see how you hold your knife and fork.'

James laughed. 'Hello? This is the twenty-first

century, you know! People don't care about that sort of thing any more.'

Caroline defended herself. 'I'm not so sure about that. They won't be up-front about it, but they still do it. Or some do. And a gallery like that would definitely subscribe to that sort of thing. Look at their clientele. Look at the people who work in those galleries. They're not exactly rough diamonds.'

James looked downcast. 'Oh dear,' he said. 'Do you think I should even bother to go?'

His tone made her rather regret having issued the warning. 'Of course you should go. I was just telling you what I thought they might be doing. And anyway, I'm sure that your table manners are fine.'

He sighed. 'I don't know. Look, when you get a bread roll, you do break it, don't you, rather than cut it?'

'You do.'

'And what do you do with smoked salmon? Do you put it on the bread and then cut the bread, or do you eat the salmon with a knife and fork and have bits of bread in between mouthfuls?'

'I always put the smoked salmon on the bread,' said Caroline. 'Then I cut it into squares. But they're not going to pay any attention to that sort of thing. They'll just want to make sure that you don't talk with your mouth full or burp.'

James thought for a moment. 'What if I do burp?' he asked. 'What do I say?'

Caroline laughed. 'My parents always told me not to say 'pardon'. They said you should say 'excuse me'. But they're such snobs.'

'Could you just say "oops"?' asked James.

'Maybe.'

'And if I need to go to the loo,' James went on. 'What then? Do I call it 'the gents' or 'the loo'? Or what?'

'My father calls it the lavatory,' said Caroline. 'I think that's the approved word in really smart circles. Not the *lav*, but the lavatory. I don't like that word much, I'm afraid.'

'What about "the little boys' room"?' asked James.

'Definitely not. Extremely twee.'

' "The washroom"?'

'American. They're very keen on euphemisms.'

James nodded. ' "Letting go" means sacking someone. "I'm going to have to let you go" means "you're sacked".'

Caroline thought: I let Tom go. But then maybe he wanted to go. And at that point, she stopped her reverie, which had been a prolonged one, drifting from James to Tom, to home, to her parents; now the lecture on Venetian painting had ended and she found that all she had written in her Moleskine notebook was: 'The boundaries of what we call the Venetian School . . .'

She snapped the Moleskine shut and followed her fellow students out of the room. She felt at a bit of a loose end; there was an essay to write but she felt disinclined to start on it. If only James had been here, she would have taken him for lunch at that bistro where they had met Tim Something. Poor James—it was lunchtime now and he would be under inspection by his prospective employers, his handling of smoked salmon being judged according to some arcane precepts of the proper way to tackle such things. Yes, poor James.

400

She decided on the spur of the moment: she would go for lunch at the bistro—she would treat herself. Why not? There was no rule against having lunch by yourself.

She walked round Bedford Square and into Great Russell Street. She liked this part of London, which was such a contrast to the garishness of Oxford Street, not far away. The shops here were small and had character, and even if she was not in the market for antiquities or first editions, she liked to see them in the windows. She paused outside the headquarters of a bookshop that was also a press. A selection of titles was displayed in the window and her eye was drawn to *Sociobiology: The Whisperings Within*. She liked that. There were whisperings within all of us; whisperings that prompted us to do one thing rather than another, whisperings that made us what we were.

'The whisperings within,' said a voice at her side. 'Interesting! Should we listen to them?'

She spun round. Tim Something was smiling at her.

'You don't fancy a bit of lunch, do you?' asked the photographer.

Caroline hesitated. She had a feeling that the answer that she gave to this question might determine a great deal for her; it was not just lunch at stake.

'Yes,' she said. 'Why not?'

It was as if the answer came from someone else; not from the cautious self which she thought ran her life, but from another self altogether, a self of more instinctive stamp, a self that beckoned from altogether wilder, more exciting shores. And she could tell, just by looking at him, that Tim's invitation, as spontaneous as was her acceptance, came from the equivalent quarter within him.

93. Crop Circles

Terence Moongrove drove Berthea back from the sacred dance in his newly acquired Porsche.

'This is a very noisy car,' Berthea observed. 'And it is also rather low. It would be very difficult to get into it if one had arthritis.'

'Oh, I don't know,' said Terence. 'The engine is deliberately noisy. Mr Marchbanks told me that it is something they do on purpose. And as for its being low, that is just the way it is. It has something to do with making it possible to creep up behind people on the road and give them a fright when you overtake them.'

Berthea gave her brother a withering look but said nothing. *Homo ludens,* she thought—man at play. And while she would normally apply any observation about man in general to women as well—particularly in the case of the term *Homo sapiens*—in this case by *homo* she meant *vir* rather than *femina.* No woman, she imagined, would find creeping up behind someone in a Porsche fun. It was just not something a woman would ever do. Indeed, when she came to think of it, most women looked at cars as functional machines and judged them accordingly. Cars got one from A to B—that was the point of them. Certainly it was nice to have a car that did this in comfort, and it was also nice to have a car that looked appealing, but that was about the extent of female interest in cars. Men, it seemed to Berthea, never grew out of their boyhood fascination with cars; there was an unbroken line of psychological continuity between the toy cars that boys played with and the real machines they later acquired as men. *Puer ludens*, she thought, and immediately congratulated herself on the term. She could use it, perhaps, as the title of a paper. '*Puer Ludens*: Men As Boys'. That was rather nice.

Already the paper was being shaped in her mind. She would postulate a hypothetical mature man— the man who confronts the world in a rational, non-exploitative way; the man who treats others with consideration and is not constantly jockeying for position in relation to other men. And then she would investigate how the vestiges of boyhood prevent most men from reaching this plateau, this resolution.

Terence dropped Berthea at the house. 'I think I shall go for a little drive,' he said. 'I need to get used to the gears.'

'Be careful,' said Berthea, and she repeated the advice under her breath as she watched her brother disappear down the drive, the Porsche's throaty roar becoming fainter.

Terence drove slowly down the road. His foot was barely touching the accelerator and yet the car's engine seemed ready to run away with him. But this was not the place to test the car's performance—he would find a larger road for that, one where he could start overtaking. He had never been able to overtake anybody in the Morris Traveller and the thought of flashing past other drivers at speed rather appealed to him, particularly if he surprised them. I have so much overtaking to make up, he thought.

After a few minutes, Terence found himself on the very edge of town. The open road lay ahead, and the traffic, he noticed, was moving faster. He eased his foot down on the accelerator and the car shot forward. He glanced at the speedometer—the needle had edged up to sixty and his foot was barely on the pedal. He pressed it down a bit further. Seventy now. Was that the speed limit, or was it one hundred and seventy? He could not remember—it had all been so hypothetical with the Morris Traveller.

He looked in the rear-view mirror. There was a car behind him, a car that looked remarkably like his own: another Porsche. That's nice, thought Terence. Two Porsches out for a run together. He looked in the mirror again and recognised the face of the driver: Monty Bismarck. So that was his new Porsche; it looked very smart, Terence had to admit. He waved, and Monty Bismarck waved back. How nice for him to see me in his old car, thought Terence.

He decided to go a little bit faster, and pressed his foot down sharply. The car responded immediately, surging ahead as the powerful engine showed its form. The sudden increase in speed alarmed Terence, and he took his foot off the accelerator and applied it to the brake. Behind him, Monty Bismarck, seeing the brake lights glow red, himself braked sharply. This prompt action avoided a collision between the two cars, but it meant that Monty had to watch powerlessly as Terence's car, although now travelling much more slowly, left the road and shot through a hedgerow and into a field of ripening wheat.

When his car went off the road, Terence's first response was to close his eyes. But he quickly reopened them once he found himself in the field, with the car obediently continuing its journey, although at a slower pace. He was relieved that the consequences of the accident were so slight; all he would have to do, it seemed to him, was to drive round in a circle and he could then make his way out through the hole that he had created when he went through the hedge.

Terence described a complete circle in the field of wheat, arriving back at his point of entry. There he found Monty Bismarck standing beside his own Porsche, anxious to check on his welfare.

'You OK, Mr Moongrove?' Monty called out as Terence drew to a halt.

'Perfectly all right, thanks, Monty!' Terence replied. 'This is a jolly good car, you know.'

'Can't beat them, Mr Moongrove. But you need to be careful.'

Terence assured Monty that he would be. He switched off the engine and got out of the car to stretch his legs. Then he saw it.

'My goodness,' he said, pointing to the field behind him. 'A crop circle. See that, Monty?'

94. A Cultural Disaster

The first thing William did that morning was take Freddie de la Hay out for a walk. The streets were quiet at that time of day, although William often encountered fellow dog-owners similarly exercising

their charges. There seemed to be a comfortable freemasonry between the owners, clear common ground in a city of too many strangers, and greetings and dog news would often be exchanged. The dogs, too, appreciated the canine contact, Freddie de la Hay being on particularly good terms with a small, rather fussy Schnauzer and an elderly Dalmatian. William wondered what it was that led to a canine friendship—was it simple recognition of shared experience, random affection, or was it some similarity of viewpoint? Or possibly smell? He wondered whether one dog liked another dog because the smell was right. Humans, he had read, made friendships on that basis—even if they were unaware of it.

The walk over, they returned to Corduroy Mansions. For some reason Freddie de la Hay seemed slightly uncomfortable, and William decided that he would watch him when he gave him his breakfast. Dogs were always hungry, it seemed, and if a dog turned up his nose at food it was a sure sign that something was wrong.

He took Freddie into the kitchen and picked up

his bowl from the floor. Freddie watched him in silence. That was strange, as he normally whined and wagged his tail when he saw his bowl being prepared.

'You not quite on form this morning, Freddie?' William asked.

Freddie de la Hay gazed at his master. His tail, which normally wagged in response to any human question, remained still.

William crossed the room to get the half-full tin of dog food that he had put in the fridge the previous morning. Then he noticed something on the floor—a few fragments of wood and some torn paper. He bent down and picked up the bit of wood. It had been chewed.

He looked severely at Freddie. 'What have you been chewing, Freddie? Come on now. Own up.'

Freddie de la Hay looked away. William, now quite puzzled, looked about the kitchen floor and saw more signs of Freddie's activity—further fragments of wood and . . . He bent down again and picked up what looked like a small fragment of paper. But it was not paper; it was canvas.

William peered at the scrap of canvas; it was bare on one side, while the other was painted dark green, with touches of red and yellow. And as he began to make out what was there, the realisation came to him in an awful moment of clarity: the image was part of a snake. The Poussin. Freddie de la Hay had eaten the Poussin.

William did not remonstrate with Freddie—the offence was too enormous—but ran out of the kitchen to knock loudly on Marcia's door. She opened it and looked at him anxiously.

'Something wrong?'

'Disaster,' said William. 'Extreme, indeed exceptional, disaster. Freddie de la Hay has eaten the Poussin. It's a cultural tragedy.'

'But I thought it was downstairs,' said Marcia. 'They took it.'

'They must have popped it back through the letterbox,' said William. 'Come to think of it, I did hear something last night. That must have been it.'

Marcia followed William back into the kitchen, where Freddie de la Hay was sitting disconsolately, looking rather uncomfortable. When he saw Marcia, the dog lowered his snout even further until it was virtually on the ground—an admission of guilt, a position of abject repentance. If an artist had been present and had wished to paint a sentimental nineteenth-century genre painting entitled *Sorrow for Past Misdeeds*, no further arrangement of subject would have been required; Freddie de la Hay said it all.

William found another scrap of canvas on the floor and passed it to Marcia for examination. 'What on earth are we to do?' he asked.

Marcia held the tiny fragment of canvas in between thumb and forefinger and peered at it. 'Imagine,' she said. 'This survived all those years. Survived the fall of empires. Two world wars. And now this.'

William was struck by the power of this observation, which underlined the significance of Freddie de la Hay's role as cultural nemesis. If a work of art was to be destroyed, he thought, then it was marginally better that it should have been done by an agent who did not know what he was doing rather than by one who did it on purpose. For a painting to be destroyed by flood, fire, or, as

408

in this case, dog, was less of an insult to the artist—
or to the values that the painting represented—
than to be torn up by one who despised it.

William repeated his question. 'What are we
going to do?'

Marcia looked at Freddie de la Hay. 'The
Poussin will be inside him, of course.'

'But . . .'

'We could take him to the vet,' Marcia continued.
'We could ask the vet to operate. To get it out of
his stomach that way.'

William did not know what to say; surely Freddie
de la Hay could not go under the knife purely to
recover a painting? There were bound to be risks
involved, as there were in any operation. Would
any ethically minded vet be prepared to do such a
thing—to place a Poussin above the life of a dog?

'I don't think that's feasible,' William said after a
while. 'And anyway, the painting will be in little
bits. I doubt they would be able to fit it together
again.' As he spoke, he thought of Dee downstairs
and her enthusiasm for colonic irrigation. Could
the Poussin be recovered by colonic irrigation? He
very much doubted it.

'Then I suspect we'll just have to write it off,' said
Marcia.

William bit his lip. 'Maybe.' It was an appalling
conclusion, but then in some respects it was really
rather convenient. There had been a major
question mark over the painting's provenance and
that was now no longer a problem, as there was no
painting to return to anybody. And there was also
the question of whether it really was a Poussin; all
that they had had so far was James's view, and he
was just a student, albeit a student at Master's

level.

William looked down at Freddie de la Hay. He would have to forgive him, because ultimately we must all forgive one another; to do anything but that merely prolongs our suffering. And if forgiveness requires apology—which is not always the case, but sometimes is—then for a mute creature such as Freddie de la Hay, this look of dejection, as heart-rending as that on the face of any expellee from Eden, was apology enough, sufficient expiation.

'All right, Freddie,' he said. 'We won't mention Poussin again.'

Freddie had no idea of the meaning of these words. He strained to make out the word 'walk', but it was not uttered. He could tell, though, from the tone of William's voice, that he was forgiven, and his loyal heart leapt accordingly.

95. A Real Job

'I was hoping that I'd see you again,' said Tim Something as he perused the bistro menu.

Caroline smiled. 'I'd actually decided to come here for lunch anyway,' she said. 'I don't know why—I just did.'

Tim Something caught the eye of the waiter. 'Fate,' he said. 'Our lives are made up of random events that determine what's going to happen to us. I've always thought that.'

'A rather bleak view, surely?'

Tim did not agree. 'Well, take us, for example.'

'Us?'

410

'Yes. We met by chance, didn't we? I happened to be assigned to take your photograph for the mag. They could have chosen somebody else—in fact, I almost didn't answer the phone when they called. But I did, and I took your photograph.'

She looked at him blankly.

'And then,' Tim went on, 'I saw you here totally by chance. I almost went somewhere else for lunch that day. But I didn't. I came here.'

Caroline shrugged. 'I don't see . . .'

'Finally,' Tim interrupted, 'I saw you in front of that bookshop. What are the odds of bumping into somebody in this city just by chance? How many million people live in London?'

Caroline did not know.

'Well, the odds must be millions to one against a completely random meeting with the person one wants to . . .'

He did not complete the sentence. The waiter had arrived at the table with his notebook open. Caroline studied the menu with renewed concentration. *The person one wants to . . .* What had he in mind? The person one wants to ask out?

They gave their orders and the waiter headed back into the kitchen. Caroline looked up from the menu.

'I wanted to see you,' said Tim Something. 'I wanted to see you about a job.'

Caroline hoped that her disappointment was not too obvious. It was another of his assignments. Perhaps he wanted her advice; perhaps it involved art.

Tim suddenly reached across the table and laid a hand on hers. 'You are going to be looking for a job, I take it, when your course finishes?'

It felt strange to have his hand on hers—it was not unpleasant, but it did feel odd.

'I suppose I will. In fact, I definitely will. But it's not easy at the moment, especially in my field—or what I would like to be my field.' She thought of James and his interview, and felt vaguely disloyal that she was having lunch with Tim Something when James was undergoing his ordeal with his would-be employers.

Tim looked sympathetic. 'It's never the right time to get a job. I remember when I started, I wondered whether I would ever get anything. I did—and now I have far more work than I can handle.'

Caroline moved her hand slightly. 'You're lucky. You're obviously good—to be in demand like that.'

The compliment seemed to be well received. 'There are people who like my work. But what I really want to do is to go in for something more . . . more stretching. That's why I'm going into partnership.'

She was not sure what the implications of this were. Presumably they were positive, as Tim's mood seemed quite buoyant.

'Who with?'

'You probably won't know anything about him— people never look at photographers' bylines, they take us for granted—but you've probably seen his work.'

'Well, I'm very pleased for you.'

He took his hand off hers. 'Now, this is where you come in.'

'Me?'

'Yes, this other photographer has an assistant. He wants me to have one too. Apparently there's

412

going to be more than enough work to justify it.'

She had not expected this, and yet the offer, not yet spelled out but already clear enough, was immediately attractive. Caroline had never before been offered a job—she had never worked—and it seemed immensely flattering to her that somebody actually wanted her to work with him.

'A real job?' she asked.

Her question amused him. 'Just because it's creative work doesn't mean that it isn't real. Of course it is. With pay.'

He was waiting for her to say something, but she could not think what to say. Could she be a photographer?

'Twenty thousand a year to begin with,' he said. 'It'll go up. And there'll be the opportunity for some freelance work of your own—if you want.'

The waiter returned with their first course. 'I don't know what to say, Tim,' she began. 'It's very sweet of you, but . . . but I'd never thought of becoming a photographer. I don't have any training in it . . .'

'I'll train you,' he said. 'It's something you can learn on the job. There's no need to go off to a college and study the history of photography. You're artistic—that's all that counts. And—'

'Doing a degree in the history of art is not the same thing as being artistic,' Caroline interjected. She was puzzled as to why he should offer the job to her. Surely there would be plenty of people more qualified to do it—graduates of photography courses who knew all about composition and depth of field and how to use light? And the history of photography too.

'But you must be,' he said. 'To be able to write

413

about painting you must be artistic—otherwise you'd be doing something else.'

'But why me in particular?'

He reached for his glass of water and took a sip. 'Do you want me to be honest?'

'Of course. Who would want anybody to be dishonest?'

'Not me. That's why I'll tell you. I like you. It's that simple. I like you a lot. I'd love to work with you.' He paused. 'I think you're fun.'

Had she disliked him, she would have been embarrassed by his directness. But she had decided that she liked him now, whatever her feelings might have been in the past, so she felt instead a flush of pleasure.

'I like you too,' she said.

'And what's your answer?'

'You'd have to tell me a little bit more about the job.'

He nodded. 'It'll be great fun. I promise you that. And there'll be bags of travel. My new partner goes to Kenya, India—places like that. He does features for travel magazines. He specifically wants me to take some of that off his hands.'

'Lucky you.'

'And lucky you?'

'All right.'

There was one last question, and she looked at him directly as she asked it. 'Is it a good idea to work with somebody . . . you like?'

He misheard her. 'Somebody like me? Don't you trust me?'

'No. Somebody you like.'

He answered as if there were only one possible response. 'Naturally.'

414

96. Three Sorts of Man Trouble

If Caroline had felt at a loose end that morning, she felt even more so in the afternoon. Her lunch with Tim Something had been concluded with an exchange of telephone numbers and an arrangement to meet for dinner two days later—'to discuss the modalities' of the job offer, as Tim put it. She agreed to this, although she was not entirely sure what a modality was—a state of uncertainty later resolved by a visit to a dictionary. They had an agreement, it seemed, and now the formalities of that agreement would have to be worked out. She wondered why he could not have said that they would meet to discuss the details—it would have been so much simpler and would have involved no dictionary. She felt slightly irritated by this, but contained her irritation; if she were to work for Tim Something, she would have to stop herself objecting to the way he put things.

She returned to Corduroy Mansions at about three o'clock and tried to begin the essay that had been hanging over her head. The topic was easy enough: each member of the class had to write a four-thousand-word piece on a painting of their choice. This was a gift, because everybody would have four thousand words to say about a painting that interested them. James, she knew, had already written two thousand words on *An Old Man and His Grandson* by Ghirlandaio, a painting he had seen in the Louvre.

'Two thousand words already,' he had remarked to Caroline. 'And I haven't even got beyond the man's nose! I'm still writing about that.'

Caroline knew the painting. 'It's a marvellous nose. So bulbous.'

'Exactly,' said James. 'The painting is all about that nose, really. And I think that's what the child is looking up at. He sees a nose. His grandfather *is* a nose to him. I could write a whole book about it, you know, Caroline. I really could. Like that whole book I've just read about Hopper's *Nighthawks*.'

She envied James his facility with words, his ability to write two thousand words, and more, about a nose. She was out of her depth, she felt, compared with people like James. There was no place for her in the world of art, and all she was was a young woman from a conventional background in Cheltenham whose only distinction so far had been to appear in *Rural Living* magazine, on a page normally dedicated to attractive, marriageable, county-ish girls whose fathers were keen to get them off their hands. It was a bleak thought.

Unable to settle down to the not-yet-started essay on a not-yet-identified painting, Caroline decided to leave the flat and go for a cup of herbal tea at Daylesford Organic. The shop was busy; the ladies who lunched had been replaced by ladies who drank tea, and Caroline had to wait a few minutes for a table. But she found one eventually and sat down to page through a magazine while she waited for her tea. She glanced about her and saw, at a neighbouring table, a man looking in her direction. She turned away, but then looked back at him and realised that she recognised him. It was the man in the flat at the bottom of the stairs—the man whom she hardly ever saw, although Jenny had spoken to him. She smiled, and nodded, which was the signal for him to rise to his feet and approach her table.

'Please forgive me for asking,' he said, 'but are you waiting for anybody?'

She shook her head. If he wanted to join her she would welcome it, given her unsettled mood.

Basil Wickramsinghe sat down opposite Caroline. 'I believe I have met one of your flatmates,' he said. 'Jenny. She and I met here just the other day.'

'Yes,' said Caroline. 'So I gather.'

Basil, who had brought his cup over with him, took a sip of tea. 'It is a very fine building, Corduroy Mansions,' he said. 'I like living there. Do you?'

She nodded. 'I do. I love it.'

'And this area is so nice,' Basil continued. 'It's so easy to walk to the parks from here. And we have all we need, don't we?'

Caroline sighed. She was thinking of her lunch with Tim Something. What was she doing? She hardly knew him, and when she had met him before she had not even liked him. How could her feelings change? Was she that flighty?

Basil Wickramsinghe was staring at her. 'You're unhappy, aren't you?'

She stared at him for a moment. He could tell. And she could tell, just by looking at him, that this quiet man could probably read her as easily as she felt she could read others. 'I'm unsettled,' she said.

Basil took a further sip of tea. 'Which means man trouble, doesn't it?'

'Yes, I suppose it does.'

Basil smiled. 'There are three sorts of man

417

trouble,' he said. 'There is one where there is no man. There is one where there is one man. And there is one where there is more than one man.'

'Mine is the third. I can't decide between two.'

'That probably seems very difficult,' said Basil, 'but it isn't. Not really. You can find the answer by doing a very simple thing. Close your eyes and then tell me which one you see.'

Too simple, thought Caroline.

'Go on,' urged Basil. 'Close your eyes. Which man comes to you? Don't think about it, just see who steps forward.'

'I'm not sure if it's that straightforward.'

'No, try it,' he urged. 'It's rather like dream analysis. Dreams are meant to tell us about our inmost desires, aren't they? But the problem with dreams is that we can't anticipate in advance which desires they will reveal. If you do what I suggest, your conscious mind can instruct your subconscious to respond. It's rather like a lucid dream, where we know we're dreaming but we continue to control the unfolding of the dream.' He paused. 'Go on. Just close your eyes and tell me which man comes to you.'

Caroline closed her eyes. For a moment there was nothing in her mind but the sounds of the café about her: the rattling of cups on saucers; the subdued drone of the conversation of others; the sound of leeks being chopped in the kitchen. But then she saw him, standing before her, smiling, his arms open, ready to embrace her.

It was neither James, nor Tim Something. It was somebody she did not know at all. A perfect stranger.

'Open your eyes,' said Basil.

418

She opened them and looked at her neighbour.

'I can tell from your expression that you saw neither of them,' Basil said. 'Am I right? You saw a stranger.'

'I'm afraid I did.'

Basil sat back in his seat. 'Well, that means that you have yet to meet the right man for you. He is out there somewhere, but you have not yet met him.'

97. The Interview

James had said that he would drop in on Corduroy Mansions round about six that evening. He had also said that he might phone and let Caroline know how the interview and the lunch had gone, if he had time. There had been no call, and so she knew nothing about what had happened until she saw the expression on his face. That revealed everything.

'You got it?' she asked.

He nodded. 'Yes. I did.'

He was standing in the doorway; she was in the hall. Now she stepped forward and threw her arms around him. 'Oh, James! Congratulations! You clever, clever boy!'

She kissed him on his cheek; she had intended to kiss him on the lips, but he moved and presented his cheek instead. He wriggled free of her embrace, not indecently soon but rather quickly nonetheless.

'I've brought a bottle of champagne,' he said. 'I bought it from one of those places that sells them

419

chilled so that they're ready for an immediate celebration.'

She took the bottle from him and went into the kitchen to fetch two glasses. He followed her through, full of news about the interview.

'I was really nervous at the beginning,' he said. 'There was this guy before me and he came out looking very depressed—defeated, really. I said to him, 'See you at lunch.' And he said that he had not been invited. I felt terrible about that.'

'Well, you knew that you had a better chance, then.'

James raised an eyebrow. 'Except for the fact that he had a Ph.D. I had spoken to him before he went in and he told me—a Ph.D. from McGill on Tintoretto. A Ph.D., Caroline, for a small job in a gallery. That's how tough things are.'

Caroline agreed; things were not easy. 'Polish Ph.D.s drive trucks. Romanian neurosurgeons wait at tables here in London.'

'So there's not much hope for somebody who hasn't even got his Master's yet,' said James. 'At least that's what I thought.'

'Were they nice to you?'

'Not to begin with. They looked me up and down and asked me to take a seat. Then somebody asked a question straight out of the blue—no preliminaries, nothing. He said, "You've heard of Marco Marziale, of course."'

'Who?'

'That's what most people would think,' said James. 'But it just so happened that I had read about him yesterday. I couldn't believe my luck. There he was, a really obscure painter who has something like eleven or twelve surviving paintings

420

to his name, and I knew about him because I had seen one in a catalogue—one coming up at Christie's in New York. And I had read that some people considered the figures in his paintings to be a bit wooden, and so I said, "A bit wooden. That Adoration that came to light recently had some beautiful passages, though. Really interesting."'

Caroline laughed. 'Served them right.'

'Yes. The person who had asked me looked really deflated. I was tempted to say to him, 'You've looked at that one, I take it.' But I didn't. Which was just as well because I think that would have sunk me. They were looking for something, you see—they were looking for coolness under fire.'

'And they got it.'

James looked away modestly. 'Maybe. And the rest of the interview went really well. The person who'd asked about Marziale tried it again, of course, with a real underarm ball about Honthorst's portrait of Charles I in the National Portrait Gallery. But again, it just so happened that I knew that one and was able to talk about it. After that, he gave up.'

While James was talking, Caroline had eased out the cork of the champagne and was now filling the glasses. She handed one to James and raised her own glass. 'To clever you. Well done.'

'And then there was the lunch,' James continued. 'They were relaxed by that stage, and so we talked about all sorts of things. It turned out that one of the directors knew my uncle. In fact he had been the best man at my uncle's wedding. So we talked about him, and his wife, and so on. All very chatty. Until one of them looked at his watch and realised

421

that it was already three o'clock. So they called for the bill and the chairman said, "The job's yours, by the way." '

Caroline did not want to cap James's story immediately, so she waited for a while before she brought up her own news.

'I was offered a job today as well,' she said. 'I hadn't been expecting it.'

James looked at her in astonishment. 'You never said anything about an interview.'

Had it been an interview? She did not think so. 'Actually, it wasn't an interview—it was a lunch. Lunch with Tim Something, the photographer.'

James looked confused. 'What's he got to do with a job?'

'He offered me one,' said Caroline. 'He's expanding his photography business and he wants me to join him.'

She could tell at once that James was concerned. 'You? A photographer?' But it was not her going to work for a photographer that worried him, she felt—it was the fact that the photographer was Tim Something. James was jealous.

She realised very suddenly that she had to say something; she could pretend no longer. 'James, listen, I think we should be honest with ourselves. I like you an awful lot—you know that—but I really don't think it's going to work between us. We can still go to Paris. But it's not going to work, is it?'

For a moment he said nothing, but stood quite still, holding his champagne glass in his right hand. The silence was such that she could hear the tiny bubbles of the wine bursting—an almost inaudible crackling sound. Then he looked at her, and his look was full of tenderness. 'No, you're right. It

422

won't. And I've been meaning to tell you something. I've met somebody else. Somebody . . . well, somebody who makes more sense for me— for the way I am.'

She felt immediate relief, mixed with pleasure for him. She wanted James to be happy.

'What's his name?' she asked.

It was a misjudged question. 'It's a she, actually. Her name is Annette.'

Caroline looked into her glass. She could have forgiven him had it been Adam or Andrew, but not Annette. And why, she thought, should another woman get him? If any woman was going to get him, then it would be her. She was clear about that.

She would get him back. She was not going to take this lying down.

98. *Martini Talk in Cheltenham*

While this yo-yo of an encounter between Caroline and James was taking place in Corduroy Mansions, in the kitchen of the house owned by Terence Moongrove, mystic and seeker after under-standing, a dinner was being prepared by Berthea Snark. Terence was giving his sister a certain degree of assistance, but not much, as he had already performed several of the tasks assigned to him incorrectly, with the result that they had had to be redone.

'We don't normally cut our potatoes into squares,' said Berthea as she contemplated the results of his attempt to prepare roast potatoes. 'Especially such tiny squares.'

'Oh, I don't know, Berthy,' said Terence. 'I really don't think I'm much of cook. I know that a man should be able to cook these days; I know that. But even if I can't cook, there are lots of other things I can do jolly well.'

Such as? thought Berthea. She could not think of a single thing at which poor Terence excelled; even his sacred dance had not been very impressive and at one stage she had seen him going widdershins when he should have been going deasil. That had almost caused the BBC cameraman to be knocked over, which Berthea thought would have been a rather satisfactory development given her unease about his presence in the first place. No, poor Terence really could do very little, if anything, and it would have been surprising had cooking been an exception to the rule.

'So rather than do anything else the wrong way,' Terence continued, 'I'm going to pour us both a little drinkie-poo. How about a martini? That would be such fun.'

Berthea thought this a very good idea. 'I'll carry on cooking,' she said. 'You bring them through and we'll have martinis in the kitchen. What a treat.'

Now as it happened, mixing martinis was another thing that Terence did not do very well. The result was two immensely strong gin martinis: tasty— perhaps by accident—but extremely potent.

'Down the hatch!' said Terence, raising his glass to his sister.

Berthea reciprocated the sentiment and sampled her martini. 'Extremely good,' she said.

'Thank you,' said Terence. 'And when you've finished that one, I'll make you another one—with the other bottle, this time.'

They continued to chat, the conversation becoming pleasantly mellow as they worked their way through their martinis.

'I saw a crop circle today,' said Terence. 'In a field of wheat. A perfect circle. It was jolly exciting. I pointed it out to Monty Bismarck and he saw it too. He said that we should phone the newspaper and get them to take photographs.'

'How strange,' said Berthea. 'Is there any rational explanation for these things? I assume that there is.'

Terence shook his head. 'They are the product of energy forces of which we have no current inkling,' he said. 'Crop circles contain ancient wisdom. Either that, or they're a warning from another planet. They're a warning that we need to heed.'

'What are they warning us about?' asked Berthea, slurring her words slightly as the martini took effect.

'This and that,' said Terence airily.

'But then why don't they give the warning in English?' asked Berthea. 'Why use circles?'

Terence smiled. 'Because the beings who make

these circles,' he explained, 'are not linear. We are linear and our languages are linear. These beings are circular. That's obvious.'

'Mmm,' muttered Berthea, draining her glass. 'Terence, that martini was divine. Be an angel and get me another. Not too strong, of course. Just like that one. My, how quickly martinis vanish as you get older.'

Terence withdrew and soon returned with another two martinis.

'Tell me about your book, Berthy,' he said, his own words beginning to slur in the same way as his sister's. 'Your un-authorised biography of Oedipus. How's it going? Have you had lots of interesting information from the chaps he knew at school?'

'Bags and bags,' said Berthea. 'They didn't like him, you know. They threw him into a pond once. Just as a joke, of course.'

'He was such a horrible boy,' mused Terence. 'I often thought that I should throw him into something or other. I just didn't get round to it.'

He looked slightly guilty after this remark, but then he saw that Berthea did not appear to have taken offence.

'Oh, I thought that too,' she said. 'You know, as an analyst I should be prepared to reveal my inmost thoughts but I've never really discussed with anybody else these feelings I have about my own son.'

'Negative feelings?' asked Terence.

'Very negative. In fact . . .' she paused, and took another sip of her martini, 'once or twice I've been visited by dreams in which I have done something terrible to him.'

Terence's eyes widened. 'What fun!' he said. 'Not

that I think we should actually do this, not in real life, but it would be such fun to electrocute him. In the same way in which I jolly nearly electrocuted myself. We could invite him to come down for the weekend and he could sleep in that old brass bed in the spare room on the first floor—you know, the one that Uncle Edgar used. Oedipus could sleep in that and we could tie an electric wire to the frame. Then, when he was asleep, we could turn the switch on.'

Berthea drained her second martini. 'Wishful thinking,' she said.

'Or here's another idea,' said Terence. 'You know that lightning conductor on the roof? It has that funny flat wire that goes down the side. Mr Marchbanks told me that it was copper. Anyway, it goes past the window of the spare room, and so we could pass a wire from the conductor and connect it to the bed. When lightning comes, bang! It would go down that copper wire and into the room and give Oedipus a jolly big shock. But they couldn't send us to prison because it would have been death by lightning and that's an act of God, isn't it?'

Berthea shook a finger at Terence. 'We mustn't allow ourselves to think like this,' she said. 'Oedipus is my son and your nephew.'

'Yes,' said Terence. 'God will punish him when he dies. Not before.'

Berthea thought about this. 'Actually, it would be much more satisfying if God punished him in this life so that we all could see. And you know what the best punishment for him would be? You know what?'

Terence shook his head.

'If God were to make him prime minister!' shrieked Berthea.

Terence roared with laughter. 'Oh Berthy, what a brilliant idea! It must be such a *horrid* job. Especially now.'

99. *Basil Buys a Blazer*

William surprised himself by how quickly he got over the loss of the Poussin. His initial reaction had been one of utter dismay but within hours of the event he had come to see it all in perspective. The painting's attribution had never been confirmed, nobody appeared to be missing it and Freddie de la Hay himself appeared to be making a rapid recovery from the ingestion of a major work of French art.

Life, William thought, was taking a distinct turn for the better. In the space of only a few days, Marcia had settled down in Corduroy Mansions very easily and was proving to be an unobtrusive and considerate flatmate. The rules of engagement had been quickly and amicably agreed: each had his or her own bedroom, William had his study, and the drawing room and kitchen were shared space. Marcia insisted on paying rent, and William put this straight back into the kitty they had set up for the purchase of household supplies. The purchase of these was undertaken by Marcia, which greatly relieved William as he had never enjoyed shopping.

'It's very nice having you here,' William observed over breakfast. 'It seems as if you've lived here for

428

ever.'

'And I'm happy to be here,' said Marcia.

No more was said. Any further observation would have been unnecessary, possibly too much: delicate understandings are sometimes best left largely unspoken. And the same may be said of feelings; a refined brush works best there too. I am happy, thought William; that was all he needed to think.

The moment seemed right to William to hold a party, and he put the idea to Marcia that day.

'Let's invite the other people in the house,' he said. 'Maybe one or two others. Not a big do—a buffet, perhaps. I've got some rather good champagne at the shop at the moment, which would probably go down well.'

Marcia agreed, and invitations were duly written out and dropped through the letterboxes of the residents. These evidently fell on fertile ground, as within a day everyone had accepted. Basil Wickramsinghe replied that he was 'deeply honoured and profoundly moved' to have been invited. Dee said that she would love to come and might she bring some elderflower cordial that she had recently made? Jenny was given her invitation at work and told William that it was 'the best idea in decades'. James was included on the coat-tails of Caroline's invitation; both said that they would 'definitely be there'. As did Jo, who remarked that she had not been invited to a dinner party for almost eight months and revealed that she had almost cried when she received the invitation.

Downstairs in the first-floor flat, on the day before the party, the invitation sparked some discussion when the four flatmates found

429

themselves around the kitchen table at the same time—a rare occasion.

'People are too tired these days to entertain as much as they used to,' said Jenny. 'When I was at university we did our best. Nowadays it sccms to bc just too much of a hassle.'

'We had great parties at uni,' said Jo. 'We used to go over for weekends to Rottnest Island and have barbies. Someone would get out a guitar and we'd sing. Out there in the darkness, under all those stars.'

'A beautiful image,' said Caroline. 'I can just see it.'

'And you, Caroline?' asked Jo. 'Remember any great parties?'

Caroline thought for a moment. The trouble with parties, she felt, was that they faded into one another so easily. There had been parties—great parties—but when did one end and the next one begin? That was the difficult part. She had met James at a party that the Institute had given at the beginning of the course. It had been a rather stiff affair, with the lecturing staff being somewhat formal and the students still all strangers to one another. She had liked the look of James and had struck up a conversation with him. Later, a group of them had gone on to somebody's flat and the party had continued there.

'The parties that you remember are the ones where you meet someone,' she said. 'You forget the others—or at least I do.'

Dee had remained silent. Now she spoke: 'The problem with parties is that they represent a shock to the system. I like them, same as anybody else, but the human body isn't really adapted to sudden

430

high-volume inputs of either food or drink. We're grazing creatures.'

All three stared at her. 'Should grazing creatures avoid parties?' asked Jenny drily.

As this discussion was taking place downstairs, upstairs Marcia was making a list of ingredients she would buy later that day. She had taken two days off and would begin cooking that evening, preparing some of the food in advance. She wrote a list: quails' eggs (two dozen), fennel, parmesan (large block), Arborio rice, dried mushrooms.

She made a mental note to be careful about the mushrooms. She had read that radioactive mushrooms—some from sylvan glades in the vicinity of Chernobyl—had been illegally imported into Western Europe and were being mixed with innocent mushrooms. One had to be careful that the container gave the exact source. *Mushrooms from various countries* was not reassuring.

Basil Wickramsinghe, for his part, was worried about what he should wear. He was an elegant dresser but he felt that on this occasion he should avoid anything too formal, and had paid a visit to Jermyn Street to see if there was something suitable. There was.

'This shirt is a very nice cream, sir,' said the young man behind the counter of one shop. 'And, if I may say so, it would be set off extremely well by this tie here. See? Look at that. Perfect.'

'I think that this occasion will be one where ties are not worn,' said Basil. 'And yet a bit of colour would not go amiss.'

'You can have colour in a shirt, of course,' said the young man. 'Or you can have it in the jacket. How about this blazer? That burgundy stripe will go very well with the cream shirt.'

Basil looked at the blazer. It had a slightly raffish look to it—it was the sort of blazer that rowers wore, set off perhaps by a straw boater. James Lock, the hat people, were just round the corner in St James's Street; should he go down there and buy a boater too? He could hardly wear a boater to a dinner party, but the summer season was under way and there would be plenty of opportunities to don a boater. There was the picnic, of course, the annual summer gathering of the James I and VI Society. A boater would be ideal for that.

He bought the shirt and the blazer and then decided to walk home, back through Green Park and Victoria, past the crowds of people, each in the world of himself, each with hopes, of varying degrees of intensity and realism, of something better for himself, and for others.

100. The End

William welcomed the guests at the door and led them through to the kitchen. There he poured them a glass of champagne or, in Dee's case, a glass of the elderflower cordial she had brought with her.

'You can add some to your champagne,' offered Dee. 'This goes with anything.'

'What a good idea,' said William politely. 'But perhaps not right now.'

Marcia was in the drawing room, where she was offering round several large plates of canapés. One plate, in particular, proved to be popular—a

432

CORDUROY MANSIONS

display of small tartlets into which a fried quail's egg had been inserted, the tiny yolk sprinkled with fresh Kerala pepper.

'The pepper's so important,' said Marcia. 'The stuff you buy in supermarkets is dreadful—ancient old stuff that tastes like cardboard. Fresh pepper should smell *green*—it should prickle the nose.'

'I love pepper,' said James. 'It's so peppery. Gorgeous.'

Marcia considered this. 'You're right,' she said. 'Have another tartlet.' She decided that she rather liked James. But was Caroline his type?

Jenny talked to Basil Wickramsinghe, reminding him of their meeting in Daylesford Organic the previous week. 'There was the tea lady,' she said, 'with her lovely rare teas. Remember? You bought some.'

'I did,' said Basil, smiling. 'I bought some of her white tea. I love that. We produce white tea in Sri Lanka, you know. The tips of the buds. It's very delicate.'

Marcia arrived at their side and joined in the conversation. She had not yet met Basil

Wickramsinghe but had been admiring his blazer from the other side of the room. Such a handsome man, she thought, and after their introduction she went on to think, *what charming manners*. Was he single? she wondered. A few questions, neatly posed, revealed that he was. And he was an Anglican too—that came up in the conversation. Could he recommend a suitable church nearby? Somewhere reasonably High? Of course he could. He smiled—such an engaging smile, thought Marcia. Would she care to accompany him sometime—he could introduce her to the vicar? She would, gladly. And at this point Marcia—quite subtly, but clearly enough—let it be known that she and William were just flatmates.

More champagne was produced and poured. Since it was early evening there was still a lot of light outside, and the now tired sun, a great red ball, was setting over the rooftops. It is all very beautiful, thought William.

Freddie de la Hay, who had greeted each guest in the hall, nosing at their shoes and ankles in a friendly fashion, now came through to the drawing room and looked about him at the human guests. He was a dog with a sense of occasion and he was carrying himself with confidence and ease. Here and there, a guest would slip him a morsel, which he received with proper gratitude. James gave him an entire quail's egg tartlet; Jenny gave him a cheese straw followed by a biscuit with pâté; and Dee gave him asparagus and a small lettuce leaf.

Then Eddie arrived. William opened the door to his son and was, for a moment, unable to say anything.

'Party, Dad?'

'Just a few people from the building. Nothing big.'

Eddie smiled—an unexpected smile. 'That's great. Nice to see you enjoying yourself.'

William looked for sarcasm but there was none. Eddie meant it.

'Come and join us, Eddie,' he said.

Eddie followed his father into the drawing room. There he saw Marcia, who paled on seeing him but recovered her colour when she received a friendly wave from the young man.

'You seem very cheerful, Eddie,' said William as he handed his son a glass of champagne.

'Yup,' said Eddie.

'May I ask why?' William ventured.

'Met a really nice woman, Dad,' said Eddie. 'She lives not far away actually. Got her own place.'

'Very nice,' said William.

'And a place in the Windward Islands,' Eddie went on. 'It's all a bit sudden but we've decided we're going to spend six months there and six months here each year.'

William's eyes widened. He would have enquired further about that but there was another question he had to ask: 'Eddie, there was a painting in the wardrobe. We found it.'

Eddie shrugged. 'Nothing to do with me. I didn't have any paintings.' He paused. 'No, hold on. There was a painting I won in the pub. Yes. I was going to throw it out. Funny thing. Some naked guy and a woman. Oh yes, and a snake. Peculiar. Did you get rid of it?'

William looked down at Freddie de la Hay-Poussin, who met his gaze innocently.

The party was now warming up. They would

435

have more to eat—the main course that Marcia had so lovingly prepared—but they would not have it just yet. For the moment, William felt that he wanted to say something. Earlier that day, in anticipation of this occasion, he had written something on a piece of paper, and now he took it out and cleared his throat.

Dear friends, now in London,
Here and there, in their various forms
Of isolation or companionship,
People begin a journey into night;
Happy they go to bed, or sad—
The choice to a very great extent
Is theirs. Happiness is a state
Which few can define—
I shall not try—but even those
Who never attempt a definition
Know from experience
That happiness flows most readily
From friendship, from the company
Of those we would rather not
Be without: a double negative
Is a way of saying that which
You really believe;
And I believe that, I really do.
Friendship is a guise of love,
And love is friendship
Dressed up for a night out.
That we are together, here at this moment,
Alive, one with another,
Is the most delicious treat;
I, for one, ask for no more,
I, for one, am replete.

After he spoke there was silence. They looked at one another, uncertain as to how anything could be added to what had been said. Marcia stepped forward, took William's hand, and held it.

CHIVERS
LARGE
PRINT
–direct–

If you have enjoyed this Large Print book and would like to build up your own collection of Large Print books, please contact

Chivers Large Print Direct

Chivers Large Print Direct offers you a full service:

• Prompt mail order service

• Easy-to-read type

• The very best authors

• Special low prices

For further details either call Customer Services on (01225) 336552 or write to us at Chivers Large Print Direct, **FREEPOST**, Bath BA1 3ZZ

Telephone Orders:
FREEPHONE 08081 72 74 75